NEXT DOOR] DADD ɪ

SECRET SHIFTERS NEXT DOOR: BOOK 1

Roxie Ray

© 2022

Disclaimer

This is a work of fiction. Names, places, characters and events are all fictitious for the reader's pleasure. Any similarities to real people, places, events, living or dead are all coincidental.

Contents

Prologue - Harley...5

Chapter 1 - Tate 29

Chapter 2 - Harley 42

Chapter 3 - Tate 51

Chapter 4 - Harley 66

Chapter 5 - Tate 76

Chapter 6 - Harley 88

Chapter 7 - Tate 97

Chapter 8 - Harley 108

Chapter 9 - Tate 121

Chapter 10 - Harley 133

Chapter 11 - Tate 146

Chapter 12 - Harley 159

Chapter 13 - Tate 171

Chapter 14 - Harley 186

Chapter 15 - Tate 203

Chapter 16 - Harley 220

Chapter 17 - Tate 236

Chapter 18 - Harley 254

Chapter 19 - Tate 276

Chapter 20 - Harley 285

Chapter 21 - Tate 302

Chapter 22 - Harley 313

Chapter 23 - Tate 327

Chapter 24 - Harley 339

Chapter 25 - Tate 352

Chapter 26 - Harley 367

Chapter 27 - Tate 382

Chapter 28 - Harley 396

Chapter 29 - Tate 410

Chapter 30 - Harley 421

Chapter 31 - Tate 430

Chapter 32 - Harley 442

Chapter 33 - Tate 455

Chapter 34 - Harley 469

Chapter 35 - Tate 484

Chapter 36 - Harley 494

Chapter 37 - Tate 504

Chapter 38 - Harley 516

Chapter 39 - Tate 524

Chapter 40 - Steff 527

Prologue - Harley

The best part about living in New York City was that there was always somewhere you could go to get your mind off things—clubs, restaurants, theaters. It was all here, damn near everything was open twenty-four hours, too. Of all the spots I could have chosen, this bar was the only one that appealed to me. It wasn't exactly a dive, but it wasn't a trendy hipster spot either. It was caught somewhere in-between—the perfect place to have a few drinks and wallow in my misery.

A couple of hours ago, I found out my boyfriend of six months had been cheating on me. Just to rub a little salt in the wound, he had been cheating with multiple women. I still wasn't sure how to feel about the whole situation. Luis was the first man I'd dated or slept with since I'd lost Sam three years ago. It ashamed me that I hadn't waited longer after his death, but the loneliness had started to eat at me. Luis had come along right at my lowest point and filled that empty space inside me. Even then, it had been forced, like I was trying too hard to move forward. So desperate to put the most painful part of my life behind me.

I should have felt rage, shame, sadness—that entire range of emotions people felt when they had been betrayed. But all I could feel was humiliation. That was the one emotion that seemed to be trying to tear its way out of my brain every ten minutes or so. Knowing that I'd been fooled so completely and thoroughly overwhelmed me. The drinks were helping with that, though.

I smiled to myself and lifted the glass to my lips. Jack and Coke—just what the doctor ordered. I'd decided not to hang out with any of my friends. They would have supported me, called Luis a douchebag and bashed his character, talked about setting me up with guys they knew, and all the other things friends were supposed to do in these situations. But all I really wanted was to be alone. At least, that was the case until I set eyes on the man across the bar.

The guy was gorgeous. He'd caught my eye, and he seemed to have noticed me, too. When his eyes locked on mine, he didn't look away—he continued to look straight at me. Most men, even the overly confident ones, would look away for at least a second if they'd been caught staring. A nervous, thrilling heat built in my stomach, and my cheeks went red. He smiled and nodded to me, raising his glass in my direction. Despite myself, I smiled back and raised my own glass in greeting.

Finally looking away, the stranger glanced down at the bar, the smile still playing on his lips. He looked like he'd made a decision. He stood, grabbed his drink, and walked toward me. My eyes widened in surprise. Was he actually coming over to sit with me? *Oh shit.* I hadn't anticipated having to make small talk. My whole plan for the night had been to have a couple of hours of lonely drinking, maybe a long hot shower, some crying, and sleep. But it seemed things had rapidly taken a new and interesting turn.

As I watched him move around the bar, I could see that his body was ripped, even with the tailored dress shirt he was wearing. One word leaped to the front of my mind. *Intimidating.* He practically oozed confidence as he took a seat next to me.

He took another sip of his drink before he spoke. "You look like you could use a friend."

I grinned and quirked an eyebrow. "Well, that's pretty bold of you to assume."

He shrugged. "Fortune favors the bold. Isn't that what they say?"

Who was this guy? It was like he'd walked out of a movie or something. So fucking smooth. The ball of heat in my stomach moved lower. I already knew what I wanted. I wasn't sure how it was possible, but I suddenly needed more than a few drinks tonight.

"I won't ask why a pretty lady like you is drinking alone. I think I can figure it out for myself."

I downed my drink and waved to the bartender for another. "I'm a walking cliché. Is that what you're saying?"

"Not at all. I just recognize the signs." His gaze swept lazily over my body before locking on my eyes again. "Looks like he's a fucking idiot to me. Dude didn't know what he had."

My cheeks were on fire, and I had to look away. The intensity of his gaze was too much for me to handle. We spent the next forty-five minutes chatting and flirting back and forth. After a while, his hand was on my lower back, my leg, then brushing a hair from my face. It was all I could do to hide that I was hornier than I'd been in forever. Each time he touched me, the wetness between my legs grew until I was almost dripping. I knew exactly where this was going, and as much as the logical side of my mind protested, the rest of me was already thinking about the feel of his sweaty, muscled body above me, the way I'd groan when the pleasure surged through me.

I forced myself to stop imagining and took another drink to calm my nerves. The stranger was pursuing me, and I hadn't realized how much I wanted that. Luis and I had sort of fallen in together, without any romance or courting per se. This? This was what I craved. To be desired, to be chased, to be wanted. The lust in the stranger's eyes lit a fire inside me that I thought had died with Sam.

There was a slight pang of sadness in my heart when I thought of him. *Was this a betrayal?* Those words always flashed through my mind when I looked at another man, when Luis had taken me to bed, when I downloaded dating apps. It wasn't a betrayal. If things had been swapped and I had died, I would have wanted nothing more than for Sam to find a lovely woman to spend his life with. I would have never wanted him to mourn and pine for me the rest of his life and live like a celibate monk. No, this wasn't a betrayal. This was life, and life was worth living.

The stranger pushed his glass away and said, "I'm only in town for one night."

I knew what he was saying, and I was fine with it. I wanted a night, a single night, to forget all the shit going on in my life. To forget what Luis did, to feel free and desired. Just one night. "That works for me."

Glancing sideways at me, he smiled faintly. "If it works for you, it works for me."

He stood, pulled two hundred dollar bills out of his wallet, and handed them to the bartender. "Keep the change."

The young man behind the bar took the bills, his eyes wide. "Sir, it was only five or six drinks."

"Have a great night." With that, he took my hand and pulled me toward the door.

I followed. His hand was warm and strong in mine. I felt like I was in a dream until the cool air outside hit me, and I realized what we were doing. Butterflies started fluttering in my stomach as he waved for a cab. If I'd rehearsed this a day ago, I would have told myself to come to my senses, give a gracious apology, then head home alone. Instead, I found myself growing ever more excited.

Fifteen minutes later, I was walking down the hallway of his hotel, toward his room. As he bent over his lock and slid the key in, my gaze drifted over his broad, muscled back. The second the door swung inward, we were all over each other. To my shock and surprise, I was the aggressor. Pulling him in close, I locked my lips to his. Arms wrapped around me, hands cupped my ass, and lifted me. Our breaths came in sharp, desperate gasps as he laid me on the bed. I unbuttoned my blouse as he pulled my skirt and panties down my legs, then threw them across the room.

Without warning, he buried his tongue in my pussy. My mouth dropped open in a gasp as his tongue flicked back and forth, making the blood rush to my head. Already, I was on the verge of a climax. I wrapped my legs around his head, pulling him closer as I unhooked my bra and freed my breasts. His hand slid up and palmed my breast, gently pinching my nipple. An explosion of pleasure rocked me as the orgasm rippled through my body, stronger than any I could ever remember.

He rose from between my legs, quickly shed his own clothes, and then kneeled above me as I tried to catch my breath. I couldn't even speak when he kissed me again.

Slowly, I regained my composure as I ran my hands through his hair, my desire already building again.

Gaze intent on mine, he slid into me. My eyes rolled back as his massive length filled me, and I came again. I bit into his shoulder, trying not to scream. My hips involuntarily thrust up to meet him, desperate for him to keep going.

He rested his weight on his hands and ground himself into me. I ran my fingers over his muscled chest, my fingertips gliding through the sheen of sweat. This man was gorgeous, and he didn't seem to be even close to finishing. The idea thrilled and terrified me at the same time. I wasn't sure how much I could take, but I was ready to find out.

Nearing another orgasm, I hissed out a breath when he pulled out and flipped me over. He plunged into me, his heavy breath on my ear sending goosebumps along my shoulders. A hand snaked under me and clutched at my breast, another wound gently into my hair. He fucked me, and I loved every minute of it. All my sadness, depression, and shame evaporated beneath him.

Finally, he started moving faster, deeper, groaning into my hair. I went over the edge at the same moment he shuddered and gasped. We came together, and I collapsed on the bed, gasping—literally gasping—for air. It was like I'd run a marathon. The room was spinning, and a satisfied warmth filled me, almost like a thick heavy blanket covered me. I didn't even remember falling asleep, but I did.

When I woke up in the morning, my head throbbed from the hangover. My body ached, in a not unpleasant way, from the activity of the previous night. I sat up and looked around the room. The stranger was gone. Christ, I didn't even know his name. A quick search of the room showed he was truly gone. No luggage, toiletries, phone charger. Nothing.

I sat, naked, on the edge of the bed. The night before played back through my mind. Some of it was fuzzy; I'd been more drunk than I thought. One thing slammed home in my mind and sent a shock of distress through me. We hadn't used a condom. A cold sweat sprang out over my body as I covered my face with my hands. How could I have been so stupid?

After freaking out for twenty minutes, I pulled out my phone. I found an STD clinic near my home and booked an appointment on their website. That done, I gathered up my clothes and went to the bathroom. There was a note stuck to the shower door.

Had a great time last night. Early flight. Stay as long as you want, but check out is at noon.

Still no name. I sighed and rubbed a hand over my face. At least he'd left a note, so he wasn't a total dick. I glanced up at myself in the mirror and almost laughed. I looked like a strung-out hooker. My hair was a rat's nest, my make-up smeared and faded, and my face was slightly puffy from drinking too much.

I gave my reflection a stern look. "You can't do this again, Harley, you can't be reckless. You have to think about your daughters."

I made myself a promise to be more careful. The girls would probably be worried sick about me. Fuck, what a mother I was. Even though they weren't little kids—Mariah was sixteen and Jordyn was fourteen—and could take care of themselves because they grew up in New York, they would be worried if they woke up and I still wasn't home. With a shake of my head, I got dressed, then rushed out the door and hurried home.

Thankfully, it was Saturday morning, and I was relieved to find that my two teenagers lived up to the cliché. It was almost eleven a.m., and both were still asleep. For all they knew, I came home after they went to bed. Sighing in relief, I took a shower. By the time I was dressed, Mariah was awake.

She was eating a bagel and cream cheese in the living room when my phone rang, Luis's name lighting up my screen. Shit. I was in no mood to answer, but it was best to get it over with. I went to my room, and closed the door before hitting the green button.

"Hello?"

"Harley? Where the hell were you last night? I texted you like ten times and called twice," Luis snapped.

I sighed and rubbed my temple with my free hand. "Luis, I told you yesterday, we're done. I don't have to answer your calls or messages."

"That's bullshit. You know it is."

Doing everything I could to control the volume of my voice, I hissed, "No, Luis. What's bullshit is that you've been fucking every woman you can find, and I was too stupid to realize it."

Luis barked out a laugh. "Harley, I'm the best thing that has ever happened to you. I pulled strings and got your girls into that private school you liked, and I paid off your credit card. I think that grants me a little leeway."

I sucked in a breath and gritted my teeth. Luis had money—*lots of money*—even though he didn't seem to have a steady job and was always cagey about what he did for work. I always felt guilty whenever he gave me anything. The police life insurance policy from Sam's death and my salary as a web designer was enough, but he would offered and wouldn't take no for an answer. Now he was holding it over my head? Rage boiled inside me.

"Luis, just because you *gifted* me something doesn't give you the right to cheat on me. You understand that, right?"

"Listen, Harley, you are mine. Nothing is going to change that. *You* understand *that,* right?"

I bit back a scream as I hung up on him and blocked his number. Fuck him and his money. I squeezed my eyelids shut and held back the tears threatening to escape. When they didn't spill, I composed myself enough to go about the rest of my weekend with the girls. I managed to slip away for an hour for my STD test, which, thankfully, came out clean after an agonizing wait of a couple of days. Other than that, the weekend ended up being very plain and lazy.

All that ended Monday morning. When I walked the girls to their school, I saw Luis standing at the corner in front of the school gate. The look on his face was one of anger and petulance.

Jordyn pointed and said, "Hey, it's Luis."

He smiled and waved. "Hello, ladies."

Clenching my jaw, I handed Jordyn her lunch box and pushed her and Mariah along. "Go on, girls. Have a good day."

I waited until they were through the gate before turning around and walking toward Luis. "Why are you here?"

Several seconds ticked by as he chewed at the inside of his cheek and looked me up and down. Finally, he said, "Have you had a chance to think about your little temper tantrum?"

I put a hand to my head. "Oh, my God. Are you serious? You're out of your mind. You know that, right?"

The look on his face went from irritated humor to… something more sinister. I'd never seen that look on his face before. It made me take an involuntary step back.

He pointed a shaking finger at me. "This is your last chance. When I'm done with you, I'll tell you I'm done. No one, no *woman*, dumps me. I refuse to let that happen."

The words came out as a hiss. He sounded like a snake. I glanced around, suddenly scared to be around him. Luis had always been intimidating, which I'd found kind of sexy and attractive. But this was different. I could finally see what I'd been blind to all these months. Luis was dangerous. I was terrified to learn what it was he did for money.

I backed toward a cluster of parents seeing their kids off. "Leave us alone, Luis. I'm sure you can find someone much better than me."

I spun on my heel and walked away as quickly as I could without running. My breath was ragged and harsh, and I kept looking over my shoulder until I got to my townhouse. I locked every door and called the super to schedule getting the locks changed. I never gave Luis a key, but the rage I'd seen on his face made me paranoid.

Instead of letting the girls walk home on their own after school, I was there to meet them. They both seemed surprised to see me. Surprised, but happy. I put on a good show, and didn't let my face show the panic when I saw Luis was still near the school. He was sitting at an outdoor café and waved nonchalantly at me as I walked away with Jordyn and Mariah.

The next several days were torture. I kept getting text messages from unknown numbers, but the content told me it was Luis.

I watched you sleep last night.

Are you ever going to respond to me? I'm getting pissed. You really don't want to see me angry.

You know, Harley, all the times we fucked, we never did any rough stuff. I'd like to try choking you the next time I have you. Maybe I'll squeeze extra hard. AND extra long.

Maybe I need to talk to the girls? Get them to talk some sense into their mother.

That last text made me hurl my phone across the room. Thankfully, the floor was carpeted, and the screen was only slightly cracked. I called Sam's old partner, Maddox. I needed some advice. Luis could threaten me all he wanted to, but going after my girls was too much.

Maddox answered after the third ring. "Hello? Harley?"

Letting out a breath, I said, "Maddox? I need you. I need advice, cop advice. Can I meet you somewhere?"

The panic in my voice must have been evident. I could hear him talking to someone, probably his wife, Julie, before he spoke into the phone again. "Yeah, Harley, name the place and time. I'll do whatever I can."

We met at a coffee shop off East 37ᵗʰ Street. It only took about ten minutes to explain everything. At first, he seemed confused, then shocked, then angry. I sucked down the coffee that had gone cold.

Maddox sighed. "First things first. Restraining order. The texts alone should be enough to get one. They're obviously threatening."

"But he's using burner phones. There's no way to know who sent them."

He chewed at his lip and glanced around before whispering, "Yeah, but… I can pull some strings. The right lawyer, the right judge? It's not by the book, but I'll do it for Sam."

I knew he was going out on a limb for me from how he was talking. "Maddox, please don't get yourself into trouble for me."

He held up a hand. "Sam saved my ass multiple times, and… well… I wasn't there to save him. It's the least I can do."

Acquiescing, I nodded in gratitude as Maddox started calling in favors and pulling strings. While he worked on helping me, Luis continued his stalking. It got to the point that I didn't leave the house except for school runs—I had groceries delivered and canceled dentist and doctor's appointments. It was like we were in prison. Jordyn was confused, but I was positive Mariah had figured it out. She hushed Jordyn whenever she asked about Luis and why we had broken up. I was grateful to her for that.

Maddox called me four days after we'd met up. "Harley, it's done."

Confused, I asked, "Don't I have to go somewhere? Talk to a judge? Something like that?"

"Like I said, I did it via back channels, had some people who owed me… big time. Luis was served with the paperwork this morning. He's aware that if he gets within a thousand feet of you or contacts you in any way, he'll be in deep shit."

I sagged against the door and breathed a heavy sigh of relief. Maybe this will get Luis off my back. Hopefully. "Thank you so much, Maddox. You have no idea how much I appreciate this."

"Like I said, it's the least I could do for Sam's memory. If you have any more trouble, don't hesitate to call me. If… if things get worse, I may have another option for you. I don't want to get into it unless things get really bad."

"Thanks," I said before disconnecting the call.

Life went on as normal for a few days, but at the end of the week, I found a copy of the restraining order taped to my apartment door. The word BITCH had been scrawled across it in red Sharpie. Luis hadn't been at my apartment that morning when I took the girls to school, but another man stood on the sidewalk.

The man was thick and burly, like a walking brick wall. He smiled at me, and I knew, instinctively, that Luis had sent him.

"Mrs. King? I think you know what you need to do. Don't you? It would be a shame if…" He glanced at Jordyn and Mariah, both shrinking under his gaze. "…you know… something was to happen. Just think about it, okay?"

He smiled again and nodded at us. I grabbed the girls and immediately led them back inside. "You aren't going to school today."

I let them sit in the living room and watch TV while I went into my bedroom to call Maddox. I was barely holding back my sobs when he answered.

"What happened?" he asked immediately.

"It didn't work. I think it's getting worse."

The panic was unlike anything else I'd ever felt. The only thing that had ever surpassed this was the day the captain had knocked on my door to tell me Sam had been killed in the line of duty.

"Okay, Harley, calm down, okay. Remember I told you I had another option?"

"Yes. Yes, that's why I called."

"So, I know you and the kids are born and raised New Yorkers, but how about getting away from the city? Away from Luis?"

I wiped tears from my eyes. "What do you mean? Like going Upstate?"

He chuckled. "I was thinking farther than that. Someplace he'll never find you."

"All right, I'm listening."

"I'm not a big city kid. I moved here with Julie after we finished college. I grew up in Colorado."

"Colorado? Like Colorado River, Colorado? Bison and trout and stuff?"

He laughed. "Right, Rocky Mountain High and all that jazz. I grew up in a little place called Lilly Valley."

The name was like a breath of fresh air. I smiled when I heard it. "That sounds like the name of a fairytale village."

"Not wrong, it's pretty gorgeous."

I couldn't get the name out of my mind. It sounded… perfect. I felt almost drawn to it, a cross between excitement and urgency. It was the way I'd felt as a child on Christmas Eve. Maddox hadn't even told me about the town, and I was already desperate to go there. It was a strange feeling.

"I still own my parents' place, the house I grew up in. My parents left it to me when they died. I thought I would be visiting all the time, but we've only been there once in the last six years. I thought maybe you and the girls could stay there for a while. I know it would be a massive change for you guys, but—"

"I'd love it," I blurted.

"Wow." He chuckled. "That was easier than I thought. I figured you could rent it from me for the summer, and if it suits you, I will sell it to you."

I sank onto the bed and smiled for the first time that week. A huge weight seemed to be lifting off me. It was like we were already on the right path. I would never be able to thank Maddox enough for this new, fresh start. After we worked out the logistics and that he would bring me a set of keys the next day, Maddox promised to have a patrol car stationed outside the house until we left.

The girls took the news of the move in stride, to my surprise. My main fear was that the girls would be devastated to leave their school and friends, but that wasn't the case. If they'd been younger, I believed it would have been a different story. Mariah had deduced what the problem was, and Jordyn had gleaned some of it from her sister. They wanted to be safe and not have to stay locked up all the time. If I were being honest, they probably wanted me to be happy, too, and I wanted to cry for being blessed with such amazing girls.

The movers arrived two days later, and within three hours, everything that had made our house a home had been packed and loaded. The girls were packing up the things they wanted to have with them in the car for the trip to Colorado. This move would be expensive, but it was worth it.

I was grabbing the last of my things from the bathroom when I noticed the box of pads beside the toilet. I frowned. In all the chaos of Luis stalking and threatening me, I couldn't remember the last time I'd needed those pads. My eyes widened as my brain did quick math, and I realized I'd missed two periods. *Oh fuck.*

I stood up so fast that my sunglasses flew off the top of my head and clattered to the floor. I did not need this right now. Making a split-second decision, I decided I needed to know right away. God, we were supposed to leave in an hour. I grabbed the keys and walked to the door.

"Be right back, need to get something at the corner store before we leave," I called to the girls.

"Okay, Mom," they called in unison.

I was back home and in the bathroom within fifteen minutes. I peed on the little stick and stared at the floor for another fifteen minutes. I didn't pray or wish for or against anything. So much had happened in the last couple of months that my brain was completely fried.

The timer went off on my phone, and without any hesitation, I stood and looked at the stick—ripping the Band-Aid off per se. And there was the little blue plus sign that said I was positive. There was no doubt—it was in sharp contrast to the white background. I was pregnant. And I had no idea who the father was. A jackass psycho? Or was it a smooth-talking one-night stand?

Chapter 1 - Tate

I'd forgotten to leave the porch light on before I'd left a few days ago, so now I stood outside, fumbling with my keys after midnight, my suitcase in one hand and keys in the other. Thankfully, my night vision was better than average due to being a shifter. Dragon eyes weren't as good at night as that of a wolf or bear, but it was still better than human sight. Finally finding the right key, I unlocked the door and stepped into my house, hitting the light switch with an elbow. The suitcase rolled over toward the couch as I unbuckled the pistol harness around my shoulders.

My three buddies and I started a security firm fifteen years prior, and the job took me out of town a lot, working as a bodyguard or setting up and demonstrating the security systems Steff had created. It felt good to be home. My body was bone tired after this two-month job guarding a pop star princess. It was a fine gig. I'd gotten to tour the country and see the sights, which was always sort of fun. The problem was that the chick was like a damned nympho and wouldn't keep her hands off me. She'd tried to fuck me five or six times over the course of the tour. She was hot, yeah, but I was a professional. I never, ever, mixed business with pleasure.

I'd made it very clear to her that I was not interested, especially after she'd tried to talk me into a three-way with her and one of her backup dancers. It got so bad that even her manager tried to tell her to find another guy to set her sights on. I'd finished the last show and deuced out before she could pull the whole *tour's over, you're not on duty anymore, let's party* stuff. Just too messy. Our firm was one of the most respected in the country, and I wouldn't risk our reputation for a wild romp in the hay.

I walked across the living room, unbuttoning my dress shirt, and glanced out the front window. There was a car parked outside the house across the street. I frowned. I'd been so dog tired when I pulled into my driveway that I hadn't registered it until now. I leaned closer to the window and saw a bunch of broken down cardboard boxes stuffed into the trash can at the end of the driveway. Definitely looked like someone had moved into the place.

I sighed. It had been nice not having neighbors the last few years. I wasn't really a people person. It was what made me good at my job. It was easy for me to tell some crazy fan to get their ass the fuck back and not feel bad about it. Now, I'd have to make nice and introduce myself at some point in the coming days.

I was starving, but my exhaustion was winning out. I'd been awake for nearly thirty-six hours. Plus, my fridge was empty. I ate a spoonful of peanut butter, tore the rest of my clothes off, and collapsed into bed.

Sleeping for over twelve straight hours, I awoke to the sound of a box truck door rolling up. My eyes snapped open, and I rubbed my eyes, feeling groggy. The clock by the bed said I'd overslept since I told the guys I'd be at the office by two. If I were going to make it on time, I'd have to hurry, especially since I'd need to pick lunch up on the way. My stomach was about to eat itself. After a quick shower, I threw on clothes and brewed a cup of coffee.

Outside, two guys were carrying boxes and furniture down the metal ramp of the truck—it seemed they were hired movers based on their uniforms. The actual new neighbors were nowhere in sight. My phone rang, pulling my attention away from the house across the street. It was Miles.

"You still coming in?"

Groggy and disoriented from sleep, I nodded before realizing he couldn't see me. "On my way. I overslept."

"Bro, it's two in the afternoon."

"Yeah, well, some of us have to work for a living."

"Very funny. I'll see you in a few minutes."

Hanging up, I jumped in my car and pulled out of the driveway. As I pulled away, I craned my neck to try and see the new neighbors. No-one but the movers. I'd have to wait till later to see if they looked like serial killers or not.

At the office, I was in for a surprise. The guys weren't in our small conference room. They were all packed into Miles's office. Miles saw me and motioned for me to come in. When I stepped inside, he nodded for me to close the door. I raised my eyes. That was unusual. This was obviously not going to be what I thought it was. I'd assumed that Blayne was going to give me a new bodyguard assignment. He typically did security analysis, but he was also the main team member who booked jobs. I was the field guy, doing the jobs that required the most travel. I was also requested more than any other guy we had on contract. But a job assignment would have been a simple open-door meeting. Three minutes and done.

Instead, I found Miles, Blayne, and Steff. No one else. We had some clerical workers, security techs, and secretaries—a staff of maybe a dozen. None of them were shifters. But every man standing in the office was.

"So," I said. "What's with the cloak and dagger?"

Miles sighed and leaned forward. "There's been a development."

Steff chuckled. "You haven't sold the company to some mercenary-for-hire group, right? Black Water or some shit?"

A look of irritation flashed across Miles's face. "Seriously? Can we be professional for one damn minute?"

"Fine, fine. What's the big news?" Steff asked as he took a seat on a filing cabinet.

"We got a call last night from an alpha in a nearby shifter pack. The wolf clan that has a spot about forty miles away."

Blayne leaned against the wall, popping peanuts into his mouth one at a time. "And what did the werewolves have to say?"

"Wolf shifters. You know we hate being called werewolves," Miles corrected.

Blayne rolled his eyes. "Yeah, sure, get on with it, my man."

"Anyway…" Miles visibly tried to push away his irritation, "…the alpha asked me if I'd noticed any strange disappearances in our area. Among shifters. I told him our pack was only the four of us, so we'd have known if one of us was missing. The guy then tells me that he's had several of his guys up and vanish. No sign, no word, just gone. Said it was like nothing he has seen before. They won't answer their phones, they haven't shown up at their homes, fully ghosted."

I frowned. "Maybe they were some sketchy dudes and took off to start their own pack?"

Miles pointed at me and nodded. "Exactly what I thought. So, I made some calls. I checked in with the other four packs within a day's drive of here. Every one of them has had disappearances. Exactly the same story all around."

Miles and I had known each other since college. We'd both been kicked out of our respective packs. After discovering each other's secrets, we'd formed our own mini-clan. Even though we weren't the same species, it helped prevent us from going feral. Having another shifter around kept us grounded. We'd found Blayne and Steff not long after and had been together ever since. We were a strange group. Blayne was a panther, Steff a bear, and Miles a wolf. I didn't know of any other cross-species clans, but it worked for us. And while none of us was officially the Alpha, Miles was the *face* of the business. Other than that, we all owned an equal twenty-five percent. Over the last fifteen years, we've gotten to know each other very well. I knew Miles even better than the other two. When he spoke about the shifters going missing, he did a good job of keeping a placid look on his face. I could read his eyes, though. He was fucking scared. Miles was almost never scared. It put me on edge.

I uncrossed my arms and leaned on his desk. The next word that came out of my mouth sent a shockwave through the room.

"Hunters?"

Steff's and Blayne's eyes widened. Miles pulled in his bottom lip and chewed at it. There were very few things in the world that could make a room full of shifters nervous. Hunters were one of those things.

Miles finally nodded. "We haven't heard any news of hunters in the area, but with these stories, we need to be on guard."

Steff shook his head. "But... hunters usually stay near bigger cities, right? More bang for your buck. That's part of why we kept the office here instead of Boulder or Denver or something. We wanted to stay out of sight and out of mind. Have you ever heard of hunters coming out into rural areas like this?"

Miles shrugged. "There's been stories. Mostly rumors. Though I've never heard of them operating anywhere near here. It may be nothing, but we need to keep an open mind *and* an open eye. This town is small, it should be easy to notice anyone who doesn't belong. That being said..." Miles glanced back at me. "Tate is the strongest of us. Being a dragon shifter means he is the best chance we have against whatever may be targeting shifters. I've suspended all his upcoming jobs for the time being. All other contract work will go to one of the other guys on payroll."

That didn't please me. I only spent two or three months a year in Lilly Valley, and that was spread out over a whole year. Usually, I was only ever around for a week or two between jobs. It made me anxious to think about sticking in one place for longer than that. I hadn't done that since my family kicked me out of the clan all those years ago. But Miles was right. Shifters were all stronger, faster, and more powerful than humans, but dragons were above even other shifters in that respect. I nodded my acceptance.

Miles looked relieved that I hadn't made a fuss about the decision. "All right. Watch your backs. If you guys see anything, hear anything, or identify a threat, let the rest of us know ASAP. Fair?"

We nodded. It was a good plan. My dragon grumbled deep inside my head. It didn't like the idea of an enemy—especially one that seemed to be dangerous. Dealing with drunk fans or horny stalkers was easy. They were no real threat. This was different.

We filed out of the office to strange glances from the staff, who were obviously wondering what had been so hush-hush. None of them knew we were shifters. Very, *very* rarely did any human ever find out about the race of beings that shared the earth with them. Honestly, it would have probably been a bigger story than if aliens were discovered. That was a threat, or unknown, that was way out *there*. We were right here. We lived next door, bagged your groceries, did your taxes, and kept handsy concert goers from groping your tits. If the news ever got out that we were here? That we'd been living amongst humans for centuries? It would be absolute anarchy.

Hunters were the humans who knew about us. They were a small, but well-trained, well-funded group, and very good at their jobs. In the distant past, their numbers had been larger, but they'd dwindled over the last two or three centuries. Most were drawn to the hunt due to a need for vengeance. They were people who usually wouldn't have followed that calling, and they burned out quickly once the reality set in that they would need to kill a living, sentient, creature. The most irritating thing about them was that they'd come about because of my own kind.

Shifters could go feral when they weren't able to band together with a pack. Once feral, we become… well, we become the monsters of movies. Bloodthirsty and violent. Legends came about for a reason, and now the rest of us had to deal with the consequences of a few feral shifters hundreds of thousands of years ago killing and eating some humans.

Looking around at our staff, I had to force myself not to wonder if one of them was an informant for the hunters. The idea was ridiculous, but paranoia could do strange things to a man.

"Tate, you wanna grab dinner tonight? Burgers?" Stef called out to me.

I waved at him as I left. "Sounds good. Text me. I'll meet you."

Outside, the warm air hit me, and I took a second to glance around. I was always in such a hurry to get out of this place for the next job I rarely ever got the chance to enjoy the views. The mountains in the distance, the bright blue sky? I shrugged and told myself there were much worse places to spend some time.

I drove home and saw that the moving van was gone. The number of broken down cardboard boxes outside seemed to have multiplied exponentially. I didn't see any cars, so I figured the neighbors were exploring the new town.

I'd never been what anyone would call *friendly*. That was especially true of my neighbors. I was usually out of town, so most of them didn't even know my name. Things being the way they were, I wasn't concerned with being buddies with these new people.

Before I unlocked my door, a thought formed in my mind. Turning, I looked back over my shoulder at the house. Brand new neighbors after three years? At the exact same time shifters were disappearing? I wasn't so jaded or paranoid that I no longer believed in coincidences, but I decided to check this out. Better safe than sorry.

My phone was out of my pocket before the door was even closed behind me. Miles answered.

"What's up?"

I spoke while looking at the house through my blinds. "Miles, I've got some new neighbors moving in across the street. You know that vacant house?"

"Yeah. Who are they?"

"Haven't laid eyes on them yet. I just thought… well. Kinda weird timing, right?"

"Someone new moves in next door to a shifter while shifters are going missing?"

"Literally exactly what I thought."

"Okay, I can try to dig up some info. May take a few days."

"Thanks, man. It's probably nothing, but it would be good to know."

Chapter 2 - Harley

Lilly Valley was as beautiful as Maddox had said. More so, even. My jaw had dropped when we pulled off the interstate and saw the place a week ago. The mountains, trees, and rivers were all picturesque. The girls had also been awed, but that awe had dissipated a bit when we drove through the "downtown" area. It was as far from New York City as you could possibly get.

On the plus side, there wasn't much commercialization. The only chain store I saw was a Dollar General on the outskirts of town. Everything else was mom-and-pop or independently owned. That made the town quaint and cute, but it wasn't a hub of activity that two teenage girls craved. There was at least a movie theater, but it looked like it was only open on the weekends and only had two screens. As far as entertainment, that was about the extent of it, but there must have been hiking trails, and probably places to have guides take you on canoe or fishing trips. That would be fun and broaden our horizons, but I could see the look of anxiety on the girls' faces.

The last thing I wanted was for Mariah and Jordyn to be miserably bored here, but I didn't know how to prevent that until we got settled in. Now, a week later, the boredom was really setting in. They'd gone on walks, and I'd even bought them bikes. They'd enjoyed that for a day or two, but they'd already ridden through the whole town. They'd seen all they could see. Thankfully, they were being good sports about it.

I decided to make my famous chocolate-chip pancakes on the morning of our eighth day in Lilly Valley. They were famous because there was usually more chocolate than cake.

I handed Mariah a jug of syrup when Jordyn let it slip. "I'm so bored." She sighed. I watched Mariah's eyes narrow and heard a soft thump under the table. "Oww," Jordyn hissed.

I put my spatula down and turned the stove off. "No, I want you to be honest. This is a family, not a dictatorship. You all know why we had to move?"

Jordyn nodded. "Luis?"

I nodded back at her. "I knew you guys were smart enough to figure it out."

"It was hard to miss," Mariah said. "You guys broke up, and then he started showing up all the time. It was… weird. I'd never been afraid of him before, but after? He didn't act the same."

I sighed as anger seeped into me. I hated that he'd scared my girls. It also reinforced the thought that I'd done the right thing by moving us here. The more distance between Luis and us, the better.

Mariah finally said, "We miss our friends. And it's still kind of hard to think of this place as home. I miss the city and everything." Being the sweetheart she was, she added, "But at the end of summer, school will start, and we'll have a ton of new friends."

Mariah was an amazing girl. She will grow up to be strong, smart, and kind. All the things a mother wished for her daughter, and I was grateful for her. She was trying her best to make the best out of a bad situation, to help her little sister feel better about this change. Knowing I relied on her so much had guilt gnawing at me. I depended on her to be––not a second parent—but a second steadying influence on our home. She was a good kid and never complained about anything. She got that from her dad, one hundred percent. I missed Sam so much, and it was nice to see little flashes of him in his children every now and then.

Before I could speak more about the move, the sound of a mower erupted from across the street. All three of us jumped. It was the first sound other than our own noise we'd heard. The street was very quiet, and the neighbors seemed to keep strange hours. We hadn't seen them at all so far other than seeing a car in the driveway.

Maddox hadn't been out here in forever and had never met them, either. The last time he and Julie had been out here, an elderly lady had lived across the street. All he knew now was that the house had been sold a few years before, and he didn't know who lived there now. It wasn't a lot to go on, and it was the last bit of info I needed. Hopefully, it wasn't some creepy peeping tom or something. The last thing I needed was to run from my home to get away from one loser, only to move in next to another one. Perhaps a family lived across the street. It would be nice for the girls to meet some kids to hang out with.

Our serious discussion was put on pause, for the time being, by the nervous excitement of meeting the neighbors. I stood and slid the pan off the stove into the sink. Before I could even turn around, Jordyn was already at the door. By the time Mariah and I got there, Jordyn had the door open and was gaping across the street. It didn't take me long to see what she was looking at.

The neighbor was pushing a mower across his lawn. His back was turned to us, and it was a hell of a back. He was nothing but rippling muscles, shining with sweat. We stepped out onto the lawn, ogling him as he cut his grass. I could practically smell the teenage hormones coming off the girls, but honestly, I couldn't take my eyes off him long enough to scold them.

I opened my mouth to tell the girls to go inside when he turned the mower around. I saw his face, and my blood ran cold. This could not be happening. There was no way this was possible. My life couldn't be this complicated and cursed. There was no denying it, though. The sweat running down his face into the close cropped beard, the nose, the chin? It was my one-night stand. The possible father of my baby.

Before I could spin on my heel and sprint back into the house, he glanced up, probably finally sensing the eyes locked onto his body. His eyes slid up to mine, the look of surprise evident on his face. The moment our eyes locked, the world seemed to tilt and spin. His eyes widened in recognition. We stood like that, looking at each other for several seconds. Each second felt like an eternity—almost like we stood there like that for years, staring each other down as the world spun and aged around us.

His look of shock slowly morphed into one of confusion. Finally, a look of annoyance clouded his otherwise handsome face. Pulling his eyes away, he leaned over and turned off the mower. The sudden silence broke whatever spell I was under, and I looked at the girls. They were both staring at me in concern.

"Go inside," I whispered, almost inaudibly.

"Mom, are you okay? Do you *know* that guy?" Mariah asked.

"No way. We just got here, she doesn't know anybody," Jordyn said.

Finding my voice, I barked, "Inside now. Please. And close the door."

I was almost never short with the girls like that. I could see the surprise on their faces, but they headed inside without protest. I was glad they obeyed because he was stalking across the street toward me. Panic flooded me, and

I had a sudden urge to run. It was like I was a cornered animal, and a giant beast was stalking me, ready to pounce. My knees shook, but I clenched my hands into fists and tried to steady myself.

The man stepped up off the road onto our lawn and crossed the last few feet in a couple of strides. He stopped, four feet from me, and stared at me again. The look on his face was not a welcome one. He looked pissed. Yanking a bandana from his back pocket, he wiped dirt and grass from his hands, looking down while he cleaned. He was clearly trying to figure out what to say.

Finally, he looked back at me, and said, "So… what the hell are you doing here?"

He spat the words at me like I had gone on some personal attack, as if my presence here was an affront to his very being. Irritation replaced my fear and panic.

I crossed my arms. "Well, the same could be said about you."

He held up a hand and shook his head. "Nope, don't try that shit. I've lived in this town for fifteen years, and I've lived in that house…" he pointed back across the street, "…for over three years. When I moved in, this house…" he waved at my new home, "…was empty. Now, somehow, a chick I hooked up with for *one night* a couple of months ago has moved in across from me. Eighteen hundred miles away from where we first met? In a fucking one-horse town with less than five thousand people? A town almost *no one* has heard of? How does that make any damned sense?"

There was no way to explain it other than a coincidence, but my God, how could something like this happen by coincidence? My head was pounding with an oncoming headache.

Holding up my hands, I said, "Okay, look. I know this is weird, but we got here a couple of days ago. This is all just a… coincidence."

By sheer force of will, I didn't wince as I said the words. One look at his face told me that he didn't believe it for one second.

Continuing, I said, "Seriously? How the hell could I have tracked you more than halfway across the country? I didn't have your phone number or address. Shit, I don't even know your name." A wave of shame slid over me, but what was done was done.

His eyes were still full of suspicion. It was almost like he was paranoid—a very far cry from the suave, confident man I'd met in New York that night.

"Lady, I don't know why you're here, but I need to make one thing clear. What we had that night was just that. *One night.* No replays, no extra fun. I don't need you getting any ideas about us. If you're looking for round two, you're out of luck."

The man—*Christ, I still didn't know his fucking name*—was pretty full of himself. "You really think I moved all the way across the country with my girls to stalk down some man? Just to ride his cock one more time? I'm a little offended you would even think that, honestly."

He sighed. "You aren't the first woman to stalk me, and I'm sure you won't be the last." He chuckled humorlessly. "This really is a bit much to hook up one more time."

That did it. I was no longer surprised, shocked, or confused. I was pissed. He hadn't been spiteful or mean when he said it. It was very matter-of-fact and straightforward, like it was obvious that was what I wanted.

"Listen, prick, you need to watch how you talk to me. My daughters could hear you."

We both turned to look at the house and saw the girls peeking through the curtains by the door. Catching sight of us, they ducked away. He laughed, and it was actually a good-natured chuckle, but the look of happiness vanished quickly. Instead of pushing things, he started backing away.

"I'll stay out of your way if you stay out of mine."

He spun on his heel and walked back to his house. I watched him go, and my hand swept across my belly unconsciously. Well, after that, there was no way I was going to tell him about the baby. The decision was made. He was mad enough to think I wanted another roll in the hay. I couldn't imagine what he'd say if I tried to convince him he may have gotten me pregnant.

Chapter 3 - Tate

It took all my control not to slam the front door as I went inside, leaving my mower in the yard. I stomped back and forth across the living room. Every few paces, I glanced out the window at the house across the street. What the fuck was happening? This was absolutely crazy. Batshit crazy, to be exact.

I went to the kitchen and yanked a beer out of the fridge, downing it in three fast gulps before I grabbed a second and flopped down on the couch. All I wanted was to get my mind off it, but that wasn't possible. I actually had to think harder on it, especially considering the information Miles had given us about the missing shifters. Was this woman involved? Was she a hunter? That sounded crazy, but maybe. Could she have marked me as a target in New York? Followed me all the way here? But what about the kids? They were too young to be hunters.

Sipping at the beer, I pulled my phone from my pocket. Maybe Miles had been able to dig up that info on her. I dialed and took another drink as it rang.

"Tate?" Miles answered.

"Yeah, hey… did you get a chance to look into my new neighbor?" I didn't go into the fact that I'd fucked her seven or eight weeks before. No need to muddy the waters.

"Actually, I did. I've been compiling all the information into a file. I can email it over in five or ten minutes."

"That would be great." Unable to control myself, I added, "Did… anything seem weird?"

A pause, then he replied, "Not really. Pretty standard stuff. I'll send it as soon as I get all the files into one folder."

"Okay, cool. Thanks, man."

"No problem."

Five minutes later, my laptop chirped with an email notification. Almost spilling my beer in my haste, I yanked it across the coffee table and pulled up the message. Eagerly scanning the information, the first thing I noticed was her name. Harley King, maiden name Stone.

I leaned back and groaned, putting my face in my hands. A married woman? That was not cool. I cringed at the idea of some poor guy sitting at home wondering where his wife was while I was banging her brains out. My moral code when it came to sex was no clients and no married or taken women. It was a simple but fucking iron-clad rule. I'd broken that rule once or twice, but by complete accident—women who had lied about being in relationships. I'd always felt like absolute shit when it happened, so I tried everything I could to prevent it.

I leaned forward, shaking my head. It was done, and there was nothing I could do to fix it. Scanning the document, I saw that I actually had no reason to be upset. Harley was a widow. That surprised me. She was awfully young to be widowed. Something tragic must have caused that. I found a couple of news articles as well as an obituary for a Samuel King. He'd been an officer with the NYPD and had been killed in the line of duty three years ago.

"That fucking sucks," I whispered to myself.

I didn't want the lady living next door, but I wasn't a total asshole. It was tough to imagine raising two young kids after your husband was killed. I could empathize with that. The kids were Mariah King, aged sixteen, and Jordyn King, aged fourteen. There were scanned pictures from a yearbook. I didn't know how Miles had acquired those.

Thankfully, their pictures matched the girls next door. No stolen identities here.

Miles had been beyond thorough. There was a copy of Harley's marriage certificate, scans of the girls' report cards, even a few hyperlinks to websites Harley had designed. I'd casually clicked them and was impressed with the job she'd done. She was good. It was also a job she could do remotely, which gave her the means to get out of the city and still remain employed. That's what I wanted to figure out next. Why the hell was she here?

A possible reason appeared in one of the last files I opened. There was a copy of a restraining order she'd filed against a Luis Ortiz a couple of weeks before she moved to Lilly Valley. A black-and-white scan of a driver's license picture popped up. He was a good-looking dude, but something about his picture put me on edge—like there was something under the surface ready to snap. I didn't like him.

The order stated that he'd begun stalking and threatening Harley and her daughters. There were a few examples, and they weren't the worst things I'd ever seen or heard about, but it had the scent of escalation. Had she not gotten out, things would probably have continued to get more and more out of hand. I had to admit, it was probably a good plan to move away from the city.

Miles had done a little digging on the Luis guy after finding the restraining order. He didn't really have any work history, but his tax returns showed he was claiming a ton of money. Weird. Several known associates were fairly high up in one of the New York crime families. There was no explicit proof, but every bit of circumstantial evidence pointed to him being connected to the mob in some way, shape, or form. This guy was dangerous on a different level. Lots of guys were pieces of shit who liked to slap around or intimidate women. Not many had the connections to make someone they didn't like disappear. If this guy was really that nuts, *and* dangerous, then he might try to follow her to Lilly Valley. That type of trouble was something the guys and I could do without. I was less than thrilled about the possibility.

I needed to talk to the guys. If I didn't, I'd go freaking crazy. I changed out of my mowing clothes as fast as I could and, making sure to get into my car and away before the new neighbors came out and saw me, I drove to the office. A quick call on the way let me know that Miles, Steffen, and Blayne were all at the office. Good, I wouldn't have to wait for them to get there. Fifteen minutes later, we were crammed back into Miles's tiny office, like the other day.

"Okay, man, what's this about?" Steff asked.

Miles raised an eyebrow. "Is this about your neighbor? Is that it?"

I sighed and leaned back in my seat, rubbing my temples. "Okay, so, you guys remember the last travel job I had, right?"

Blayne nodded. "The pop star? Nineteen-year-old chick who tried to suck your cock every night?"

"Yeah, right. Anyway, a few weeks before that tour was over, she did a two-night event in New York. On the second night, after she passed out drunk as shit on her tour bus, I decided to go out on the town. Have some drinks since I'd gotten off early for once."

"Does this story have a point?" Steff laughed.

I glared at him. "While I was out, there was a gorgeous woman sitting across the bar. I introduced myself, we drank and flirted, and one thing led to another and… well… you know."

"You… played Jenga?" Blayne said.

"You made sand castles," Steff said, nodding and snapping his fingers.

"You obviously watched a marathon of *Downton Abbey*," Miles said.

I snarled. "Oh, for fuck's sake. We had sex, all right? Fucked, screwed, made the beast of two backs, did the nasty. Stop being assholes."

The guys chuckled but nodded for me to go on.

"So, we do the thing, and it's fucking amazing, Maybe the best night of my entire life. I had a flight out at like five in the morning, so I bounce before she ever wakes up. I flew out to meet the singer chick in Los Angeles for the next leg of her tour, and I have a great memory of the lady in New York. Fast forward a few weeks, and I'm back home. Miles tells us shifters are disappearing and going missing. Be on the lookout for anything strange?"

"Well, two freaking hours ago, I'm mowing my yard. Not a care in the world. I turn the mower around, and look up. My new neighbors are across the street, staring at me. Two teenage girls and a mom. Guess, if you can, who the fucking mom was?"

They all stared at me for several seconds. All three of them had confused looks. I would have, too, if I'd been them. Even after talking about the lady in New York, it was hard for them to fathom how she could possibly be my neighbor. It was literally so unlikely that I'd made it as obvious as possible, but their minds refused to make the connection.

Blayne was the first one to get it. His eyes went wide. "No… fucking… way."

I nodded. Steffen and Miles looked confused. Blayne smiled and said, "His one-night stand chick. She's the new goddamned neighbor."

Steffen's jaw dropped, and he said, "Wait, what? How is that possible?"

"Right…" Miles said, "…the odds of that are like, a billion to one. You'd have a better chance of finding a dollar on the street, buying a lottery ticket, and winning the lottery than for this lady to somehow wind up being your neighbor in itty bitty, middle-of-nowhere Lilly Valley."

"This is what I'm saying."

The other three looked at each other and laughed.

"What's so funny?" I asked through gritted teeth.

"The thought that you have to wave at this lady every morning when you get your newspaper is pretty funny," Steff said.

Blayne raised his hand, pretending to wave. "Hey, Miss. It was really nice rubbing my genitals on yours that one time. Welp, see you tomorrow."

I hissed a breath out my nose. "Would you guys quit?"

"Okay, okay, all done," Miles said, though he was smiling with the rest of them. "I'll have to dig more into it. Though, I sent you pretty much everything there is to know."

I rubbed my head. "Miles, man, this can't be a coincidence, there's just no way. I—" I stopped to think about how I reacted to her and winced inwardly. "I was kind of a dick to her. Not kind of, I guess I was a total asshole to her. I was freaked out by her showing up there, and the whole story about the shifters going missing. I guess it wasn't a great introduction."

Steffen looked at me and raised an eyebrow. "You mean you weren't your usual double-oh seven? Usually, you have ladies eating out of your hand."

I shrugged. "Like I said, I was suspicious and on edge. If she's on the up-and-up, I'll go over and apologize or something."

Miles glanced down at my hands. "Are you sure you're good?"

Confused, I glanced down. I'd been twisting my fingers, popping my knuckles, and rubbing my fingers together. I was fidgeting like crazy, and I hadn't even realized it.

"All right, listen, I know you aren't used to being in one spot for very long. This whole neighbor lady thing is making you antsy as all hell. We need you here, but I don't want you going stir crazy." He pulled a manila envelope from his desk and handed it to me. "Here's a new job that came in this morning. Some tech billionaire needs a bodyguard for some R&D trip in Europe. His usual team will be with his wife and kids on a trip to Jamaica. It should get you away for a couple of weeks. Let you get some distance and some perspective. Sound good?"

I let out a deep sigh. I really hadn't understood how stressed I was, or how caged in I felt until he gave me the out. I was grateful. I couldn't wait to get home and pack. I took the envelope and left, barely saying bye to the guys as I went.

Not wasting any time, I started packing as soon as I was home. I was zipping up my garment bag of suits when the doorbell rang. Glancing over my shoulder, my eyes narrowed as I looked down the hallway to the front door. I had a sneaking suspicion who was at the door.

A few strides later, I yanked open the door. My suspicions were confirmed by the new neighbor standing on my porch. *Her name is Harley,* I reminded myself. She looked nervous as hell.

Before I could say anything, she started speaking. "Listen, I know this is weird, but I wanted to clear the air. This is not what I'd imagined when we moved out here. We sort of… left some things unsaid earlier. I want you to know that I am, in no way, a stalker or whatever you think. This wasn't a plan, or a plot, or whatever, Mr…"

I blinked, realizing I now knew her name, but she didn't know mine. "Sorry, yeah. I'm Tate, Tate Mills."

Harley nodded and flashed me a tight smile. "Mr. Mills. My late husband's partner offered the house to me out of the blue because…" She paused, and I could see her mind racing. She must have been running from the Ortiz guy, but she didn't have a clue that I knew that.

She gathered her thoughts and finished. "Because we needed a change of pace. An adventure, maybe."

I grinned and nodded. My suspicions were fading. This lady did not seem like she was hiding anything, or being shady. Could it really be some mind-boggling improbable accident? As hard as it was to believe, it was looking more and more like it was a possibility.

"So, I want you to know that my daughters and I won't cause you any problems, we'll stay out of your way."

The tension that had been building in me since the moment I'd looked up and saw her standing on her lawn had almost totally faded. "It's fine, really. Sorry I was such a dick earlier. We're all good."

She visibly relaxed and smiled. "Great. Nice to meet you, uh, again."

"Right. Listen, I've got a business trip to pack for and a flight to catch."

She held up her hands and turned toward the steps. "Got it. Well, we'll see you when you get back. Have a safe trip."

"Thanks," I said and watched her go down my steps.

My heart suddenly sped up. In an instant, it felt like I had just gotten done sprinting a mile. Dizzy, I stepped back inside and closed the door. I leaned against it and gasped for breath. I pressed a hand against my chest as sweat ran down my forehead. What the hell? I slid down to the ground and took several deep breaths. It took a few minutes, but the feeling slowly faded.

I stood and went back to packing my bag. Nothing like that had ever happened to me before. It made me even more determined to get the hell out of this town for a few weeks. After zipping up my big suitcase, I packed the backpack I usually took along, then threw it all in the back of the car. I pulled away and forced myself not to look at Harley's house as I left for my assignment.

Chapter 4 - Harley

After three weeks, it seemed like the girls had finally settled in. The only real excitement we'd had was meeting our new neighbor. Thankfully, the girls had been smart enough not to ask about that. Honestly, I was surprised they hadn't. Our little showdown on the front lawn had to have seemed really strange to them. Why wouldn't it? Some stranger had confronted their mother in front of their house a few days after we moved in. It hadn't helped that it had been obvious that we knew each other.

Tate hadn't been around for almost two weeks. He'd said he had a trip, but two weeks seemed excessive. It was hard to talk myself out of the idea that he was staying away, so he didn't have to see us.

One of our other neighbors, Mrs. Rose, introduced herself a few days after he left and informed me that he worked for some type of security firm. That tidbit of info would have been welcome in most situations. Knowing your neighbor was paid to protect people could come in handy. At least, that would have been the case if it didn't seem like he despised you.

I jerked awake in the middle of the night. I rolled over and glanced, bleary-eyed, at the alarm clock. It was three in the morning, and as I woke up, I realized what had ripped me out of sleep. Music. Loud music. Coming from across the street. I swung my legs from under the sheet and walked to the window. Pulling the blinds aside, I looked over at Tate's house. There was one light on in the bedroom, and the music was definitely coming from over there. It pissed me off that he didn't have any more respect for us than that. This noise would wake up the girls.

Grudgingly, I slipped on sweat pants, an old tee-shirt, and flip-flops and made my way downstairs, and out the front door. As I walked across the yard, I noticed that the car in Tate's driveway wasn't the one that was here when he was. Nowhere near it. I stopped walking and gaped at the bright yellow Ferrari. What the hell? After staring at the car for several seconds, I continued to the front door.

I knocked twice, but no one came to the door. The music was too loud. It didn't even have vocals, it was just electronic dance music. I pounded harder on the door. It still took nearly a minute before someone came to the door.

The door swung inward, and I winced. The music was at least three times louder now with the door open. But it was nothing compared to the sight that greeted me. A woman stood in the doorway, a glass of champagne in one hand, the other on her hip. She wore dark red lingerie that left nothing to the imagination. Literally. The lacy fabric rose up to cover her breasts, but the fabric was so thin and delicate, it was translucent. My eyes locked on her nipples before I realized what I was doing. I quickly glanced up at her face. How could anyone answer the door dressed like that?

"Well, who the fuck are you?" the woman asked.

"I, uh, live across the road. Your music woke me up. Can you turn it down before you wake my kids up?"

The woman looked me up and down. I'd felt the eyes of a lot of men in my life. Noticed them doing the same thing. In all those instances, they were checking to see if I was something they wanted. This *inspection* was different. It was almost like she was grading me. Somehow, it was worse than a drunk guy ogling me. She must have judged that I wasn't a threat—I wasn't sure how I felt about that—because she smiled at me. The smile was not nice, though. There was a hateful quality to it. There was also something vaguely familiar about the girl. And she was a girl. No way she was more than twenty-one.

She opened her mouth to say something, but her face went blank. She'd looked over my head toward the driveway. Her eyes glazed over, and she looked worried. Turning, I saw what she was looking at, and my blood ran cold. The music had been too loud for us to hear his truck pull into the neighborhood and park on the curb. Tate was unable to get into the driveway due to the Ferrari sitting there.

He looked pissed. Of course he did. I'd apparently stumbled on and ruined his welcome home party. A party that was supposed to consist of exactly two people. It appeared I was the third wheel. I glanced again at his *welcome home present*. I still couldn't believe she was wearing that. I told myself I wasn't jealous, but if I were being honest, there was a twinge of jealousy.

If Tate was angry, he wasn't directing it toward me. Instead of glaring at my face, he was staring daggers at the woman in his house. Strange.

"Tate, baby, I thought you'd never come home," the girl purred. She acted so familiar and sexual that I had a hard time not thinking they'd been intimate in the past.

Tate didn't answer her, but instead, he continued up the walkway and mounted the porch steps. One of his hands gently slid around my waist. It was surprising how tender he was as he moved me aside. I went without question, stepping into the shadow beyond the light of the porch bulb. His gentleness was even more surprising when I heard what came out of his mouth next.

He sneered at the woman. "What the fuck are you doing here? And how the fuck did you get into my goddamned house?"

Her calm, sexy, façade broke a bit, and the cocky smile on her lips faded. "Uh… well… I missed you, is all. Umm… I thought it would be nice to get together."

Tate's face twisted into a mask of disgust. I had never been so uncomfortable in my life. I wanted to be anywhere but here, but Tate was blocking the stairs with his body. Unless I wanted to jump over the hand rail and make a fool of myself sprinting back to my house, I was out of luck.

Almost as though he had read my thoughts, he turned his eyes to me. "Why were you over here?" he asked in a, blessedly, much kinder tone.

I swallowed hard, and said, "The, uh, music woke me. I came over to ask for it to be turned down so the girls wouldn't wake up."

I didn't think it was possible, but that enraged him further. He spun on his heel and glared at the woman again. She'd finally realized how ridiculous she must look and had crossed her arms to cover her basically naked breasts. Tate brushed past her and stomped into the house. Five seconds later, the music abruptly shut off. The silence was deafening after the blaring electronic music. I sighed gratefully and eased over toward the steps to go back home.

Tate stepped back out the door and saw me trying to leave. "Don't leave," he growled.

I froze at the top step, eyes wide, terrified to move a muscle. He turned back and loomed over the girl again.

Tate took a deep breath and tried to calm himself. "You have two minutes. Two. Fucking. Minutes. Get dressed, get your shit, and get the hell out of here." He stopped and frowned, like he'd just remembered something. "Wait a minute. In Chicago, when I lost my keys and wallet for a full day… Did you steal my stuff? Is that how you got in here? You got my address off my license and made a copy of my house key?"

The girl's eyes dropped to the ground, and even I knew he'd hit the nail on the head. Tate shook his head and smiled without humor. "Britt, if I ever see you here again, I'll call your manager, *and* I'll leak to the press that you're batshit crazy and a stalker. We'll see how many albums you sell after that shit hits the fan. You got it?"

That was when I realized where I recognized her from. I'd seen her face every day for the past two years. Except, it was usually made up in garish makeup with an over-the-top hairstyle. She was on the poster above Jordyn's bed. The girl—whose freaking nipples I'd seen five minutes ago—was Brittany Leigh. Her stage name was BrittLeigh, and she was Jordyn's favorite pop star. There was *no way* in hell I would ever tell my youngest daughter about this. I was actually fairly surprised she would go to such lengths to try to get into Tate's pants. She was a sex symbol all over the world. Men from Los Angeles to Tokyo would probably cut off their left nut to get a chance to roll in bed with her, and Tate was tossing her out on her rear like it was nothing.

Britt scooped up the clothes from the living room floor. Struggling to grab them all and stay covered herself at the same time, she called out, "Tate, I just wanted to have fun with you. I tried for months. I'm sorry, please calm down and don't be mad."

By the look of exhausted disdain that settled over his face, Tate was over the whole situation. "I won't say it again. You've got one minute now."

She didn't bother changing. Instead, with tears in her eyes, she ran out of the house and threw her clothes and purse into the passenger seat of the sports car, then she sped away. I was still standing on the top step of the porch. Without any idea what to do next, I inched my way down the steps.

Tate glanced over and stopped me. "Don't leave yet." He sighed and stuffed his hands in his pockets. "Are you guys okay?"

So far, I'd known two sides to Tate. A guy hot enough and charming enough to get me to throw caution to the wind for a one-night stand, and a paranoid, irate, and angry neighbor. But this side of him was different. There was concern in his voice. He really did care whether we were fine.

Before I could answer, he added, "My life shouldn't touch you or your girls. I'm sorry. I'll make sure it doesn't happen again."

His words bothered me. I didn't want to be totally shut out. At best, we would be neighbors, and it would be nice to have a cordial relationship. At worst? He was the father of my unborn baby, and… well. Making sure my feelings weren't written all over my face, I nodded and backed down the steps.

"Thanks for handling all that," I said before turning and walking across the street. I tried to convince myself that his eyes weren't on me as I went.

The next morning, Tate's truck was gone. Which was strange since he'd gotten home so late, and I'd woken up around six-thirty. Had he even slept before leaving again? I wouldn't get an answer to that. That truck wouldn't be in his driveway again for two weeks. Each day, I'd look out the window and rub my belly absently. I was three months pregnant and still not showing. What would I tell Tate when it became obvious I was pregnant?

Chapter 5 - Tate

I felt *like shit*. I'd been away from home for about two weeks, ever since that ridiculous performance Britt put on at my house. I'd been so embarrassed by her behavior that I'd headed out without sleep, just dropped my dirty clothes in the hamper, and packed fresh, then I was out the door. It was good to leave again, but now? I was miserable.

It had started a couple of days after I arrived in Toronto to do security for a hedge-fund guy. What started as a melancholy sort of depression had morphed into an ache that wouldn't quit. The only thing I could associate it with was homesickness, which I'd never had before in my life, not even as a kid—there had maybe been a little of that when I got kicked out of my pack.

All I did was think about going home and being back in Lilly Valley. It got to a point where I was struggling to concentrate on the job. The Fourth of July weekend started in a few days, and that also had me on edge. Back home, the little town of five thousand would balloon up closer to ten thousand. Tons of people came to swim in the lakes and rivers, go hiking and camping—all the fun outdoorsy stuff. That also meant a ton of new and strange faces in town. The fact that hunters may have been active near town made the thought of thousands of strangers almost panic-inducing.

Thursday night, Miles called me. I was still on duty, but my client was in a penthouse suite with three or four high-end working girls. I was blessedly out in the hall and didn't have to witness the disgusting debauchery.

When the phone buzzed, I answered eagerly. "Miles? What's up?"

"Hey, Tate. I have a question for you."

"Shoot."

"Do you know anyone who could take over for you on the job you're on?"

"I know of one guy who's probably free. I saw him yesterday. He's a professional. We had a drink last night after I got off duty. Why?"

"Well, there's been another disappearance—"

"Steff and Blayne?" I asked, panic rising in my chest.

"No, no, no, another pack about an hour outside town. It's got us more on edge than before. You know how the Fourth can get out here. Too many faces, too many scents, not enough of us to keep track of everyone. We all want you back, at least until the holiday is over. I know you wanted to be away, but—"

"I'll fly out tonight," I cut in.

"Wait, seriously? Can your guy get there that soon?"

"I'm sure he can. He's… well, he works for a competitor. Hope that's okay."

"Dude, I couldn't care less right now. Get a hold of him and get back home. I'll see you in the morning."

I hung up and dialed my buddy Darren, an ex-Army Ranger, and a good dude. We'd worked together twice before on big security jobs. Ten minutes later, after a quick negotiation on price and an info dump on the client, he was on his way.

While I waited, I shot him a secure email with all the itineraries and files he'd need for the job. He arrived less than an hour later. From the sounds coming out of the penthouse, he had a while yet before the client would be done. Dude must have taken a Viagra or something. I left Darren once he was settled in and confident with the assignment.

I got to the airport less than an hour after that. There was only one seat open on the flight to Colorado—first class, something I never splurged on, but I considered it a good investment. Otherwise, I would have had to wait until the following morning.

I became more and more antsy as I went through security and waited at the gate. It was like I couldn't get home fast enough. The homesickness had started fading as soon as I realized I was going back. So weird.

After a four-hour flight and an hour-and-half drive from the airport, I was home. Pulling into the driveway, I couldn't help but glance over at Harley's house. I didn't like how I'd left things with her, and I was a little ashamed for having Miles dig up dirt on her. It was pretty obvious she wasn't a hunter, or working with hunters. Somehow, someway, her arrival in Lilly Valley had been a total coincidence. As strange as that was, it was the only explanation. She'd come here to get away from her psycho, mob-connected boyfriend. And me, being the gallant gentleman I was, had treated her like shit the moment I saw her. God, I was such an asshole sometimes. Deciding it was probably better for both of us if she just ignored me, I went inside and collapsed in bed.

The next morning, I met the guys at the office. None of them looked very laidback. Steffen and Blayne looked tense and more serious than usual. Yeah, they were all on edge.

"Okay…" Miles started, "…we can all have a nice calm weekend, but we have to have our heads on a swivel. There's no other way to explain these disappearances except that the hunters are here. We are the only shifters in this town, so if they come here, we are the only targets. Make sense?"

We agreed solemnly. Our typical banter and ball busting was non-existent, but I had to admit even with the heavy atmosphere, I felt freaking great. Ever since I got back in town, it was like a weight had lifted off my chest. I couldn't explain it, and as we filed out of the office, I found myself walking down the sidewalk to the park.

In all the time I had lived here, I couldn't remember ever going to the park, but I was in a fantastic mood and wanted to enjoy the fresh air for once. On the way, I noticed that some sort of food festival was going on in the park. There were around twenty little tents set up with different food vendors, with tons of people milling around. It looked like a great place to set up, and people watch. Maybe one of them would be a shitty actor and show himself to be an obvious hunter.

I leaned against a lamp post beside a Greek food tent. The smell of falafel and gyros had my stomach grumbling, but I was a professional, and I kept my composure as I scanned the crowd, looking for anyone that didn't seem to belong in one way or another.

A young girl jogged up to me and playfully slapped my arm. I frowned and looked at her. She acted like she was familiar with me, but I didn't recognize her. Her jet black hair was waving in the breeze, and her hazel eyes looked at me playfully.

"Uh, can I help you, young lady?" I asked, sounding like the old dumb guy I probably was.

She smiled and said, "Duh, I'm your neighbor, Mr…"

Oh shit, Harley's daughter? I'd only glanced at them when I confronted Harley in her yard. My eyes had been glued to her, not her kids. But now that I knew, I could see the resemblance, especially in the eyes.

"Well, good to see you again, I guess," I said.

She grinned. "Why are you gone so often?"

"I work," I answered.

"Mom works, too, but she's always home. Do you sleep where you work? What do you do, anyway?"

I answered as best I could—unsure why I was entertaining her. "I go out of town and work in security. I protect people, train others to protect people, and help install security systems. Burglar alarms and stuff like that."

"That's cool, I guess."

Something about the girl called to me. Her spunky little attitude and openness was appealing. I liked her. We continued chatting, and I found myself laughing at some of her dumb jokes. A few minutes into our conversation, I glanced up and saw Harley and her older daughter walking toward us. Harley stopped dead in her tracks when she saw me, causing the older girl to almost collide with her mother. My heart jackhammered in my chest when I saw her, and something deep inside me roused from slumber.

My dragon had been in a long, dormant sleep. Not being in a pack with other dragon shifters, I very rarely felt the need to shift or fly alone. Steffen, Blayne, Miles, and I formed a makeshift pack, but it wasn't the same. It gave us camaraderie and prevented us from going feral, but it didn't give our beasts the species-specific bonding they needed. I couldn't remember the last time I'd shifted or felt my dragon stir, but for some reason, seeing Harley had awoken it.

The deep rumble in my chest meant the dragon saw something it wanted. Usually, this only happened when we spotted deer while flying, which made this… unusual. Being away from its kind made the dragon lonely, which bled over to me as well. The sight of Harley perked the beast up, and that scared me more than I could say. It had never reacted to a human like this. It hadn't reacted all those months ago in New York when I first met her. What was different now? It had been years and years since the dragon had taken such interest in *anything.*

Thinking back on it, maybe the dragon had stirred in that bar in New York. Something had made me look up and notice her. This was an altogether different matter though. It filled me with want, need, and desire. It was almost physical in its power. I bit the inside of my lip to pull myself together as Harley continued toward us.

She stepped up and grabbed the girl's hand. "Sorry about that. Jordyn's never met a stranger she didn't like. Pretty terrifying, actually."

I nodded. "Kinda dangerous walking up and talking to any person you see."

Jordyn shrugged. "I don't talk to *everyone*."

Harley and the other girl gave her a look that told me she was stretching the truth. The way she'd walked right up to me and started talking made me think the older King women had the gist of it. The older girl looked exactly like her mother, but thinner and taller. Harley was of average height, but with curves in all the right places.

Unbidden, my dragon dragged out a memory. My hands sliding across Harley's breasts, my tongue on her nipples, between her legs, her moist lips as she moaned beneath me. I blinked the memory away, my breath catching in my throat. Despite my best efforts, I caught myself staring again, and I had to shake the thoughts away, terrified I might pop a boner right there in front of the entire family. I'd be damned if I'd let my dragon do that to me in public, especially in front of children.

During the awkward silence accompanying my internal struggle, Jordyn whispered something to Mariah. The golden-haired girl shrugged and nodded.

Jordyn turned to me. "We've got a spot all picked out for the fireworks later. Our picnic blanket is already there. Do you want to watch them with us?"

"Jordyn…" Harley hissed, then added, "…um, I'm sure Mr. Mills has other plans for the evening." Her face reddened.

I made a disappointed face toward Jordyn. "Unfortunately, I'm working right now. On duty, you know? I won't be able to make it."

She pouted and kicked at the grass. Her disappointment almost made me feel bad. Not sure why. I didn't dislike kids or anything. I barely knew the girl. I guess I didn't like disappointing her.

Harley put an arm around her girls and turned them back toward the food festival. "Well, we need to get going. We don't need to bother Mr. Mills anymore."

I smiled. "She wasn't a bother. We were having a very good conversation."

Jordyn grinned at that as she and her sister turned to follow Harley. I couldn't help but smile as the little girl turned back to wave. Watching Harley walk away made my stomach ache painfully. I winced as my dragon stirred and whined, literally whined, inside my head. It was going crazy. Nothing like this had ever happened in all my life.

I ducked behind a tent and knelt, trying to gather myself. I couldn't actually talk to my dragon—it wasn't like I had multiple personalities or anything. That being what it was, I was so confused I didn't know what else to do.

"What the hell is going on?" I asked, focusing the question internally, toward the dragon.

What happened next sent a shockwave of fear through me. There seemed to be a massive struggle within me, and I nearly fell over as the will of the dragon desperately tried to claw to the forefront of my mind. I placed a hand on the grass to steady myself. Then my lips began to move, and a voice, deep and gravelly, whispered through me. *"Mate."*

My eyes bulged, and my head snapped up. I caught a glimpse of Harley through the crowd, buying a massive tower of cotton candy for the girls. The longer I looked at her, the more insistent the dragon became. It was desperate for me to approach her. Sweat beaded on my forehead as I fought the beast within.

Again that alien whisper escaped my lips. "*Mate.*"

I dug my fingers into the grass—confusion and fear filled me in equal measure. "What the fuck?"

Chapter 6 - Harley

The girls and I did a full tour of the food stalls and got something at nearly every stall. We made our way back to our picnic blanket, our arms laden with every kind of food and drink imaginable. The pregnancy cravings were kicking in big time. Usually, I would never splurge on food like this, but everything looked so damned good.

As we arranged everything on our blanket, my mind slipped back to the baby. I still hadn't told the girls I was pregnant, but the first trimester was over. I hadn't started showing until the fifth month with both of them, so I still had some time. Even with that, I had decided to tell the girls soon, just to get it out in the open. That would be a relief, but I had to think of Tate.

He'd eventually notice I was pregnant. Sooner or later, it would be evident. Would he even care enough to do the math? He'd have to put two and two together. Would he ask about it? Would he ignore it? I had so many questions, but I had no one to confide in or talk to.

I had a doctor's appointment soon, and then I'd have a better idea of the conception date. Luis and I had been having trouble before I found out he was a cheating bastard. We hadn't had sex in about three weeks before I spent the night with Tate. The dates were pretty close, and there was no way for me to know for sure who the father was until that appointment. Already, I'd resigned myself to raising the baby alone. Luis was a psycho, and Tate seemed aloof and distant toward me.

I stared down at the Cuban sandwich I'd ordered earlier and picked at the bread. Lost in my own thoughts, I didn't even notice the people setting up blankets and chairs around us. When I took a bite of my sandwich, I glanced over and saw a young woman struggling with a lawn chair, cooler, thermos, and blanket. She could barely move as she tried to set her chair next to our blanket.

Quickly putting my sandwich aside, I stood, and said, "Can I help?"

She looked at me with obvious relief. "Oh God. Yes, please."

I laughed and took the cooler and thermos from her. It freed her hands enough that she could put the chair down. She sighed, and her shoulders slumped dramatically.

"Thanks. I was about to die." She extended her hand. "My name is Emily."

Shaking the offered hand, I replied, "Harley, nice to meet you." I gestured to the girls. "These are my daughters, Jordyn and Mariah."

The girls went full teenager and barely looked up from their food to nod. I rolled my eyes and smiled. "Kids, right? Are you from Lilly Valley?"

Emily opened her lawn chair and sat down, then said, "Not really. I got here a few days ago. I came to help move my grandma into a nursing home. I'm the only grandchild and wanted to be here for her. Between getting her moved in and starting the process of cleaning out her house and listing it to sell..." She shrugged. "Today has been my first break in almost a week."

Settling back down on the blanket, I took another bite of my sandwich and started chatting with her. It was nice talking to someone else who was new in town. I asked her about her grandma, where she was from, and the usual things. She didn't go into detail. It may have been a sore subject. Our conversation flowed, and it was almost like we'd known each other forever. It was so nice to have someone to talk to.

"Harley, how did you and your two girls there end up in a small town like this?" Emily asked.

"I needed a change of pace. We're from New York City, and a friend of mine had a house down here that he rarely ever used. He offered it to us, and we jumped at the chance."

"Wow. That's a hell of a culture shock."

I shrugged. "To say the least."

"Have you met anyone since you've been here? Any tall, dark, and handsome men in this one-horse town?"

That subject was not something I wanted to get into, so I skirted around it.

It went on like that for an hour. Emily seemed really interested in my life, the girls, who my new neighbors were. I hadn't realized how much I'd missed talking to an adult. My work was digital and kind of isolated. The girls were… the girls. And my closest neighbor was a complicated mess. It felt good to spend time with someone who really wanted to know about me. Thankfully, I stopped myself from unloading every tiny detail on her, even though it seemed like Emily wanted nothing more than to hear about it. Before the music started, we made plans to hang out later in the week.

The first massive boom of the fireworks ended our conversation. I settled in with the girls, watching as colors arced across the sky and the echoing explosions bounced around the valley. The first few minutes were exciting, but I had a nagging sensation that someone was watching me. It was the same sensation I got when Luis was stalking me, and I could feel his eyes on me before I could see him. For a moment, I was terrified that Luis had found us. Was he here?

Glancing away from the show in the sky, I looked around the crowd. I wasn't sure I would see anyone, and I hoped to hell I wouldn't see Luis. I glanced about, hoping to see security or police in case I did see Luis. Instead, off in the distance, I saw Tate. He was standing by a T-shirt display, staring right at me. Our eyes locked, and the look on his face was the most intense expression I'd ever seen in my life. It was as if he was trying to look directly into my soul. Involuntarily, I shivered, and tore my gaze away from him. It was pretty obvious he still wasn't a fan of me being in town. The rest of the show went by in a blur, with me barely watching the fireworks. Instead, I thought about that thousand-yard stare he'd given me.

Later, after saying bye to Emily, the girls and I loaded up our things and headed for the car. As I put the blanket in the trunk, I noticed Tate walking toward me. My stomach lurched at the sight of him. It made no sense why he seemed to be so angry at me. I'd done nothing to cause him to react this way. Our last interactions had been calm, cordial, and almost friendly. What had happened between the meeting at the food stalls and the start of the fireworks?

I called out to the girls. "Get in the car, guys. I'll be there in a second."

He made it plain by the way he was moving that he was coming to talk to me, and I didn't want that to happen near my kids. Stepping away from the car and moving out into the parking lot, I met him. He still looked upset but also confused and more frazzled than I'd ever seen him. Even when he'd found a half-naked pop star in his house at three a.m., he'd had a quiet control that had seemed rock steady. Now, he had the air of someone on the verge of a panic attack.

He stepped up to me, and without preamble, he asked, "What are you?"

Frowning, I said, "A woman? A mother? What kind of question is that?"

Tate winced and shook his head. He looked at the pavement, and had some weird kind of solo conversation with himself. Was he crazy? He mumbled something about being human, but I couldn't make out exactly what he was saying.

He stopped whispering to himself and looked at me. "I don't trust you."

The words caught me off guard. They hurt me, and they pissed me off.

"Oh, you've made that very clear." I sneered. "I know you think your dick is some kind of fucking wonder drug, but it wasn't good enough to make me uproot my whole life and my kids' lives for the chance to sit on it again. Get that shit out of your head right now, once and for all. Get over yourself. Our move here was for the safety of me and my kids. That's it. That is, one hundred percent, the only reason. If you dislike me that much, then keep doing what you've been doing. Ignoring me and disappearing. You seem to be really good at both."

My heart hammered in my chest. I couldn't remember ever being so pissed. My mind played out scenarios where I kicked him in the balls or slapped his face. Anger was making me say things I would never have otherwise. Though, for some reason, along with the anger, there was an undercurrent of heat that I couldn't suppress. I've never been so angry, but somehow I also had feelings for him. Not quite sexual tension, but it was close. It only made me angrier with myself. It was a dangerous game to play.

Something ominous seemed to bubble up within Tate. It wasn't visible, but it was like an aura or a mood that I could sense. It was intimidating, and I had the weirdest feeling that I wasn't looking at a man but some beast. Something deep and dark lurked just below the surface.

Calming myself, I reminded him what he'd said before. "Remember when you said your life shouldn't touch ours? Well, it goes both ways. I don't want our life touching yours, either."

I whirled around and practically sprinted to the car. I got in, locked the doors, and pulled out of the parking lot without looking back. I didn't speak to the girls; I just drove. The girls could obviously tell I was in no mood to chat or even talk because when we got home, they said goodnight and went straight to bed without me asking. That made me feel like shit, too. I'd turned a fun day and evening into a tense, weird night. Great, really fantastic.

An hour later, I lay in bed, unable to sleep. As I absently rubbed my stomach, I realized my pillow was soaked with my tears. I hadn't even noticed I was crying. I rolled over and buried my face into my bed. I really couldn't have picked two worse people to be the father of my child.

Chapter 7 - Tate

The holiday weekend had gone by without any incidents. I hadn't seen anyone acting shady or strange. Though, that wasn't true. I had been acting strange. My dragon had taken over my body and had used my voice and mouth. That had never happened before—not to me, and not to any other shifter I knew. After that, I'd probably been pretty shit at looking for hunters. Hard to concentrate when the beast inside you was demanding to mate with a human.

Steff and I were at the office early on Monday since we'd all planned to meet up and debrief over the weekend's activities. Blayne and Miles were running late, so we started without them.

"Weekend was a wash. No sign of anything other than drunk tourists, screaming kids, and partying college students. I never saw anything remotely close to a hunter. Not that I'd ever seen one before," Steff said.

"Me neither. Pretty quiet." I didn't go into detail about the weirdness that was my weekend.

Steff leaned back in his chair and sipped at his coffee. "Do you think Miles might be wrong? About there being hunters, I mean. If they were here, you'd think they would have acted by now, don't you think?" he asked.

I shrugged. "Maybe they're being cautious."

His expression said he didn't buy it. "The last attack was pretty far from here and actually going in the opposite direction of the others. Even if they are in the area, maybe they're moving away from us."

"Miles said it was an hour outside of town. That sounds pretty close to me," I said.

"Okay, yeah, but an hour's drive is still like seventy-five miles away. To me, that's pretty far."

"Well, either way, until they act or show themselves, we're at a dead end."

Steff looked at me and frowned. "Are you okay, Tate?"

Immediately anxious, I asked, "What do you mean?"

He glanced down at my leg. I followed his eyes and saw my leg bouncing nervously while my right hand was picking at the fabric of my jeans.

Steff said, "You seem a little more on edge than usual. Are you sure you didn't see anything strange this weekend?"

I'd gone over what had happened with me and Harley a hundred times since Friday night, and I was coming up blank. The dragon had been clear. The words that had come out of my mouth hadn't been mumbled or incoherent. *Mate*. It had needed to get that into my head. Steff was one of my best friends, but I had no idea how to broach this subject.

Finally, to break the awkward silence, I said, "Have you ever heard of a shifter being mated to a human?"

Steff's head jerked up, and he shook his head, almost like I'd thrown a glass of water in his face. "What?"

"It's just a question. Have you ever heard of that?"

Steff shook his head slowly. "Nah, man, because it's not a thing. Shifters aren't fated to mate with humans. A fated mate is always another shifter. At least, that's the way it is with bears."

I'd asked Harley what she was, thinking the abrupt question might throw her off guard and get her to reveal herself. Instead, she'd looked at me like I was crazy. None of my senses picked up anything magical about her or her kids. As far as I could tell, she was a hundred percent human. What the hell could have happened to cause my dragon to react the way it did then?

Steff was looking at me with concern. "Why are you asking about this?"

I could almost see the wheels turning in his head. He was smart enough to figure it out. I slumped in my chair and opened my mouth to tell him, but the others walked in before I could. I clamped my lips shut.

"Hey, guys," Blayne said, taking a seat beside me.

I nodded and watched Miles close the door and sit on the desk. From the corner of my eye, I saw Steff studying me. Trying to ignore him, I went back to bouncing my leg and plucking at the seam of my jeans.

"Anything?" Miles asked.

Glancing over at Steff, I noticed the realization dawning on his face. He'd figured it out, or at least was on his way to it. It was now or never.

"Yeah, something did happen actually," I blurted.

Miles and Blayne's eyes widened, and they leaned forward.

"What the hell was it?" Blayne asked.

"So, my New York chick? The new neighbor?"

They all nodded, looking like children ready to hear a ghost story around a campfire. Rapt attention. Sweat pooled in my armpits.

"Friday night, she and her kids were at that food festival in the park. I was chatting up with one of her daughters, and then Harley came up. This wave of, I don't know, sickness, swept over me… Dizziness, sweating, racing heart. When they left, I watched her go, and it got worse. It was so bad that I had to go behind a tent and get on my hands and knees. Like, I was absolutely pouring sweat. My dragon was going crazy inside, too. That's where it gets weird."

Miles looked shocked. "Wait, this isn't even the weird part?"

I shook my head. "No. I'm sitting there trying to pull myself together when my dragon suddenly takes control of my body. It used my mouth to say a word. Not once, but freaking twice."

A shocked silence descended over the room. Our beasts were always inside, and a significant part of who we were. What I saw in their eyes told me that this was as crazy for wolves, bears, and panthers, as it was for dragons.

"What did it say, man?" Steff asked, sounding desperate.

I looked at each of them in turn. "It said: mate. When I looked at Harley again, it said it a second time."

The air seemed to get sucked out of the room, and they all looked like I'd slapped them. Steff looked less shocked, as I was pretty sure he'd already had it figured out before I said it. I sighed and relaxed in my chair, relieved to have it out.

"Are you sure that's what it said? Maybe you misheard it," Blayne said.

Miles nodded. "Right. You said you weren't feeling well when it happened, so it may have been something else."

I shook my head. "Nope. It used my voice, my mouth, my tongue. I didn't misinterpret that. It was clear as day. It was telling me that Harley is my mate."

Steff said, "She doesn't know what you are, right? You didn't let that slip at some point in New York?"

It was a ludicrous question. Humans did *not* know about shifters. It would cause a panic and be incredibly dangerous for us as a race. Hunters were a small but dedicated group, and even then, they caused fear and chaos amongst shifter clans around the world. If everyone knew, the number of hunters would grow exponentially. We would have to go into even deeper hiding than we were now.

The few humans who did know about us were very high-ranking government officials. Presidents, joint chiefs, people like that. Other than those, a few very select people and very close friends were sometimes let in on the secret. Shifters did sometimes take humans as lovers, but they were not mated to them. Being a fated mate was a much deeper, more intense connection than simple human marriage. If I had to gauge it, maybe a tenth of a percent of a tenth of a percent of the entire human population knew. Probably less than that, honestly.

"No, bro, of course I didn't tell her. I'm not insane."

Steff leaned back and raised his hands in a defensive gesture. "Sorry, just had to cover all the bases."

"This is bananas, guys. What are we even talking about?" Miles said. "Humans and shifters cannot be mated."

Blayne, who had gone very quiet, spoke up. "I think it can actually happen."

I pinned him with my gaze, eager to hear what he was going to say.

"My brother loved a human woman. Fell head over heels for her. And she loved him right back. It was super intense. He even revealed to her that he was a shifter, and she didn't bat an eye. I'm not sure if they were fated mates, but they might have been."

Blayne's face became very solemn. His brother had died not long before we found him. Blayne was nearly feral when we did, almost too far over the edge to come back. Losing his last living relative had almost stripped him of everything but the animalistic needs he had. Steff, Miles, and I had brought him back, but just barely. None of us thought for a moment he was lying or exaggerating.

Hearing this made me wonder if a shifter and a human really could be mated. The pull I had toward Harley was real and undeniable. I even remembered how homesick I had been in Toronto. At the time, I just thought I wanted to go home, but maybe it was Harley. My body and soul had been so desperate to get back to her it made me physically ill. I'd woken up every day feeling more and more like shit. That had never happened before, so maybe it could be true.

We let Blayne's story settle, then Miles asked, "Did you feel anything when you first saw her?"

My mind drifted back to that night, and I went over every detail as best I could remember. I shook my head. "I know my dragon took notice, but it was nothing like what it's doing now. It was purely noticing that Harley was a pretty woman and alone. I did the rest. There was no pull, no racing heart, nothing like this, and I definitely didn't have a desire to claim her as my mate."

"This isn't natural," Blayne mumbled. We all nodded in agreement.

Steff looked up. "What if she's a witch?" he asked, almost sheepishly. "Maybe she cast some sort of love spell."

I laughed, so did Blayne and Miles. Witches were real, yes, but incredibly rare. They weren't the goths who liked to play with tarot cards and herbs and worshipped nature you saw all over the internet and in bigger cities. They were the real deal—spell casters, soothsayers, mystical beings similar to shifters. None of us had ever seen one, but even though I'd never met a witch, I had a hard time believing Harley was one. I said as much, and the others agreed. Even Steff, though grudgingly.

Miles stood and walked around to the computer on his desk. "I need to do some more digging. Maybe I missed something."

There was very little chance that was the case. Miles was the resident private investigator for our firm, and he was incredibly good at what he did.

"Hang back until we're sure Harley isn't a true threat. Stay away from her," Miles said.

That pissed my dragon off. A sudden surge of irritation and anger flared within, and a deep reptilian growl escaped my throat. When they looked at me in surprise, I sighed and slumped in my chair. The winged beast inside me was absolutely not on board with staying away from Harley. If I even tried, it would give me hell for it.

Chapter 8 - Harley

By Wednesday morning, I was a nervous wreck. The waiting room in the doctor's office was too quiet. There was only one other woman waiting, and no music played to set me at ease. That left me with nothing but my thoughts as I waited.

I couldn't even concentrate on the book I'd loaded on my phone. I kept reading the same sentence over and over until irritation made me shove my phone back into my purse. Instead, I stared at the floor, trying not to be too emotional. All I could think about was going in there alone. I'd never done this alone before. Sam had always been there. He'd been right beside me every step of the way with both girls—every appointment, birthing class, and baby registry.

Thinking about being alone only reminded me that Sam was gone. I bit back tears that threatened to fill my eyes. I'd be damned if I would be that lonely woman crying at the OB-GYN's office. Not happening.

A faint thought flitted across my mind. *I could still get an abortion.* But the thought made me just as sick as it had when I first contemplated it. There was no way I could get rid of the child growing inside me. I'd messed up, and I needed to live with that. Just because both possible fathers were shits didn't mean the baby would be. That was up to me and the girls. We would give the child a loving and healthy home. I would love the child as fiercely as I loved Mariah and Jordyn.

"Mrs. King?"

I jumped at my name. I hadn't noticed the nurse opening the door. Snatching up my purse, I stood and walked into the adjacent room. The door closed behind me, shutting off the waiting room. I couldn't help but imagine the door was not only cutting off the room, but cutting off the life I'd known before. Almost like I was stepping into a different universe.

The doctor was a very sweet and pleasant older woman, who didn't make a fuss about me being on my own. The cold gel for the ultrasound was a shock to my system and not entirely pleasant. The exam was pretty simple and just as thorough as the exams I'd had in New York. One of the fears I'd had was that rural medicine would be a lower tier, but the opposite seemed true. Without so many people coming and going, she was able to spend more time on my questions and care. By the end, I was much more relaxed than I thought I'd be.

The doctor glanced at her chart and said, "Things are looking very good. I don't have any worries at the moment. Baby is measuring well. From what I see, I would think you're right at three months along. As you saw during the ultrasound, it looks like we have a little boy on our hands. Your history says you have two daughters, so that should be exciting. A whole new adventure."

A shaky sigh escaped my chest. If I really was at three months, there was no way Luis could be the father. It had been almost four months since we'd had sex. So Tate was the father. I didn't feel any relief. Neither men were ideal. Though I had to admit, if I had to choose, I was happy Luis had been ruled out. I could deal with Tate. Things with him were already strained, but Luis was crazy and possibly dangerous. If he had been the father and found out about it, I had no doubt he would somehow use it to manipulate me. I put that out of my mind and focused on what she'd said. A boy. A whole new adventure. I wasn't in the mood for adventures.

I nodded. "Thank you so much. No, I don't have any questions."

"Sounds good. If you have no questions, then we're all set here. I'll let you get dressed. The nurse at reception will set you up for your next appointment."

My clothes went on robotically, almost like someone else was dressing me. I grabbed my purse and walked down the hall to the little window where the nurse sat. We had a conversation, but I only knew it because I could hear our voices, but I was somewhere else. Barely listening or paying attention. All I could think of was how Tate had treated me the week before and after the fireworks. He had been so distraught and angry. How would he react if he knew his child was growing inside me?

I was able to get out of the doctor's office before the tears started. It didn't build up slowly, either. I went from dry-eyed and in control to sobbing in seconds. Tears and snot poured down my face. Anyone on the sidewalk would see my breakdown, but I couldn't stop it. All I wanted was to get to my car, so I could fall to pieces on my own.

"Harley?"

My head jerked. I turned, wiping my eyes. Emily stood on the sidewalk, looking concerned.

"Sweetie, what's wrong? What happened?" she asked.

I straightened and did my best to calm down and tell her I was fine. Instead, I burst out in another crying fit. I wasn't even able to excuse myself and run away. I was too distraught to do anything but stand there and cry. Emily put an arm around me and led me down the sidewalk. I leaned against her, not paying attention to where we were going. Five minutes later, we were seated in a little café, and I was clutching a menu.

Emily ordered me a glass of water, then took my hands in hers. "Harley, what the heck is going on? Do you want to talk about it?"

Her tone wasn't judgmental. She genuinely wanted to hear my problems. I'd wanted to keep everything a secret, but I might explode if I didn't unload. I told her about the baby, how alone I was, and how frustrated I was that the father wanted nothing to do with me. Basically, every dreadful thought I'd had at the doctor's office spilled out as one big verbal vomit to a woman who I'd only met five days before.

The server must have realized things were a little emotional because she waited until I was done to swoop in and drop off our drinks. The look on her face let me know she felt awkward after watching and hearing my emotional breakdown.

"Well, ladies, what can I get you?"

Emily smiled and said, "Chef salad, please. Italian dressing."

"Got it, and for you, miss?"

I looked at her and said, "What's the greasiest, fattiest thing you've got?"

"Um… well, we have our double cheeseburger and fries… uh… I can add bacon to the burger and add chili and cheese on the fries?"

"That sounds like a heart attack on a plate. Bring me that."

The server chuckled and walked away with our orders. My tears were fully spent, but after all the crying, I had a splitting headache. Emily looked stunned by all the information, but not judgmental, which was a relief.

"Harley, that's a lot to deal with. I know you said you didn't want an abortion, what about giving the baby up for adoption?"

The thought of my child out in the world, being raised by someone else, never knowing me or his sisters, offended me more than I thought it would.

"Absolutely not. This is my child. I will raise it," I snapped.

"No, I'm sorry, I was giving you options. You seemed so distraught and torn up about the whole situation."

"Sorry, I know you're trying to help. I could never do that to a child I birthed. I'm so close with my daughters, and the thought of losing the closeness I could have with another child is too much to imagine. I'm just so alone."

Emily leaned forward and took my hand again. "You are not alone. I understand it must be overwhelming, but I'm here. I know we just met, but I think we were meant to cross paths. I want to help any way I can."

New tears tried to well in my eyes as I smiled. "Thank you. I really needed a friend. I'm glad I met you, Emily. You could have brushed me off as some crazy lady crying on the street. You have no idea how grateful I am that you took the time with me."

Emily squeezed my hand. "Girl, I got you."

The lunch was fantastic. My hunger had returned by the time the food got to us, and I devoured the burger and chili fries. After I'd wept like a baby, it tasted like the best thing I'd ever put in my mouth. By the time we were done, I felt a thousand times better. Outside, I hugged Emily and passed her my phone number.

She typed it into her phone. "I'll text you soon. Maybe we can get together again?"

"I would love that," I said, then headed to my car.

Driving home, my mood was much improved from what it had been when I'd left for the doctor. I felt so much better that when I saw Tate in his yard as I pulled in, I didn't even feel the urge to cry. That was a win in my book. I parked and checked my email on my phone before getting out of the car. Casually glancing up, I saw Tate watering his garden. My gaze lingered on him as he moved the hose back and forth across the flowers in the bed. He was as lean and muscled as he had been the last time I'd seen him. He must work out like a maniac.

Without realizing it, my gaze started sliding up and down across his body. Before long, the pregnancy hormones running roughshod through my body sent my mind to a place I didn't want it to go. It was easy to remember how it had felt to slide my hands across the muscled back as he thrust into me.

I blinked, and the horny thoughts morphed into irritation. Without thinking, I was out of my car and walking toward him. There was enough time for me to ask myself what the hell I was doing before I stepped up onto his lawn.

He glanced up, surprised, and nodded to me. "Hey."

"Hey? Do you even own a shirt? Christ, I've got young impressionable girls over there. Do you think it's appropriate for them to see you walking around half naked?"

Instead of answering me right away, he went back to watering his flowers. He did that for several seconds before turning the hose off and looking at me.

"This is my house. I own it, and the land it sits on. If I want to sit on my porch butt ass naked and drink a beer, I will."

My mouth dropped open. The thought was horrifying. At least I told myself that even as my body betrayed me, and there was a warm tingle between my legs. Keeping myself composed, I went to speak again, but he cut me off before I could start.

"Don't worry," he said, giving me a placating look. "I'm not an exhibitionist or a nudist. I wouldn't do something like that with kids around. Give me *some* credit." Tate looked at me and grinned slyly. "Now, if you wanted to see me naked again, I think we could work something out."

The tingle between my legs turned into a pulse, and I hated the way my body reacted to him. His eyes smoldered and burned into me. Tate was looking at me differently than he had the last time we'd spoken. It was almost like he could read my thoughts. He stepped forward and brushed his fingers across my arm. Trying to hide a pleasurable shudder, I stepped back and turned to walk away.

"Just remember your shirt next time, Tate," I called over my shoulder as I hurried back home. I didn't trust myself to stay that close to him.

He called to me as I mounted the porch steps. "Come knock if you ever change your mind."

Closing the door behind myself, I leaned against it and took a deep breath. I was fucking horny. I'd wanted him so bad. After everything that had happened, all he'd done and said, I still wanted to fuck him. What was wrong with me? My skin was on fire. I needed to cool down, and get my mind off what I was thinking about. I needed a cold shower. It would cool me, and maybe extinguish my libido.

In my room, I stripped my clothes off and jumped into an ice cold shower. My breath caught in my chest as I adjusted to the freezing temperature. But even as I put my head under the cold spray, the same thoughts flipped through my head like a picture book. I suffered the cold as long as I could before cranking the knob back to warm. In seconds, steaming hot water coursed over me. I shivered at the change in temperature.

Still, the thoughts persisted. The way his tongue had felt inside me, his strong hands kneading my breasts. I let my fingers glide up my skin and gently pinched my nipples. A deep sigh escaped my lips as I circled my nipples, the skin puckering and getting firm. I thought of

Tate's throbbing dick brushing against my clit before he slid into me. My pussy was wet just from remembering it.

My right hand grazed across my stomach and then across the hair between my legs. I could feel the heat there. I let out a trembling breath, and for an instant, I tried to talk myself out of it, but my body's needs overwhelmed my mind's hesitation. As I caressed my clit, my breath caught in my throat. The small bud was engorged and more sensitive than it had ever been. I circled it, still imagining Tate fucking me.

I could almost hear him gasping for breath as his cock slammed into me. I slid two fingers into myself and whimpered. My legs nearly buckled as I moved them in and out, the movement making my palm graze over my clit. With my free hand, I tugged at my nipple, almost hard enough to be painful, which increased the pleasure between my legs. Sucking in shallow breaths through my nose, I worked my fingers faster and faster. A groan escaped my throat as my hips worked in concert with my fingers.

I sank to the shower floor, afraid I would slip and fall. My mouth dropped open on a moan as I spread my legs, my fingers thrusting into my pussy as my other hand worked my clit. I was still imagining Tate's flexing muscles above me, his tongue flicking across my nipples as we fucked. The orgasm came hard and fast, almost pulling a scream from my throat. I jerked and bucked my hips, hands still working. It went on for several seconds, powerful contractions radiating across my body. I collapsed and rested under the hot spray of the shower.

The warm glow of the orgasm faded, and I shook my head at myself. What the hell was wrong with me? Fantasizing about Tate was stupid. There was no way this was going to work. I'd just uprooted my girls' lives. Dragged them halfway across the country, and now this was what life was. Living across the street from my baby's father, and he didn't even know. A small part of me was pretty sure this was the most depressed and broken I'd been since Sam died.

I didn't cry in the shower—I, at least, had enough pride to not turn myself into that cliché. Instead, I dried off and pulled on a robe. I settled into the chair in my bedroom with a book and tried to think about anything but Tate.

Chapter 9 - Tate

The day before Harley had accosted me in my yard and berated me for gardening without a shirt. It had been weird, and it should have pissed me off, but my dragon had calmed my temper. Hell, I'd even flirted with her. My cock had hardened when I watched her walk back to her house. My dragon had nearly purred like a cat. I was thinking about how ridiculous the entire thing was when my phone rang.

"This is Tate," I answered.

"Hey, are you free?" Miles asked, his voice almost vibrating. He sounded more nervous than I'd ever heard. "Can you get here? I think I found something about Harley. Something you'll want to see."

It hadn't occurred to me that Miles would actually find more info because the file he'd compiled was beyond thorough. Whatever information he found must have been buried somewhere, or it was new.

"I'll be there as soon as I can," I said, then disconnected.

As I sped to the office, I tried to think what Miles could have found. A police report? Some connection to the hunters? A picture of her over a cauldron casting spells? The last image made me laugh as I turned into the security firm's parking lot.

As I walked into Miles's office, the first thing I noticed was how nervous he looked. He was pacing back and forth across the room and seemed upset. He didn't even notice me until I cleared my throat. He stopped pacing and blinked at me before closing the door.

"You know, I usually don't do things like this. It's like my moral compass is spinning. No true north, you know what I mean?"

"I have no idea what the fuck you're talking about," I answered honestly.

Miles winced in irritation. "I had Blayne do some heavier digging. We went for medical records."

Blayne worked as our security analyst, but before his brother died, he'd been a pretty good hacker. There was almost nothing he couldn't get into. Miles was good, but nowhere near Blayne's level. If he'd called him in to dig, he really did want every single piece of information out there.

Miles went on. "I don't often go for medical. It's usually nothing applicable to what we do as security providers. But while we were looking into it yesterday, a new addition was logged in Harley King's file. It blew our damned minds, and I've been trying to figure out how to tell you since. You have to see it for yourself."

Miles picked up a thin stack of paper stapled at the top corner and handed it to me before sitting on his desk. It was like he'd been running a race and had finally crossed the finish line. He looked exhausted and relieved all at once. With a frown, I glanced at the packet. At first, I didn't even know what I was looking at. Then I noticed there was a range of dates and what looked like medical notes. It was from an OB/GYN. The first page was from a doctor's office in New York. Harley's name was listed on every date. I only skimmed through it before coming to another page that was dated the day before, at a local county doctor.

I looked up. "Man, why do we care about when her last pap smear was?"

Miles rolled his eyes. "Can't you read? She's freaking pregnant."

My eyes widened, and I went back over every single word. This time I did notice a positive pregnancy test on the first page. I flipped to the very back and found an ultrasound image captured yesterday. The black-and-white image clearly showed the curled body of a fetus.

I shook my head and raised my eyes. "So, the Luis guy knocked her up. Is that what you're freaked out about?"

"Look at the damned dates, Tate. The form says she's three months pregnant. That lines up almost exactly with the one night you guys had in New York."

What he was hinting at was crazy, and I looked at him like he was. "Miles, this is like elementary school shit. Shifters and humans can't have kids. She was dating Luis at the same time. Damn, she could have had sex with him the day before."

Miles ran a hand across his face. "I had Blayne pull phone records, too. I read through her texts to the Ortiz guy. It looks like they were maybe having trouble for a few weeks before you guys hooked up. Some pretty pissy stuff back and forth, definitely didn't look like a happy couple that humped every Wednesday and Saturday."

He was getting on my nerves. "Look, Miles, humans and shifters can't have kids. Facts. Simple as that."

Miles raised an eyebrow. "And until a few days ago, it was a *fact* that shifters couldn't be mated to humans. What does your dragon have to say about that?"

The words slammed into me like a hammer. My dragon purred deep inside my mind in answer to Miles's question. It was content and excited. Could it sense a baby within her womb? Could it actually tell if it was ours? For the first time in my life, I felt like there was a stranger inside me. The dragon and I had always been intertwined and connected. Now, it was speaking a language I didn't understand.

Should I confront Harley? How could I do that without letting her know I'd pried into her most confidential secrets? No. I couldn't ask her about it without rocking our already shaky relationship. If the kid was mine... Geez, I had no idea what I'd do. I'd never even considered having a child. I pinched the bridge of my nose when I felt the impending headache.

Frowning, I asked, "Why couldn't I sense the baby?"

"Huh?" Miles looked confused.

"Pregnant women. You know what I mean."

Shifter senses were incredibly enhanced compared to human senses. We could hear and smell things normal people could never imagine. I'd been surprised by Harley being across the street that first day because the smell of cut grass had overwhelmed everything else. Once I was in front of her, I recognized her scent. But pregnancy filled a human with hormones, enzymes, and every other thing you could think of. Often, I walked through a store and could immediately tell which women were expecting.

Understanding dawned on Miles's face, and he looked thoughtful. "Maybe because it's yours?" he said with a shrug. "It might be that a human-shifter hybrid is, like, invisible or something. Not sure."

I tossed the papers onto his desk. "I need to get out of here. I've got some stuff to think about."

Miles nodded. "Yeah, I got it. Let me know if you have everything you need."

Five minutes later, my truck rumbled down the highway, my mind still reeling from what I'd just learned. Everything was mixed up, yet somehow it made both total sense and seemed impossible at the exact same time.

My hope that the drive would clear my head turned out to be fruitless. Three hours later, I found myself parked in a pull-off to a hiking trail. The sun had set two hours ago, so the spot was secluded and deserted—the perfect place to shift. I wouldn't be seen here, but I wasn't worried about that. I just wanted to be free, to feel the wind rushing beneath my wings as I let every problem I had fall away.

Jumping out of my truck, I took a deep breath of the fresh air, then sprinted toward the forest. I was already morphing, my body twisting, elongating. Scales replaced my skin, and my arms transformed into wings. In seconds, I was aloft, the wind blowing across my dragon's face. The beast was content to be out, but it didn't mask the lingering sadness deep within.

This was new. My dragon had always been full of base emotions: hunger, anger, suspicion, happiness. It had never felt anything deep like depression or sadness. Only lonliness, but that wasn't quite the same thing as being sad. Using my mind, I asked the beast if it was sure about

Harley. The massive head bobbed in an obvious nod as we flew. Allowing my dragon to dive and sweep across the sky, I thought it through. I'd never ignored my dragon, but it had never *wanted* anything before. Wincing inwardly, I wondered if I could let it have it. If not, what would that mean?

After my dragon had a good relaxing flight, with a nice hefty deer for dinner, I made my way back home. Harley's lights were on when I pulled into my driveway, and when I got out of the truck, I heard the girls laughing through an open window. I turned to listen. It sounded like they were watching a movie or something. When I heard Harley's voice, my gut stirred.

From what I'd witnessed so far, Harley looked like she was a fantastic mother. Their small family was full of happiness and love. Would this new baby change that? Would she even want to keep it if it was going to change everything? Would she tell me about it soon? Would she keep it a secret and then give up the baby for adoption? I wouldn't blame her if that was her plan.

That thought brought forth a swell of anger from my dragon. He obviously did not want that to happen. He was already protective of the child growing inside Harley. Miles was right. The baby was mine.

Steff was the only one of the pack out of the loop, and I figured it was time to get his input. Leaving the sounds of laughter and happiness, I headed into my house to call Steff.

He answered on the first ring. "Tate? Where have you been, man? I tried calling earlier. Miles said I needed to get a hold of you."

"Sorry, had to clear my head for a few hours. I headed out to shift and let loose. It was desperately needed."

"Okay, well, spill it, dude."

I took a deep breath and let it all out. I even went through all the internal arguments between me and my dragon. As good as my shift had felt, getting it all out was even more cathartic. Hopefully, Steffen would have some good advice.

"Do *you* think she'll tell me about the baby?" I asked.

"You want my honest answer?"

I wasn't sure if I did or not, but I nodded and said, "Yes."

"You've kind of treated her like shit since she moved in. Other than a few good interactions, you've accosted her in her yard, accused her of being a witch, and told her you wanted nothing to do with her. Am I missing anything? Honestly, bro, I wouldn't blame her for keeping her pregnancy a secret. You haven't given her any reason to trust you, man."

It was a punch to the gut. It made me sick. I hated that he was right. My friends were the closest thing I had to family. Still, it irked me that they were always able to see what I couldn't. I really was a dick sometimes.

"Steff, I don't think I'm ready to be a father. I've never wanted a family of my own. You know that."

They understood the trauma I carried from having been thrown out of my pack. That betrayal from my own flesh and blood had soured the idea of having my own family. The trauma ran so deep that I had trouble trusting the mating bond that seemed to be happening with Harley.

"What if she planned all this? Intentionally gotten pregnant for some type of plot against me?"

"Are you being serious right now? Listen to yourself. I know you don't believe in coincidences, I get it. Tate, you have to be honest with yourself and accept that this may just be fate. Don't get pissed at me, but I think you're dead set against it because you're fucking terrified. This is a journey you've never been on, and that is scary. You don't really think any of this stuff you're spouting, do you?"

I sighed and gripped the phone tighter, not sure how to answer. It was emasculating to admit I was afraid. I'd spent years building up walls, trying to forget my family's betrayal. All this time, I'd been relying on my three best friends, pushing away any idea or possibility of more.

"Steff, I gotta go. I have to think about this."

"Yup, sounds like you do. Love ya, brother."

I walked out to my porch. Flopping down on my patio chair, I leaned back and stared up at the night sky, which I'd soared across only hours before. This day seemed like it had been going on for years. There was so much to think about. As I contemplated my life choices, I heard the sliding door across the street open. I forced myself not to look, but my dragon whined and asserted its will. It wanted nothing more than to see Harley again. Groaning, I tilted my head and glanced across the street.

Harley was pacing on her porch. She looked anxious and nervous, lost in her own thoughts as she rubbed her belly. My heart lurched at the sight. Harley tilted her head down, looking at her stomach. With my enhanced hearing, I could pick up what she was saying even this far away.

"Momma loves you. No matter what, I'm going to love you more than enough for me and your daddy."

My dragon was overcome with an intense longing to go to her, and the feeling was almost strong enough to get me to obey. The love it felt for her was beyond description, but it wasn't just that. It was in love with the baby growing inside her. It was so fierce that I knew it would die for both of them. Could it really be possible? Was that, somehow, beyond all explanation, my baby? And if it was, what would I do about it?

Chapter 10 - Harley

My eyes snapped open as my stomach roiled. I lurched from the bed and stumbled across the room, barely making it to the toilet before my stomach expelled its contents. Heaving twice more, my stomach muscles started to spasm, and tears tracked down my cheeks. I couldn't stop until every drop of undigested food and liquid had been expelled from my body. Barely able to catch my breath, I gagged one more time before I was done.

After wiping my mouth with a towel, I stumbled back to bed, collapsing on the sweat-soaked sheets. This didn't feel like morning sickness. I'd had it fairly bad when I was pregnant with the girls., but this was something else, I could already tell. My body was feverish, and I had aches, night sweats, and a splitting headache. I had not experienced these symptoms with my previous pregnancies. The thought that it was only because the baby was a boy seemed a little outlandish. All pregnancies were different, but this was too much. I'd never felt this awful.

I'd had stomach flu, food poisoning, morning sickness, and none had even been half as bad as this.

After a few minutes, I forced myself to slowly sit up, then I got up and got ready. There was no way I'd lie in bed and let the girls worry about me. It was like my body was made of lead. Every muscle shook as I dressed myself and got shoes on. Afterward, I sat on the edge of the bed, dripping sweat. By sheer force of will, I made it to the bathroom and made my face and hair somewhat presentable.

I planned to tell Mariah and Jordyn about their new baby brother today. The problem was that no matter how many different ways I thought about doing that, none sounded right. The other issue was that they would automatically assume that Luis was the father, and there was zero-percent chance I was going to tell my girls what had actually happened.

"So, girls, Mommy got a little tipsy in New York and met a hot guy. We fucked our brains out all night and didn't even ask each other's names. That's the daddy. Oh, and by the way, the same walking slab of muscle and dick lives next door now. Okay, have a great day now."

Not a chance in hell. My attempts to prevent a full panic attack while thinking about it had been pretty fruitless. All I could do was keep telling myself that I needed to stay calm. Things would work out fine. My girls were strong, smart, and intelligent. Still, no matter how much I tried to talk myself up, worry nagged at the back of my mind. No amount of positive self-talk could keep me from wondering how it would play out.

The girls were in the kitchen eating cereal when I came down. Each step was like a full thirty-minute workout. I grabbed a granola bar from the pantry and sat down, hoping the girls couldn't see the sweat already beading on my forehead. I was still sick to my stomach but wanted to appear as normal as I could. When I took a bite of the cereal bar, I regretted my choice of breakfast. The dry, crumbly texture sucked all the moisture out of my mouth. I chewed, the granola going from crunchy to gummy. I swallowed hard and kept a neutral expression as I fought not to vomit all over the table.

Jordyn glanced over at Mariah and whispered, "Ask her."

"Ask me what?" I mumbled, trying to work up the courage to take another bite of the bar.

Mariah smiled shyly and looked back at Jordyn. "Would it be okay if we went to the mall? To do some school shopping?"

My nausea and exhaustion forgotten for the barest moment, I looked up in surprise. They were smiling. The hopeful expressions on their faces would have been over-the-top and silly, had I not already known how bored they were. A shopping trip and lunch were usually nothing exciting. But after being in Lilly Valley for several weeks, the trip to the next town over probably sounded like the excursion of a lifetime.

"By yourselves?" I asked, praying the hopefulness wasn't evident in my voice.

Mariah chewed at her lip before speaking carefully. "I have my permit. You said I was doing really good. Plus, it's only like ten miles away. What do you think?"

They were also getting tired of being around Mom all day. I could relate. Normally, it would have broken my heart a little. Today? The thought of being able to go lie back down for a while without having to put on a show of health sounded like nirvana. Though, I couldn't seem too urgent to get them out of the house.

I worked up my best mom voice, and said, "Okay, but no speeding. Seatbelts, and use your turn signal like I told you. *Before* you hit the brakes, not after."

Surprise flashed across their faces. Mariah was already nodding, a smile forming on her lips.

"I'll give you my card. Two hundred bucks each. Not a cent more. Got it? And go ahead and get lunch there while you're out. There's a food court, so take your pick, but no damned desserts. I don't want you having cinnamon rolls or ice cream for lunch."

"Okay," both girls said in giddy unison.

They nearly leaped up from the table to put their bowls in the sink. I took a breath and heaved myself up out of my chair. I found my purse by the door and dug out my card. Handing it to Mariah, I pulled her close and said, "If you guys wanna catch a movie, go ahead. Make a day of it if you want. Just be home by three."

Mariah grinned and nodded. "Thanks, Mom." She tilted her head and looked at me closely. "Are you okay? You look really pale."

"Fine. Just fine. Didn't sleep well last night."

"Okay," she said, sounding unsure. "See you this afternoon."

A few seconds later, I watched as Mariah backed the car out of the garage and out onto the street. Before the garage door was even closed, I walked back to my room. It felt like I was on fire but also freezing to death. Maybe I had the flu or something? Before I could get to my bedroom, another massive wave of nausea struck me, and I dived into the guest bathroom and threw up the water and two bites of granola I'd just had. Instead of feeling better after throwing up, I felt worse.

Once I was in bed, exhausted and drained, I couldn't sleep. I choked down some Tylenol, hoping to lower the temperature I knew I had. It went on like that for over an hour. One minute I was rolling around in bed, first freezing and huddling under the covers. The next minute I was sweltering to the point I threw the blankets and sheets off, pulled my clothes off, and tossed them on the floor. Even naked under the ceiling fan, my body was on fire. It worried me that I seemed to be getting worse. If I had any friends here, I could call someone to help me, but all my friends were fifteen-miles away.

Then a thought occurred to me. Emily. She was the closest thing I had to a friend here. As little as I wanted to impose on someone I'd just met, I wanted my girls to find me like this even less. Chills were creeping back into my joints, and I tried to find my pajamas and panties again as I grabbed my phone from the nightstand.

I texted Emily, telling her I was sick and asking if she could come over and help me. To my surprise, she responded within a minute, asking for my address. She didn't even ask what was wrong; she was eager to come help. Gratefulness washed over me, so strong that my eyes welled with tears. I sent her my address and told her not to worry about getting here in a hurry and to take her time.

Thirty minutes later, Emily knocked on my front door. Too tired and weak to make it back downstairs, I called out to her. "Come in."

Thankfully, the house and neighborhood were quiet, and she heard me. Emily appeared in my room a few seconds later, carrying a bag of groceries.

Her eyes went wide when she saw me. "Harley, no offense, but you look like absolute shit."

I gave her a tired smile. "Thanks. You're pretty hot yourself."

"Sorry. I brought some stuff. I wasn't sure what you'd need." She dug in the bag and listed everything. "Cold and flu medicine, Pepto, chicken noodle soup, saltines, Gatorade, and bananas."

"Sounds great, everything a lady needs for a full tune up," I attempted to joke, but my voice was monotone and listless.

Emily put the bag down and pulled out the medicine. "I'll be right back."

She returned a few minutes later with the bright green liquid in a small plastic cup. Looking at the viscous drink made me want to hurl again. I didn't think I could stomach it, but Emily was insistent. Thankfully, it had a minty flavor and wasn't as thick as other medicines. It went down easily, and I lay back on the bed. Emily dug into her purse and pulled out several small bottles.

She held them up. "Essential oils. I'm not a hippy or anything, but I am a little crunchy, I guess."

She dabbed some on my forehead and temples, then raised my shirt to drip another oil on my stomach. The smell was… weird, but it did ease my nausea. Emily had been here less than ten minutes, and I already felt better. Mentally, I congratulated myself on making at least one good decision in the last three months.

Emily pulled the chair close to the bed and smiled at me in concern. "Harley, are you sure you don't want to go to the hospital? You really don't look good."

I shook my head. "It's just the flu or something. Maybe the flu and food poisoning? It's not that serious."

"Yeah, but it can't be good for the baby if you can't keep anything down. You have to think about that, right?"

She had a point. I hadn't thought about what the tiny person growing inside me was going through, and I couldn't remember the last time I'd peed. Maybe I was dehydrated. That had to be dangerous for a fetus.

I waved at the brown shopping bag. "Can I have a Gatorade?"

"Sure." She handed me the bottle.

I sipped at it at first, worried I would spew it back up immediately. Instead, when the lemony drink hit my tongue, a devastating wave of thirst washed over me. I was ravenous for liquid. I gulped half the bottle before Emily snatched it away.

"Hang on. Go slow," she said with a chuckle.

I nodded. "Okay. I'm going to try to sleep. I promise, if my fever hasn't gone down, or I get worse, I'll go to the doctor."

"Okay," Emily said. "I'll stay here as long as you need. I brought a book."

If I'd been less exhausted, I would have thanked her, but instead, I slipped into a deep sleep. I dreamed about flapping wings and a *thwap-thwap* sound all around me as I was lifted into the air. They weren't my wings, though. At first, I couldn't see anything or what was lifting me, then a set of gold reptilian eyes stared at me out of the darkness. It should have been a terrifying dream, but for some reason, both things were almost comforting. It was a strange dream, to say the least.

Sometime later, I woke and found Emily still beside me. She was leaning back in the chair, her left leg draped over her right, holding the book in one hand. I felt human again, and I could tell my fever was gone, as were the body aches and nausea. There was no way I would rate myself as one-hundred percent, but based on before the nap, I was a solid eighty percent better.

When Emily noticed I was awake, she put the book on her lap and leaned forward. "How do you feel?"

Slowly sitting up to rest against the headboard, I said, "Actually? A lot better."

Emily looked relieved but still worried. Setting the book aside, she dug into the bag and pulled out a can of soup and a pack of crackers.

"Hungry?" she asked.

My stomach rumbled, and not in a bad way. I nodded vigorously. "Yes, please."

She handed me the crackers, then went to the kitchen to heat the soup. I had eaten half the pack and washed it down with Gatorade by the time she got back and handed me the warm bowl and spoon. I ate, groaning in pleasure between bites.

Emily placed a hand on my thigh. "Harley, I think you should think about telling Tate about the baby."

I snapped my eyes up to her, nearly dropping the spoon into the bowl. "Absolutely not. The guy already hates me. This would just give him another reason to despise me."

Emily sighed and shrugged. "I think he'll be more receptive than you think. He might surprise you."

Unsure of how she could possibly think that, I asked, "How do you know that?"

"I don't *know* it, but I've got a hunch," Emily said.

After I ate, I felt even better. By the time Emily left, I was close to my old self, which was a good thing since the girls got home a while later. They showed me all the things they'd gotten for school. Mariah had done a good job of helping Jordyn pick out things on sale or clearance, and they both got a surprising amount of things for the limit I'd given them. They gushed about the newest epic superhero movie, and it sounded like Jordyn had a crush on the leading man, which I found rather hilarious. I felt so good that I didn't even give them a hard time when I found the Cinnabon receipt at the bottom of one of the bags.

As I cooked dinner, my thoughts slipped back to what Emily had said. How would I deal with things if I told Tate about the baby and he rejected it? There was no scenario I could run in my head that had us still living across the street from him if he shunned our child. No possible way I could handle that type of reaction.

Another small part of me wondered though, what might happen if he did accept the baby and, by association, me. I didn't know him, not really. We were still basically strangers. What if our baby acted like a bridge? What would happen if we were brought together? What would that life even look like?

Chapter 11 - Tate

With every sweep of the hose over my car, I glanced at Harley's house. I'd been washing my truck for about twenty minutes longer than I usually would, using it as an excuse to look over there. Since I'd found out she was pregnant, I was desperate to talk to her again. The problem was, I couldn't think of a way to approach her. Especially after the way I'd treated her the last few times I'd been around her. Along with that, my dragon's reaction to her put me on edge. Not the nervous, irritated edge. No, it was the excited edge, like a kid getting ready for bed on Christmas Eve, or waking up on the morning of their birthday. It was annoying. Even though he hadn't reared his head, I could still feel my dragon's lingering emotions.

While I was lost in my thoughts, I neglected to realize Harley's door had opened. As I scrubbed my truck's rims and cursed my dragon's uncontrollable needs, the youngest King girl had made it across the street and was standing behind me.

I scented her before I saw or heard her. My head snapped around, and I blurted a very unmanly yelp of surprise.

"Damn, girl. You scared the hell out of me." I chuckled.

She grinned like she was proud of herself. It took a second for her name to pop into my mind. Jordyn. While I turned off the hose, she walked around my truck, checking it out. I couldn't tell if she liked it or not. She bounced around on her toes and looked to be just as full of energy as at the fireworks show.

I put my hands on my hips and asked, "How's it been going?"

She studied her reflection in the chrome of the truck's grill. Without looking up, she said, "Pretty good." She then looked me in the face and unloaded a barrage of words I was barely able to keep up with. "My sister and I went shopping yesterday. We got a bunch of new clothes for when school starts. We went to get pizza in the food court, and then got a giant cinnamon roll to share. Mom didn't want us to, but we did anyway. She didn't get mad. We saw a movie too, do you like superhero movies?" Before I could even answer, she went on. "Anyway, we saw the new one, and then we came home. Mariah drove there and back, and we didn't even die. Pretty impressive on her part. So, how have you been? Haven't seen you much since the Fourth of July."

My eyes widened as I tried to take in everything she'd said. Once I had it mostly sorted, I replied, "Been good. Working a lot. How… uh… how's your mom?"

Jordyn made a face. "Not so great. She was sick yesterday, which is probably the only reason she let us go to the mall alone."

My dragon stirred at the news that Harley wasn't well. Not just my dragon, I realized; I was worried too.

"She stayed home and slept."

"Is she feeling better now?" I asked.

Jordyn shrugged. "I think so, but not all the way. Plus, she's got more to worry about now. The air conditioning went out, and the water isn't getting hot anymore. She called the number for the maintenance guy, but he's busy and can't get to us for a few days. My Uncle Maddox—well, he's not really my uncle, he was Daddy's partner—anyway, Uncle Maddox has a company he uses to take care of the house, but it looks like there's quite a bit that needs to be done. It's a nice house… just… sort of sick? I know houses can't get sick, but you know what I mean."

I was familiar with the maintenance company. I'd seen the truck parked there every other month. It was the same company that maintained a lot of the rental cabins, and since we were in the peak of summer, they were probably busy as hell. Harley and the girls didn't have a man around who could fix little things like that. God, that sounded sexist even in my head, but Harley obviously needed help if she was calling the repair guy.

Desire flamed in my chest, fed by my dragon. I should step up and help them. Jordyn was talking about how nervous she was about going to a new school, but I barely registered her voice. All I could think of was helping them. My dragon was almost physically clawing to get out and do some good.

I interrupted Jordyn. "Hey, I'll come over later and fix your stuff. You know, so your mom can feel better without worrying too much."

Jordyn's eyes widened in delighted surprise, and a big smile appeared on her face. "Oh my gosh, that would be great."

I'd always been a pretty stoic guy. I wasn't a crier or sensitive about most situations, but it was hard to ignore the immense satisfaction I felt when Jordyn gave me that smile. Even my dragon purred with delight.

I was suddenly struck with a possessive feeling toward Jordyn—a familial possession. My dragon was imprinting on her as someone to protect and care for. It was viewing her as a fledgling dragon.

Before I could even process all those new feelings, Jordyn grabbed my hand. "Come on. Let's go. It's so dang hot in there."

Mariah's face had a comical expression of surprise when I came in. She gave Jordyn a questioning look, trying to be subtle. The younger girl didn't seem to get it.

She shrugged. "What? I found a repair man. What more could you want?"

The house was boiling. It had to be at least eighty-five or ninety degrees inside. Even with all the ceiling fans going, it was miserable. Coming to my senses, I gently removed my hand from Jordyn's.

I glanced around the house. "Let me go grab my tools. I can't do anything without that. Where's your mom?" I asked, trying to sound casual.

Mariah nodded at a closed door. "She's taking a nap. Said she was tired."

My eyes slid toward the door. "Okay, I need to peek in there real quick to… see how many air vents are in there." I added the last as a bullshit reason to see Harley. The number of air vents didn't mean shit to getting the air con to work. "I won't wake her up."

"Okay. Jordyn, did you do the dishes like Mom asked?" Mariah said, her attention already away from me.

"Ugh. I want to help Tate. Dishes suck."

I left the girls to argue and quietly turned the knob on Harley's door, doing my best to be silent as I opened it. In the shadowed bedroom, there was a lump under the blankets. My dragon eyes had no problem seeing in the dark, and I could easily make out Harley's form. Her eyes were closed, her mouth slightly open as she breathed deeply. My dragon rumbled as it laid eyes on her. Want, need, desire, and the urge to protect her warred within me. I shook my head. How had this happened? Not just a mate, but a human mate? Was this really possible? I forced myself to push the thoughts aside. After closing the door, I went to grab my tools from my garage. I needed to get the girls some cool air and hot water.

Mariah showed me to the corner of their garage where the water heater stood. One look revealed to me the problem. They had moved in and placed a bunch of boxes near the water heater. Now, one of the boxes was leaning against the pressure relief valve, keeping it partially open. I went outside to the relief hose. It was steadily spraying a small amount of water. The spray wasn't loud or super obvious, so they'd never noticed, but the tank was slowly emptying water into the backyard before the heater could heat it. Not only would they have cold water, but their water bill would be enormous.

Back inside, I moved the boxes and discovered that the valve was loose. A few turns of the wrench, and it was good to go. The air conditioner was another story. It was on the other side of the house, and once I got the metal plate off, I found the coils completely corroded. The unit was old and needed replacing. If I replaced the coils, it should last for the rest of the summer and fall. I'd need to go to the plumbing and HVAC supply store outside town, and see if they had these parts in stock. I wrote down the serial number and went inside to tell the girls I needed to leave for a while.

"I'll come with. I'll be your assistant," Jordyn said.

I laughed. "I don't think your mom would want you riding with the neighbor."

Jordyn punched my arm playfully. "It's not like you're a stranger. It'll be fine. Right, Mariah?" she asked.

Mariah shrugged. "I think it's fine. Mom wouldn't care."

The fact that the girls trusted me made both me and my dragon happy and content, though I couldn't help wondering if Harley really would be fine with it. Not wanting to disappoint, I agreed.

"All right, shorty, let's go," I said.

Jordyn followed me outside, mumbling, "Who're you calling short?"

"You, because you are." I laughed as we climbed into my truck.

The drive to the store was filled with conversation, as was the rule with Jordyn from what I'd noticed so far.

Thankfully, the store had the coils in stock, but they were pricey. Grabbing new air return filters as well, I swiped my card—it was the least I could do after treating Harley like shit. When we arrived home less than an hour after we left, Harley was still asleep. She must have been exhausted.

Jordyn and Mariah stood outside and watched me fix the unit. They asked questions and seemed to enjoy learning something new. I was no expert but knew enough to fix it and explain what I was doing. After I got the new part on, we went inside, and I turned the unit on while I changed the air filter. Mariah stood by a wall, holding her hand to one of the floor vents.

She sighed with relief and smiled up at me. "Cool air."

Jordyn laughed and got down on the floor, putting her face over the vent. The silliness of the situation made my heart swell with happiness. I'd done something for them, but it had been for *me,* too. I could already feel the temperature going down. Before I could get the air filter vent back on, I heard mattress springs creaking in Harley's room. She was up. I experienced a moment of panic. What would she say when she saw me? Would she call the cops? Kick me in the balls?

Harley stumbled out of the bedroom, still half asleep. She glanced at the girls and laughed, seeing them on the floor with their hair blowing in the cool breeze from the air conditioning.

Harley rubbed her eyes. "How the heck did you guys fix the air?"

Mariah looked at Harley. "We didn't fix it, he did." She pointed down the hall at me.

Harley turned and spotted me on my knees as I replaced the vent cover. She froze, face strained, body rigid, and stared at me for several long seconds. I couldn't blame her for reacting the way she did. What had I done other than treat her poorly since she'd moved here?

"Why are you here?" she asked.

Before I could answer, Jordyn said, "He fixed the hot water heater, too. Now you can take that hot bath you were talking about. We were all miserable, so I went next door to see if he knew how to fix this stuff. And, well, he did." She laughed and went back to letting the cool air blow on her face.

Harley's face softened, not a lot, but a little. She actually looked a little stunned. I stood and watched several thoughts go through her head, a range of emotions playing over her face.

She straightened. "Well, thanks. How much do I owe you?"

The innocent question shouldn't have irritated me, but it pissed me off for some reason. When I responded, I did a pretty good job of keeping the anger out of my voice.

"I didn't do it for money. I did it so you and the girls would be comfortable. Shorty over there said you guys were sweating your butts off. Honestly, you might want to go ahead and get a little shower in, you're a little damp yourself."

"Well, I really would feel better about paying for the service," Harley said.

"Service? I'm not a plumber, only a concerned neighbor. It really isn't necessary."

"Be that as it may, I'd like to at least pay for the parts you had to buy."

"Seriously, I'm not taking your money." I paused to taper the feeling of anger and frustration. "It was the least I could do after… well… I'm not going to let you pay me for it."

Harley sighed and put her hands on her hips. "Fine, but I really would feel better if I paid you somehow. What can I do for you?"

Before I could answer, Mariah surprised both of us. "Why don't we cook Mr. Mills dinner?"

I flinched at being called "Mr. Mills". "Please don't call me Mr. Mills. I'm just Tate."

Harley raised a hand in warning, irritation flashing on her face. "I really prefer my kids to respect adults and not call them by their first name."

Jordan pursed her lips in thought. "Well, since you call me Shorty, I'm gonna call you Big Guy. Sound good, Big Guy?"

I laughed, then looked at Mariah. "Okay, and you just call me whatever you're comfortable with."

Harley sighed in obvious exasperation. "Fine, dinner it is. I'll send Jordyn over to get you when it's ready."

"Oh, Mom," Jordyn said. "Make your famous chocolate cupcakes. For dessert, I mean, not for dinner."

Harley looked like she was going to object, but Mariah spoke up, and said, "Oh my gosh yes. You haven't made those since we moved. Please?"

"Good lord," Harley said, "Fine, cupcakes. Are you all happy now?"

My heart almost jolted out of my chest as I watched their little family interaction, and a longing I'd never noticed lurking inside me resurfaced. It wasn't just my dragon who wanted to protect them. That was becoming easy to see, yet not as easy to understand. I left with a smile, pondering everything I'd seen and felt.

Chapter 12 - Harley

My forced smile stayed in place while I waved at Tate as he left. It slid away the second the door closed. I turned and looked at Jordyn, who had left her spot on the floor by the air vent and was rummaging in the pantry for a snack.

"Jordyn, what on earth possessed you to ask Tate to fix our things?"

She looked at me over her shoulder, frowning in confusion. "You weren't feeling well. It was hot and miserable. He's a big guy, and I figured he might know how to fix some things. I don't see what the big deal is."

My sigh was one of frustration. "The big deal is that he's a stranger. We don't know him."

Jordyn looked at me like I was speaking Spanish. "He's not a stranger, he's our *neighbor*. Besides, he doesn't have to be a stranger if we don't want him to be. He's really nice."

Jordyn seemed hellbent on befriending Tate, and I had no idea why. If I had time to think about it, maybe I could figure it out, but I didn't have time. The girls had me on the hook for cooking dinner *and* baking cupcakes. Since I made the cupcakes from scratch, it would take almost two hours just to get them done.

It was irritating, but I'd been sweating buckets with the AC broken. I should have been grateful. The air in the house was much cooler than it had been. If I'd been in my right mind—and the situation was different—I'd have showered the guy with thanks and praise. But with the way things were now, him being around just put me on edge. If he came around more often, it would only be a matter of time before he noticed my belly bulge when I started to show.

"Mariah, can you help me get started on the cupcakes? They'll take longer than anything."

"Sure. I'll get the flour and sugar," Mariah said as she went to the cabinets.

It took a few minutes to gather everything needed to bake the cupcakes. As Mariah measured out the dry ingredients while I started the frosting, we discussed dinner.

"What do you girls think Tate would like?"

Mariah shrugged. "He's a pretty big guy. Something filling? Pasta maybe?"

"Nah," Jordyn said. "That guy is a steak and potatoes dude if I ever saw one."

I couldn't disagree with that. It seemed to hit the nail on the head. "Okay, I like that. Steaks, baked potatoes, maybe a salad?"

The girls nodded, and Mariah said, "That sounds good. I'm getting hungry thinking about it. We didn't eat lunch today. First, it was too hot to eat, then we were busy helping Tate. I'm starving."

"Well, we have everything for a salad. What we don't have is potatoes and steaks. We've got sour cream and butter and all that. Why don't you two run to the store real quick and get everything else? You can grab the list off the fridge and get the other things we need."

Mariah brightened. "Yes! Jordyn, road trip."

I rolled my eyes. "You aren't going to Malibu, you're going to get groceries. It's a three-minute drive, not a road trip."

Mariah grinned. "We're taking a *trip* to the grocery store, while *driving*, on the *road.* Hence, a road trip."

"You better end up being a high-profile lawyer when you grow up. Fine. Grab the list and my wallet, then get out of here."

Once the girls were out the door, I slid the cupcakes into the oven. I set the timer for twenty minutes, then decided to take a shower while I waited. In my room, I stripped down naked before jumping into the shower.

A groan escaped my lips as the hot water cascaded down my body. I mentally cursed Tate. Why did he have to be the one who fixed it? I didn't know how to show my gratitude. Pushing the thought from my mind, I lathered soap over my body and scrubbed the sweat off my body. Once done, I sat on the shower bench and enjoyed the feel of the water streaming over me.

I'd lost track of time when I heard the front door open. "Shit."

I jumped out of the shower and pulled on a pair of shorts and a white tank top, not even bothering with a bra. My phone said I still had three minutes till the cupcakes were ready, which gave me a minute to help the girls with the groceries.

I jogged down the stairs, hair still dripping, and almost slid to a stop. Frozen in place, I stared at the front door, where Tate stood holding a paper grocery bag. My eyes locked on him, his on me. His gaze traveled down my body, and I was suddenly aware of the thin white tank top. The dark outline of my nipples was probably visible. Heat crept into my cheeks, and I had to force myself not to cover my chest with my hands.

The heat in my face drained away, and a chill ran up my spine when I saw that Tate wasn't looking at my breasts but at my slightly rounded belly. The girls hadn't noticed the tiny bump, and I'd thought I was still safe from discovery. Obviously, from the look in his eyes, that wasn't the case.

The girls stood by the kitchen door, awkwardly watching us stare each other down. The looks on their faces said they were confused by the strange standoff. I wished they didn't have to be here for this.

Tate, never taking his eyes off me, handed his bag to Mariah. "Girls, go put the groceries away. I need to talk to your mom."

Instead of questioning it, surprisingly, Jordyn and Mariah did exactly what he asked of them without a single protest. Tate walked up the steps toward me. When he got to the step below me, he placed a warm hand against my stomach and unhurriedly guided me back up the stairs.

I clutched at the banister and slowly walked backward, keeping my eyes locked on his. What was he thinking? What was he feeling? Did he know? How could he know? I didn't look pregnant yet, just bloated—maybe a little more than just regular bloat. The look in his eyes was intense but not dangerous. Nothing about the situation made me fearful. I was terrified, but in a different way.

He gently steered me into my bedroom and closed the door behind us. He turned to make sure it was latched, and I finally came back to my senses. Panic flooded me. What did he want? How many different ways could the next few minutes play out? Screaming, yelling, crying, accusations—all of the above? God, could this day get any worse? Why were so many damned questions spinning through my head?

"What are you doing?" I asked, my voice cracking.

Ignoring my question, he turned to face me, staring right at me. He didn't speak or move; he just looked at me.

It could have been that he was trying to think of what to say, or what to ask, but he looked almost like a statue. Immovable. Uncaring. Perhaps he was waiting for me to say something again.

I repeated my original question, putting more strength and conviction into my voice. "What are you doing, Tate?"

"Is there something you need to tell me?" he asked, ignoring my question.

He did know. Somehow, he realized I was pregnant. All coherent thoughts fled my mind, replaced by abject, unblinking fear. I fell back to my only defense. Denial.

"What are you talking about?" I asked, hoping the confused derision in my voice sounded genuine.

"You don't?" His gaze flicked to my belly, and he tilted his head. "Looking a little rounder than when you moved in, aren't you?"

I sputtered, not even sure how to respond to such a direct accusation. I wanted to be shocked or offended, but… he *was* fucking right.

Forcing the shocked look on my face to morph into one of irritation, I said, "Tate, it's not really polite to point out when a woman's gained weight. You may not have a lot of experience with that, but it's pretty rude, actually."

Tate threw his head back, rolling his eyes, before fixing me with a knowing grin. "Is this why you've been feeling sick?"

I wanted to respond with another lie, anything to get him out of here, but he continued speaking before I could.

"Your girls are worried as shit about you. That tells me they don't know either…"

He was piecing everything together. I'd been an idiot to think I could keep it hidden. All the ridiculous thoughts and plans I had to keep the baby a secret were unraveling because he was too damned smart—because he couldn't keep his damned nose out of my business.

"This isn't your concern. It has nothing to do with you," I said.

Tate stepped forward, uncomfortably close but not touching me, his face soft and calm. "Are you sure about that?"

"Y-yes. It's—" I thought for a split second and made one last attempt at lying. "It's not yours. It's my ex's, but he's not a great guy. That's why we moved away. I wanted to raise the baby away from him."

That was a pretty decent story. It was honestly as close to the truth as I could get. If Luis had been the father, I still would have moved away. It made sense. It was believable. It was logical. He should have bought it hook, line, and sinker.

He smiled at me and said, "Well, a DNA test will prove it one way or another."

"What?" It was like a slap in the face.

He winced and looked at my belly again. "I never planned on being a father. Figured it was something that would never be for me. Though, if this is my baby? I'm not going to be some deadbeat, piece-of-shit father. I won't abandon my child."

I waved my hands in the air between us, as if, by doing so, I could wave his statement away. "No, this isn't how this was supposed to be. It was a fucking one-night stand. One night of really great sex, no names, no history, no future. It was supposed to be a pleasant memory I could pull up later in life. It was not supposed to lead to… to… this." I gestured at both of us. "I don't need you to be involved. I'm not some delicate flower who *needs* a man to help me raise a baby. I've done fine on my own with Mariah and Jordyn for the last three years. Since…" I trailed off, not wanting to say Sam's name. Not here, not like this, not arguing with Tate.

Tate nodded at me, as though he understood, but the look on his face was anything but defeated or acquiescent. "That's fine, and I respect that. The problem is, at the end of the day, you might be carrying my child. I can't walk away from a responsibility like that."

He opened his mouth to say more, but Mariah called from downstairs, "Steaks are marinating. I got the oven on to bake the potatoes."

Tate grabbed the doorknob and looked back at me before opening it. "I'll give you some time to think about things. About how you want to handle this, but…" he looked me in the eyes, "I'm not going anywhere."

Without another word, he pulled the door open and strode out. I followed, thinking I could stop him, grab him by the shoulders and talk sense into him. Instead, I stopped right at the top of the stairs when I heard him talking to the girls.

"Good job, guys. These look great. How long are they supposed to marinate?" Tate asked.

"The package said thirty minutes," Jordyn replied.

"Awesome, I'd go ahead and put the potatoes in. They usually take forever. I'm going back to my place for a bit, but I'll be back. And don't get any ideas, I'm grilling those bad boys. I've got a knack when it comes to barbecued meat. See you in a little while."

"Bye," the girls said in unison.

Jordyn added, "See you soon."

My body numb, I leaned against the newel post, reeling from what had just happened. In ten minutes, my entire world had been thrown upside down. Not only that, but the girls seemed to *really* like Tate. They were excited to have him around, and all I wanted was for him *not* to be here.

A thought struck me then, and it devastated me. Did they enjoy Tate's company because of what they were missing? Did they miss Sam's male influence? It had to be difficult being without a father figure for so many years. Were they starved for that type of interaction? My heart broke a little.

Nothing about this made sense. The last thing I wanted was for my girls to get attached to Tate. The problem was, he'd told me his intentions. He wasn't going anywhere. There was no scenario where he would just disappear into the shadows again.

I had no choice now but to tell the girls. When, though? Not tonight. I couldn't do that. I was too drained. The timing was terrible, but I had to tell them. Eventually.

Chapter 13 - Tate

That… had gone poorly, to say the least. Thoughts raced through my mind as I walked across the street. It was true—she was pregnant. It took a lot for me to stop my dragon from leaping forward and embracing Harley the whole time we were arguing. My dragon had actually gotten irritated with me for making her uncomfortable, which was weird. It was kinda like my right hand getting pissed at my left hand. The fact that she didn't want us in her life had been hurtful but not unexpected. I'd given her no reason to want me in her life.

It took me fifteen minutes to take a quick shower and get redressed. Then I spent a few minutes at my front door, staring at Harley's house. My courage had flagged after leaving, and now I was trying to build it back up.

"Oh, hell, let's do this," I muttered.

A few minutes later, I was back in her kitchen, helping Mariah chop cucumbers and carrots for a salad while the grill heated up outside. Harley was at the kitchen table, talking to Jordyn. I'd gotten to know the youngest

King girl pretty well today, and I was trying to get to know Mariah. She was quiet and softspoken, the polar opposite of Jordyn.

"What grade are you going to be in this year?" I asked.

Mariah glanced at me. "Junior."

"Big year," I said.

She was pretty like her mom. The boys would be falling all over themselves for the chance to date the beautiful girl from the big city. My dragon stirred, its protective instincts rearing its head at the thought. Was this what it would be like to be a father? Constantly wanting to protect and take care of the ones younger and weaker?

It made me edgy and uncomfortable. I'd never wanted something like this. It seemed the dragon had staked its claim on the entire family. This girl wasn't my responsibility, but there would be hell to pay if I tried to tell my dragon that. As far as it was concerned, they were already part of its family, and I wasn't sure how I felt about that. I couldn't deny that I enjoyed being around them, though.

Harley seemed to be on edge with me here. No surprise after our showdown upstairs less than an hour ago, which definitely had not been part of the plan. I'd seen the girls taking in the groceries and gone to help. When I walked in and saw Harley's belly, the dragon had taken hold, reacting on instinct. As soon as I touched her belly, the dragon *knew*. I hadn't intended to take her to her room, but I needed to speak to her alone.

When Miles had told me that the baby might be mine, I'd done everything I could to deny it or make excuses. That was all over now. I knew in my gut the baby was mine, as did the dragon. I had some ground to make up, though. I didn't blame her for trying to keep me at a distance and hiding the truth from me. After all, I had been a dick to her. I needed to try and mend that fence. She needed to give me a chance to do that. Something between us had to give.

When the food was done, we sat at the table to eat. It was awkward. Harley sat across from me at the other end of the table, with Jordyn and Mariah on each side. The first few minutes were really quiet, which only made things worse, but then Jordyn piped up and filled the silence with her endless chatter.

"Did I tell you I was starting high school this fall?" she asked me.

I bit back a groan. Jordyn was a very friendly person, and high school was full of assholes and bitches who would take advantage of that. She could end up with fake friends who only wanted to use her, or a shitty boyfriend who would make her life hell. Neither me, nor my dragon, were particularly fond of the idea of her getting hurt. Instead of telling her all that and damping down her excitement, I went with the safe response.

"Nice. Are you excited?" I asked.

"Yeah, it'll be cool. Not sure if it'll be easier or harder to make friends in such a small school. I think the whole school, like all four grades, is as big as my freshman class would have been back in New York."

I shrugged and made a face to show my understanding. "That's to be expected. Colorado is not a hub of humanity like New York."

"What do you do for work, Tate?" Mariah asked.

"I'm part owner of a security firm here in town. Three of my best friends and I started it about fifteen years ago."

Mariah frowned. "So, like, you do network security or something?"

"Eh, one of the guys does stuff like that. I'm actually in charge of personal security. I'm a bodyguard, more or less. I get to be around a lot of cool people."

"Anyone famous?" Jordyn asked, eyes widening in excitement.

I chuckled. "A few. I can tell you who as long as you don't spread it around."

The girls nodded eagerly. Jordyn said, "Spill it."

I laughed and started dropping names. "Jacob Vance, quarterback for the Jets. Patricia Long, the actress in that new vampire movie. Let's see, hmm, Sebastian Justice, the tech billionaire. Just between us, his real name is David Walker, he changed it to sound more mysterious and important before he launched his company, and he's a real douchebag. My last long-term job was going on tour with Brittany Leigh."

Jordyn gasped. "BrittLeigh? Shut up. You were BrittLeigh's bodyguard?"

Too late, I remembered Brittany had been the half-naked woman Harley had found in my house a while back. I glanced across the table. She was stiff, robotically stirring sour cream into her baked potato and doing everything possible not to look at me.

"She is, like, my absolute idol," Jordyn gushed.

I put a hand out to slow her down. "Look, it's totally fine to enjoy her music, but I would find a better person to idolize. Brittany is... well, to be honest, she is a spoiled, entitled brat. Not fun to be around. She also has a hard time hearing the word 'no.'"

Jordyn's face fell slightly. "Ugh, seriously? That sucks. But if you say it's true, I believe it."

Furrowing my brow, I wondered why she took my word on it so easily. Her trust in me and my judgment was strange since we barely knew each other. For whatever reason, she trusted me, and it warmed my heart. I grinned and shook my head, thinking how strange this all was—in a good way.

The rest of the dinner continued in a similar fashion. The girls and I had great banter and conversation. Harley, stiff and uncomfortable, only contributed a word or sentence here and there. She avoided making eye contact with me the whole time. The girls cleared the table after dinner, and Harley went to get the cupcakes. Mariah and Jordyn wouldn't let me do anything, since dinner was a thanks for fixing the water heater and the air con.

The cupcakes were amazing. Homemade cream cheese frosting, which had the perfect balance of tangy and sweet, atop the soft, spongy cake. Freaking mind-blowing. I ended up eating three of them.

"Harley…" I said between mouthfuls, "…these are the best cupcakes I've ever had."

I was happy to see her blush and smile a little, even though she still wouldn't meet my eyes. I waited until she finished her cupcake.

Pushing away from the table, I said, "Ladies, do you mind if I borrow your mom for a second?"

Harley's gaze darted to mine, fear, and uncertainty written all over her face. I nodded toward the back porch door. Reluctantly, Harley pushed her own chair back and followed me. The girls watched us go—Mariah with a raised eyebrow, Jordyn with a goofy grin. I wasn't sure what they thought about the whole situation, but I'm sure they were starting to piece some things together. They were smart kids. We really needed to sort all this out soon.

I opened the door and let Harley through first. Once the door was closed, I said, "Can we talk?"

Harley walked around the deck in a big circle before taking a deep breath and saying, "Okay, sure."

I sighed. "Good. Look, I'm not trying to wedge my way into your life. If you really want me to back off and not come around as much, I will. That doesn't mean I'm going to ignore the fact that you're possibly carrying my child. The only reason I was here today was because it seemed like the girls wanted me around. I didn't want to let them down or reject them."

Harley's eyes flashed with surprise. "Why would you care about that?"

That felt like a bit of a kick in the balls. Jesus, did she really think I was that big of a piece of shit?

"Harley, I'm not an asshole. I have no reason to be a dick to your kids. Hell, I didn't have a reason to be a dick to you, either. I'm sorry. Anyway, they're good kids. If I had to guess, this whole thing today was more about you than about feeding me. They were worried about you and wanted you to feel better. You've done a really great job raising them. I'm sure you'll do the same for the baby. You should be proud as shit of yourself for what you've done as a mother."

Harley's eyes welled with tears. "It wasn't *all* by myself. Their dad did a lot to make them who they are, too."

I didn't press for more information on her husband. I'd already read about him and knew what had happened. She would either tell me in her own time or not—totally up to her.

"I'll be right across the street whenever you're ready to discuss what we should do moving forward. About the baby, I mean."

Harley was going to say something, but the ringing of my phone interrupted us. I silenced it, gesturing for her to go on. "I'll talk to you once I've had time to think. Okay?"

I nodded just as my phone rang again.

"Shit, hang on," I said. Steff was calling, "Let me take this real quick."

Harley nodded.

"Steff, I'm in the middle of something right—"

"I need you right away. Get your ass to Cooperton," Steff said, his voice wavering with something like panic or fear.

"Hey, hey, hang on. Steffen, what's wrong?"

"Tate, just get out here. I'll text you my location."

"Bro, I'm not driving a damned hour without a legit reason. Why do you sound so…" I looked up to see Harley's face. She looked concerned and confused by my end of the conversation. I altered what I said. "You sound a little out of it."

"Tate, Blayne found a dead shifter. He said it looks like he was murdered. Miles is already on the way. I'll meet you there. Go. Now."

All the blood rushed out of my face, and I was clammy and cold. I still held the phone to my ear even though Steff had ended the call. Harley stepped forward, putting a hand on my shoulder.

"Tate? What's wrong? What was that call about?"

"Uh." I thought quickly, a lie that might work springing up into my mind in an instant. "My friend Steff. He, uh, he had a little too much to drink. Got in a wreck out near Cooperton." I shoved my phone into my pocket and pulled myself together. "He wrapped it around a tree. He's totally fine, but I need to go get him. Right away. I'm sorry."

Harley's face told me I was in the clear. She said, "No, that's fine. I get it. Go help your friend. I'll let the girls know you have to help someone."

"Thanks." I had to stop myself from leaning forward and kissing her cheek. Jesus, that would have been embarrassing. "Um, I guess I'll see you later?"

She nodded and walked over to the door. "Bye. Be careful, Tate."

"I will."

She had no idea how careful I needed to be if someone was killing shifters. If what Steff had said was true, things were getting out of hand. Missing shifters were one thing—they could have run off with a girl or decided to start their own pack or something. A body? One that indicated murder, no less? That was heavy shit, and a whole new level of terror. It confirmed that there were hunters nearby.

The drive to Cooperton usually took about forty minutes, but I pumped the gas, hoping there wouldn't be any cops on the road. I arrived there in just over thirty minutes. All the guys had tracking apps on their phones so we could find each other on the very rare occasions when we all worked a job together. It came in handy at times, just like tonight. I followed it until I came to a small pull-off at the side of the road on the outskirts of the town. Steff's, Miles's, and Blayne's cars were all parked there—they were huddled around the hood of Miles's car.

"You got here fast," Miles said as I stepped out of my truck.

"Well, hell, of course. After what Steff told me. Is it true? Blayne, did you actually see a body?"

He nodded. "I came out here to shift and have a run. Catch a deer or something for dinner. As soon as I got out of my car, I smelled it. I tracked it… it's about three hundred yards down the path, and then another hundred or so yards off the path to the right. As soon as I saw it, and realized what I was seeing, I booked it back here and called Steff."

I tilted my head to the sky and pulled in a deep breath. I could smell it, too. A body, freshly dead, and definitely a shifter. It smelled sort of like Miles, so probably a wolf. The night took on a surreal quality as we all turned and started the hike into the woods.

We walked in silence, flashlight beams bouncing along in front of us as we went. The closer we got, the stronger the smell became. The body wasn't rotten and putrid yet—that would have been a different scent. This smelled of blood. Lots of it.

"Oh shit. Do you smell that?" Miles whispered.

"Yeah, man, I smell that. What do you think we're following?" Steff said.

"Not the blood. Something else. Are we almost there?" he asked.

Blayne nodded, lifting a hand to point. "Right here. Should be right behind that tree and shrub."

I took the lead, taking Steff's flashlight and pushing through the underbrush. What my light fell on was awful. I pulled up short, my feet sliding in the leaves on the ground. The others stepped in beside me, a muffled chorus of curses and disgusted sighs erupting from them.

Shifters weren't like the werewolves or vampires of mythology. We weren't immortal, everlasting creatures. We were born, we grew old, and we died. We were stronger and faster, and we could withstand a lot more injury wise and heal fast, but a bullet to the head or heart? A knife across the throat? Yeah, that killed us just as dead as a human. This man had died, and it didn't look like it had been quick.

Steff and I circled the body, looking at the wounds. He'd been cut dozens of times with a blade of some sort. There were burn marks around each wound, like the knife had been hot or something.

"Fuck," Miles said. "Can't you smell that?" He was shaking.

I sniffed the air, and picked up the faint metallic scent that wasn't the iron scent of blood. "What is that?"

"Fucking silver, man. His whole body reeks of it. They used silver knives on him, that's why he's burned. Bullets, too."

Being a wolf shifter, Miles was much more sensitive to silver. He avoided it like the plague. Some myths did have a kernel of truth to them. Passing the light over the body again, I spotted several bullets—three in each leg, another in each hand, two in the stomach, and one in his forehead. The kill shot. But the others? The others had been meant to injure. This shifter had been tortured, viciously and without mercy. Bile rose in my throat. I didn't know this man, but in a sense, he was a brother. A shifter like me, hiding among the human population, and he'd been hunted down, tortured, and murdered.

"We need to look into this, but I think our gut was right. Hunters. No way anyone else would do something like this. That means none of us are safe," Steff said.

I looked up at him, an overwhelming sense of fear and uncertainty settling over me. If they found out about Harley and the baby, would they go after her? The baby might be born shifter or human, but there was no way to know. If they found out, they would kill my child just like they had killed this man. Hunters had a reputation. They would bash the baby's head in while it slept in its crib, all because they wanted to eradicate our race.

My dragon's anger flashed, my own raging along with it. Whether I was a family man, or whether Harley would allow me to be a part of her life, I wouldn't allow this. There was no way I would let those sons of bitches anywhere near my child, the woman who carried it, or her daughters. I would die before I allowed that.

Chapter 14 - Harley

Sunday was makeover day. I'd promised the girls we would go get their hair done and have mani-pedis the weekend before school started. I'd put it off on Saturday, taking the day to rest and catch up on work. Luckily, the salon in town was open on Sundays. So, here we were, three ladies on the town, ready to get pretty.

It had been a week since the showdown with Tate. He'd been good on his word and kept his distance, giving me time to process. There had been a lot to think about, and most of my thoughts surrounded when and how to tell the girls. Today was the day.

We all got trims and simple styles. I'd vetoed Jordyn's request for a crazy trendy haircut and Mariah's pleas for red streaks in her hair. The relaxing effect of the manicure and pedicure evaporated as soon as it was over. Anxiety, fear, and dread swirled in my chest as I paid and left a tip.

"You want to get lunch while we're out?" I asked the girls.

"Oh yeah. I'm starving," Jordyn exclaimed.

"There's a pizza place down the street. That okay?"

"That sounds good. We haven't had Colorado pizza yet. Do you think it'll be as good as New York?" Mariah asked.

I had a hard time not smiling. "I'm sure it'll be fine, but I doubt it. Let's go give it a try."

We walked in silence. It was an enjoyable day, but I still didn't know how to broach the subject with the girls. I had multiple ideas, some too silly, others too serious. By the time we got to the restaurant door, I had decided to be straight forward.

The scent of sourdough crust and tangy tomato sauce greeted us. The restaurant looked like a lot of the pizza places around Manhattan. I grinned at the little slice of home. The bell above the door jingled, and a small man with white hair, a mustache, and an olive complexion came out to greet us.

"Such lovely ladies. Hello, what can I do for you today? Pizza? Stromboli? Pasta?" His voice had a familiar lilt I couldn't place.

"Um, pizza," I said, smiling at him.

He tapped his ear and widened his eyes. "For the ladies? Anything. What can I put on the pie for you?"

I ordered our usual. "Half pepperoni and mushroom, half sausage and onion?"

"I will take care of it. Sit, sit. I'll bring you drinks."

"I'm sorry, your accent? Where are you from?" I asked, despite myself.

He patted his chest. "Born in Sicily, raised in Brooklyn from the age of six."

"Oh wow," Jordyn said. "We're from New York, too."

He looked pleased. "Fellow New Yorkers? For you? Free cannoli after lunch. Welcome. Let me get started for you."

We sat at a booth, surprised to have run into an Italian New Yorker who owned a pizza place in Lilly Valley, Colorado. It seemed like a sign. Like the universe was telling me: *You're in a comfortable place that reminds you of home. Time to spill the beans.*

I put my hands on the table, twisting my fingers together. My nerves had to be obvious on my face and in my body language. I took a breath and steadied myself. Jordyn and Mariah were looking at me with puzzled expressions.

"I have something really important I need to tell you about."

Mariah raised an eyebrow. "Okay?"

Taking a deep breath, I said, "I'm pregnant."

Jordyn and Mariah looked at me, their faces blank. They stared at me for several seconds before glancing at each other and smiling. The little buttheads thought I was lying? Surely not. Why would I lie about something like that?

"I really am."

Mariah grinned and shook her head. "Mom, we don't think you're lying, we just… kind of already suspected."

I jerked back. "What? How?"

Again, they exchanged a look before Mariah said, "You've been pretty sick. You've also been napping, like, a lot."

"Yeah, and you've had mood swings and stuff. Grumpier than usual. Crying more often. Like that commercial last night on T.V. had you sobbing," Jordyn said.

I crossed my arms over my chest. "Well, it was sad."

"Mom," Jordyn said. "It was a commercial for dog food."

I pressed my lips together, not wanting to respond.

"Plus, you've been eating crazy stuff," Jordyn went on. "You were dipping corn chips into grape jelly the other day. Then you put hot sauce on that bowl of vanilla ice cream last night." She wrinkled her nose.

My cheeks flushed. I'd had the same weird cravings when I'd been pregnant with both of them. It was a little disconcerting that the girls had been so aware of my actions.

Mariah nodded toward my midsection. "The kicker was that we both could tell your belly was getting bigger. It all sort of fit together."

My embarrassment irritated me. So much for thinking I'd done a good job of hiding it. I was surprised that the girls didn't seem overly concerned. In my mind, it had been a foregone conclusion that they would have thought it was the end of the world. Now I realized I could breathe easier.

Mariah's smile faded away. "So, does this mean Luis will be coming around? Is he going to move out here?"

My heart lurched. This was why the girls hadn't brought up their fears. Not because they were worried about having a new sibling but because they were afraid of Luis. They assumed Luis was the father. Why wouldn't they? Jordyn also looked concerned. I needed to ease their fears.

"Luis is not part of this. You shouldn't be concerned about him. He doesn't know where we are, and he won't be part of this family. Ever."

They looked relieved at that. Just then, the little man running the restaurant brought out our sodas and our pizza, and we dug in, devouring the entire thing. It was indeed as good as New York pizza. Another delightful surprise to the day.

"Mom, I'll help. When I'm not in school, I'll do whatever you need to help with the baby," Mariah said.

"Me, too. I'd love to babysit," Jordyn said.

I smiled around a bite of pizza. "Thank you. I'm sure I'll need help, but I don't want you to let this rule your lives. It's my responsibility, but I do appreciate the offer, and I'm sure I'll take you both up on it at some point."

We walked out of the restaurant a while later, full and happy. The day seemed glorious now that my heavy secret was out in the open. It felt like a whole new day. My chest and shoulders felt much lighter now that the heavy weight had been removed. Things were looking up.

Lilly Valley was a small town, and usually quiet. Through my reverie, I heard murmurs of conversation ahead of us. I glanced past the girls who were walking ahead of me. A group of people were huddled around the side of the road near where our car was parked. Frowning, I pushed past the girls.

There were around twenty people standing around my car. They were blocking my view, so I couldn't see what was wrong. Panic flooded me. People wouldn't be huddled around a car if it only had a flat tire. Something else had to be wrong. Then the group parted, and I saw what they were gawking at.

I stopped dead, nearly stumbling as I looked at what had happened to my car. The windshield was smashed. All four side windows were gone, just chips of glass remained. All four tires had been slashed, and the car sat on its rims. Across the hood and side of the car, there were words spraypainted in red. WHORE. BITCH.

I covered my hand with my mouth. Luis had found us. Somehow, he'd tracked us all the way here. He was in this town, and he'd done this. In broad daylight. Why had no one stopped him? Had they watched and laughed, or were they too afraid to do anything? I was starting to shake when thick, strong arms wrapped around me. I jerked and screamed. Luis was grabbing me, trying to pull me into a car. I lashed out, trying to fight him off.

"Harley. Harley, stop. It's me. It's Tate."

His voice cut through my panic, and I looked up into his face. I collapsed into his arms, tears streaming down my face. The girls were behind him. I hated that they'd seen the graffiti on the smashed car.

"Let's get you out of here," Tate said. "Girls, follow me."

He put an arm around my shoulders and ushered me to his truck. Jordyn and Mariah hurried along behind us. I wanted to comfort my girls, but fear had a vice grip on my chest. Luis was dangerous. He was the reason we'd moved here. But I never expected him to follow us halfway across the country and vandalize my car. That was more than dangerous—it was psychotic.

The girls and I buckled ourselves in, and Tate pulled away from the scene. He was speaking, yelling instructions into the phone, but I was in too much of a haze to take in what he was saying. Even as dazed as I was, I was surprised by how happy and relieved I was that Tate had been there.

"Momma?" Jordyn asked in an uncharacteristically meek voice. "Did Luis find us?"

I couldn't answer. Simply couldn't get the words out. Mariah answered for me.

"Yeah, I think he did."

We got home, and Tate hustled us into our living room. A few minutes later, there was a knock at the door. Before I could let myself believe Luis was outside, Tate opened the door, and three strange men walked in, each shaking Tate's hand as they stepped past him. I breathed a sigh of relief. Tate knew them. Mariah and Jordyn sat on either side of me.

Tate pointed at each new arrival. "This is Miles Kelly, a private investigator. That's Steffen James, security program developer, and Blayne Walker, our security analyst. These are the guys I work with. I trust them with my life, and so can you."

Miles sat down on the ottoman in front of me and looked me in the eyes, "Mrs. King, do you have any idea who might have done this to your car?"

"Luis. It was him. I know it," Jordyn said, her voice just a step away from a yell.

Miles glanced at Jordyn before his questioning gaze landed on me again. I took a breath and steadied myself.

"Luis is my ex. We dated for several months." I sent a sideways glance in the girls' directions. I didn't want to air my dirty laundry in front of them.

Tate seemed to read my mind and gestured to the girls. "Hey, guys, how about we get you into your rooms? Your mom needs to give Miles all the information she can. No need for you to be here for that."

For a moment, I thought they'd argue, but they stood and went upstairs. I let out a small, relieved breath. I loved my daughters, but there were some things they didn't need to know.

"Luis is my ex. A while back, I found out he was cheating on me. Had cheated on me multiple times with different women. When I broke things off, he started stalking me, texting me, showing up at the girls' school, always being visible. But it got more intense and scarier. I finally got a restraining order. That was when he had some associate approach me to threaten me *and* the girls if I didn't withdraw the order. That was the last straw. A friend of mine offered to rent me their house out here so I could get away from Luis. It looks like he found me..."

Miles glanced at the other men. "I think you're right about it being this Luis guy. If I had to guess, he hired his own investigators to track you down."

"Is it really that easy? I didn't tell him where we were going. Only my friends knew. They wouldn't have said anything."

Miles nodded. "Fifty years ago, a private investigator's job was much harder. Now? Even if you're extra careful, any PI worth a damn could track someone down. Really great when you're the one looking, not great when you're the one trying to run. He probably had a team pull up your medical records too. I'd say he knows about the baby, which might be what brought him out here."

My eyes widened, and I glanced from Miles to Tate. Tate didn't look ashamed or embarrassed. Miles shrugged. "Tate's not just my business partner, he's also my best friend."

Of course he would have told his friends that he may have knocked a woman up, and that she now lived across the street. I wasn't even mad. In fact, it was a relief not to have to go through the entire story with someone else.

Miles asked me more questions, but it was a struggle to focus with Tate walking all around the house and murmuring to Blayne. The two of them pointed at windows and doors, then at the ceiling. I narrowed my eyes when Blayne started marking spots around my house with a pencil.

Ignoring Miles, I called out, "What the hell are you guys doing?"

They turned around, their faces bearing twin expressions of surprise.

"Sorry, um, we were marking the best areas for the security system. Spots for alarms, heavy locks, cameras, motion detectors, the whole shebang," Blayne said.

I blinked. "That sounds really expensive, I can't afford that," I said, addressing Tate.

Tate shook his head and waved me off with a dismissive gesture of his hand. "Don't worry about it. You aren't paying for it."

"What? Tate, no. I can't let you pay for such an extravagant gift, or whatever you want to call this."

Tate sighed. "Harley, are you pregnant with my child or not?"

The room went quiet. Steff suddenly seemed to find something very interesting on my blank living room wall. Miles's eyes widened, and he dropped his head to stare at his shoes. Blayne, who stood next to Tate, looked like a deer caught in headlights.

When I said nothing, Tate continued. "Do you want to sleep easy knowing your home is safe and secure? That no one has pried a door or window open and is creeping down the hall to your bedroom? I know that's maybe an exaggeration, but isn't that what you want? To be totally safe? I can give you that, so let me."

I couldn't argue against that. I nodded and gave him a weak smile. The grin he shot me was dazzling, then he and Blayne went back to what they were doing.

Miles cleared his throat. "I'll be looking into the vandalism of your car. I'm sure the sheriff's department was already called and they have been out there and completed a report. I've had dealings with them, so I can get whatever info they may have."

The front doorbell rang, and I almost jumped off the couch. Steffen held up a hand. "It's okay. It's okay. It's our installation crew. We called them as soon as Tate let us know what was happening.."

My jaw dropped. "Already? This only happened thirty minutes ago."

Steffen shrugged nonchalantly. "Helps when you own the company. When the bosses call, other stuff gets dropped. Tate figured it would be best to install it ASAP."

A half dozen men filed into the small living room and started unboxing items, unrolling cables and wire, and pulling out drills and tool belts. It was overwhelming, and I was suddenly dizzy.

Miles took my hand. "Harley, you're gonna be fine." He gestured at Tate. "I've known this guy longer than almost anyone in my life. He won't let anything happen to you or your family."

His words seemed to break the inner dam I'd built up, and tears of gratitude slipped down my cheeks. I tried to utter the words *thank you*, but all that came out was a blubbering sigh.

Seemingly uncomfortable now that he was faced with a sobbing woman, Miles said, "Um, maybe you should lie down or something? A nap would be the best thing for you, I think."

I nodded and stood to go up to my room. Fearful and angry thoughts roamed freely in my mind. Luis had found us so quickly. We'd barely been able to get settled in, and he was already making our lives hell again. Only, this time it was worse. Back in New York, it had been subtle, vague. Terrifying but in a quiet, controlled way. This was more overt and aggressive.

As crazy as it was, I appreciated Tate's help, and I understood why he was doing it. It was only natural for him to want his unborn child to be safe. Was that all, though? I had a feeling that there was more to it than that, but my brain was too fried to entertain such thoughts. My bed looked like the most amazing thing I'd seen in my life. Not even bothering to take off my shoes, I collapsed onto it. The sounds of men working and talking downstairs drifted into the background, lulling me into sleep.

Chapter 15 - Tate

Steff and Blayne had their heads bent together over a laptop. Steff's systems were of the highest quality and nearly completely impenetrable. In all our time owning this firm, I'd never known anyone to break through what he cooked up. I'd requested our top-of-the-line system to be installed in Harley's place. We only installed two or three of them a year, and the last one we'd installed had in Vail at the Speaker of the House's vacation home. It was as safe as I could make Harley's house without stationing an armed guard at each entrance.

Leaving Blayne and Steff to work and direct the team, I went over to Miles. He was working his way through more background information on Luis and his known associates. He wanted to be sure we had every scrap of information we could on him.

I slumped down on the couch beside him. "How bad?"

Miles stopped typing and looked at me. "Well, let's look at it. Broad scope. Ninety percent sure he knows

Harley is pregnant. He's traveled across the country." He held up a finger. "Mind you, he traveled that far without so much as warning Harley. That already tells me he has bad intentions. Then he vandalizes her car. It was almost manic in its thoroughness. That shows psychological instability. This makes him dangerous, and makes it very difficult to predict his next move. He still has a sense of self-preservation, otherwise he would have attacked her right on the street. As awful as that would have been, he probably would have been stopped by bystanders or police and been arrested. Harley may have been injured, but we'd know he was safely locked up."

"That being said, the most dangerous thing I've found is the possible ties to the mob. It would be less worrisome if I could find something overt—an arrest record, court summons, things like that. I can't find anything. He has known associates that go back to his time in freaking middle school. Almost all of them are deeply entwined with the mafia. Two and two always makes four, but from everything I'm seeing, I can't guarantee it. But if he does have mob ties, he's dangerous. More dangerous than the typical jilted boyfriend. Shit, man, he could be a killer. I don't like it."

Miles's description of the situation was not reassuring. This Luis guy was trouble, and not the typical type of trouble. He was dangerous and unpredictable.

First hunters, and now this? I sighed and rubbed my temples to ease the headache forming behind my eyes.

"All right," I said. "Looks like you guys have all this handled. I'm going to check on Harley."

Miles had already turned back to his laptop screen. "Sounds good."

It was quiet upstairs. I could hear the girls' murmuring voices coming from the room at the end of the hall. Harley's room was dark, and when I peeked my head into the room, it looked like she was sleeping. Not wanting to be creepy, but still wanting to check in on her, I stepped over to the side of the bed.

She was curled into a ball, hugging the pillow tight. Mascara tracks ran down her cheeks and onto her pillowcase. She'd been crying in her sleep. I clenched my jaw as my dragon snarled and gnashed inside my head. It was as pissed as I was at seeing her so vulnerable and sad.

Without thinking, I eased myself onto the bed and pulled her into my arms. Half of me hoped she would accept the comfort; the other half readied itself for her to lash out and slap me for assuming she would. To my relief and surprise, she not only accepted it, but cuddled closer to me. Her body molded to mine as she burrowed deeper into my arms and chest. My heart began to race, and I hoped it wouldn't wake her.

But then she spoke, and I did my best to listen and take it all in. "I'm so afraid, Tate. I don't know what to do. I really thought moving out here was the best thing for us. But now? I'm scared. Luis is dangerous."

"Why did you ever get involved with this guy?"

She sighed into my chest. "He put on a good act. When we first met, he seemed so nice. He took care of me, he was nice to the girls, and he offered to help in any way he could. He even pulled some strings and helped me get the girls into a private school. Everything was great for the first few months. I'd been hesitant to take things from casual to more serious. It was just so difficult. Sam had been gone for almost three years when I met him, so it was tough. Things started changing when we were officially a couple. He treated me more like a possession. Controlling and manipulative. Then I started suspecting that he was cheating on me. It was a week or two before I met you, but he tried to make me think I was crazy."

"I'm sorry." It was all I could think to say.

"Yeah. Me, too. It was a toxic situation. I'd finally gotten proof of his cheating, and I broke things off over the phone. He actually tried to tell me I'd brought it on myself. And then the stalking and the harassment started. When I was getting the restraining order, Maddox—Sam's old partner on the force—told me he, Luis, might have targeted me years ago. Sam had been investigating the mob, and… well, I might have caught his eye back then. I never knew anything about that part of Luis's life, but after all that has happened, it makes sense."

"Holy shit," I murmured.

She nodded against my chest. Then, surprisingly, she chuckled. "My life is pretty fucked up." She lifted her head and looked at me. "I wanted to get away from Luis, but then I found out I was pregnant. I felt terrible. I didn't even know who the father was."

I grimaced. "I'm also to blame. I didn't think to use a condom."

I couldn't tell her that I never wore condoms because I had no need for them. Shifters couldn't catch or transmit STDs. Also, until not that long ago, I didn't believe a shifter could impregnate a human woman. In all my life, I'd only known shifter men and shifter women to have kids. It was so damned crazy, but there was nothing I could do about it now.

"I'm sorry I put you in this position. I should have done more for you," I said.

Harley raised herself on her elbow and looked at me. Her face was a mask of confused surprise. It sliced my heart that she was surprised by my apology. Had I really been such a dick that it was too unbelievable to think I would apologize? Shit, what kind of asshole had I been?

I cupped her face with my hand, the skin of her cheek warm and smooth against my palm. "Harley, I promise you aren't alone. Not in whatever is happening with Luis, and especially not with the baby. I'll do whatever is in my power to keep you safe. You, the girls, and the baby. No matter what it takes."

Harley smiled and snuggled into me again. After a while, her breathing deepened and evened out. I lay there holding her, my head a mess of thoughts and feelings. My need to protect Harley and her family was growing stronger with each passing second. Fed by the dragon inside me, it was almost primal in its strength.

Harley, fully asleep, rolled away from me, and I used that moment to slide out of her bed. She didn't even stir as I packed her pillows around her to take my place. Before I closed the door, I glanced back at her. She looked peaceful and calm. That was good. She'd been through enough. She deserved to rest a little.

The door to the girls' room was open, and they were nowhere to be seen. The noise and commotion the guys were making downstairs must have stirred their curiosity.

Sure enough, I spotted them at the bottom of the stairs, watching the chaos. Steff had set up several laptops on the kitchen table and was working on them. When I got to him, I realized most of the devices weren't his. There were two laptops, phones, and a tablet, which probably belonged to Harley and the girls.

"Are you doing what I think you're doing?"

Steff looked up and nodded. "Yeah. Firewalls. That way, no one can hack them. No trackers, no slave cameras or speakers, fully secure. I don't want that jerkoff getting a foothold inside the house after all the work we're doing to secure the place."

Everything he said made sense, but I was having a hard time listening. Instead, I was stifling a laugh. Steff stopped and frowned at me. "What's so funny?"

I leaned toward Steff and said, "I think you have an admirer."

His frown deepened, and he spun in his chair. Jordyn saw him turn to look and quickly darted her eyes away."

"Oh lord," Steff said. "What am I? Like the hot teacher or something? Gross. I mean, don't get me wrong, she's a nice kid, but... gross."

"Bro, I spent the day with her a while back. She's going to be a force when she gets older. Anyway, how're things looking on the install?"

Steff glanced around then said, "Looking good. Should be done soon."

"Okay, I'm gonna check on the kids."

Mariah and Jordyn saw me coming toward them, and they smiled weakly. "Ladies, you want to come have a seat? Take a load off?"

They nodded and followed me to the table. Steff moved his computers aside and smiled at the girls. Before I could sit down, Mariah asked, "Is Mom okay?"

I raised my eyebrows. "Yeah, she's up in her room, napping. Are you guys all right?"

I didn't believe their quick nods of assent. I could tell they were pretty shaken up. How could they not be, though? The day had been traumatic for a grown woman. How could anyone imagine her kids would fare much better?

Mariah stared down at her feet. "Please protect our mom. Please." Her voice was thick with unshed tears.

"She's all right—"

"I'm scared of Luis," Mariah cut me off. "I'm afraid he's going to take her like he took our dad."

Steff froze mid keystroke and shot a questioning look at me that said *what the fuck?* I sat up straight in my chair, not sure what she meant. The implication was there, but not the full thought.

"Mariah? What does that mean?"

Her lip quivered, and tears shone in her eyes. Jordyn lowered her face to the table and covered her ears with her hand. They suddenly looked much younger than teenagers. Young, scared, and carrying some terrible secret.

Mariah sucked in a trembling breath, then spoke in a forced, calm voice. "Our school—the private school we went to before we moved—it was a pretty nice school, and a lot of the kids were rich or well off, you know? Their parents were doctors or lawyers, CEOs, and stuff. Except, some of those kids had dads who were… I guess… criminals or something? Mafia people?"

"I get what you mean," I said.

"Well, after Mom broke up with Luis, some of those kids started talking. They said he hung out with their dads. There was a rumor going around that Luis…" She took a shuddering breath. "That Luis killed our dad so he could get my mom. Like, he liked Mom and killed Dad so he could date her. That's crazy, right? It has to be crazy."

I leaned around the table and gathered Mariah into my arms, holding her close as she sobbed into my chest. Steff glanced at me, wide eyed, and mouthed, *holy shit.* This was a fucking nightmare. No child, no matter their age, needed to know and deal with this kind of shit.

"I promise I'll do everything I can to keep the two of you and your mom safe," I said.

Mariah sniffled as she pulled away from me. "Thanks. Um, is it okay if I start dinner??"

"Yeah, totally fine. Let me know if you need anything."

"I'll help," Jordyn said as she slid her chair back.

She came over and wrapped her arms around me in a tight hug. The moisture from her tears soaked into my collar. My heart felt like it was going to burst. Mariah nudged Jordyn, then they headed into the kitchen. When I turned back to Steff, he was smiling at me.

"What?" I asked.

Steff gestured at me. "This whole family-man thing looks good on you, bro. It suits you." I glared at him, but he merely laughed. "Quit with the big-bad-bodyguard routine. Let your heart feel what it feels."

After everyone had finished and cleared out, Harley woke up from her nap. She came down the stairs, rubbing her eyes and yawning, as we were putting the dinner dishes in the sink.

"Where is everyone?" she asked.

"They left. The crew finished up, and my guys helped them get loaded up and out. We saved you some dinner. Hungry?" I said, wiping my hands on a dish towel.

"Sounds great," she said.

"I'll heat it up, Mom. Tate was going to show you the security system," Mariah said.

Frowning, Harley came the rest of the way down the stairs. "The girls already know how to operate it?" she asked.

I shrugged. "Kids easily pick up on stuff like this. Here, let me show you."

Leading her to the wall beside the door, I pointed out the new control panel. "This will set and control your security system. There's also a display where you can pan through and see all the cameras." I clicked through each displayed as I named them off. "Outside back door, outside front door, outside garage door, inside back door, inside front door, and one at the top of the stairs aimed at the landing. That should be enough to cover all the bases. Steff set up your phone so these feeds go right to you. You can bring up the video feed anywhere and anytime. You'll see a new app on your home screen for it. The camera feeds also go to the server at my office."

"We also installed firewalls on all your devices, the girls' included. It's probably way over the top, but you can't be too safe. Blayne had them put in some reinforced door locks, too. Much stronger than what was on there before. I'm pretty happy with it all. What do you think?" I was like a child trying to show off, but I couldn't help myself. The team really had done a magnificent job.

Harley shook her head in disbelief. "It really does seem like too much. Is all this really necessary? I was thinking a simple alarm would be sufficient."

I slipped a hand around her waist and pulled her to the side, away from the girls. The feel of her skin through her clothing sent a pleasant shiver through me, but I didn't let it show on my face.

I leaned in and whispered, "The girls are really worried. When I showed them everything, it made them feel better. They are very worried about you."

Sadness cloaked her eyes, and she gave a sharp nod. "Okay. It's fine, really. I just didn't want to impose too much."

My hand slid down to her lower back, and flashes of our night together in New York played through my mind. My hands had been all over her. Every inch of her body knew my touch. Heat slowly moved up my spine, and I pressed my body against hers. I could hear Harley's breathing start to pick up. I wanted a replay of that night. A second chance to feel her writhing beneath me, gasping and clutching at me. The dragon growled deep in my chest as she moved closer to me.

"Tate?" Harley whispered as my face inched closer to hers.

Her hand moved up and slid along my stomach. I was barely able to control myself. I was inches from kissing her, tasting her again, when Jordyn called out.

"Mom, dinner's ready."

We broke apart, coming back to our senses. I bit back a curse as Harley disentangled from my embrace and moved toward the kitchen. I stood there for a moment, taking a few deep breaths to calm myself. Had she felt the same way? It had seemed like she had wanted this as much as I did. There was no way to be sure now. I shook it off and went back into the kitchen with everyone else.

While Harley ate, I hung around, talking to her and the girls. We laughed and enjoyed each other's company. It was a great night, even though the day itself had been pretty terrible. It was nice. Harley sent the girls to bed early since they started school the next morning.

"I'm not really sure how I'm going to get around after they get to school," she said after they went to bed. "My car is trashed."

"Don't worry about that. I'll get you guys wherever you need to go."

"Tate, you've done too much already. That's a kind offer, but Emily can probably help out."

"Who's Emily?" I asked.

"She's a new friend I made. I met her on the Fourth of July. She's really nice. I think she'd be fine giving us a ride if we needed it."

"Okay. Well, if you do need anything, please call me."

"Tate, I live across the street. I think I can find you."

"Nope. What if you're not at home? Or I'm not at home. Here." I grabbed her phone and dialed my number, then saved it. "Now, you can get me whenever you need me."

Not wanting to overwhelm her anymore, I stood to leave. She needed to rest. An impulse came over me to finish what I'd started earlier. We'd been interrupted before, but the girls were in bed now.

"I'm going to head home. Goodnight, Harley." I leaned down and kissed her.

My lips pressed against hers. She stiffened in surprise, then relaxed a moment later, her lips parting to kiss me back. When the kiss broke, I let myself enjoy the look of stunned surprise I left on her face.

"Make sure you lock up as soon as I leave."

"Uh… okay, yeah. Good night."

Outside on the porch, I stood by the door. I didn't leave until I heard Harley punch in the code. Once I heard the beep that indicated the alarm was activated, I headed home. What the hell was I actually doing?

Chapter 16 - Harley

Even after all that happened the day before, I didn't let it bring me down as I helped the girls get ready for school. It was Jordyn's first day of high school. Nothing could stop me from being there for her on a day that stressful and exciting.

To their credit, the girls were up before me. When I came down the stairs in my robe, Mariah was already pouring a bowl of cereal for both her and her sister. I stopped on the stairs and watched them—Mariah working on breakfast, Jordyn running a brush through her hair. They looked so grown up. Soon, they would be adults. Women. Tears started to burn in my eyes, but I took a breath and kept it under control.

"Good morning," I said as I descended the rest of the stairs.

The girls turned and looked at me. Mariah smiled. "Morning, Mom. Did you sleep well?"

I nodded and took a seat next to Jordyn. "I did. Are you guys excited?"

Jordyn said, "Yes. I can't wait."

Mariah set their bowls down, and they ate while we discussed the day. The strangeness of the day before hadn't made things weird between us. It was as if nothing had happened. Still, it was difficult for me not to cast an eye toward the security panel by the door or the cameras.

After breakfast, I helped the girls pick outfits and shoes. While I braided Jordyn's hair the way she liked it, I started having reservations about sending them to school. I didn't let that show or tell them, but the fear was there. Almost as though he read my thoughts, my phone buzzed with a text from Tate.

Good morning. Wanted you to know not to worry about the girls at school. I've got guys on it.

On it? That was comforting but also a little heart breaking. Why did I have to have *guys*? Why did they have to be *on it*? Though I couldn't ignore the fact that having Tate watching out for us made me feel much better about everything.

I texted back: *Thanks. That means a lot. You read my mind.*

Tate responded seconds later: *It's what I'm here for.*

We walked out the door to stand on the curb and wait for the bus. Out of the corner of my eye, I caught movement across the street. Tate stood on his porch, leaning against the rail, sipping on a cup of coffee. He was shirtless, enjoying the warm late-summer weather. I couldn't help but remember him kissing me the night before. My cheeks flushed as I took in the ripple of his muscles as he raised a hand to wave at us.

Jordyn waved ecstatically. "Tate. I'm going to high school. Can you believe it?"

He chuckled and nodded. "I *can* believe it. Have fun."

It was crazy how quickly the girls had taken to him. Even with the way the two of us had acted around each other at the beginning, the girls seemed to really enjoy his company. As the bus pulled up, I smiled. It was good that they had someone they could trust right across the street. Mariah and Jordyn waved to me through the window of the bus as it rolled away. Once it pulled away, I saw that Tate had gone back inside. Had he come outside just to see the girls off? Then, before I could go back inside, and before the bus was out of sight, a black sedan drove out from a side street farther down the neighborhood. A moment of fear took hold, but as it passed, Tate's friend Blayne nodded and waved at me from the driver's seat as he followed the bus toward the school. *On it?* I guess so.

Ten minutes later, while I drank my coffee at the kitchen table, my phone chimed, notifying me that someone was at the front door. After a few seconds of fumbling with the new app, I was able to find the feed for the porch camera. Tate stood there, waiting. It took a few more seconds for me to get the security system deactivated, and the door opened.

Tate smiled at me. "Hey."

"Hey. Why didn't you knock or ring the bell?"

He shrugged. "Wanted to test the system and make sure the notifications were working right. Looks like we're good. Can I come in?"

Realizing I was blocking the door, I blushed. "Sorry, yeah, come in."

We went to the kitchen table. After we sat, Tate said, "Okay, just an update. The cops did get some photos of your car, and they towed it off yesterday. Miles got the name of the garage. They were going to hold it until the owner claimed it. We went ahead and got that taken care of. The repairs on it are starting today. Steff and I gave the cops everything we have on Luis, and we let them know we are pretty much one-hundred percent sure he's the perpetrator."

It was a very funny feeling, having someone look out for me. It had been so long since anyone had done something like this for me. It was nice. Comforting. Warm. But it also made me feel like I was taking advantage of him. I wasn't even sure how to respond.

"Thank you, Tate. I really appreciate all this."

He just stared at me. It wasn't an angry or irritated stare, it was more like he was searching for something. Looking deep inside me, literally trying to read what was going on in my head. Heat rose in my cheeks when he finally leaned back, breaking the moment.

"Okay, I'm taking you out for breakfast. Go ahead and get dressed," he said, startling me.

I shook my head. "I'm not really in the mood for all that. I'd rather stay in today. I'm sorry."

He smiled. "No problem, I get it."

He stood and walked to the kitchen, then started pulling out some pans. He grabbed eggs and a pack of bacon from the fridge. It took a few seconds before I could process what I was seeing. I finally broke the paralysis that had taken hold once he stood.

"What are you doing?" I asked.

Without looking up from the stove, he said, "I'm making us breakfast. I'm starving. Plus, we need to talk." He glanced at me. "There's a lot to go over, and we need to go ahead and get it all out in the open. I don't really want to drag all this out until the baby is born. No reason not to do it over a plate of eggs, toast, and bacon. Crispy or floppy?"

"Huh?" I asked dumbly.

He raised his eyebrows. "Your bacon? Crispy or floppy?"

"Oh. Uh… crispy. Maybe a step or two away from being burnt," I said with a smile.

He pointed at me with a spatula. "I knew there was a reason I liked you. Consider it done."

Twenty minutes later, he put a plate in front of me with perfectly cooked bacon, scrambled eggs, and buttered toast. I hadn't realized how hungry I was until the food was in front of me. I took a bite of bacon and eggs and had just stuffed a piece of toast into my mouth when Tate started talking.

"When is your next doctor's appointment?"

My eyes jolted up to meet him. My mouth was stuffed with food, in the most embarrassing, least ladylike way I could have imagined. Already, this little breakfast meeting was going poorly on my end. "What?" I mumbled through a full mouth.

"Your next appointment. I want to be involved with everything from here on out. I want to go with you to the next one. Plus, since I'm going to be around a lot more, we should get to know each other a little better. Right?"

Finally getting the mouthful of food swallowed, I shot him a surprised look. This was not how I'd thought this would go.

Before I could answer, he said, "I mean, we're going to be raising a kid together. Shouldn't we know each other a little better?"

"Well, sure. Can we maybe start with the background stuff? You know, the things people usually find out *before* having hot, sweaty sex."

He actually blushed a little at that, which helped me feel a tiny bit better about the whole conversation. I could keep him off kilter, too, it seemed.

"Okay, okay," he said. "What do you want to know?"

I shrugged. "What was your childhood like?"

He glanced down at his plate and ate an entire piece of bacon before answering. "Well, I guess my childhood was pretty normal. Things didn't get weird until I was older. My family pretty much disowned me and kicked me out when I was eighteen."

That should have been one of the craziest things I'd ever heard, but my own life was similar. When Sam and I got pregnant with Mariah, my parents demanded I have an abortion or put her up for adoption. They'd absolutely refused to even entertain the thought that I would marry him. When I did, and I kept the baby, they'd cut me off. I hadn't seen or spoken to either of them since I was pregnant with Mariah. I couldn't imagine anything my girls could do that would make me want to cut them out of my life. To send them into the world without someone to lean on or confide in sounded heartless and brutal. It *was* heartless and brutal. It was even worse when it was done by someone you loved and trusted. Tate and I had more in common than I thought.

"What made them do that?"

Tate shrugged and stirred his eggs around his plate. "I... I didn't want to follow the path they'd laid out for me. I'd met a girl that they thought I should marry. I didn't love her, though. I was just with her because everyone wanted me to be with her. When I broke up with her, my family tried to force me to get back with her. When that didn't work..." Tate made a slicing gesture with his fork, "...cut off. Never to return."

"I'm so sorry." I proceeded to tell him my story. His eyes widened with surprise when he realized we had very similar experiences.

We talked for hours, long after our food was done. We talked as we did the dishes, as I brewed coffee, while we sat on the couch. It was companionable, easy, and enjoyable. It had been a long time since I'd been able to converse this easily with a man. Luis had talked, but the conversations had always been very one-sided and narcissistic. This was a give and take, and it was fun. I hadn't had this sort of connection with someone since Sam.

After a while, Tate sighed. "You know, I'd decided a long time ago that I would never have kids. I'd never even considered it. Still, as soon as I realized you were pregnant with my kid, I couldn't walk away. There was no way I could abandon my child the way my family abandoned me. So, how do you want to do this?"

It wasn't an easy question, especially since I didn't really know how this was going to work.

"I'm in the same boat. I never dreamed I'd be pregnant again, much less with a—no offense—complete stranger's baby."

Tate nodded in agreement. "No offense taken. How about this? We take the next few months to, sort of, hang out. See if we're compatible? I don't really like the idea of my kid growing up in separate homes, getting shuffled around on weekends and holidays, but if things between us aren't what we want, that could work. I'd really like things to work out, though, or at least try to see if they could work out."

His proposal hit me hard and fast, and I leaned back, stunned and shocked. Tate had basically just said he wanted to spend the next few months seeing if we could be an item. Like, a live-together, raise-a-kid-together, have-a-home-together couple. There was nothing wrong with that idea. He was gorgeous, kind, smart, and really seemed to want what was best for my girls and me. The only problem was that if things didn't work out, there was a chance my heart might get shattered into a thousand pieces.

"I guess we can see how things go," I said after a moment's hesitation.

Tate grinned. "Sounds great. I've got to go. There's some work stuff I need to take care of. Call me if you need anything."

"I don't think I'll need anything. I wouldn't want to burden you or anything."

He rolled his eyes. "Harley, you'll have to get used to the idea that I'm going to be around more often if we want this to actually work."

"Right." I closed my eyes, embarrassed as hell. "Sorry, you're right. It's just a ton of stuff to get used to and deal with."

"I get it. It is a lot. I'll go at your pace, but I warn you, I've never been a patient man," he said with a wink.

Tate stood to leave, then leaned down to kiss me goodbye. Warmth shot down my neck to my chest and stomach when his lips touched mine. I didn't pull away, instead I opened my lips and flicked my tongue out, exploring his lips. The kiss deepened, becoming more urgent and passionate. For a second, I thought I heard Tate growl.

When he finally pulled away, his eyes seemed to burn with hunger. The warmth I felt as he kissed me changed. That look was like nothing I'd ever seen in anyone's eyes before, and the warmth seeped down from my stomach to between my legs.

"I'll see you later," Tate whispered, then turned and left without looking back.

My body felt scorched once he was gone, seared by that look he'd given me. It sounded bad, but it wasn't. It was pleasurable. Something I thought I might like to experience again. I blushed thinking about it and talked myself out of taking a cold shower.

When the girls got home later on, I was inundated by Jordyn's stories about all her new teachers, the new friends she'd made, the way the school was laid out, even the options for sides they had at lunch. It was a lot, even for Jordyn. Her excitement was palpable. Mariah looked at me at one point and rolled her eyes, which told me she'd probably already heard all this on the bus.

Finally, Jordyn smiled mischievously and glanced at Mariah. "Mariah needs to tell you about the boy."

Frowning, I glanced at Mariah, who was turning red. I looked back at Jordyn. "What boy?"

"There was a cute guy waiting out at the bus stop for her."

Mariah sighed. "Stop making a big deal out of it, Jordyn. Kayden just wanted to give me back the binder I forgot in fourth period. He was just being nice."

"He's super cute, like a full-on heartthrob." Jordyn batted her eyelashes at Mariah. "Oh, Kayden, thank you *so* much for my binder. Maybe I can say thank you with a big wet kiss."

Mariah pulled a chunk off the banana she was eating and threw it at Jordyn. The white flesh of the fruit struck her right above the eye and splattered across her face. All three of us burst out laughing, Jordyn was nearly crying by the time she was able to stop laughing and catch her breath.

"Okay, that's it, watch your back. I'll get you for that one," Jordyn said, grabbing a paper towel to wipe her face.

I wiped the tears of laughter away from my eyes as my mind went back to the idea of boys. Of the two girls, I knew Jordyn was the one who would end up being the most boy crazy. It showed. Mariah and Jordyn were both gorgeous, and I'd be crazy to think they hadn't already caught the eyes of boys at school.

After wiping off her face, Jordyn said, "Okay, I'm going to go add a bunch of my new friends on social media. Bye."

She ran upstairs, and I glanced at Mariah. She was finishing what was left of her banana. "So, Kayden?"

"Oh my gosh, Mom," she said with a laugh.

"I'm just asking. Sounds like he's got his eye on you."

"Good Lord. Okay, sure, he's cute… well, really cute, I guess. He really was only returning my binder, though."

"Okay, I'll leave it alone," I said with a smile.

Mariah's face changed. It was like she'd instantly thought of something. Her brow furrowed, and she chewed at her lower lip. She glanced at the stairs, almost like she was looking to see if Jordyn was coming back. It was a strange shift.

Before I could ask what was wrong, she said, "Um, is Tate the father of the baby?"

It was like I'd been standing on the beach, enjoying the warm sun, relaxing and happy, and then a massive freezing wave had slammed into me. Tumbling under the water, barely able to breathe, cold and shocked. My eyes widened in surprise.

After a few seconds, trying to collect myself, I stammered, "What… what are you talking about, Mariah?"

"Mom, I heard it last night. When they were putting the security system in, he asked if you were carrying his baby." She sighed and shrugged. "I heard it. I just wanted to know if it was true."

"Mariah, it's a really long story. Complicated and weird, and… well, I promise I'll tell you about it soon."

Mariah shook her head and smiled. "It's fine. Take your time. I really like having Tate around. It's nice, you know? Anyway, I'm going to go read for a bit."

I watched Mariah walk up the stairs, still shocked by what she'd asked. She knew. What's more, she seemed fine with it. The girls had really taken to Tate, had embraced him even. Once again, I wondered if I was making the right decision by bringing him into our lives. It was a huge risk. Not just because my heart was at stake here, but theirs as well.

Chapter 17 - Tate

If Harley knew where I actually had to go, I was sure she'd change her mind about allowing me into her life. Miles had set up a meeting with an Alpha from a wolf shifter clan to the south. They'd also had pack members disappearing, but unlike a lot of the others, they'd found the bodies. We wanted to talk to him and try to figure out what he might know. We also wanted to see if the body we found and had buried was one of his. If so, we'd give them the location so they could get some closure.

We met him at a rest stop off the highway halfway between our towns. The spot was always pretty deserted, which made it a good location to meet up. No one would hear what we were talking about. The others were already there when I pulled up.

Steff, Miles, and Blayne were already in conversation with the Alpha as I walked up. The Alpha glanced up and said, "Is this the other guy?"

Miles glanced at me. "Yeah, this is the last of us."

He stepped forward and put his hand out, "Doug. Good to meet you."

"Tate. Likewise. So, what did I miss?"

Miles said, "We were talking about the body we found. It's not one of theirs."

Doug nodded. "Yeah, the description doesn't match any of my missing guys. Doesn't sound like anyone I know from the other wolf packs around here. Could be a guy who was on his own, maybe getting close to going feral. Sorry I couldn't help with that. I'll keep an ear out if I hear anyone looking for somebody."

"Have you or your guys noticed any new people around? People who have maybe just moved in, or somebody who came to town for work or something?"

Doug mulled it over for a minute. Then he shook his head. "Nothing that rings a bell, but there was something I wanted to bounce off you guys."

My ears pricked up. "What do you have?"

"Well, we've lost several members. Two of them we... found, afterward. Both were in similar shape to the one you guys found out in the woods. Tortured, killed." He paused and looked off into the distance. I could only imagine how tough it had to be to find a member of your pack, a friend, like that. "Anyway, both of them had something in common before they went missing. They each mentioned seeing a woman. Someone following them. She wasn't familiar to either of them. They didn't think anything of it, just thought it was weird. I didn't either until the second guy disappeared."

We all looked at each other. Strange. Shifters sometimes dated human women, but it was always a short-lived casual affair. For the most part, we never told anyone what we are, plus you couldn't mate with or have kids with humans. Well, at least we thought that couldn't happen—until me. The same woman hanging around shortly before two shifters were abducted, tortured, and killed? Pretty damning evidence.

"Hunters?" Miles asked.

Female hunters weren't unheard of. They weren't even that rare. The thing was, it took one special kind of woman to take down a wolf shifter. Usually, men led the way when it came to attacking and killing shifters. That's the way it had been for hundreds of years. Things could always change, though.

We nodded in agreement. Nothing made sense other than it being a group of hunters. The only one who didn't nod was Steff. He'd been standing off to the side, staring at the ground, deep in thought. He finally pulled a folded manila envelope out of his back pocket and stepped forward.

"It's a witch," he said.

We all froze and stared at him. Witches were not a common occurrence, even in the world of shifters. Oh, they were out there, but I'd never had any dealings with them.

"What makes you say that?" Doug asked.

"This," he said, holding up the envelope. "Pictures I took of the body we found." He pulled them out. The image of the desecrated man brought a new wave of nausea to my gut. "The cuts here all across the body. Some of them are from a silver knife or something, sure. Miles smelled the silver, but most of these wounds aren't from a blade, they look more like a whip or a lash. Look."

We passed the pictures around. I was the last in line, and I had to force myself to look at the wounds. He was right. Most of the wounds were thin and even, like a slice of a knife. The bigger wounds were laid open, like the skin had split. It did look like he had been whipped. I frowned as I handed the pictures back to Steff.

"A silver whip?" I asked, thinking it sounded stupid even as I said it.

Steff shook his head. "Not possible. They could have maybe had a custom-made cable woven from silver and used that, but the wounds would have been even bigger. No, this is magic. Witches can use their spells like weapons. In my old pack, we worked with a coven once. I watched them use their magic like that, like a weapon. One of the spells they used the most was like a whip of mystical energy. It worked just like that. When I saw this body, I knew the wounds looked familiar, but it took me a little while to remember where I'd seen it before. Either a witch is hunting shifters, or even worse, a group of hunters has recruited a witch to help them."

The news slammed into us. Hunters were dangerous in their own right. They knew about us, had learned how to track and find us over the centuries, had specialized weapons and equipment, but to also have a witch working with them? It was like giving a nuclear missile to a splinter terrorist group. There was nothing worse.

"Well, the only way I know of to catch a witch is with the help of another one. I know who to call. I'll be gone for a couple of days. She doesn't have a cell phone or anything," Miles said.

"Are you sure that's safe?" I asked.

He nodded. "I'll be fine, I'll keep my head on a swivel. I'll text you guys every few hours so you know I'm good. I better get going."

With that, our little group broke apart, scattering to the wind as we left in our separate cars. I drove back to Lilly Valley, my mind swirling with the implications of what we'd discovered. A witch? Fucking terrifying. A human I could kill. Another shifter? I knew how to fight that. A witch? I was in the unknown. Unlike Miles and Steff, I'd never met one. How would I know when I met one? Would I have any way *of* knowing?

Once I got back to town, I stopped by the auto shop to check on Harley's car. It would take another day for the repairs, and yet another day for the paint job. Leaving, I called Harley to see if she had any plans for dinner.

"Hello?" she answered.

"It's me. How's it going?"

"Things are fine. Is your work meeting all done?"

"Yeah, I stopped to check on your car. Still another day or two until it's ready. I wanted to see what you guys were doing for dinner?"

"Well, the girls made some new friends and went out for pizza with them."

I laughed. "Didn't you guys have pizza yesterday?"

"Tate, they're teenagers, they'd eat pizza for every meal if I let them."

"Fair enough. What are you going to have for dinner?"

"With the girls out, I was thinking maybe a bowl of cereal or a grilled cheese, something like that."

"How about I pick something up? Bring it over there. Is there anything you've been craving?"

There was a long pause, then she finally said, "Tate, you don't need to do that, I wouldn't want to put you out."

I sighed. "Harley, I'm getting myself food anyway. I'm going to take it home to eat, and I live like a hundred feet from you. It is literally no trouble. In fact, it will be more trouble if I don't bring you dinner. I'll be over at my house eating a delicious meal, thinking about you sitting by yourself eating grilled cheese. Now, what are you hungry for?"

She laughed. "Pasta. I want carbs. All the carbs. Please and thank you. Garlic bread, too."

I laughed, happy that she was letting me do this little thing for her. "Okay, cool. I'll call it in and be there in a little bit."

I called in an order to the little Italian place in town. I liked the place. The little old man who ran it was a funny character and made great food. When I pulled in, I was surprised to see Mariah and Jordyn sitting inside with some other kids. Harley had told me they went out for pizza. I shouldn't have been surprised to see them here since this was the only Italian place in the whole town. There were a few boys sitting with them, and my dragon gave an irritated growl at the way the boys were looking at them.

I got that under control, and went inside to pick up my food. As soon as I walked in, Jordyn spotted me and waved at me like a crazy person. Her arm swung back and forth so madly that she almost elbowed the boy next to her in the nose. I chuckled as she got up and ran to me. It was funny but also made me feel really good. To be wanted and needed was something I wasn't used to. I thought I could maybe get used to it.

Mariah followed Jordyn over. "What are you doing here?"

I nodded toward the counter. "I stopped by to pick up dinner for me and your mom."

The girls locked eyes, mischievous grins blooming on their faces. Jordyn turned back to me. "So, do you like our mom? I mean, do you *like* her?" she said, drawing the word out dramatically.

I rolled my eyes at them and walked toward the counter. "You girls have a fun night, now."

Jordyn shrugged. "Fine. See you later."

She went back to the table with her new friends, but Mariah hung around while I paid for the food. I looked at her questioningly.

She seemed nervous. "I know you're the dad of Mom's baby, I mean. I heard you say it to her while the guys were installing the security system."

"Well, shit," I muttered.

Mariah waved that off. "It's okay. Adults make mistakes, too. I mean, it's not a big deal as long as it's a happy mistake, right? It is a happy mistake, isn't it?"

I studied her, then I said, "I think it might be, yeah."

She nodded. "Good." She then turned serious and lowered her voice. "You know, it's been a long time since we felt safe or protected. Basically since Dad's been gone. Plus, ever since he died, Jordyn and I have thought Mom seems so lonely. She's really alone, and we're always worried about her. When she first met Luis, we thought maybe she'd found someone, but we never really liked him. There was always something about him that seemed… fake." She looked at me with eyes far too old for her age. "What I'm trying to say is, I'm glad you're the father of the baby. I have no idea how that happened, but I don't really care. I just want my mom to be happy."

The seriousness evaporated as she walked backwards to her table. "Enjoy your night together," she said with a smile, then turned and joined her friends and sister again.

I watched her go, and my connection to the girls clicked into place. Almost like there was a switch inside my chest that had been teetering on being flipped, and it had just been switched over.

The owner of the shop appeared from the back, carrying packaged meals. "Ah, Mr. Mills. Here is your order. Good to see you again. Everything good?"

I smiled at him. "Yeah, I think they are."

When I got to Harley's house a few minutes later, I could tell she'd been thinking about my earlier proposal. She had a hard time looking me in the eye, and kept twisting her hands together like she was nervous. It was weird. We'd spent hours together earlier in the day talking, but now it had gone back to being awkward. At first, I wondered if I'd done something wrong. I assumed that she was still trying to figure out how to act around me.

I was pulling the containers out of the paper bag in the kitchen when I asked, "Are you okay?"

"Huh? Yeah, why?"

I leaned against the counter. "You know, this whole shy, unsure, timid thing you've got going on is cute."

She frowned. "What does that mean?"

I nodded at her hands. She was twisting and untwisting the hem of her T-shirt. She glanced down and immediately stopped fiddling with it.

"The thing is, I've seen you naked, Harley. I know what your moans sound like. After all that, I don't know why I still make you nervous."

Her face went scarlet, and her jaw dropped slightly. She finally grinned. "I was drunk, okay."

I laughed. "You weren't that drunk. But if that's the excuse you want to use for all the dirty things you did, then I'll let you have it."

Harley gasped but was smiling when she did it; her face grew even redder. "What a jerk."

I laughed and went back to the food. "I got the garlic bread and pasta with cream sauce, pasta with red sauce, and a side of meatballs too. I wasn't sure if you wanted some protein to go with your carbs. And there're two pieces of cheesecake for dessert."

"Oh god," she groaned as she saw the food. It was an almost sexual sound, and I was immediately aroused.

I shook the thoughts away. "When I checked on your car, it actually looked pretty good. It was all just surface damage. Nothing mechanical. It should be good as new once they're done."

"Thank you again, Tate. For everything. I don't know what I would have done without you."

"No problem at all. I'm happy to help with everything." Changing the topic, I said, "The girls were at the restaurant when I picked up the food."

"Yeah? I guess that makes sense."

"Mariah came up and told me she knows."

"Oh," Harley said. "Yeah, she told me she knew, too."

"Are you going to tell Jordyn soon?" I asked.

She sighed and slumped into a chair with her plate. "I want to, but she's so young. I'm not sure she'll really be able to get her head around the situation."

I sat beside her with my own plate and nodded reluctantly. "I can see that, but do you really want her to be the only one in the dark? The longer it goes on, the more likely she'll put it all together. She may be hurt if she realizes she was the only person who didn't know. Even small secrets can hurt a family. Mine, for example, was big on secrets. It was part of what drove us apart."

I didn't elaborate on the biggest secret they kept. The fact that they'd planned a mating ceremony without my knowledge or consent. Had demanded I mate with the girl they'd picked for me, and then disowned me when I refused. Secrets were not a healthy thing. Thankfully, Harley didn't pry.

"I guess you're right. I can't have her stumbling around in the dark while the rest of us knows. I'll have to find the right time to tell her. It'll take me some time to figure out how to explain it."

"Well, I'll be there with you, so that should make it easier," I said.

She seemed surprised by my offer. I smiled and shook my head again. "We *are* working on being together. If I'm in your life and the baby's life, then that means I'll be in Jordyn and Mariah's life. It's only right that I'm there for things like this. I'm not just in this for you or the baby. If this works out, I want to be what those girls need, too."

Harley's eyes misted over, and I had an overwhelming urge to comfort her—in fact, my dragon demanded it. I lifted her and set her on my lap, gently wiping away the tears that had spilled down her cheeks.

"I'm sorry. I'm a big blubbering mess. I think it's the hormones."

I didn't want her to apologize for something I understood. "It's okay. You can cry whenever you need to. I've got a shoulder ready to cry on any time."

Harley smiled and looked at me. Our eyes connected, and I couldn't look away. She stared into my eyes, and it was like she was staring right into my soul. Neither of us spoke as the tension built. Our eyes stayed locked on each other as the seconds ticked by, and each second increased the feeling that something needed to happen. I knew exactly what I wanted. I stared into Harley's eyes and remembered the way we'd been all those months ago in New York. The taste of her nipples, the sound of her moaning, her hand on my cock.

"Fuck it," I mumbled and kissed her.

This wasn't a quick peck on the lips like I'd done before. It wasn't even the deeper kiss we'd shared earlier today. This was hard, wet, and intense. Our tongues twisting and fighting, our breath mingling as our breathing got heavier. Harley's hands ran through my hair, and I picked her up and carried her to the couch.

The kiss broke for a moment as I laid her on the couch. She had a hungry, demanding look in her eyes that told me she wanted what I wanted. My dragon was ready to claw its way out of my chest if we didn't get to it. I peeled her clothes off until she lay naked beneath me. The girls would be home soon, so this would need to be fast. I'd take my time to fuck her brains out next time. Right now, it was going to be all about her.

Sliding to my knees in front of her, I grabbed her legs and nudged her toward me. She laughed until I slid my face between her legs and slid my tongue along her pussy, flicking her clit with the tip of my tongue. Her laugh turned to a gasping moan. Her fingers dug into my hair as I slid my tongue in and out of her. One hand slid around and massaged her clit while another grabbed her breast, gently pinching the nipple. She rocked against my face, in time with the thrusts of my tongue.

"Fuck," she breathed out as I started moving faster.

I slipped my tongue up to circle her clit and her back arched, a trembling breath escaping her lips. The sound drove me crazy. I slid a finger inside her, her body went rigid, and then shuddered. I sucked on her clit as I fucked her with my fingers.

"Oh God. Oh God." Her hips were nearly vibrating as she edged closer to orgasm.

Harley grabbed her breasts and massaged them. Her mouth opened in a silent moan, her eyes half-lidded and staring at me while I worked her closer to climax. She looked so fucking sexy I had to bring a hand down and free my cock from my pants. I stroked myself hard and felt myself already getting close.

I went faster, flicking my tongue across her pussy, sliding my finger in and out of her. She was getting close. I could tell by the way she writhed beneath me that she was ready to explode. Like she wanted it, but was afraid of it. Afraid it would be too strong. That was exactly what I wanted. I wanted to blow her mind, to leave her spent and exhausted. I pressed my lips to her pussy and slammed my tongue into her. Each time I pulled it out, I slid it across her clit.

Harley clutched at the fabric of the couch, her head thrown back, her entire body quivering uncontrollably. She nearly screamed as she came. Her face was red, veins showing on her neck; her body bucked, and she pressed her hips into my face. Unable to control myself, I came just as she climaxed. I jerked myself off right there on the hardwood floor as she shivered and collapsed on the couch. Harley was spent and already nearly asleep. I sat back on my heels, breathing heavily.

Suddenly headlights shone through the window as a car pulled into the driveway. "Shit!"

As fast as I could, I pulled my shirt off, and used it to clean up my mess. I kicked Harley's clothes under the couch out of sight and scooped her up, rushing up the stairs and into her room with her clinging to my body. The bedroom door swung shut behind us just as the front door opened. I chuckled, thinking how awkward *that* would have been. Harley was already asleep in my arms as I gently set her down in her bed. She groaned quietly in her sleep as I tucked the covers around her. For a few seconds, I watched her sleep. Deep inside me, the bond with her deepened. All my life growing up, I'd watched mating bonds develop and grow. Seen the way men acted when it came to their mates—those protective instincts, the urge to always be near their mate, that unbridled *need*. My heart fought to break free from my chest, and I knew, by some strange miracle, that she truly was my mate.

Chapter 18 - Harley

"Mom…" Mariah started, "…can Jordyn and I go out to a movie and dinner tonight with some friends?"

They'd been home from school for only twenty minutes when she asked. Their first week had gone remarkably well. I'd truly been scared that they would hate the new school, but as always, my daughters surprised me. They'd really taken to the kids they'd met and were home a lot less than they had been over the summer. It filled me with joy that they weren't miserable here. Plus, Tate had guys out watching them whenever they left the house. They were as safe as we could make it.

"Sure, that's fine. What are you guys seeing?" I asked.

Mariah laughed. "No idea. The movie theater only has two screens, so there are only two options. They don't even have a website. It's like this town is stuck in the nineties or something."

I didn't like the way she made the nineties sound like it was as far away as the nineteen-forties. "I grew up in the nineties, Mariah."

She looked at me like I'd said something obvious. "Right. That's what I'm saying. Ancient."

"Okay." I laughed. "That's it. No movie, no dinner, just hard labor for the next two years until you're eighteen."

"Yeah, yeah. I'm going to tell Jordyn we get to go," Mariah said, jogging up the stairs.

I shook my head and walked over to the window. The familiar black sedan sat halfway down the street in the driveway of a vacant home. Who did Tate have watching out for us today?

Thinking of Tate sent a delicious shiver through my body. The things he'd done on Monday night with his fingers and mouth had been beyond anything I could imagine. He'd played my body like an instrument—a well-tuned and well-practiced instrument, no less. Every time I thought about it, I wondered when it would happen again. I was like a horny teenager, but I really didn't care. It had been days, and I still found myself thinking back on that night several times a day.

Almost as though he heard my thoughts, his truck turned off the main road into our neighborhood. I'd known he was coming. He had an update on my car. It was supposed to have been done a few days ago, but some of the busted glass had gotten down into the driver's side window and ruined the electric motor. They'd had a hard time getting the part in.

He got out of the truck and walked up the steps. Even though he'd pretty much been over here almost all the time since Sunday night, he still rang the bell or knocked each time he stopped by. True to habit, he rang the bell as soon as he got to the top of the stairs. Once I let him inside, he gave me a quick kiss on the cheek.

"Hey, how's it going?" he asked.

"Oh fine, my teenagers are being smart asses. Just another day. Did you hear about my car?"

He smiled. "Good news. They finally got that part in. It'll be ready in a couple of hours. We can pick it up today. I have to go out of town for a few days for work, so

I'm going to have some of the guys pick it up and drop it off."

"You don't have to do that. I'll call Emily, she can take me out there." Emily and I had met up a few times over the last week, and I knew she wouldn't mind.

Tate frowned and pulled his phone out. "Okay, but I'm going to text you Steff and Blayne's numbers. You can call them if you have any trouble. All right?"

"That's fine, there shouldn't be any issues."

After texting me the numbers, he gave me a stern look. "I have to go pretty soon. I won't be gone long, but while I'm away, make sure you set all the alarms anytime you guys are home. Remind the girls, too."

It was cute how worried he was about us.

"Will do. Don't fret about us."

Then, as though he'd done it a million times, he stepped close to me. He slid one arm around my back, the other went to the back of my neck, and kissed me. Our tongues mingled and twisted around each other. I sank into him, my legs turning to jelly beneath me. I trembled as the memory of Monday night came back again. The way his mouth felt, his hands on my body.

Tate pulled away, gently nibbling on my lip. "I'll see you later."

Without another word, he turned and left, leaving me wet and covered in gooseflesh. All I could do was watch him walk out and close the door. I went to the window and watched him walk away, admiring the way his ass moved in his jeans. The sight gave me a pleasurable ache between my legs.

I texted Emily to see if she could give me a ride. I needed to get my mind off Tate. Emily replied that she was happy to and would pick me up in an hour. The girls got picked up for their movie and dinner about ten minutes before Emily pulled up to get me. It was good to see her, otherwise I would have sat there in the house fantasizing about Tate. A little girl time would help get my mind out of the proverbial gutter.

"Hey, girl," Emily said as I climbed in.

"Hey. Thanks for the ride. I've been miserable without a car. I really appreciate it."

Emily made a face that said it was no problem. "My pleasure. Hopefully, you'd help me out if I needed it."

"Yeah. How are things going with your grandma's place?" I asked.

She shrugged. "It's going. I've got all the final stuff together for the sale. I think I'm going to do an estate sale first, see what I can get rid of before renting a dumpster. I tell you, the worst part of selling a house is getting all the shit out of it." She put a hand on my thigh as we turned onto the main road. "Sorry I haven't been in touch the last day or two, it's been crazy getting all that stuff ready."

"Emily, seriously, it's fine. Do you want to grab dinner before we pick up my car? It's a little early, but I thought it might be nice."

"Oh, we can grab the early bird specials." Emily laughed.

"Exactly," I said.

We pulled into the diner down the street from the garage and sat down for dinner. I was having a hard time deciding what to eat. My adult brain pushed me toward grilled chicken or a salad, but the baby growing in my belly was urging me to order the chili cheese burger or the fried pickles.

"So," Emily said. "How are things with the guy?"

I put the menu down and blushed, all thoughts of food evaporated for the moment. "I'd say it's going pretty good. I told you about Monday night, right?"

Emily rolled her eyes. "Uh, yeah. How have things been since then?"

"I guess I'm a little conflicted. I'm really starting to like him, but it's hard to open up to him completely. I'm worried that if I bring him fully into my life, things might go wrong. It would hurt me, and it would break the girls' hearts. They've really taken to him, and I don't know if I could live with myself if they had to lose someone they were starting to care for. I keep thinking maybe I should leave things as they are. Not go any deeper, you know?"

Emily reached across the table and took my hand. "You've got to try. It seems like this might be something special. I really think you guys can make it work. You just have to open up and let him in. Really show him how amazing you are. Tate probably sees that anyway, and he knows what he's missing out on. It's probably why he's pursuing you now more than before."

I sighed, uncertain. "Maybe, but shouldn't I try to take things slow… uh… slow*er*. I don't want us to start humping our brains out before truly getting to know each other."

"Take it from me, the fastest way to get to know someone is in bed. That's my personal experience. You should give it a shot. Next time you two are alone, just go to town. Surprise the shit out of him. Yank his pants down and suck on that big cock before he even knows what is happening."

I burst out laughing, my face flaming. Emily made a compelling argument. The mental image of me sliding him into my mouth sent a hot jolt through my body. She really seemed to want me to make a go of it with Tate. She seemed almost desperate to see me with him. It made me wonder how lonely she might be.

"Speaking of…" Emily said, leaning close to whisper, "…let's hear about the sex."

My eyes widened in surprise, and I glanced around to see if anyone had heard. "What do you mean?"

She rolled her eyes. "Spill it, sister. I heard about the tongue action, but you haven't really gone into detail about that night in New York. What was it like?"

"Oh geez, uh, it was a few months ago—"

"Sweetie, you know as well as I do that women don't forget things like this. Was it hot and heavy? Did he like… growl or bite during sex? Animalistic stuff like that?"

Her questions were getting a little weird. I wasn't sure how to answer them. "Um, well, there's been no biting. I guess when he does get really worked up, there's some kind of growling sound he makes."

"What kind of growl? Can you describe it?"

She was making me uncomfortable. I held my hand up. "Emily, what the hell? You're getting super personal."

She seemed to realize she'd pushed a little too much. She blushed and leaned back. "I'm sorry. I've been going through a dry patch the last few months. Well… a year and a half actually. I can't help but be jealous and wanted to know all the dirty details. The closest I've had to a sexual relationship is naming my vibrator. His name is David, by the way."

I chuckled, still a little uneasy about her line of questioning. I told her it wasn't a problem. Though even after the waitress took our order and brought out our food, I couldn't shake the feeling that she'd been trying to dig some other information out of me. It left me with a bad taste in my mouth. I tried to play it off, but when she dropped me off at the auto shop, I was a little relieved to be away from her. Once she was gone, though, I felt pretty stupid for thinking that. She probably was just horny and wanted to live vicariously through a friend. I told myself to forget about it as I walked into the garage.

"Mrs. King?" the attendant asked as I walked up to the counter.

"Yes. I had the car that…" I trailed off, not knowing how to finish. *You know, the car my psycho ex had trashed. I'm sure you remember, it's the one that had the word whore spray painted on it.*

He nodded, and I didn't have to finish what I had been about to say. Thank God. "I gotcha. Mr. Mills came by to check on it earlier. I have you all set up."

He came around the counter with my keys. "It's in the lot out back."

I followed him through the garage and out the back bay door. He walked me to my car, and I was surprised at how good it looked. The entire exterior had been repainted. You couldn't even tell anything had happened. The attendant unlocked the door and opened it. My jaw dropped. The interior had been detailed. The carpets and upholstery looked like they'd been shampooed, and there wasn't a speck of dust or dirt anywhere inside. The whole car, literally, looked brand new.

"Wait," I said. "Is this really my car?"

He looked confused for a second and did a double take before saying, "Oh, I see. Mr. Mills paid for a full detail job. He said he wanted it perfect for when you came and picked it up. Had us go ahead and put new brakes on her, too."

I smiled to myself. It was a sweet gesture to go above and beyond like this. I thanked the clerk, then took the keys and pulled out my phone. I sent Tate a message, thanking him for taking care of things for me.

Normally he would have texted back almost immediately, but there was no response, and my phone was silent on the drive home. It got me wondering what kind of job he was on that forced him to go radio silent. Hopefully, he was safe. I didn't like thinking that he might be in danger.

The house was eerily quiet when I stepped inside. For the last several days, either the girls or Tate had been here with me. The silence was welcome, but also a little strange. Once all the doors were locked, I tried to find something to pass the time while I waited for the girls to get home.

There was literally nothing I wanted to watch, and I had no book in my to-be-read pile. After ten minutes, I decided to mop the floors. I couldn't remember the last time I'd done it, so it *had* to be about time for a thorough cleaning.

Once I had the mop bucket full of sudsy water, I went about cleaning the floors. The mindless work kept me busy. Moving from the living room hardwoods backward to the kitchen tile, I was both happy and disturbed to see how much cleaner they were as I worked. Apparently, teenage girls weren't good at wiping their feet.

I was backed up against the sliding patio door, dunking the mop into the bucket of water again, when I heard the sound of breaking glass. The explosive sound made me freeze. Then the sound of raining chips of glass pattering around the tile had me glancing down, scared I was going to get cut. Never in my life would I have thought to run. An icy spike of fear lodged deep in my gut when the man in the ski mask and gloves walked through the broken door. In that split second, I realized I'd set the front door alarm, but had forgotten to set the back door.

Frozen in place, I watched him step through the doorway and reach out for me. My brain was still frozen, like it was on a delay. It was still processing the sound of breaking glass and hadn't even begun to process the intruder reaching out for me. When it finally did send the signal to my legs, it was too late to run. His arm shot out like a snake and wrapped around my neck, yanking me toward him. His arm went across my throat, tightening like a steel band as he pulled me against his chest. I tried to rip away, but my feet slid on the wet floor. I stumbled, but he tightened his grip to hold me up. All the oxygen was cut off from my air canal. I gagged, trying to breathe and beating at his arm as hard as I could. Fear unlike anything I'd ever felt flooded through me. Adrenaline pumped into my body, and I clawed at his sleeve, trying to pull the arm away to catch a breath.

A whole new terror erupted when he started dragging me toward the door. He wanted to take me away, into the night, away from my home. An instinctual, animalistic panic chittered through my mind. If he took me, I would never come back, I knew it without a doubt. The pain in my neck was almost unbearable, and I wasn't able to fight back like I wanted. The pull toward the door seemed like an inexorable finale to this nightmare I was living.

He began stepping through the door, pulling at me harder, as I still tried to fight. My vision was blurring and going dark around the edges. I was about to pass out from the lack of oxygen. My lungs burned and ached, every nerve in my body screaming for oxygen. He pulled me through the door, and all I could do was reach out and clutch at the frame. His pant leg hooked on a shard of glass, and he stopped to pull it free. That was when I managed to stretch the final inch I needed to grab the one thing I had left—the panic button installed on the door frame. Tate's crew had put one at every entry door and in every room.

My hand slapped at where I thought it was. I couldn't see it because of how the man was holding my neck. I couldn't find the button. *I couldn't*. Where the fuck was it? He freed his leg and pulled me again. I held tight with my right hand and slapped the wall one last time with my left. The tip of my ring finger brushed against the button, barely clicking it. Even a millimeter either way, and I wouldn't have activated it. I would have been taken.

The shrill, earsplitting alarm erupted like an explosion in the night. Even though I knew it was coming, it shocked me with how loud it was, immediately making me want to cover my ears. My assailant was equally surprised, and the grip around my neck loosened. Even oxygen starved and already exhausted from the struggle, I used the chance I'd bought. Planting my feet, I yanked myself forward and ripped fully out of his grip. Once I was free, I sprinted away from him. For a terrifying second, my feet slipped and slid on the wet floor, but by a miracle, I stayed upright and ran for the stairs. The attacker screamed a curse, but the alarm drowned it out. His feet pounded on the floor behind me, but he wasn't as lucky as I'd been. I heard the squeak of shoes on the wet floor and then the thunderous rattle of him falling to the ground. Grabbing the stair rail, I turned and took the steps two at a time, running with more speed and force than I knew I possessed. I came to the first room I found and ran inside, slamming the door and locking it behind me. The girls' bathroom. I sat and put my back against the door, braced my feet on the vanity, and waited.

My breath hissed madly in and out of my nose as I waited for the thumping of his feet to come up the stairs, but I didn't hear it. Had the alarm scared him off? My phone rang, and I screamed, actually screamed in fright. I put a hand to my mouth and tried not to whimper as I pulled the phone out of my jeans pocket.

Before I could say anything, Tate's voice burst from the speaker. "Harley?" he yelled. "Harley, what the hell's going on? My phone alerted me. A panic button got activated."

I took a shaking breath and said, "Tate, someone broke in. He... he... he tried to take me."

"Oh shit. It's okay, my guys got the same notification. They should be there soon. Is he still there? Do you hear anyone?"

I turned and pressed my ear to the door and listened as best I could, but I couldn't hear anything above the siren of the alarm. Almost as though the system had read my mind, the alarm abruptly stopped.

From downstairs, I heard men shouting, "Harley? Harley? It's Steff and Blayne. We're here. Harley?"

I sobbed in relief and spoke into the phone. "Tate, they're here. Your friends are here."

"Thank Christ. Let them know where you are."

I cracked the door of the bathroom. "Up here," I called.

In seconds, Blayne and Steff were in the bathroom with me. Blayne was awkwardly rubbing my back, trying to comfort me.

I put Tate on speaker. "Steff, you there?"

"Yeah, bud, we're both here," Steff said.

"Okay, cool. Don't leave until I get there. I'm on my way. Harley, did you hear that?"

Feeling more in control of myself, I said, "Yes. I'll see you soon."

"We'll be here," Steff said. "We'll work on whatever repairs we can do."

For the next thirty minutes, I sat on the couch and watched as Steff worked on the door and Blayne pulled up the security feeds from my house. Steff cleaned up the broken glass as best he could, and then called multiple hardware stores trying to find someone to come out and replace the glass or the door itself.

Blayne finally came over to me and said, "I have all the footage compiled. Do you want to look through it?"

I nodded. "Sure."

Steff came over to watch, and Blayne hit the play button. The video was in high definition and very clear, unlike a lot of security footage I'd seen on the news. The rear camera showed a shadowy figure hunched over and walking toward the back door through the shrubs behind our house. The sight of him filled me with dread. I looked down at my lap, afraid to even glance at the video.

After a few seconds, I settled myself and looked back at the footage. I could see the man trying to pull me through the door. I called him *the man* in my head, but I knew exactly who it was. It was Luis. Of course it was Luis. There was no other threat to me but him. The entire struggle only lasted fifteen or twenty seconds, which didn't seem right. It felt like we'd fought and struggled for minutes. How could that only have been a few seconds? Another camera outside caught sight of him sprinting away from the house. He ran down the street and jumped into a black car before speeding away.

I pointed at the car. "That's a Lexus. It's literally the only car Luis will drive. He refuses to buy anything else. He likes them black with dark tint. It has to be him."

Steff pulled out his cell and dialed. Before I knew what was happening, he was barking orders to someone, telling them the description of the car. Before I could ask any questions, the doorbell rang. Blayne got up and opened it, letting in a crew of carpenters. They were carrying a sheet of replacement glass with large suction cup holders. It had to be seven o'clock at night. How had they managed to get these guys here so fast? Again, I wondered what kind of strings Tate and his friends were able to pull to get things like this done so quickly.

Once again, my house was a hive of activity. The girls would be home in a couple of hours, and I had no idea how I would explain all this to them. It couldn't be helped, though. Instead of worrying, I watched the men at work. Steff helped the crew replace the glass. Blayne printed out pictures of the car and made some more phone calls. For about the millionth time in the last hour, I was grateful Tate had insisted on putting in the security system. Otherwise,

I'd have been taken. I also chastised myself for not setting the back door alarm. Things might have gone better if I had.

Tension suddenly surged through me, and I knew without a doubt that Tate was here. He burst through the door and ran straight toward me. When he reached me, he crouched in front of me and ran his hands over my body, searching for injuries. His frenetic energy seemed to fill the room. Everyone went quiet and turned to watch him, as though they were afraid of offending him by moving while he checked me over.

"Are you all right? Is the baby okay?" he asked.

I nodded. "I'm good, *we're* good. I was pretty shaken up, but the guys took care of me."

Tate glanced at Blayne, an unspoken question on his face. The long-time friends seemed to be able to read each other's minds.

Blayne nodded. "Looks like it was the Luis guy."

"Motherfucker," Tate hissed, a look of such profound rage on his face. He looked ready to kill. "That's it. I'm moving in until this shit with Ortiz is settled."

I looked at him blankly, thinking I'd misheard him. "What? You're moving in?"

Tate raised an eyebrow. "I won't be able to sleep at night, knowing what this asshole is up to. As long as this piece of shit slime ball is out there threatening you and the girls, I'm sticking close. I'm not taking 'no' for an answer. I'll sleep on the couch if you want me to, but I'm pretty sure the girls have figured out something's going on between us."

"Tate, it's fast. I don't—"

He held up a hand. "I'll keep the boundaries, if it makes you feel better. Just know that I'm not leaving you all alone."

Multiple arguments spiraled through my mind, but the memory of that arm wrapping around my throat silenced them all. I had no rebuttal that wasn't pathetic or pointless, but that didn't mean I had to like Tate forcing his will on me.

"You can be one pushy bastard, you know that?" I said.

He merely shrugged. "I don't mind being pushy if it means you are all safe."

The butterflies that filled my stomach in response to his words were hard to ignore. The fact that he cared so much for us so soon was surprising. We'd really only known each other for a couple of months, and already he was ready to go to war for me and my girls. It was nice to know someone had their backs. Also, why would I deny my girls the protection Tate was offering freely?

"Okay, fine. You can stay." It was a moot point at that moment. Tate had already made up his mind, no matter what I said.

Chapter 19 - Tate

Once Harley was calmed down, Steff and I helped the construction crew finish up with the door. Their boss had been a client a few years back. Miles had tracked down his runaway daughter in some weird religious cult, and I'd extracted her and safely returned her to her home. He owed us one. We wouldn't have gotten the door fixed that fast if not for that. Even with that advantage, Jordyn and Mariah still got home before we finished.

Their friends had dropped them off in the driveway just as the crew was loading up their van. The girls gawked at the van, which was understandable. It was nine o'clock at night, and there was a construction crew at their house. They'd have been crazy not to think something was amiss. I cursed under my breath as they walked up the path to the porch.

Mariah walked in and saw Harley on the couch. "Mom? What the hell?"

"Hey, language," Harley said.

Jordyn shook her head. "No, Mom, this is definitely a what-the-hell moment."

Harley sighed and patted the sofa, indicating the girls should sit down. They did, but not before glancing at me for some sort of hint. All I did was nod toward their mom.

"Someone tried to break into the house and broke the glass in the back door. The alarm went off like it was supposed to, and scared them off. Tate and his friends showed up, then they called some people to fix the door." Harley was calm as she recounted the events of the night.

"Holy crap, Mom, are you serious?" Mariah asked.

Jordyn looked beyond worried, which seemed more terrible since she was always so boisterous and happy. To me, she looked on the verge of a breakdown. I wanted to comfort her, but knew Harley needed to handle this.

"Also..." Harley said, looking nervous for the first time since the girls had walked in, "...until things are totally safe and settled, Tate will be staying with us. Just to make sure nothing else happens."

In unison, Mariah and Jordyn sighed in relief. They didn't even flinch at hearing that I would be staying. I had the feeling that Harley thought they'd freak out, but I was sure they would be fine with it. In fact, Jordyn perked up almost immediately after hearing I'd be staying over. I did a poor job of hiding my smile.

"Okay, girls, go get ready for bed. It's getting late," Harley said.

"I'm going to head home quickly to pack a bag. Steff, can you hang out till I get back?" I asked.

Steff nodded. "No problem. I've got to reset the control panel for the security system anyway."

I looked at Harley. "I'll be right back, okay?"

She nodded and collapsed back onto the couch, looking exhausted. The houses weren't very far apart, and I could go back over anytime to get stuff. The problem was, I didn't feel comfortable leaving Harley. Even now, walking out the door and heading to my house made my chest ache. The whole time I'd been away today had been the same. The longer I was away, the sharper the pain got. My dragon was also more on edge and anxious when I was away from her. The pain was the worst. It wasn't something I'd ever heard of happening with a mating bond. Very strange. In fact, the whole damned situation was strange. All I wanted was answers, but I didn't have any idea where to even start.

Once I'd tossed some clothes in a bag, I grabbed my toiletries, and headed back to Harley's. She stood in the living room with the girls. Harley held a blanket and looked at the living room furniture with pursed lips.

She glanced at me when I walked inside. "Tate, how tall are you? Which one looks big enough to sleep on?"

Before I could answer, Jordyn said, "Mom, he'll catch a cold down here on the couch. That's what you always tell us when we fall asleep on the couch."

"That's not the same thing, I'm—"

Mariah cut her off. "Jordyn's right. Plus, we'd wake him up if one of us got up to use the bathroom or something."

Steff glanced at me, the corner of his mouth quirked up in a grin before heading out the front door. I covered my face with my hand to hide my own smile. I'd been right, the girls had figured out there was a thing between me and Harley. Now, they were basically arguing for me to sleep in her room. It was their version of giving me their blessing.

Harley looked ready to spit, until it dawned on her. That gorgeous shade of red bloomed on her cheeks. All I did was grin at her and walk up the stairs to put my clothes in her room.

Once the girls were in bed, I walked the house, double-checking every door and window. I didn't want to leave anything to chance. After checking those, I turned the floodlights on for the backyard and scanned for any movement. Leaving the lights on, I went to the front door and unlocked it, then walked out. The neighborhood was quiet and deserted, at least at first glance. Down the street, I spotted a black car in a driveway. I'd lived here long enough to know which cars belonged and which ones didn't.

It sat there with its lights out, but I saw a shadow moving behind the tinted glass. My dragon eyes were better than most shifters, but even I couldn't see completely through dark tinted glass from this distance. The only thing I knew for sure was that someone was sitting in that car, with the engine and lights off, at a house they didn't live in. All of which were bad signs.

Walking to the edge of the porch, I made sure I was visible to anyone watching. Then I turned and stared at the car, trying to bore through the windshield with my eyes. After a few seconds, whoever was in the car realized they'd been spotted. The headlights kicked on, then the car slowly pulled out of the driveway. It crept down the road, slower than I would have anticipated. There was no way to know for sure who was in that car, but I had a very likely suspect.

Most people considered me a big, intimidating guy. Normally, I didn't play that fact up. Most of the time, especially in my work, it was better if people didn't realize how imposing you were. As the car cruised past, though, I played up the fact. I stood tall and glared menacingly at the windshield, hoping I was making eye contact with the asshole. I wanted to make it clear that I was here to stay, and that he better not get within fifty feet of this house. Once the car was out of sight, I waited a couple more minutes to be sure it was gone before I went inside.

Once everything was locked and the system set, I headed upstairs. Harley was pacing the floor and looked freaked out.

"What's wrong?" I asked.

She was on the verge of tears. "I don't know why, but while you were checking the house, I started looking back at a bunch of old text messages Luis sent me. To delete them and get them totally out of my life and off my phone. They went pretty far back. Even before we broke up, some of the things he said seemed… out of place."

"What do you mean?"

She sighed. "There was this long chain of messages in which he talked about how he'd always thought I was beautiful and was glad to finally get to be with me. This text was only a few days after we'd met, but he made it sound like he'd been watching me for a while. I didn't think anything of it until I reread it just now."

"It made me think about a fight we'd had not long before I broke up with him. He'd said something like he'd done a lot to get me, some very bad things to get me, and he wasn't going to give me up that easily. Tate…" She took a deep breath, and a single tear slipped down her cheek. "I think Luis killed my husband." The tears came in a flood then. "Did he murder my Sam just to try and have me?"

I was at her side in two strides, taking her in my arms and pressing her to my chest. There was no way I could tell her that Mariah had heard rumors at their old school alluding to the exact same thing. That was not something I'd felt comfortable divulging before, and I would definitely not tell her after everything she'd gone through tonight.

"I can't stand the thought that I dated… that I fucked the man that killed my husband. The man that killed my daughters' daddy," Harley whispered against my chest. "It really makes me want to lose my mind. I'm such a shitty person. How could I have not seen it?"

I pushed her away slightly, placing my hands on her shoulders and looking into her red eyes. "Harley, he's a sociopath and a narcissist. No one is better at hiding who they are than someone like that. You can't blame yourself for not seeing him for who he truly is. It's not on you, it's on him. We blame him for all this, never you."

I put my hand on her stomach. "This baby is mine, *you* are mine." I nodded toward the stairs. "Those girls are mine. I will protect you all with every fiber of my being."

Harley was looking at me with a combination of awe, confusion, and shock. "How can you feel that way so fast?"

Once shifters found their mate, they didn't look back. There was no time limit on loyalty or love, no set amount of days it took to feel these things. Once the mate was found, it was one-hundred percent. My instincts were screaming at me to protect these women, and by God, I was going to. Plus, baby or no baby, Harley was my mate, and I would die to protect her and her kids.

I didn't say all that, though. "I'm a firm believer in following my gut. And my gut is telling me this is where I belong. I'll keep earning your trust, but I've fully made up my mind about what I want. I want you, and by you, I mean all of you."

Harley was crying again, but it seemed to be happy tears. She grabbed my face and kissed me. It was not passionate or sexy, but it was still intense. Intense and full of what I hoped was something deeper.

Chapter 20 - Harley

I woke up to the now familiar disorientation of an arm draped around me. For the last several nights, since Tate moved in, he couldn't sleep unless he had me in his arms. It had been awkward for me at first, but I always fell asleep and had the most restful night ever. It had been so long since I'd been held like that, I'd almost forgotten how good it felt. Luis had, not surprisingly, not been very affectionate. It had been years since I'd had the experience of melting into someone else as we fell asleep. I hadn't realized how much I missed it.

Having Tate around helped me feel more balanced, too. With the stress of the move, the pregnancy, *and* the threat of Luis, I had been on the verge of a mental breakdown. I'd been jumpy and half crazy. The last few days with him had really calmed me down. It was almost like I was a new person.

Tate stirred and pulled me closer, pressing my back against his chest and stomach. He breathed deeply and sighed, making my hair flutter around my neck.

He leaned close to my ear and said, "I'll get breakfast ready for the girls. You need to rest."

As Tate rolled out of bed and headed downstairs, I rolled onto my back and closed my eyes. There was no way I was going back to sleep, but getting more rest sounded amazing. Not only had it been a long time since I'd had the physical connection, but it had also been just as long since I'd had help with the girls. Now that they were older, they didn't need much help, but any help at all was a huge help, and very appreciated.

As I lay in bed listening to Tate pulling pans out, I heard Jordyn's voice. Both girls were already up. It sounded like Jordyn was giving Tate a hard time.

"Hey, Big Guy. Are you gonna burn us some eggs or something?" Jordyn laughed.

Tate responded, "Nope, gonna blend up some broccoli and onions for a smoothie. Sound good?"

Jordyn giggled. "Eww, gross."

"Can I help you?" Mariah asked.

A smile played over my face as I listened to the three of them together. How had we gotten to this point?

Six months ago, if someone had told me I'd be in Colorado, pregnant, and living with the sexy guy I'd met in a bar once, I'd have called them something even crazier than crazy. Now? Well, here we were. Were we turning into a family? God, it was insane to think about.

Dangerous to wish for.

Before my mind was able to spin down that rabbit hole, the doorbell chimed. I groaned and finally got out of bed. I wasn't expecting anyone, so I had no idea who it could be. Maybe it was one of Tate's friends stopping by.

Tate called toward the door, "One minute. Be right there."

I slipped on my fluffy robe and got halfway down the stairs by the time Tate got to the door and opened it.

I saw Emily at the door, and immediately grinned. She gave Tate a blazing white smile and put her hand out. "I'm Emily. You must be Tate. I've heard so much about you."

Tate took a half step back and... sniffed. Was he smelling the air? That was weird. Then he glared at the hand, not taking it. The look on his face was not friendly at all, which was strange. What was wrong with him? Emily didn't seem to mind, though. She dropped her hand and stepped inside, brushing past Tate. Under his breath, Tate breathed a word that sounded like 'witch.' Or maybe he said 'bitch?' Emily's steps faltered a bit after he said it, but she regained her composure quickly and smiled at me. I watched their interaction with a mild mix of confusion and horror.

Emily acted as though nothing had happened. She also acted like she'd never met Tate before in her life, but the way Tate was scowling at her made me think there was some history there. I attempted to keep the look of uncertainty off my face as she stepped forward and gave me a quick hug. I glanced over her shoulder at Tate and tried to catch his eye, but he looked uneasy and wouldn't take his eyes off Emily. In another situation, I might have felt slighted, but the look in his eye was not of attraction or lust. If it was anything, it was rage and hate.

After we hugged, I noticed the velvet bag in Emily's hand. Trying to put the weird vibe between her and Tate at the back of my mind, I said, "What's that?"

She looked at her hand, like she'd forgotten she was carrying anything, and laughed. "Oh, this? I almost forgot.

I brought you and the girls some jewelry. It's stuff my grandma had, that I thought you guys might want."

The girls' eyes lit up when she mentioned jewelry. I shook my head. "You guys are gonna be late for the bus. You can go through it tonight when you get home."

"Ugh, fine," Jordyn said, grabbing her backpack.

I glanced at Tate, who had moved from the doorway over to the girls. He was still looking at Emily like she was a rabid dog. I wanted to tell him to stop, but didn't know how without making things awkward.

I nodded toward the door. "Tate, did you want to take the girls out to the bus?"

"Yeah. Sure." His clipped words didn't go unnoticed by the girls. They both raised an eyebrow at each other before walking to the door.

Tate walked backwards with them, almost like he didn't want to let Emily out of his sight. It was the most bizarre thing I'd ever seen in my life. Even more bizarre was the way Emily was acting. If a man Tate's size had looked at me like that, I'd have been terrified. She acted like he wasn't even there.

As Tate stepped through the door, he said, "I'll be *right* back." He emphasized the word 'right', almost like he was warning me. Or warning Emily? From the corner of my eye, I thought Emily smirked.

"Umm, are you sure you and Tate don't know each other?" I asked.

She shook her head. "No. Never met him before. He's cute, though. Good job, sis."

I sighed, not even trying to hide my confusion. "It just seems like he's a little… hostile toward you."

Emily waved a hand in dismissal. "He's probably worked up about the whole kidnapping attempt. Speaking of, how are you doing after that? I freaked when you called and told me."

Caught a little off guard, I said, "Uh, good, doing good."

I didn't really buy her excuse about Tate. She didn't look anything like a masked grown man. There was no way she was involved in what Luis was doing. Except, there was no other explanation.

"Anyway…" she said, "…I need to get going. I've got a few more things to do before grandma's house sells."

Forgetting my misgivings, I asked, "Does that mean you'll be leaving soon? If the house sells, I mean?"

She nodded sadly. "I will. Unfortunately, my work here is done."

That saddened me a little. Emily was the only friend I'd made since I got into town. I didn't want her to go, even though things had been a little strained between us the last week. Maybe some distance would be good.

Tate came back inside a few minutes later, and he did so rather quickly. I had to tell myself he hadn't sprinted back to the door. Emily grinned at me as he stepped inside.

"I need to head out." She hugged me. "Don't worry, we'll keep in touch. Plus, I'm sure I'll see you again before I leave."

She turned and walked to the door. Neither of them tried to hide the way they looked at each other as she passed. Tate's face was just as it had been, but maybe more angry rather than suspicious like it had been before. I could only describe the look Emily gave him as one of disgust. Like he was something to be wiped off her shoe. She disappeared out the door, and Tate stared out the window as she walked away.

I crossed my arms. "So, what the hell?"

Tate glanced back at me. "Huh?"

I gestured to the door Emily had closed behind her. "That? You acted like she was here to kill us all. The looks you were giving her? It was weird as shit, Tate."

Without holding back, he growled, "I don't trust her."

I furrowed my brow. "Why?"

"Trust me. I have my reasons. I've got to make a call." Without another word, he grabbed his phone and stepped out on the porch.

I tried to figure out what the hell had happened, but realizing there was no way to figure it out without more information, I decided to look at the gifts Emily had brought. Once I poured the jewelry out onto the counter, my jaw dropped. It was all gorgeous. It was crazy that she'd want to get rid of it all. Some of the pieces looked pretty valuable. All my hesitations about her evaporated.

She really was just being nice, even though she was a little odd.

An opal necklace caught my eye almost immediately. When I reached out for it, I could almost swear I felt energy pulsing out of it. The stories of people saying crystals contained energy sprang to mind. In my life, I'd never experienced it and had thought it was silly—until now.

The necklace was hypnotic. I stared at the stone, almost enraptured at its beauty. My heart raced as my fingers closed around it. As I lifted it, light danced across the opal, making circular patterns in it. Beautiful orange, pink, and white colors wavered as it turned in the light. It almost felt like the necklace was calling to me, asking to be worn. And I wanted to wear it.

Just as I was about to put the chain over my head, Tate's hand clasped over my wrist. I jumped, surprised. I'd been so focused on the opal, I hadn't even heard him come back inside.

"What are you doing?" I asked.

He relaxed his grip but still had an intense look on his face. This time, it wasn't the angry aggression he'd shown with Emily. There was fear in his eyes as he stared at the necklace.

"Don't put that on," he said.

"Why?"

"Just trust me, please." He glanced at the other things on the counter, too. "Don't put any of it on. Don't let the girls wear it, either."

"Tate, you're acting crazy. What's this all about?"

"It's like I said earlier, Harley. I don't trust her, and I don't have a good feeling about this stuff." He waved a hand at the jewelry.

I didn't like that he seemed to be accusing my friend of something. What exactly he was accusing her of was a mystery, though.

"Why don't you trust her, Tate? *Do* you know her?"

He sighed and rubbed a hand over his jaw. "Look, I've got some guys looking into her, is all. Until we figure out what her angle is, I'd prefer you not get too close to her."

"You have guys watching Emily? My friend? Why are you investigating my friend?" I snapped in irritation.

Tate was visibly frustrated and winced, almost like he was in pain, before he finally opened his mouth to reply. "Harley, don't you think it's a little weird that she showed up in town almost the same time you did? And then, within a couple of weeks, Ortiz found you? That Luis somehow located you halfway across the country?"

"What? Do you think she's like… a private investigator or something? That she's working with Luis?"

He held his hands up in defense. "I'm just saying that I want to play out all possibilities and turn over every stone before we let our guard down. Doesn't that sound reasonable? I care too much about you and the girls to leave it all up to chance. If I can stop something bad from happening, then I want to. I want you and everyone around you to be safe." He placed the necklace on the counter and pulled me close, placing a sweet and gentle kiss on my lips. Then he looked into my eyes. "I promise, I'm not trying to steamroll you and control your life, or who you can be friends with. All I'm doing is trusting my gut, and my gut is telling me something is off about Emily. If I end up being wrong, I'll eat all the crow you want me to. Until then, please trust me."

The idea that I'd been played horrified me. Even thinking that Emily might be working with or for Luis made my skin crawl. After listening to Tate, all the weird things she did came to mind. Strange ways she'd acted, offhand comments that seemed a bit off, the way she'd acted earlier with Tate. It all *was* a little strange. Maybe he was right. Besides, she was leaving soon anyway. I slid all the glittering bracelets, rings, and necklaces back into the velvet bag and handed it to Tate. For the first time since Emily walked in the door, I saw him relax as he took the bag from me.

He kissed me again. "I promise I'll get to the truth about Emily." A smile slowly reappeared on his lips, and he said, "Okay. How about you go get dressed? I've got somewhere I want to take you."

"Um, sure. I'll be right back."

Ten minutes later, we were driving to the outskirts of town. He pulled his truck into the parking lot of a random strip mall. There was a nail salon at the far end and a tax place at the other. The center portion was unmarked. The windows and door were black with the darkest tint I'd ever seen in my life. I doubted you could see inside even if you peered in through cupped hands.

"Where are we?" I asked.

He gave me a wry smile. "This is how I make my living. I thought you might like to check out the security firm."

Surprised, I smiled and nodded. "That sounds kind of neat."

"Let's go."

Tate climbed out of the truck, and I followed close behind. When he got to the door, he punched in what seemed to be a ridiculously long code on a keypad. When the door opened, my jaw hit the floor. I wasn't sure what I'd expected. Maybe some bland white or beige walls, a few mismatched desks, and cubicles, with some early two-thousands-era computers. I was not prepared for what I saw—sleek stainless steel, glossy glass, light gray paint, it was like walking onto the deck of a futuristic starship. If he'd been trying to impress me, he succeeded.

Inside was a desk, and a pretty young lady typing at a frantic pace. When we stepped forward, she looked up and smiled at Tate.

"Good morning, Tate. How are you today?" Her voice had a flirtatious lilt to it, and I watched her lean forward, obviously letting her cleavage show a bit more than was necessary—or appropriate.

"Doing great. Kennedy, this is Harley. She's my guest today. Just giving her the grand tour."

"Morning," Kennedy said to me in a clipped tone.

She didn't look happy that I was here with Tate. It was all I could do to hide my smile. She was young and hot, but Tate had made it very obvious what and who he wanted. I stood a little closer to him after that, even though I wasn't intimidated by her at all.

Tate moved deeper into the building. I followed him as he led us past a small cluster of cubicles. Each one looked like they were filled with top-of-the-line computer equipment. I couldn't even guess as to what some of the stuff was used for. Down a hallway, we came to a small conference room. Four men sat inside and were looking at a map. Once I had a second to orient myself, I could tell that it was a map of my neighborhood.

Tate swept an arm around the room. "These are the guys who have been watching out for you guys." He pointed them out, and he named them off. "Mitch, Carl, Terry, Shawn. You may have noticed the black SUV that's been hovering around your house for the last couple of weeks? It's been one of these guys."

The men in the room smiled at me and waved. I waved back awkwardly. "Uh, thanks, I guess."

"They'll be there all the time now after what happened the other night. We hadn't thought twenty-four-seven surveillance was necessary, but we learned our lesson." He waved at the guys and turned to leave. "Thanks, guys."

Putting a hand on Tate's arm, I said, "I feel bad. I'm like a drain on your resources. I'm sorry."

"Don't be sorry. We do really well. It's not a drain. Like I said before, there are perks to being an owner."

Further down the hall, we came to another office, and I saw Steff and Blayne. Their eyes widened when they saw me with Tate.

"Holy shit," Steff said, "A female in the inner sanctum?"

Blayne laughed. "Yup, looks like it. Mrs. King, you are the first woman Tate here has ever allowed in the man cave. I hope you're thoroughly impressed, as that's no doubt the entire reason he brought you."

"Hey, shut up." But he was grinning when he looked at me. "I'm not trying to impress you. I'm… just showing you what I do."

From his tone, I had a hard time believing him. He spoke to them for a couple of minutes, and I saw some pictures and personal items around the office. From the pictures, I assumed this was probably Steff's. We left and went down the hall, where we entered a sterile and unadorned office.

"This is my office. I don't spend a ton of time here, but it does get some use between jobs," Tate said. "You can hang out here for a bit. I've got a quick meeting. It won't be long. Are you cool with that?"

"I'll be fine."

He grinned. "Great. Like I said, not long. Fifteen, twenty minutes max. See you in a bit."

I looked around the office when he left. After seeing Steff's office, it was a little weird how bare it was. Steff's office had been positively lively compared to this. No photos, no personal items, not even kitschy little knick-knacks or paperweights. I would have been happy to see the obligatory Newton's cradle or Rubik's cube. Honestly, it made me sad.

Tate had told me he was estranged from his family, but I hadn't realized to what extent until now. Lots of people said they didn't get along with their family, but even then, their mother or grandmother sent pictures or cards. This looked like a desert. A desert of the heart. While I sat reading on my phone, and occasionally glancing around at the spartan environment, I had an idea. Something the girls and I could to thank Tate for everything he'd done. We could bring some life into this office.

Chapter 21 - Tate

Leaving Harley in my office, I hurried back to Steff's office and stepped inside, closing the door behind me. Steff had his phone on the table and had already dialed Miles. It rang several times before he answered.

"Are we secure?" Miles asked.

Steff nodded to himself. "Yup, this is the secure cell. You're good."

"Okay, is everyone there?"

"Here," Blayne said.

"Right here, Miles," I said, sitting down beside Steff.

"Okay. I'm on my way back. Not more than ten minutes out, but we need to get started. So, first off, I was able to do some digging on this Emily chick."

When I'd gone out on the porch that morning, I had called all the guys and told them I'd found a witch. Miles had told us he'd look into her ASAP. I sat forward, eager to hear what he'd found.

"So, first off, Tate, do you want to give us a little more about your interaction with her? You were pretty rushed this morning."

"Sure," I said. "When I opened the door, I was hit by the reek of magic. Like it was absolutely mind-blowing. I think she tried to pull it back in some way after she saw me. She must have been caught off guard. As soon as she stepped in, the smell dissipated rather quickly, but I knew what I'd sensed. Pretty sure she knew that I knew, too. She was being coy and giving me these big fake smiles and whatnot. I'm positive she's a witch. No other explanation."

"Okay," Steff said. "But are we sure she is the same witch who has been torturing and killing shifters?"

"No way to be sure," Miles said. "I have to say, the odds are not good. Two different witches? At the same time, in and around Lilly Valley, Colorado? Seems a little outlandish. Or am I wrong?"

He wasn't. The money was on Emily being the witch we were looking for. Fear itched up my spine. It chilled me that she'd taken an interest in Harley.

"Something else happened after I got off the phone with you guys." I pulled the bag of jewelry out and set it on the table.

The bag fell open slightly, and Steff and Blayne both winced and leaned away from it. The stench of magic was not necessarily repulsive to shifters, but it was strong and shocking. Overpowering and easy to spot. It kind of slapped you in the face—or nose, as it was. Again, it wasn't an altogether bad smell, but potent and unmistakable.

Blayne picked the bag up and looked inside. "Jewelry?"

I nodded. "She gave it to Harley this morning. Whatever they are, they are not safe. She almost put a necklace on before I stopped her. I have no idea what to do with it."

"I can help with that. I've found some help. You guys just need to hold the fort down until I get there."

"We can do that, but first, we need to figure out what the hell this Emily chick wants with Tate. Why is she targeting Harley?" Blayne asked.

"To get close?" Steff asked.

"None of the Alphas I spoke to remembered anyone else being involved with the missing shifters. They had a couple of reports of a random woman, but that was it. If I had to guess, that woman was probably Emily," Miles said.

"Maybe they didn't have a mate," I said with a tightness in my chest. "She's my mate. That's a much deeper connection than just a random part-time girlfriend or something."

"Right." Steff nodded. "If she's a hunter, then she would know about the mating bond. She could have somehow figured out that Tate and Harley are connected like that, then used it to gain access to his life."

Emily was no match for me, at least, I didn't think so. I'd never fought a witch before, but now that I knew what she was, I was certain I could take care of myself. The problem was that she wasn't just targeting me. If it was me against her, I'd throw down and go to battle anytime. She was coming at me through Harley, though. It made the situation sticky and difficult to control.

"All right, guys, I'm pulling in the lot. See you in a second." Miles's line went dead, and we all sat in silence as we waited for him.

Seconds later, the intercom buzzed, and Kennedy's voice came over the line. "Mr. Kelly is here."

"Thanks, Ken," Steff said.

Miles walked in a few seconds later. A woman trailed behind him. She looked older and gave off the scent of old magic. She was an elder witch, for sure. I'd never met one, but I could tell instinctively.

"This is Siobhan. I helped her a long time ago, so I called in a favor. She's here to give us some help and a little guidance."

I pointed at the jewelry. "Can you tell us about this stuff?" I dumped it all out on the desk.

The woman stepped forward and glanced at it, then at me. "This was given to you?"

I shook my head. "No." I hesitated. "To my mate."

She touched each item in turn, slowly, almost lovingly. She placed them back after handling them. After she was done, she glanced at us and smiled.

"There is magic in these, but it is not harmful. It's more like simple charms. Spells for luck." She pointed at the opal necklace Harley had almost put on. "That one has a protection spell on it."

Had I heard that right? Protection? "So, this Emily woman is trying to protect Harley and her daughters?"

Siobhan stared at me for a long time without answering. It was like she'd not even heard my question. She just held me with her eyes. For a minute, I was certain she was reading my soul, or my mind.

Finally, exasperated, I asked, "What the hell are you staring at?"

Siobhan took a deep breath. "The town. There's a spell on the entire town."

A stunned silence fell over us. Shocked silence was more accurate.

"The entire town? What does that even mean?" Miles asked.

She looked at him like he'd asked the dumbest question she'd ever heard. "It means what I said. Someone has cast a spell over the whole town. Don't ask me what kind of spell, I can't sense that. All I know is that as soon as we crossed over the Lilly Valley city limits, I felt it."

"Is there any way to figure out what it is?" Blayne asked.

She sighed, as though she were tired. "Let me focus. I can try my best."

She stood in the center of the room and held her hands out at her sides. We gave her complete silence to help her focus. After a few seconds, I felt a prickle along my arms, almost like static electricity was playing across the hairs of my forearm. I'd never felt anything like it. She seemed to be changing the energy in the room. Her hands vibrated slightly, but not like she was doing it, more like some force encircling her was influencing the movement. Eyes closed, Siobhan winced and flinched. As calm as she looked, it also looked like she was working really hard. At last, when she looked ready to collapse, she opened her eyes and wobbled on her feet. Miles jumped up to steady her.

She took a breath, then said, "There's definitely a spell." She moved her finger around the room, pointing at all of us. "And the threads of the spell are all attached to the four of you. Threads that come from the epicenter of the spell and center on you all."

Blayne looked at himself like he would be able to see what Siobhan saw.

"No, boy. You can't see it. It's all I can do to make it visible to myself. It's like a wispy golden vapor rising off you in a thin stream. As for you…" she nodded at me, "…your thread is attached to someone down the hallway. I can see it turn the corner there."

My heart stuttered. Harley was down the hall. This spell was somehow attached to us. How could this be happening? Why was this happening?

"What does all this mean? What will the spell do?" I asked.

She shook her head. "My opinion? By how the spell feels? I think a fate spell has been cast on the town, on you four specifically."

Steff had gone pale, and his voice had a nervous lilt when he spoke. "Fate? Explain that?"

"I can see faint red threads in the spell. The red thread of fate. If it's what I think it is, a witch has cast a fate spell that will force a mating bond. Bending your will to the whims of the witch and the spell." She shrugged and shook her head. "I'm sure there's more to the spell, but without either being there at its conjuring or speaking to the witch herself, I can't tell you more. This is like nothing I've ever encountered. I can't tell you the pros or cons of the spell, either. All I can tell you is that it has connected you all to your fated pairings. Whether you want pairings or not."

Miles pointed at me. "Tate is the only one with a mate so far, but she's a human. How can a shifter be mated to a human? That's nothing I've ever heard of, have you?"

"No, not in all the history of your species. All I can imagine is that the spell was so strong that it somehow defied our natural, and supernatural, laws. It's allowed a pairing that has never happened before."

The next question had to be asked, so I went for it before I lost my courage. "My mate. The human woman down the hall. She's carrying my child. A baby, that is mine, one-hundred percent. Could this spell have caused that pregnancy, too?"

Siobhan had looked so calm and composed since she entered the office, that the look of shock on her face now was almost comical. She leaned forward, her mouth open in surprise, and looked me dead in the eyes.

"A human is carrying a shifter baby? You're sure?"

"Yes."

"Well, if such a thing truly has happened, then there is no doubt the spell is involved. Quite a powerful spell indeed," she said to herself.

A spike of fear and dread shot through me. What if the spell had done more than force a pairing? If it was powerful enough to create a human and shifter child, it could do other things, too. Things that were too scary to think about.

"What about the feelings we have for each other? Did the spell create that, too?"

Siobhan seemed to come out of deep thought. Her face creased into a smile. "My boy, unlike folk and fairy tales, there is no such thing as a love spell. Nor a love potion. Yes, the spell perhaps forced you to meet or come together. Any feelings you felt after that are entirely yours. You and the woman. Love is love," she said, smiling even more broadly.

I sat back, breath shuddering out of me in relief. That relief was quickly overcome by the questions. There were so many. There was only one way to get the answers to those questions. I glanced at Miles, then Steff, and Blayne. They each looked back at me with the same determined look. They knew as well as I did what had to be done. To get our answers, we had to capture Emily. We would find out her motives, why she killed those shifters, and why she'd cast a spell on us. But how did one capture a witch?

Chapter 22 - Harley

Tate's meeting had ended sooner than he said it would, but it seemed like it hadn't gone well. When he'd come to get me, he was tense and introspective. He spoke in short one-word answers when I tried to talk to him. He wasn't angry, I could see that. It seemed more like he was worried or confused about something really important.

The drive home was a little tense. He was so damned edgy. I didn't bother even trying to talk to him as we drove home. Tate stared out the windshield, silently chewing his lower lip and scowling. His free hand was patting his knee nervously.

It finally got to be too much, "Are you okay?"

He jerked as if I'd startled him. The truck swerved to the wrong lane for a half second before he righted it. Once he had the vehicle stable, he gave me an apologetic smile.

"Sorry, you scared me there."

"Did you forget I was sitting here?" I asked, only half joking.

He shook his head. "I'm sorry. I have a lot on my mind."

His face softened, becoming more like his usual self. Tate took my hand and brought it to his lips, kissing my knuckles. "I'm okay. I promise. Let's stop and get lunch before we head home. Good idea?"

The thought of food made my stomach rumble. The little person growing inside me had increased my appetite threefold. Ignoring the hunger would only cause me to binge on ice cream and chips later. Better to eat now and have some control over what I put into my body.

"That sounds great."

We stopped at a small restaurant. The smell of food inside didn't do anything to quell my hunger, and I patted my stomach. In my head, I said, *Easy little one. Soon.* Tate was closer to normal by the time we sat and had our menus.

Glancing over his own menu, he asked, "Harley, what do you want for the future?"

I nearly dropped the menu. The question caught me off guard. All I'd been thinking about was whether I wanted a cheeseburger or a salad—the cheeseburger was in the lead. The deep, somewhat existential question threw me off. Trying to maintain my mental balance, I thought quickly, and came up with what I thought was a good answer. It was the first thing to come to mind, and it made me smile.

I shrugged. "I want my daughters to be happy. To enjoy their lives, and grow up to be good women."

Tate looked at me, his smile spreading to a grin. "That's a given, Harley. You're a great mom, and you've raised some really great young women. That's not really what I was asking about. What do you want for *you* in the future? What do you want for yourself?"

It should have been a simple question. I almost laughed, thinking the answer was easy, but stopped when I really thought about it. All I could ever remember was being a mom. My life before that was almost totally forgotten. So distant that it was almost like another universe, in some alternate reality that barely drifted around my memory. Thinking about it, I realized what I wanted was fairly simple.

"I want to be comfortable," I said, slumping as though a weight had been lifted from my shoulders. "I want to wake up every day knowing that I'm safe and loved. I thought I had forever once. That my happily ever after had already happened. Things didn't work out the way I wanted, but I do still believe in happy endings. If it's in the cards, I want to grow old with someone meant for me." I shrugged a shoulder. "And at least one more kid."

Tate laughed. "One more after that little nugget?" he said, pointing to my belly. "You looking to start a basketball team?"

I raised an eyebrow and gave him a crooked grin. "I've always wanted a big family. Being an only child, the idea always seemed appealing."

The server came and took our orders and removed the menus. Tate leaned back in the booth and looked down at the table. He seemed to be thinking about something. When he didn't speak for a minute or two, I prodded him.

"What's going on in there?" I asked, pointing at his head.

Snapping out of his reverie, he smiled. "Sorry. It's just that, until all this, I'd never imagined having a family.

Now? It's like it's all I can think about." He looked me in the eyes, his gaze so intense I nearly shivered. "I want to do my best every day to be what you need."

His words surprised me, not only by what they implied, but by how serious he was when he said it. "Where is this all coming from? No offense but, originally, you didn't seem to want anything to do with me."

"I've lived my whole life fighting things. Fighting my family, fighting myself, fighting the world. I think I was used to fighting against anything that felt different. I'm starting to see that some things aren't meant to be fought. Sometimes they need to be embraced. I don't want to fight what I feel is building between us. Not even a little bit."

The same idea had been bouncing through my mind for a while. Hearing him say it out loud was reassuring. For the past week, I'd been trying to ignore the fact that I liked having Tate around. The girls liked it, too. They'd been missing that male presence. If I was honest with myself, so had I. I liked Tate even more than I'd been letting on.

Before I could respond, he reached into the pocket of his jeans and pulled out a ring attached to a thin gold chain. The ring was beautiful. A black obsidian jewel was embedded in the ring. The ring itself looked like it was platinum or white gold. It looked old but well kept. Tate didn't seem like the type of person to have such a beautiful piece of jewelry.

He held it out by the chain so I could see it better. "This is the last thing I have from my old life. It's a reminder of where I came from and who I am now." He reached under the table and pressed a hand against my stomach. "This ring is my legacy, and I want our boy to have it. Passing it down to our son would make me very happy. But for now…" he lifted the chain and put it around my neck as I fought back tears, "…I want you to have it. It represents power and strength. Two things I think you have, and I'm sure our son will have as well. This ring is important to me, and so are you. That means it's meant for you to wear."

Our food came out, and I had to turn my head so the server wouldn't see me crying. The hormones roaring through my body wanted me to break down blubbering, but the little boy growing inside me demanded food. The tears dried up, and I went to work on my burger. Tate and I continued to steal glances at each other as we ate. We ate in silence, but it wasn't awkward. It was a comfortable silence between two people who had finally opened up to each other. It was one of the best meals I'd ever had in my life.

The rest of the day went by in a blur. We'd gone home and did a few chores before the girls got home from school. Tate had impressed us by making a dinner of meatloaf, mashed potatoes, and roasted Brussel sprouts. The girls and I were pleasantly surprised by how tasty it was. Jordyn even made a comment that he was in charge of dinner from now on.

"I don't know that I'm ready for such a big responsibility," Tate had answered.

Later on, after the girls had gone to bed, I decided to take a shower. Leaving Tate to read on his phone, I went to the bathroom and stepped under the spray. I would have preferred a really hot bath or shower, but doctor's orders said that wasn't a good idea when pregnant. Instead, I settled for a very warm shower. Once I got in, I lathered my body and thought back on the talk Tate and I'd had at the restaurant. I felt much closer to him after that, especially after he gave me the ring. The last week had been a little strange and awkward having him around. After today? I couldn't think of anyone I wanted here more.

After the shower, I dried off and stood in front of the mirror, I looked at my body and saw how my belly bump had grown. My breasts were also getting bigger, like… a lot bigger. The ring hung between my swelling breasts. I leaned closer to the mirror to inspect it. The black stone caught the light and shimmered. Seeing it, I remembered his words from that afternoon. I was a little scared to believe everything he said, but he'd been so earnest. Everything he'd said had been truthful, and knowing he meant every word filled me with happiness. All I wanted was to be fully with him.

My mind drifted back to that night in New York. Tate's hands on my breasts. I lifted my hands and gently stroked my nipples. I thought of the other night, when his face had been between my legs, sliding his tongue into me. My nipples hardened and ached as I stroked them. I imagined him sucking on them, and heat flashed across my chest and between my legs. I knew exactly what I wanted.

Turning from the mirror, I stepped out of the bathroom, and into the bedroom, wearing nothing but the ring necklace. Tate glanced up from his phone as I walked out. His eyes widened, and I smiled coyly. He looked at me, sliding his eyes from my face down my body before locking on my eyes again.

His voice was deep and husky when he spoke. "You know you're playing with fire, right?"

More sexually confident than I'd ever been in my life, I replied, "I guess it's a good thing I like the heat."

Tate threw his phone aside and made a sound like a snarl as he stood and crossed the floor in two quick strides. He pulled me in close, pressing my naked body to his as our lips locked. I was almost dripping wet between my legs, and as we kissed, I ground my pelvis against his thigh, rubbing my clit across the muscles beneath his pants. I moaned into his mouth as his tongue moved between my lips. I imagined what his cock would feel like in my mouth and nearly came just thinking about it. I was as horny as a teenager, my hands already working at his belt and fly, desperate to get him undressed.

Before I could complete my work, he slid his hands under my ass and picked me up. I gasped at his strength. He lifted me like I was nothing, and his show of strength only heightened my arousal. Tate laid me down on the bed and stripped his shirt off. I gazed at the rippling muscles of his chest and stomach hungrily. He was fucking hot. I'd almost forgotten how good he looked naked. Through half-lidded eyes, I watched him yank his boots and pants off. Then his underwear. His cock was already throbbing and rock hard. I looked at it and bit my lower lip. I usually thought penises looked strange, but right now, nothing looked sexier. I spread my legs and laid my head back, never taking my eyes off him.

Tate knelt on the floor in front of the bed, kissing my legs. Working his lips up from my knees, closer and closer with each kiss. I was breathing heavily when the warmth of his breath breezed across my pussy. I moaned and looked up at the ceiling. My clit was throbbing, engorged, and pulsing. I'd never experienced anything like this. I was so hot for him, and he was teasing me. I shivered, except I was the opposite of cold; it was like my skin was on fire, and only he could put out the flames.

Instead of stroking me with his tongue, he lifted his head and kissed up my stomach toward my breasts. I whimpered when he didn't slide his tongue into me.

"I need you to fuck me," I panted.

Glancing up at me, he murmured, "Oh, I will."

Without another word, he took my breast into his mouth. I cried out, "Oh shit," and nearly came from the warm, wet touch of his tongue on my nipple.

While his lips played with me, I reached between his legs and wrapped my fingers around his dick. I stroked it twice, and he pulled his mouth away, grunting in pleasure. The tip of his cock was already wet, cum already starting to seep out. I slipped my finger around the slippery head. Tate's face was a mask of ecstasy as I touched him. I felt empowered, knowing what I wanted to do. I pushed him back and knelt between his legs. I locked eyes with him and slowly slid his dick into my mouth. He groaned as I took every inch of him.

His cock was thick, warm, and hard as steel between my lips. Nothing had ever felt as erotic as staring into his eyes while I moved my head up and down, fucking him with my mouth. His hips started to thrust unconsciously as I worked him. My wetness was dripping down my leg. I wouldn't be able to hold out much longer, but I was enjoying the power I had over him. The fact that I could bring this big, strong man down into a puddle, the same way he'd done to me, was fucking hot. I didn't want it to end.

"If you don't stop, I'm gonna come," Tate gasped.

For a moment, I almost did it. Almost sped up the movement of my tongue and lips. The mental image of his back arching, fingers digging into the sheets, spurting cum into my mouth, was almost tempting enough, but I wanted to come with him. I pulled my mouth away, sucking the head as I did. He breathed a deep sigh and looked at me with a fiery hunger, which, at any other moment, would have terrified me. Instead, I returned it with the same fire.

Tate rolled over and grabbed my hips, lifting me so that I flopped onto my back on the bed. I laughed as he straddled me. Instead of entering me, he kissed me deeply. I moaned, stroking the muscles of his back. Then, without warning, he slammed the full length of himself into me. I let out a low throaty moan. It was loud, but I couldn't worry about it.

He chuckled against my mouth. "Quiet now."

I looked at him and gasped, "Shut up and fuck me."

"Oh, is that what you want?" he whispered.

"Uh huh." I nodded.

Without answering, he moved his hips against mine, slipping in and out of me. My moaning and gasping grew more insistent with each thrust. Each time his cock filled me, the wave of pleasure grew higher, closer to cresting. Tate's breathing grew heavier, and I could tell he was close. Warmth started to build in my pelvis, the first waves of pleasure beginning to pulse from my clit. I wrapped my arms around Tate and thrust my hips against his, increasing the speed. Desperate for a climax. There was nothing else in the world except for Tate and me.

Three more quick thrusts, and Tate's body went rigid. He grunted, almost screamed as he came. As he buried himself in me, the wave finally crashed over me. I bit into Tate's shoulder to stifle my scream. Wave after wave slammed into me. The world spun, and electricity seemed to sizzle across my skin. My body jerked spasmodically, causing his dick to slide into me again and again, the pleasure almost too much to take. It was truly almost too much—I'd never come so hard in my life. I was on the verge of blacking out when he finally pulled free of me and collapsed beside me.

I lay there, my body jerking every few seconds. My breath vibrated out of me in uneven gasps and sighs. Tate lay beside me, taking huge, shuddering breaths. After a few seconds, his arm snaked around me and pulled me close. He kissed my shoulder, then my collar bone, then my nipple, which sent me into a fresh set of shivers, and finally kissed my lips. I was only awake for another two or three seconds before I slipped into the deepest sleep I'd ever experienced.

Chapter 23 - Tate

I'd been living with Harley and her girls for two weeks. The transition had been fairly simple and easy, and it helped that I enjoyed being around them. It was nice to have people at home when I got off work. It was nice not to enter an empty bed each evening. It was nice hearing the talking and laughter that was always going on. It reminded me of how quiet and lonely my house had been before.

There hadn't been any more signs of Luis. No further kidnapping attempts, no sign of the black car. My guys still followed the girls to school each day. Their reports had been bland and vanilla. Nothing exciting, other than the fact they got to watch two freshmen boys get into a fist fight in the parking lot one afternoon. Carl and Terry had both laughed until they'd almost cried when they'd described it. Apparently, the boys had basically been having a slap fight, and neither had done a very good job proving his manhood. I'd laughed along with them, but I was still on edge. There was no way Ortiz had just up and left. It did not seem like his style. For now, though, things were quiet and calm.

At least it would be if not for what was going on tonight. Mariah was bringing home a boy for dinner. The fact that I wasn't her real father was not lost on me. The fact that my dragon, and by association, my own mind, didn't give a damn also had to be taken into account. For all intents and purposes, I felt like a father figure. I wanted to protect and take care of all the girls. Mariah included.

Mariah came down the stairs and called out, "He just texted me. He'll be here in a minute or two."

Harley grinned at her. "Okay, sweetie. He does like steak and potatoes, right? Potatoes are already in the oven, so I can't really turn back now."

"Oh yeah. Who doesn't like grilled meat?" Mariah said, shrugging off the question.

"Vegans don't," Jordyn said.

I raised an eyebrow. "No offense, Mariah, but I don't think I could stomach it if you brought home a vegan."

Mariah rolled her eyes. "He's not, trust me. He eats the school hamburgers and pepperoni pizza. We're good."

Jordyn leaned against the counter, her eyes bright with mischief, and said, "Kayden's so pretty. I can't wait for you to see him, Mom."

"Just a hint," I grumbled. "Boys prefer the words handsome or sexy over pretty."

Jordyn tilted her head. "Pretty is pretty. Doesn't matter what he prefers."

I rolled my eyes right as the doorbell rang. I was the closest, so I stepped to the door, put my shoulders back, and placed a serious and intimidating look on my face before turning the knob. As I swept the door open, the young man with perfectly tousled hair grinned, then caught sight of me. The smile quickly slid off his face as he gaped up at me. I was six-foot two-inches of solid muscle, and it was obvious. The dragon in me gave an approving hiss at the look on the boy's face. In my personal opinion, he looked like he was ready to shit a brick. He was a good-looking kid, healthy and strong for his age, but I could have picked him up and broken him over my knee, and he realized it, too. It was also a very small town, so the kid probably knew who I was and what I did for a living.

I stepped back and smiled, waving a hand inside. "Come on in, Kayden. Nice to meet you," I said, with my best gracious host voice.

"Thanks, uh, Mr. Mills. Um, I didn't know you and Mariah's... well, it's nice to see you," Kayden stammered.

I had never seen the kid before in my life, but I nodded. "Good to see you again, too."

Jordyn chimed in, "I forgot to tell you guys. Everyone at school knows Tate and his three friends. The girls call them The Crew, and everybody thinks they're super-hot. Hotties with bodies, they say."

"Jordyn," Harley hissed in a near-yell. She looked aghast, but I had to bite my lip to keep from laughing.

"What? I didn't say it. I'm just telling you what everyone else says."

Kayden cleared his throat. "Well, she's right. Every kid knows who Mr. Mills is. Most people know what he does for a living and think he's..." he paused and blushed a little, "...they think he's a badass."

I would love to say that having a fourteen and seventeen-year-old say all these things about me was silly, and that I didn't care. But the awkward kid I had been when I was younger, the one who had wanted nothing more than to be cool, did perk up a bit. As silly as it was to say, my ego definitely took a boost.

Mariah looked like she wanted to crawl into a hole and die. She grabbed Kayden's hand and walked toward the stairs. "We're gonna go watch a movie until dinner is ready."

"Keep the door open," Harley said.

"Mom!" Mariah gasped, her face turning blood red.

I glanced over Mariah's shoulder and gave Kayden a look that told him everything I wanted him to know. He saw my expression, and the smile that had been on his face slipped away. He gave me the faintest of nods in acknowledgment. He understood exactly what my look meant. If he even *thought* about touching Mariah, he'd find out how much of a badass I really was.

Harley and I went to sit on the back porch with a couple of glasses of lemonade while the potatoes cooked, enjoying the early evening weather. It was warm but comfortable. A question bounced around in my head—it had been ever since Harley told me Mariah was bringing a boy home. There wasn't a subtle way of bringing it up, so I just went for it.

"So, Harley, random question, but is Mariah on birth control?"

Harley choked on her drink and leaned forward, coughing and gasping, spitting out what had been left in her mouth onto the concrete. I grimaced, thinking I could have timed the question better.

Once she recovered, she said, "What the hell is wrong with you? No, she's not."

I held my hands up, warding off her anger. "Hey, I'm just asking. All I'm saying is I was a seventeen-year-old boy once, and I know exactly how they think. That's all. Mariah is a beautiful girl, and I guarantee boys have noticed that. And when boys notice things like that, they try to get into a girl's pants."

Harley wiped her face with her sleeve and said, "Mariah is a smart girl. She's not going to fall for some goofy kid's overtures."

Her naivety was cute. I looked her up and down. "Looks like you were probably pretty hot in high school.

And I bet you were really smart, too. When did you start having sex?"

She stared at me, defiant at first, then as the question worked its way into her mind, her face paled.

She leaned back and groaned. "Shit!"

I laughed, hard. Harley, even in her state, chuckled along with me. After I got myself under control, I said, "It's easy to think that your kids won't make the same mistakes you made, but you can't be blind to the fact that they probably will. Ignoring it won't make things any better."

She put her glass on the ground and climbed into my lap, leaning against me. "Okay, Tate, you win. I'll talk to her. Maybe set up an appointment."

"Good. You talk to her, I'll talk to Kayden."

Harley swatted my chest. "Don't run the boy off. Mariah likes him."

"Okay, okay, I'll try my best."

We sat there, simply enjoying each other's company for a few more minutes. My dragon was so content it worried me. I'd never been this content or at peace with anyone. Was it just the mating bond? Was it simply the way Harley made me feel? She was depending on me, which stoked my protective nature—the dragon loved being needed. Being able to keep them safe. Even when we didn't exactly agree, she still listened when I knew what needed to be done. I loved her for that.

My eyes widened in surprise. Harley didn't notice the sudden stiffness to my body. Love? Had that word really just tickled the edges of my mind? My heart thudded hard against my ribs. Was I really, truly, falling in love with Harley?

I did the best I could to cover my surprise at what I'd been thinking about. We went inside to check on the potatoes. They were getting close, so I pulled the steaks from the fridge while Harley put the salad together.

While I seasoned the meat, Mariah and Kayden came down the stairs. "How's dinner coming along?" Mariah asked.

"Good. If you want, you can help me cut veggies for the salad," Harley said. "Kayden, do you want to help Tate cook the steaks?"

Kayden swallowed hard, then, to his credit, he smiled. "Sure."

The boy and I stepped outside and turned the grill on. "How do you like your steak cooked?"

"Medium rare, a little closer to the rare side."

I pointed at him with the spatula. "Kid, I think there's hope for you yet. If you'd said well done, I'd have thrown you out on your ass right then and there."

He laughed at that, and I decided I actually liked him. Grudgingly, but I did. He seemed like a good kid. He was brave, too. I didn't know whether I would have gone out on the back porch with a guy that looked like me at that age.

"What do you do at school? Any clubs or sports or anything?" I asked.

He nodded as he handed me the plate of steaks. "I play baseball. Love baseball, actually."

I frowned, something tickling my memory. Had I heard this kid's name before?

"Are you the kid that had the walk-off homer in the state finals last year? Won Lilly Valley High the state championship? Didn't you guys upset the reigning champs?"

He reddened a bit. "They were the four-year running champs. It was a lucky pitch, though. The pitcher had a dead arm. His coach should have pulled him at least an inning before. It was just luck."

Modest, too? Well, shit. The guy was fucking Prince Charming. "What are your plans for life after school? College? Work?"

His eyes lit up. "I like baseball, and I'm pretty good. There are several pretty big schools offering me scholarships, I want to go to one that has a really good veterinary program. I want to be a vet. That's the first thing Mariah and I found out we had in common."

I had no idea Mariah wanted to be a vet. My mind began to spin through scenarios, doing math with my savings accounts and investments I'd made. Both girls would need college funds. I was sure Harley had plans for that. There'd probably been life insurance from when their dad passed. All well and good, but if I was going to be around, I would make sure the girls didn't want for anything.

Kayden went on. "Upstairs, all Mariah could talk about was you. Mr. Mills, she really likes you. I thought you should know that. All she could talk about was how happy she was that her mom found you, and that she wasn't alone anymore."

Son of a bitch, this kid was freaking awesome. That sealed it. He was all right with me. In fact, I didn't think Mariah could have done any better. I smiled wryly to myself and thought, *they still needed to leave the door open when they were in her room.*

Once the steaks were done, I handed the plate to Kayden to take in. Inside, I closed the door and walked over to Mariah, then kissed the top of her head. She looked at me in surprise, but then smiled when she looked into my eyes. I had a family again. I'd already known it, but looking into Mariah's eyes really pushed it home. It would take all the hosts of heaven and all the demons of hell to pry me away from these women.

Hours later, after dinner, after Kayden went home, and after the girls were asleep, Harley and I lay in bed, panting and sweaty after another mind-blowing evening of sexual adventures. Teenagers tended to sleep like the dead, but we'd still done our best to be quiet. I wasn't sure how successful we'd been.

"So?" Harley asked. "Did you and Kayden have a good talk outside? I assume you did, since he looked much less like he was going to piss himself when he came back in."

I laughed. "I have to say, he's a good kid. Smart, athletic, polite, the whole nine yards. I'm pretty sure that he knows he's found a prize with Mariah. We're good buddies now."

Harley wrapped her arms around me and whispered, "Good," before slipping into sleep.

I held her and listened to her gentle breathing. Over and over again, the same words played on repeat in my head. *Love, family, mate, love, family, mate.* It was strange, but in the best damned way. I fell asleep smiling.

Chapter 24 - Harley

Even after Tate had explained that he didn't trust Emily, I still had a hard time not thinking of her as a friend. A friend who was acting weird as hell, but a friend, nonetheless. I wasn't concerned exactly, but I needed to know what was going on. It had been over a week since I'd heard from her, and despite everything, I was worried about her. She said she'd see me again before she left, so I knew she hadn't left town.

It was early September, and a beautiful day, so I decided to see if she was home. I knew it shouldn't have bothered me, but the curiosity was almost overwhelming. One way or another, I had to figure out what the hell was going on.

Emily had told me where her grandmother's house was. I'd always meant to go out and see it, but life had kept me occupied. I got into my car and headed out. The chance of her being there was pretty small, but I had nothing better to do, and there was still a chance. She would probably be there, doing some gardening to spruce it up before it got listed. Improving the curb appeal or whatever.

I turned the radio up and rolled the windows down, enjoying the cool late-summer air. One thing about Colorado: it was a much different climate compared to New York. It was warmer but less humid. It felt cooler than it should, and I loved it. My body was already going through hot flashes with the pregnancy, so any respite was welcome.

Finding the street Emily had mentioned was easy, but I had no idea which house was the one she'd talked about. When I turned onto the street, the choices were pretty simple. It wasn't really a *neighborhood* per se. It was just a dead-end street with three houses and an empty lot where an old house had once stood. All that was left there was a crumbling chimney.

Frowning, I cruised down the street, checking each house to see which one was correct. The first house was a small one-story ranch-style. A middle-aged man was out mowing the lawn, and there were toys scattered around the porch. That couldn't be it. The second house was similar to the first but a little bigger. There was a small car and a minivan sitting in the driveway, neither of which was Emily's car. Sitting on a porch swing was a younger couple having a conversation. It had to be the third house. When I pulled up to it, confusion swept over me.

It was abandoned—not just that it was obvious that no one lived there. The yard was overgrown, the windows were dusty and dirty, and the paint around the windows was peeling and faded. This didn't look like a house someone had spent weeks getting ready to sell. It also didn't look like a home that had been lived in. Not for a very long time.

I sat there trying to figure out what was going on. Was Emily having financial trouble? Maybe she didn't have the money to fix the place up on the outside. Was that it? Had she used what money she had to fix up the inside instead? Doubtful, but wanting to know for sure, I pulled into the driveway. A quick walk up to the first window and a peek in told me that was *not* what was going on. The inside was caked in dust. Cobwebs hung freely from the ceiling, and it looked like some type of black mold was growing on a wall in the living room.

What the hell? I was positive this was the road she'd mentioned. The other houses didn't look like they'd been newly bought. Even if Emily had listed it and sold it on the same day I'd seen her last, it would have taken at least two weeks for all the paperwork and stuff to clear. No one could have bought and moved into a new house that fast. It didn't make sense.

I walked slowly back to my car, wondering how I'd find Emily. As I got back in the car, a lightbulb went off in my mind. Her grandma. She said she was in a home, and there was only one nursing home in the whole county. Emily had said she was there. If I could find her anywhere, I'd find her there.

Fifteen minutes later, I walked into Harmony Grace nursing home. A small part of me hoped to see her car in the parking lot. I hadn't. I thought she might be inside in a waiting room of some sort. Again, no luck. The nurse at the reception desk smiled at me as I walked up.

"How can I help you, ma'am?" she asked.

"Yes, I'm here to visit Ms. Heath?" I said, using Emily's last name. There was a fifty percent chance her grandmother shared it with her.

The nurse frowned but tapped at the keyboard for a moment. "That's what I thought," she said to herself before looking back up at me. "Yes, ma'am, I'm afraid we don't have a patient by that name here."

Well, that hadn't worked. I smiled back at her apologetically. "I'm sorry. I assumed they shared a last name. I'm friends with her granddaughter, she's her caretaker. It's her only family. Can you find her by the guardian's name? Emily Heath?"

The nurse typed at her workstation again and shook her head again. "We don't have any guardians by that name. We don't have anyone with the first name Emily."

What the hell was going on?

The nurse looked at me, concerned, and said, "Are you okay, miss?"

Snapping out of my daze, I said, "Oh, I'm sorry to have bothered you. I must have… I guess I was misinformed."

"No problem at all, ma'am. Have a good day."

This time, the walk back to my car was filled with swirling thoughts and questions. Emily had lied about this? Why? Tate said he didn't trust her, and I'd been hesitant to believe him. Was he right after all? I refused to believe that she was working with Luis. It made my skin crawl to even think about it. But if not, what was she doing?

I drove around town, stewing on all the questions, for thirty minutes. My stomach growled, and since I was already out and Tate was working, I decided to treat myself to lunch. Giving it one last shot, I dialed Emily again as I waited for my food. Still no answer. An uneasy feeling had filled my chest as the day drew on, as more things started to not add up. After my food came, my next call was to Tate.

"Hello, beautiful," he answered.

Despite my misgivings about Emily, I blushed, and said, "Hello, handsome. How's your day?"

"It's fine. Just going over some contracts for jobs later this year. What are you up to?"

I hesitated. I still wasn't a hundred percent sure Emily was sketchy, but something was going on, and I needed his opinion. In the end, I decided to be honest.

"Well, here's the thing. I haven't heard from Emily since she gave me that jewelry. She hasn't answered her phone or responded to texts. I decided to stop by her grandma's house, the one she's been fixing up to sell."

"Yeah?" Tate said, his voice wary.

"So, I found the house, but it's a dump. Looks like it hasn't been lived in for at least thirty years. The yard isn't even mowed. So, then I went to see if she was visiting her grandma, but there is no grandma at the nursing home. Emily's name isn't on the register as a guardian. It's... it's like she's lied about everything. Maybe you were right."

There was a long pause before Tate said, "I'll look into it. I can have the guys check the nursing home admittance. There's always a chance that maybe grandma died. Could also be that Emily put her on a secure list, and no one is allowed to visit or ask about her. If that's the case, it could be why the nursing home said they had no one registered by that name. That's all pretty unlikely. For now, I'd prefer it if you didn't reach out to her anymore. It sounds like it's really possible she's involved in something and tried to wedge herself into your life for some reason."

My worries had become much more pronounced after talking to Tate.

"Yeah, you're right. No more calls, no more texts."

"Good. Where are you right now?"

"Um, out to eat. This little boy is gonna cause me to gain a hundred pounds."

His chuckle sent a thrill down my spine. "Okay, but I'd like you to head straight home after. Set the alarms and stuff."

"Got it, captain. See you tonight."

"See you, be careful."

My food didn't look as appetizing as it had when it came out. The conversation about Emily had robbed me of most of my hunger, but I still managed to eat half of my meal. The other half went into a box, and I left, doing exactly what Tate told me to. The drive back home seemed longer than usual. Every time a car passed, I glanced at it to see if it was Emily. Before, I'd wanted to know she was safe. Now? I wanted to know if she was following me. Or stalking me.

My arrival back home was not a relief. As I put the car into park, I glanced up and saw a package sitting on the porch. Even from this distance, I could see it was a silver box with a black ribbon. Distinct packaging. The exact same packaging Luis had always sent me gifts in. A diamond necklace, tickets to a Broadway show, an invitation to a fancy dinner—they'd all come in a silver box with a black bow. There was only one person who would have put that on my porch.

My stomach was full of lead as I got out of my car. As soon as I was out, I couldn't shake the feeling that there were eyes on me. Glancing at my watch, I realized that the girls would be home soon. I didn't want them to see the box. They'd recognize it. Trying not to run, I walked to the porch, unable to shake the feeling of being watched but unwilling to give Luis the satisfaction of seeing me hurry. I scooped up the box and walked inside, closing the door and setting the alarm as fast as I could.

My breath was shaky as I leaned against the door to compose myself. We'd only had Tate's guys follow the girls to school, and then they did a drive-by of the house every hour or so once it got dark. We hadn't thought it necessary to have them at my house all day every day, but that might have to be revisited after this.

There was only one thing to do. Tate needed to hear about this. I called him again.

After three rings, he answered. "Yes?"

I flinched at his voice. He sounded irritated and short. It was probably my fault. I was putting too much on him, asking too much of him. Guilt spilled over me, and I wanted to crawl into a hole.

"Uh… sorry, I'm bothering you. I'll talk to you later."

"Harley, wait, no." He sighed tiredly. "I'm not frustrated with *you*. I've got a client being a dick. They already signed the contract, but now they're adding all kinds of crazy stuff. I've been dealing with it all day."

"I don't want to be the one piling more on your plate."

"I sat myself at your table. I expect to be well fed, so pile that baby full. What's wrong?"

Another part of me fell for him, then. He was so genuine when he said it. He truly did want to take on whatever I was willing to give him. It wouldn't help my guilt, but it was nice to know that he was there.

"Luis left me a package on the front porch."

"What?" he nearly shouted.

"It's in a package that he knew I'd recognize. It's got to be from him."

"Do not open it."

"You don't have to tell me that."

"Okay, good. I want you to make sure the coast is clear, and then bring that package to me at the office."

"But the girls will be home soon. School lets out in about forty-five minutes."

"I'll text Mariah and tell her to take Jordyn to the little ice cream joint instead of getting on the bus. Shawn's watching them today. I'll let him know there's been a change of plan. I'll even send her some money in a cash app or something. That way, they won't be home alone."

"I can text her and let her know," I said.

"No, I'll take care of it. I just need you to get your fine ass down here as soon as possible."

I hung up and did exactly what he said. I made sure the coast was clear. No sign of Luis or his car. Then I got my fine ass into my car, locked the doors, and pulled out of the driveway. That feeling of being watched swept over me again, making my blood run cold. Once I was out of the driveway, I hit the gas a little harder than usual, the tires squealing as I went.

I pulled up to Tate's office not long after. He was already standing in the lot, waiting for me. I got out of the car and was in his arms within seconds. He cupped my face and looked into my eyes, then kissed me hard. For a few seconds, I forgot about the day. He pulled away and swept me into the office. Terry stood at the door, staring daggers out through the window, scanning the surrounding area. It looked like Tate had already informed his team about what was going down. I liked knowing we weren't alone in this.

Tate took my hand and led me to the conference room where Blayne, Miles, and Steffen were waiting for us.

"Give me a second, guys. Don't open it until I'm back." Tate guided me down the hall and into his office.

I gasped slightly as we entered the room. It was different. Instead of the stark spartan furnishing, there was decoration. There was a picture of me with Jordyn and Mariah n his filing cabinet. We were sitting on the couch laughing—I remembered the night well. On his desk stood a framed picture of one of my ultrasounds. The gray blob that was our baby sitting right where he could see it anytime he wanted. I looked at Tate, who was staring back at me. I knew what it meant for him to have these pictures in here. The man who'd had no one but his friends until now. My eyes welled with tears as I looked back at him.

Tate pressed his hand to my belly, and we both felt the baby kick. I was six months along, and though I'd felt him shifting in there, it was the first real kick I'd noticed. I gasped and laughed.

"Did you feel that?" I asked.

Tate's eyes were wide and beginning to tear up, too. "Holy shit. I did." He kissed my forehead. "I'll be right back. Okay?"

I nodded and watched him go. Placing my hands on my belly, I felt the baby kick again. It was the best thing that had happened all day. It was a reminder that even on bad days, good things could happen. I took a seat at Tate's desk to wait for him to get back.

Chapter 25 - Tate

Steff was looking at me expectantly as I came through the door. Blayne and Miles were hunched over a computer and didn't notice me until I closed the door. The box in my hand was like a lead weight pulling at my arm, even though it only weighed a few ounces.

Steff nodded to the box. "Whatcha got there?"

Holding it up so they could see it, I said, "Ortiz decided to leave Harley a little gift. On her fucking front porch."

"Shit," Blayne hissed, "Did you see him on the cameras?"

"Pretty sure it's him. I think he knew they were there. He wore a hoodie and had it pulled way down over his face. Had sunglasses on, and kept his face to the ground. You can tell it's a guy by the build, but that's about it."

"Okay," Miles said. "What are we thinking? Like, how crazy is this guy?" He pointed at the box. "Vial of his own blood crazy or dead mother's engagement ring crazy?"

"Only one way to find out." I pulled the ribbon and opened the box.

Inside the black box was another box. It was a familiar light greenish-blue jewelry box. I'd never bought anything there, but I knew the place well. I'd walked past the storefront near Rockefeller when I was working in New York. Inside that box were two items. A small velvet drawstring bag the same color as the jewelry box. Beside that were two embroidered baby booties. Sky blue for a boy.

As I lifted the booties, my dragon's irritation sparked. Then I read the embroidery. One bootie read: *Baby Boy*. The other read: *Luis Jr.* Breath hissed from my nose, and I crushed the booties in my fist, grinding the cotton together until my knuckles cracked. Glancing down in my rage, I saw a slip of paper still in the box. My hands shook as I opened it and read:

Hey, babe. I'll be in touch soon so we can talk about my son. -Luis

My vision went red; my dragon was absolutely raging inside. It knew that the baby was ours as much as I did. We could feel the magic growing inside Harley. The connection to her was undeniable, and there was only one explanation. My son growing in her. Ours. The fact that he was trying to claim him made me more furious than I could have ever thought possible.

I was on the verge of slamming my closed fists onto the conference room table when Miles put a hand on my shoulder. Had I been anywhere else, I would have swung at him, thinking he was Luis. Thankfully, I remembered I was in a safe place with friends before my fists flew out at him.

"Bro? Are you good?" Miles asked.

Looking up, Steff and Blayne were staring at me, a combination of fear and concern on their faces. I took a breath to calm myself before throwing the note and booties into a waste bin under the table.

"I'm fine. That guy's just an asshole. What was in the bag?" I asked, looking at Steff.

Steff tipped the little bag out into his palm. Two earrings tumbled out. They were both teardrops, with a blue gem in the middle surrounded by diamonds. They were gorgeous and looked expensive.

Steff pulled out his phone. "Okay, I've got to see how much these bad boys are worth. Hang on a second."

While Steff tapped and swiped at his phone, I stewed on how angry Luis had made me. I was synced with the baby inside her. The magic the child gave off was so similar to mine that I could almost taste it. Surely he felt the opposite. Could he feel any connection to the baby inside Harley's belly? Did he even try? Or was he too concerned with taking what he thought was his?

"Holy fuck." Steff gasped. He looked at us and laughed humorlessly. "These freaking things are fifteen-thousand goddamned dollars. Who the hell is this guy?"

I was already on edge with everything Harley had told me about Emily. Not only did we have Luis skulking around town, making life miserable, but we had a witch to deal with as well. A witch whose intentions weren't entirely clear, but were more than likely nefarious. It was enough to drive me crazy.

Trying to get my mind off Luis, I asked, "What have you guys dug up on this Emily Heath chick?"

Miles and Blayne shrugged almost in unison. Miles said, "It's like she doesn't exist. We couldn't find anything on her. Could be a totally fake name, but she's a witch. With her magic, she could stay fully dark to the web. If she doesn't have any need for credit cards or I.D. or anything else we could track, then there's no reason to think she isn't living on the fringes. Biding her time."

"Biding her time until what? What is her end game?" I asked.

"I don't know. Is she torturing and killing shifters to get some kind of information? Is there some spell she's trying to complete that needs shifters? Is she just a fucking bigot and hates us? Your guess is as good as mine. Basically, we have no idea." Dejected, Miles flopped into his chair.

The unknown was scary. The dragon didn't like it; neither did I. It meant we needed to up the security for Harley and the girls. There were two direct threats now. One was known, understandable, trackable, easily dealt with once caught. The other was unknown, confusing, untraceable, and of unknown strength. Luis and a witch. It seemed life was getting much more difficult with every minute that passed. We needed to find Emily, whatever it took.

"We gotta call the cops, right? At least about Luis. I doubt they'll believe a rogue witch is on the loose," Blayne said.

We all exchanged a look. The cops in Lilly Valley were not huge fans of us, and we all knew it. Part of the problem was that we didn't have a lot of respect for them. We were more thorough in our investigations. Even their best detectives weren't as good as Miles, and their forensics teams couldn't hold a candle to Steff and Blayne. It caused tension. So much so that we rarely even took jobs anywhere within the tri-county area. Instead, we focused on bigger clients in larger cities. Blayne was probably right, though. If nothing else, they needed to know Luis was in town and stalking Harley, especially since the order of protection was still active.

Steff sighed and stood. "Okay, I'll head over to the station. Out of all of us, I'm the least grumpy and most friendly. They won't give me too much hell. I'll need those little gifts out of the trashcan, Tate. Tell them about that restraining order and whatnot. I'll give them everything we have about him. I may even mention we've spotted him with a woman. Give them Emily's description. Cops won't be able to do much against a witch, but it could flush her out if they're looking for her."

"Good call," I said. "I need to make a statement to Ortiz. He needs to know that Harley and that baby are mine. It's childish, but I want to do something to hit back. Any ideas?"

Blayne raised his eyebrows. "In-vitro DNA tests are a thing now. I mean, they've been a thing for a long time, but they're super safe now. You could do that with Harley. It would go on her medical paperwork, too. If this Ortiz guy has a team monitoring her, then he'd see that pop up. It would be a slap in the face."

I winced. "That might offend Harley. Like I don't believe the baby is mine or something."

"It's all in how you present it," Miles said. "You're wanting to have it on file or whatever. Present it like it's the best thing to solidify your fatherhood. I'm sure you'll think of a way to keep her from getting pissed."

"Easier said than done, but I guess you're right. Once he sees the kid isn't his, he may give up and go home."

"Okay, that's all we can do about Luis for now," Blayne said. "The witch needs to be the main thing we focus on. She's killed shifters, allegedly, and I think she's the bigger threat at the moment. How do we catch her? We have to do that to get the answers to our questions."

Miles sighed. "Harley. That's the connection we have to exploit."

"The hell? You want to use her as bait?" I rarely got in arguments or fights with the guys, but I really wanted to slug Miles for suggesting it.

"What else do we have that can bridge the gap between us and Emily? Answer me that, and I'll pull it off the table."

Glaring at him, my mind flipped through any possible scenario, then I finally said, "That Siobhan lady? Your friend, can't she…" I waved my hands vaguely, "…track her magic or something?"

Miles shook his head. "She already said she couldn't. The spell is over the whole town, and it's a strong conjuring. If she's in town, all that magic from the spell will hide her. No go."

No other thoughts came to me. Blayne and Steffen were no help; they both looked like they agreed with Miles. Grinding my teeth together, I nodded in reluctance.

"The jewelry she gave Harley all had protective spells placed on them. Maybe she really is trying to protect her. She may be watching her to make sure she's safe," I said. "We can figure out a plan. But under no circumstances is she to be placed in harm's way. I'd rather be extra careful and not catch her than get sloppy and have something happen to Harley. Understood?"

The guys nodded. We spent the next ten minutes coming up with a plausible story as well as a plan. Blayne created a few documents to help sell the lie. It wasn't great, and I hated the idea of lying to Harley. The only other option was to tell her the truth. That I was a magical shape-shifting half-man half-dragon. My other friends could turn into wolves, bears, and panthers. Oh, also your new friend is a witch, like a real-life witch with magic powers, and she might be trying to murder me and my shape-shifting friends. Sound good, sweetie?

That shit wouldn't fly. Best-case scenario, she'd get mad we were telling stupid stories. Worst-case scenario, she'd run screaming from the building and buy silver bullets.

We had Kennedy get Harley from my office and bring her to the conference room. She looked confused and a little irritated. I'd left her there longer than I thought I would. Things would already be difficult enough without her being pissed at me. I sat with her and put an arm around her shoulders.

Miles sat at the table in front of us. We'd decided he would lead the discussion and explain the plan. Better him than me. I wasn't sure I could pull off lying to Harley the way he'd have to.

"Emily Heath?" Miles said. "This is the woman Tate said you've been looking for?"

Harley looked unsure. "Um, yeah."

Miles nodded, looking like he'd heard exactly what he wanted to hear. "Tate had us look into her. Turns out she's a known scam artist. Do you know what a grifter is?"

Harley shook her head. "I think I've heard it before but... wait, what are you saying?"

"This Emily is a wanted criminal. She's traveled all over the U.S. and Canada, pulling off these small-time swindles. Pretending to be someone she isn't. She inserts her way into people's lives, scams them out of money, and then disappears before she's caught. She usually preys on the elderly and single older men. Jumping from town to town, staying one step ahead of the law."

Harley leaned away from me and looked into my eyes. "Is he serious? There's no way."

By some amazing strength of will, I didn't look away. Instead, I looked her dead in the eyes and said, "It's true. We've seen the proof."

Miles went on as Harley looked around the room like she had found herself in the middle of a circus. "Her latest victim was a lady in the nursing home you visited. She used a false name and pretended to be her long-lost grand-daughter. Got the lady to sign over her power of attorney. The bank account has already been cleaned out."

Harley put a hand to her mouth. "Oh my god. This can't be happening."

Blayne stood and pulled two pieces of paper from the printer, then handed them to Harley. She looked down, and I looked over her shoulder at the papers. Blayne had put together two shockingly realistic pages. One looked like a screen grab of some regional paper in the north east which gave an accurate description of Emily as well as a rundown of the crimes she was accused of. The other was an FBI wanted poster. He'd used a picture from Harley's security cameras, but had altered the hair color and the background. While Harley stared at the pages and read, I looked at Blayne and raised an eyebrow. He'd done amazing work in fifteen minutes. If he wasn't already a partial owner, I'd have given him a damned raise.

Harley was close to tears when she finally handed the pages to Miles. "I thought she was my friend."

The sadness in her voice was almost enough for me to stand up and call the whole story off. I didn't do that, but it was damned close. My dragon was actually mad at me. All it wanted to do was protect and care for her, and here I was making her cry with this sham.

Managing to get my voice, I said, "She's wanted by the FBI. They've been looking for help capturing her. We think you may be able to help with that. Like Miles said, her latest victim has already been taken advantage of. She's not going to stay in town much longer."

Harley sighed. "You have some sort of plan?"

Miles nodded. "She gave you the jewelry gifts, so we think she does actually care for you as a friend. Or, if nothing else, she may view you as a secondary mark she can swindle before bouncing out of town. Our plan is that you and Tate *break up*, somewhere public. Lots of witnesses. Then in your distraught state, call Emily for comfort and support. It's a long shot, but she may agree to meet. You guys talk for a bit, and when you go your separate ways, the authorities move in and arrest her."

It was a good plan. If we could keep her in public, it would be easier to capture Emily. She wouldn't dare use her magic in front of humans. It would be as dangerous as me shifting in broad daylight downtown.

Harley chuckled humorlessly. "It's almost like you guys wrote a scene for a movie."

The four of us exchanged a nervous look before Harley said, "Okay. I'll do it. If what she's been doing is true, she needs to answer for it. I can't believe this is happening. It's crazy."

Later that night, when we lay in bed, Harley curled into my chest, and said, "With everything that happened about Emily, I forgot to ask. What was in that box Luis left?"

My heart skipped a beat, and for half a second, I thought about lying. That idea fell apart fast. I'd already lied through my teeth today. There was enough being held back from Harley. In this one thing, I could be honest. I told her about the booties, the earrings, the note, everything. I also told her what I wanted to do to get back at Luis. After I was done, I held my breath, waiting for her response.

Finally, she said, "God, he's such an asshole. I'll take the DNA test. It's not because I question who the father is, but because I want to shove it in his face. It'll be for my peace of mind and to put it to rest once and for all."

I squeezed her close and said, "It makes sense to me, too. I'll schedule an appointment for the test after our fake break up."

"Oh lord, I forgot about that. I hope I don't screw it up. I was never a very good actor."

I'd thought the same thing about myself until today. Sometimes you surprise yourself. I said, "You'll do fine. Honestly, I think part of why you felt like someone was watching you was that Emily might have someone watching the house. We really think you might be her next victim."

"Maybe. It would make sense. It sort of breaks my heart that I was starting to trust her, and she was lying about everything."

"I'm sorry," I said automatically.

"Why are you sorry? You didn't have anything to do with it."

I said nothing—partly because I didn't know what to say, and partly because I was fairly certain it had everything to do with me. If anything happened to Harley because of what I was, I'd never forgive myself.

Chapter 26 - Harley

Breaking up was always hard. It was a lot harder when it was on the day you were scheduled to get a paternity test. It was even harder when the break up was fake. There'd never been a time in my life when I considered myself a good actor. Now, I was being asked to pretend to break up with Tate, make it believable, and then go running to Emily. Not only that, I had to keep acting like Emily was my bosom buddy. Could I fake cry? Would I need to? It was so stressful to think about it that I had a hard time focusing on what the doctor was saying.

I was sitting on the exam table, holding Tate's hand, the doctor's voice droning on and on. "…a very easy and simple procedure. It's non-invasive and ninety-nine percent accurate. There really is nothing to worry about. You and the baby will be fine."

None of what she'd said before had stuck, but I did understand that part. This was all safe. My baby was safe. That was what mattered the most. Secondarily, I could finally find out, for sure, if Tate really was the father. He was sure, and so was I, but knowing would take more stress out of our lives.

The doctor looked at Tate and smiled sadly. "Unfortunately, there can't be anyone else in the room while we perform the procedure. Mr. Mills will need to exit the room for a bit while we proceed."

Tate's hand tightened on mine. "Well, can't I sort of… stand in the corner? I'll be quiet. I'd really like to be here."

The doctor smiled again. "Again, this is a very safe procedure. No need to worry. Besides, I have a nurse ready to take your oral swab. You can go with her and get that taken care of. Once you're done, it will just be a few more minutes, and we'll be finished. It's simply our policy, I'm sorry."

Tate looked like he was ready to argue, but I gave him a nudge. "Tate, it's fine. It's just some blood. I'll be done in no time. You go on."

He looked at me and nodded. He gave me a quick kiss before leaving with a nurse. After worrying so much about it, I was a little surprised at how easy it was. Anticlimactic, in fact. All she did was take a vial of blood.

If I'd known it would be that simple, I probably would have argued for Tate to stay.

The doctor labeled the blood vial and patted my arm. "All done. You need to rest, and not stress about anything. We should have results in a few days."

Tate and I met in the hallway after we were both done. I asked, "How was yours?"

He raised his eyebrows. "She put that swab halfway down my throat. Not very pleasant, but I've experienced worse."

We stepped into the elevator. We were alone, and Tate said, "Are you good with the plan? The story seem believable?"

"I think so."

"Okay, we have to remember, if she doesn't bite, I'll need to stay at my place for a few nights. We'll have to make it look real in case she's watching. Don't worry, I promise I'll have extra eyes on you to make sure you're safe. You will be okay. No matter what."

He pulled me close and kissed me long and hard, making my knees weak. It was almost like a goodbye kiss.

That wasn't what I wanted, but I knew the next part would be difficult. It was his way of telling me he didn't mean any of what he was about to say. It was hard to hide the smile on my face when he pulled away.

The elevator doors opened, and he held me back, leaning out and looking around the foyer of the doctor's office. Then he leaned back in, and said, "Show time."

He stiffened, and a look of irritation and anger masked his face as he stomped away from me. I followed a few seconds later, already caught off guard by what a good job he was doing. Tate slammed his hands into the glass door and shoved it open. Every motion of his body exuded anger. He was intimidating like this, but I did my best to channel my inner movie star and pushed through the door with what I thought was a moderate reenactment of how he'd gone out.

The doctor's office was in a building right on Main Street. Lilly Valley was a small town, and most of the activity was located here. A strange combination of terror and excitement filled me when I saw how many people were out and about walking by. Excitement that there would be plenty of witnesses to our 'break up' and terror at how many people were going to watch as Tate and I pretended to nuke our relationship.

Tate spun on a heel and pointed at me. "You know what? I think it's horseshit you even asked me to do this damned test. Christ, if you'd been on the pill, we wouldn't even be worrying about this."

He seemed so angry that it took me a second to screw up my courage and reply. "Well, no one held a gun to your head and told you *not* to put on a condom. We both screwed up, don't pin it all on me."

Tate scoffed sarcastically. "Oh, okay. It's like that? Obviously one of us is at fault. Shit, I'm the one in here getting fucking DNA taken to prove I'm the father. How many guys did you fuck anyway? Jesus."

He was acting, but his words seemed so vitriolic that I actually felt a little hurt, and responded waspishly. "Well, if you're sticking your dick in every woman who walks by without putting a condom on, maybe I need to get another type of test."

A ghost of a smile flashed across Tate's face. He was fighting a laugh. He pulled himself under control and deepened his scowl. It was nice to see. I'd been ready to cry until then. We were being mean and nasty to each other. It felt like we were saying all the hateful things we wanted to say months ago when things had been awkward. Like it had all built up and was exploding right here and now. That trace of a smile kept me grounded, but there was still an ache in my chest.

"You don't even want this baby. Admit it. You just want to duck out on your responsibilities and do nothing. That's a shitty way to be a father."

People up and down the street had stopped to watch and gawk at our screaming match. I hoped Emily was watching. This was rough, and I hoped it was all worth it. Tate took three big steps backward and put his arms out to his sides, like he was being crucified.

He screamed, "You know what? You're right. Fuck off. Get out of my life, never talk to me again. You and that brat in your belly."

He spun on a heel and stomped away, jumping into his truck down the street and laying a strip of rubber on the road as he roared off. We were acting, it was a show, I knew that. The problem was, we'd done a really good job, and my body was pulsing with hormones, and I was still stressed beyond belief. Which meant that, despite me worrying if I could cry fake tears, I started sobbing and sank to my knees right on the sidewalk.

My hands fumbled at my purse, trying to dig out my cell phone to call Emily. The plan had always been for Tate to leave me stranded, making himself look like a total asshole. What no one else saw or knew was that Steff was waiting in an unmarked car in a nearby parking lot to swoop in and pick me up if Emily didn't take the bait. It made it a little better knowing that someone who knew what was going on was watching me, making sure I was safe.

Finally pulling the phone free, I dialed Emily's number. I prayed for her to answer as I wiped tears and snot off my face with a tissue from my purse.

When I was about to give up, she answered. "Harley?"

Obviously still crying, I said, "Emily? I need help. Tate's gone."

There was a long pause before she said, "What do you mean gone?"

"We had a fight. It was awful. He blew up at me and left me here at the doctor's office. He said he didn't want anything to do with me or the baby. I need you." My voice was clogged from the tears, and I was shockingly proud of my performance. "Please, can you come give me a ride? I don't have any way to get home. I'm so alone."

"Oh, sweetie. I'll be there soon. Just wait for me, okay?"

"Okay," I said miserably.

Hanging up, I stared at the phone, astounded that the plan was actually working. She was coming. I wiped the tears away, as I wasn't upset anymore, and sat on the sidewalk. The bystanders had all gone back to going about their business. Several folks looked like they were ready to ask if I needed help. I was torn, because they were being nice, but I was also lying. I didn't want some good Samaritan to use up a good deed on an act. I was both happy and sad that no one ended up checking on me. It was strange.

While I waited, my phone buzzed, and a single text from Tate came through: *I feel terrible about saying all that, but I think we did a good job selling it. Are you okay?*

I typed back: *All good. Emily is on the way. We should be in the movies lol.*

He sent me back a laughing face emoji. We were okay. Thank goodness. It made me feel better, but I also knew Emily would be there soon, so I tried to get my face back to the wretched mask of sadness and misery I'd had a few minutes ago.

Emily pulled up about fifteen minutes after I'd called. She nearly leaped out of her car and ran around to me. She knelt and helped me up.

"Oh my God. That piece of shit, I can't believe he did this to you," she said, wrapping me in a hug.

She let me go and wrapped an arm around my shoulder, guiding me to her car. She was supposed to get arrested. The cops had to be around here somewhere. They were probably waiting on Steff's word to run in and take her into custody. What if they were farther away than that, though? If I was in the car and driving away, it would be really hard to arrest her. I stopped right as she opened the passenger door.

"Emily, it's okay. I need a few minutes to get myself under control," I said.

She took my shoulder and not so roughly pushed me into the car. "You're distraught. You need a ride. I'm not letting my friend go through this alone in public. Let's go."

Emily closed the door behind me. I surreptitiously checked the handle, and a spike of fear hit me when I found the child locks were on. I couldn't open the door. My eyes were big as saucers by the time she circled the car and jumped in. This was not part of the plan. Where was Steff? Where were the cops and Tate? Emily's tires squealed as she pulled away from the curb.

One last glance back told me I was on my own. My heart pounded. Emily was a scam artist. She milked old people out of their money. She didn't kill anyone, she wasn't violent. At least, I hoped she wasn't.

"Um… where are we going?" I asked, as she passed the turn that I would usually use to go home.

Ignoring my question, she punched the steering wheel, making me jump. "Filthy damned animals. Disgusting. I can't believe this."

Her voice was almost out of control, vibrating with anger and… what? Revulsion? The car slowly ticked up in speed. Going from thirty, to fifty, then to seventy miles an hour. Stealing glances at her, I clutched at the armrest and wrapped another hand around my growing belly.

Emily continued staring out the window and mumbled, "They all need to be eradicated. A full cleansing of the earth. It's all they deserve." Snapping out of her strange trance, she turned to me and said, "I'm so sorry. This isn't how I wanted all this to go."

"For… what? How *what* was supposed to go?" I asked, my fear building with every second. She seemed unhinged.

Emily shook her head and chuckled ruefully. She looked back at the road, and I noticed something impossible. Her hands. I had to be hallucinating. All the little creases in Emily's knuckles were glowing. Almost like light was shining through them. I blinked, and instead of the light disappearing, it seemed to have spread. Now, the light was faintly radiating from both her hands. What the hell was going on? The world had taken on a surreal quality. So much so that I dug my nails into my leg, hoping to wake myself up from whatever fevered dream I was in. Unfortunately, I was already awake.

"This is all my fault," Emily said, sounding apologetic. "It's my fault that piece of shit found you."

Snapping my head toward her, I said, "Luis?"

"No," she said, exasperated. "Tate. He would have never found you if it wasn't for me. You'd have gone your whole life without ever knowing it was even alive. But I forced it to find you."

Nothing made sense, and why was she calling Tate *It*? Already I was wondering if, maybe, Miles had been wrong. Had she done more than steal money? Was she dangerous? My God, what if she was a serial killer or something? Every word she was saying sounded insane. I continued to huddle close to the door, putting as much space between Emily and myself as I could. Then the car picked up a little more speed, and I swallowed hard. We were rushing into the mountains, the wilderness.

"Don't worry, Harley, I'm going to take care of everything. Tate will be the first to pay. I'll make sure of it."

"Wha… what does that mean, Emily?"

She looked at me, her eyes wild with rage and anger, psychotic eyes that sent shivers of terror into my soul. This was not the woman I'd gotten to know over the last few months. This was some other person entirely.

She hissed, "Every shifter, every single one of them, needs to be eradicated."

"What the hell is a shif—"

Before I could finish my question, I felt a thump behind us as the car was rear ended. A short yelp burst out of my mouth, and I tugged at my seatbelt, only to realize I hadn't buckled it. I clicked it home and looked at Emily. She was checking her mirror, her teeth bared like an animal.

"You know, you've got shit taste in men, sweetie. First, you fuck a gangster, then you bed a damned shifter. You've got to try better, Harley."

There it was again. What the hell was a shifter? Emily was deranged, that was the only explanation. Before she could say anything else, another car shot in front of us. It wasn't the car that had hit us. Glancing over my shoulder, I could see it was a white van, but the windshield was too dark for me to see the driver. I recognized the car in front of us as Steff's car. I took a breath, knowing he was here. I wasn't alone, but why just him? Where the hell were the cops? They'd said the cops would be nearby.

Emily leaned on the steering wheel and screamed at her windshield, "You'll all pay. All of you animals." Spit flew from her lips and spattered the glass as she screamed, fully unhinged now.

Another car slammed into the back of us. Emily's hands slipped from the wheel as we were pushed into the car in front of us. Steff's rear end spun around, and he slid off onto the shoulder. Our car began to spin out of control, pushed along by the car behind us. My hands dug into the upholstery, my teeth bared, bracing for impact. We were going at least seventy when the rear tires went off the road, and hit a tree stump. The car lifted, and we flipped through the air. I wrapped my arms around my belly, asking every God there might be in the universe to save my baby.

As my stomach did barrel rolls while the car spun in the air, a strange pulse of energy burst through the car. It rippled through, and it almost was like the air itself became thick and viscous. The car's flip slowed and then stopped. While we were still in the air. I opened my eyes and saw Emily, her hands thrust out, glowing like miniature suns. Sweat beaded on her face and dripped down her cheeks. She looked like she was straining hard, almost as though she was holding the car up herself, but that was impossible—as equally impossible as the glow of her hands. Knowing that my mind must have snapped, I leaned back as the car slowly lowered to the ground and came to rest against a tree that we'd been about to slam into when... whatever it was had happened.

My breath hissed in and out of my lungs like I'd run a marathon. I looked at Emily. She was slumped over. If I *felt* like I'd run a marathon, she looked like she'd *actually* run three or four in a row. She looked absolutely exhausted.

"Emily?" I gasped. "What in the hell just happened."

Emily lifted her head as though it weighed a hundred pounds. Her eyes were half-lidded. She opened her mouth to speak, but she never got the words out. Her groggy eyes snapped open in surprise. Instead of speaking, I heard her scream, then I heard the passenger window behind me shatter. Before I could turn, a hand slid around my head. A gloved hand pressed something against my face. I slapped at the hand once, and then everything went dark.

Chapter 27 - Tate

Things had gone sideways in a bad way. My truck literally couldn't go any faster, no matter how hard I stomped on the gas. My panic was almost enough to make driving dangerous. My heart was jackhammering, and I was sure it would tear free of my chest any second now. I'd never been so worried in my life.

Steff had called me about twenty minutes after Harley and I had our fake break up. He hadn't sounded like I thought he would.

"Tate? Bro, I don't know what happened."

"What do you mean? Is Harley okay?" I asked, already getting anxious.

"I have no idea. Emily took the bait, for sure. She came by and got her into her car, and took off. A van pulled out with them, though. It was following Emily. Tailing them. It was pretty obvious. I'm following them now. Emily is fucking flying. The van is keeping pace. They've got to be going seventy-five or eighty on these little back roads. It's dangerous."

I'd already jumped back into my truck. "Where are they going?"

"Heading north on highway twelve. Hang on, I'm going to try to get around both cars. If I can get in front of them, I may be able to force them to slow down and stop."

Dirt spun under my tires, and I pulled my truck out onto the street, heading toward Steff's directions. "Steff, be careful."

"I'm in front… I'll just… shit, shit, shit—"

"Steff? Steff? Steffen, are you fucking okay?" It felt like my heart was going to explode.

Steff coughed. "I'm good. They pushed me off the damn road. Car's fine, I'm trying to get back on the highway. I…"

Steff trailed off. At first, I thought the phone had cut out or something, but I could hear him breathing. Finally, he whispered, "Holy shit. This witch is legit."

"What?" It was torture having to listen to all this being relayed through Steff's phone. I just wanted to be there and see what was happening.

"The van ran Emily's car off the road. It flipped into the air, but sh… she caught it with magic and lowered it. Dude, I've never seen anything like that in my life. It's crazy. How far away are you, Tate?"

"I don't know, I'm heading toward where you said. What's wrong?"

"I can't tell for sure. A couple of guys got out of the van. Shit! One of them has Harley!"

My heart was nearly bursting out of my chest. All I wanted was to be there. I pressed my foot harder on the accelerator, willing the truck to go faster. "Steff, what do you mean they have her?"

"Wow, oh Christ. Emily just blasted one of the guys. It's bright as shit. That's crazy, Jesus. Tate, what do I do? Do I stop and try to catch Emily or follow the van? What do you want?"

"Steff, don't you lose her. You hear me? Don't you lose Harley."

"I'm doing my best. I shot Blayne a text right before I called you. He should be right behind you. Maybe you guys can get to the scene before Emily gets away."

I'd hung up with him at that point. Then all I had for company was the screaming sound of my truck roaring down the highway and the buzz of my tires on the road. Five minutes later, when I finally saw the car resting off the side of the road, leaning against a tree, I let out a hiss of anger. Seeing that car was proof Harley had been taken. I punched the steering wheel to keep my mind off the fact that my heart was breaking. Pulling to the soft shoulder, I slammed on the brakes and jammed it into park. I was out of the truck and running before it had fully come to a stop.

Steff had been right, Emily had taken out someone. There was a guy on the ground. He wasn't dead. His left hand was absently pushing at the dirt and grass around him. Like he was trying to get up, but had no idea how. A quick glance into the car showed me Emily wasn't inside. Kneeling, I grabbed the guy by the collar of his shirt and dragged him to the car.

I had him up and against the car when I heard screeching tires behind me. Thinking I'd see Luis or a pack of hunters jumping me, I was relieved to see Blayne leaping from his car and running toward me. Baring my teeth, I turned back to the man in my grasp.

The guy's head was lolling around, almost like he was dead, but his eyes flicked around. I wasn't sure what type of spell Emily had hit him with, but it had fully thrown him for a loop. Jerking his collar then slapping him in the face seemed to help. He blinked and looked more or less awake.

"Who the fuck are you?" I growled.

The man glanced back and forth between me and Blayne before he said, "Ortiz hired me. He ordered me to follow this Harley chick. Said once she was away from you and secluded, we take her."

I growled at him, deep and throaty—and unmistakably inhuman. The man pressed himself against the car, his eyes growing wide and fearful. "I... I wasn't going to hurt her. We ran them off the road, but that was a last-minute order. Once Luis knew the other guy had followed us, he told us to."

"That makes it better?" I screamed in his face, "Someone ordered you to purposely wreck a car with a pregnant woman in it?"

"I'm sorry." The guy sobbed. "I wasn't even driving. I don't even remember what happened. I got out and ran to the car, I busted out the window, and…" He trailed off, eyes going distant. "The lady in the driver's seat screamed and threw her hands up. There was a flash of light, and then…" he paused, shaking his head, "…I woke up on the ground with you jerking me up."

Before I could say anything else, a sizzle ran up my back. A feeling of perceived power, almost like I was standing next to a high-voltage power line.

I glanced at Blayne. "Do you feel that?"

Frowning, Blayne asked, "What?"

Then I heard the snapping twigs. Spinning around, I dropped the man and looked toward the surrounding forest. From behind a massive oak tree, Emily strolled out. She smiled without humor and raised an eyebrow at me. Blayne stiffened beside me. She wasn't the same as the last time I'd been near her in Harley's house. The power pulsing out of her was almost beyond description. Siobhan was nothing compared to Emily. This was a witch on a totally different level. The scent of magic was almost so overpowering that I couldn't smell it anymore. I felt it in my pores, and in my hair follicles. It was terrifying. It may have been affecting me more than Blayne since I was a dragon shifter. My species had a closer kinship to magic than bears or wolves or other earthly realm creatures.

"You're a piece of shit boyfriend, Tate. Why couldn't you protect Harley?" Emily spat. She looked furious. "Damned shifter garbage. You didn't deserve Harley. She needs something better than one of you filthy animals. If I could undo the spell, I would."

I pointed at her. "Explain that! What did you do?"

Emily smirked at me, like a teacher who knew the answer, and the student was too stupid to figure it out. I wanted to lash out at her, to attack her. Blayne's body was humming next to me, wound tight and ready to spring. He felt the same way. Both of us knew we had to get information. We had to control ourselves to hear what she had to say.

"I tracked you *things* to this town. I created a spell, a very special one. I cast it across the entire town of Lilly Valley. It was supposed to force any shifter into a mating bond. Create fated mates that you couldn't pull yourselves away from." She smiled and winked. "You see the beauty, right? Pull you and another shifter together? Two birds with one stone? Well, two dead birds and one stone."

"Bitch," Blayne whispered.

"See, I can see all the connections. I can see what my spell is doing even though you can't. Faint golden threads surrounding the shifters, leading to other gold threads of your mates. But I knew I'd fucked up when your gold thread was wrapped around Harley. Human threads are white, and that should *not* have been possible. I followed your thread and found you. Disgusting thing that you are, I could almost follow my nose. Dragon shifter, aren't you? Very rare. You'll make a good trophy."

"When I saw that gold thread tied to Harley, it was all I could do to keep my composure. I didn't think it was even remotely possible. I had to inspect my spell again. On second look? There are some interesting things I've done, very interesting."

I growled. "Will the spell kill Harley? Will it?"

She looked at me like I was an idiot. "I like Harley, I care for her. I don't attack humans. I don't murder, pillage, and feast on humans. Not like you filth. No, humans have to be protected from things like you." She raised an eyebrow, and a psychotic grin lit on her face. "Now, as for that abomination growing in her belly? That will need to be taken care of."

It was so fast. I didn't know I could move that fast. In a blink, I was on her, covering the twenty feet between us in less than a second. I slammed into her, wrapping my hands around her throat, throttling her. She was so caught off guard, she couldn't even summon her powers. My fingers dug into the soft flesh at the back of her neck, my thumbs pressing into the weak skin of her throat. My dragon's rage spilled out of me as I choked her.

Emily beat at my arms with her hands, then choked out, "I have more to tell you."

The words bounced off me, almost completely unheard. All I wanted was to watch the life spill out of her eyes, and then my dragon would incinerate her body so her ashes could scatter in the wind. Emily's face grew red as I squeezed tighter.

"You'll… you'll all die if you deny your mates… souls… ripped apart."

Blayne was at my side, pulling on my arm. "Tate. Tate, let her go, man. You aren't a killer, come on."

Blayne was one of my best friends, but in this, he didn't know what he was talking about. At this moment, I most definitely was a killer. I would kill her, and I was sure that I wouldn't regret it. She'd threatened my unborn baby. Neither I, nor my dragon could let that go unpunished.

Emily was slipping away, barely able to keep her eyes open, then she hissed, "Human... mates... if they're... claimed... they'll become shifters, too."

My fingers jerked open on a spasm, the words hitting me like a shotgun blast. Emily dropped to the ground, retching and gasping for breath. She sat on her knees, dry heaving and trying to get air into her body. Blayne's eyes looked just as wide as mine must have been. Had we heard that right?

"If you claim Harley, she'll become a shifter?" Blayne asked.

"But if I don't claim her, I'll die. That's what she said."

Emily, now partially recovered, chuckled maniacally. "How about you do us and the world a favor and don't claim Harley. I'll sit outside your house and listen to your screams as you die the most painful death you can imagine. Besides, if you claim her and make her into a shifter, then she's as unclean as you. She'll be a target for the hunters."

My blood ran cold. She stood, wiping the dirt off her jeans, and took a few steps away to put distance between us. My hands were still clenched into claws. I could still imagine her neck between my fingers.

"Tate, this is not what I'd planned. We'll call it a happy accident. One way or another, my spell will be the end of your kind."

Before I could say anything, my cell rang. I pulled it from my pocket and answered when I saw it was Steff.

"Where's Harley?" I barked.

"I'm still following the van. I haven't lost sight of them."

Emily was walking back into the woods. She called back to us, "I'm going to save Harley, Tate. Do us a favor and go die. Alone."

The seething hatred in my heart for Emily was screaming for me to go after her. To sprint into the woods, shift into my dragon, and tear the flesh from her bones, but Harley was my first priority. I watched her disappear into the shadows and reluctantly turned back to Luis's hired man.

I knelt next to him. He looked beyond confused by everything he'd just heard.

I held the phone to his ear and said, "Details. Where did Luis instruct for Harley to be taken? Now."

The guy spoke into the phone, giving Steff the details and location—somewhere deep in the mountains. When he was done, I let out some of my frustration by slugging him in the jaw and knocking his ass out again. Blayne started tying the guy up, and I went back to the phone.

"Did you get all that, Steff?"

"Yeah, I know the place. Real ritzy joint. Been up for sale for years. Want to meet me there?"

I nodded. "Yeah. We'll leave this piece of shit tied up here. I'll make an anonymous call to the cops and give them the location. Go ahead and call Miles. We'll have the whole crew there to fuck up Luis's plan."

"Don't you want to tell the cops about this?" Steff asked.

It would have been the smart thing to do, but I wanted these assholes for myself, so did my dragon. "No. This is personal. No cops."

"If you're cool, I'm cool," Steff said and hung up.

After the guy was tied up and secured to a nearby tree, I pulled the guy's cell phone out and dialed 911. I dropped it a few feet away and let it ring. They'd trace the call and find him here. Blayne and I went to our cars.

Before we got in, Blayne asked, "Do you think she was telling the truth? Emily, I mean."

My gut instinct told me she was. Something about how powerful my connection was to Harley and how much discomfort I was in when I was far away from her made too much sense. I nodded.

"Shit," Blayne said and got into his car.

I climbed into my truck, mentally cursing Emily for this. All of it. As though I didn't have enough to worry about. First hunters, then a mate, a baby, Luis, and a witch. Now this double-edged sword. If I denied the bond, I would die. Harley, the baby, and the girls would be left behind, alone and broken. If I claimed her? She would become like me, a shifter, and her life would be at risk.

Chapter 28 - Harley

The first thing I noticed was the nausea. Keeping my eyes closed because I didn't want anyone to know I was awake, I tried to listen for any clue as to where I was. My head was cloudy, I was awake, but it was like I was stuck halfway inside a dream. What had happened to me?

Footsteps clicked nearby, approaching. I swallowed despite myself, pushing the sick feeling in my stomach away. The steps stopped right beside me—whoever it was stood right above me. Trying to appear like I was still asleep, I forced my body to stay still. Apparently, I did a poor job pretending to be asleep.

"Mrs. King, I know you're awake. Can you open your eyes?" The voice was male, deep, and calm.

Knowing I had no other choice, I opened my eyes, then immediately closed them again. The brightness of the room sent slivers of pain into my head. Not only was I sick to my stomach, but my head was throbbing. Had they drugged me? Squinting against the light, I opened them again.

The man standing above me looked at me impassively, his arms clasped behind his back. As my eyes grew accustomed to the light, I could take in the room around me as well. It was almost gaudy in its luxury. The bed I lay on was a four-poster with hanging curtains of thick velvet. The lights and fixtures were gold accented, a bookcase in the back and a desk beside it were dark, rich-colored wood—mahogany if I had to guess. The room itself was huge for a bedroom, and it gave me the impression that I was in some sort of mansion.

The man took a glass from beside the table and held it out to me. "Please drink."

The last thing I wanted was to take anything from this man, but my throat was so dry I could barely swallow. It was like I'd swallowed a mouth full of sand. I took the glass and sipped at the water. As much as I hated it, that one drink was heaven, and it was all I could do to not sigh in satisfaction. Looking into the shimmering water of the glass, the last few hours slammed back into my mind. The doctor's visit, Tate and my break up performance, Emily, the wreck.

The stranger said, "My name is Javier. I'm here on Mr. Ortiz's orders. I'm to keep you safe and comfortable until the situation is completely handled. Once he's done, Mr. Ortiz will come to collect you."

"Collect me?" I asked. Like I was some trunk of knick-knacks he was getting from a yard sale?

Javier looked me dead in the eye, and a ghost of a smile played across his lips. "We are going to take out the trash, so to speak. Once a certain person is out of the way, you and your girls will be moved back to New York. Mr. Ortiz will have everything prepared so that your family can truly begin. Then he can welcome his new son and be there to help raise him in his rightful home."

He said it all with such emotionless formality that it took a second for me to understand what he'd meant. The guy was like a prim and proper butler or something, but there was danger lurking beneath the surface. His hair was perfectly combed and slicked back, but there were what looked like prison tattoos on his hands, fingers, and neck. The suit he wore appeared to be off-the-rack and ill-fitting. It was like Luis had dressed up some thug and given him a script to read to make things less terrifying. It did the opposite, actually. It showed that Luis was very serious about all this. He'd made plans, and called in friends. All of which with two goals in mind. One, he wanted to get me and the kids back to New York. Two, he was going to kill Tate and anyone who tried to stop them.

Javier stared at me. He tried to look at me impassively, but there was something underneath. A hungry glint in his stare. I had the distinct feeling that if he hadn't been scared of Luis, he might have tried to give me more than a glass of water. I had to choose my words carefully. There was no way to know what might set the man off and make things more difficult.

"Do you really think Tate is going to let me go without a fight? He's just going to roll over and let Luis take us?"

Javier cocked an eyebrow. "If Mr. Mills feels the need to make things difficult, a bullet to the skull should do the trick. Most people tend to give up once their brains have been blown out the back of their heads. We have plenty of guns to choose from."

My heart revved up, hammering against my ribs. My face remained an emotionless mask, but inside I was freaking out. They meant it. They really did. My panic caused my thoughts to spiral, bouncing through my mind.

They focused on Emily in an attempt to forget about what was happening with Luis. It seemed that she wasn't working for or with Luis, but if that was the case, what was she doing?

She'd definitely been on the verge of some type of breakdown in the car. She'd been talking crazy, and that weird light that had come from her hands? Had that really happened or had that been a hallucination on my part? Then there were the things she was saying. Shifters? What did that mean? What was a shifter? Was it some synonym she had for a liar or cheat? Nothing made any sense. Was Emily crazy? Was I?

Javier was examining my breasts in great detail when we heard a commotion outside. Screams and muffled gunshots. Javier's calm demeanor faded as he turned his head to the window.

He stepped toward the window, murmuring, "What the fuck?"

Before he got there to see what was happening, a radio clipped to his belt cracked, and a panicked voice screamed out, "Javi. Javi. Where the fuck are you, man?"

Javier unclipped the radio. "I'm here, what the hell is going on?"

The man screamed over the sounds of gunfire and… something else, a screeching roar of some sort. "They're taking us down. I need back up. What the fuck are they—"

The man's words cut off, replaced by a high-pitched agonized scream, then the radio went silent.

Javier's eyes widened as he stared at the quiet radio. He threw it to the ground and sprinted to the window, trying to see what was happening to his men. From my bed, all I could see was the blackness of the window. I could see Javier's eyes widen even more, then an orange flash from outside lit his features. It was like someone had shot a blast from a flame thrower outside. Javier's shoulders slackened, and he slowly backed away from the window.

Whatever he'd seen had shaken him to the core. His face was almost ghost white, and his eyes were glassy. It looked like he was in shock. He slowly went to his knees, trying to steady himself.

The last thing he said before he fainted was a single whispered question I could barely hear over the chaos outside. "Dragon?"

He fell forward, unconscious, his head bouncing off the wooden floor like a basketball. For a split second, I thought about sprinting to the window to see what would cause a hardened criminal to pass out from fright, but I'd seen this movie before. There was only one thing to do. As much as my curiosity demanded to know what was happening, my fight-or-flight response was stronger. I ran. I ran faster than I'd ever run in my life.

The bedroom door was unlocked. Javier must not have thought to lock it while he was in the room with me. Not knowing which way to go, I chose directions at random. I didn't even pay attention to where I was, I just kept going, taking stairs downward whenever I found them. If I was going to get out, it had to be down, right? After what seemed like an eternity, I found myself in what was obviously the kitchen. I snatched a massive butcher knife off a magnetic knife rack and opened a door that looked like it led outside.

Almost stumbling on the edge of the door, I stepped out onto a concrete patio. The sounds I'd heard coming from outside had died down, and everything was almost eerily quiet. There was a faint glow from the left of the patio, and I assumed that must be the driveway, so I ran toward it. Hopefully, one of the cars would have keys in the ignition. After I rounded the corner and came to the front of the house, I slid to a stop and gaped at the sight in front of me.

Men were lying everywhere. Face down, face up, one was lying on top of a car, the roof crumpled in like he'd been dropped from twenty feet up. They were everywhere. I couldn't tell if they were unconscious or if they were dead. It was like a war zone.

Before I could even process what I was seeing, I heard a familiar voice barking orders. "Inside. Check inside. Harley, where are you?" Tate bellowed.

I ran for his voice, like a child waking from a nightmare. Safety was at hand. Once I was in Tate's arms, things would be better. That was when he ran from behind a decorative hedgerow. I dropped my knife and slid in the grass, thumping onto my butt. A whole new terror flooded into my body. He looked... enraged. His eyes were blazing with anger and panic. They weren't just blazing, they were actually glowing. Gold, like the hottest coal of a fire. He almost looked inhuman, like something deep inside him was angry and trying to rip free. Tate didn't seem to notice the terror on my face. He stepped forward, his face going almost completely back to normal. I did my best not to flinch away from him.

He turned and called back over his shoulder, "Miles, I found her. Blayne, Steff, over here."

Without another word, Tate started running his hands over me, looking for injuries. All I could do was look at his eyes. They still glowed with that strange gold light I'd seen a moment before. Without the snarling, angry face, it was less terrifying. It was fading, but still obvious. It was impossible. That was a word I'd thought a lot of the past few hours. That was when I remembered what Emily had said. *Shifters*.

"Tate," I whispered.

"Huh?" He grunted, checking my knees for scratches.

"Your eyes are glowing."

His hands froze above my knee cap. He blinked several times before raising his face to meet my eyes. When I got a look at him, the glow was gone, but he looked tense and worried.

He caressed my leg. "We need to go."

He helped lift me, and I took his hand, following. My feet were moving, one in front of the other, but where yesterday I would have been happy and content to walk with Tate and hold his hand, now there was a tinge of fear. What was happening? Emily's voice was in my head again.

Every shifter, every single one of them needs to be eradicated. That word again. Shifter.

Tate escorted me to his truck and helped me get in, and buckled me up. As he closed the door, Blayne, Miles, and Steff came jogging up to him. With the doors closed, I couldn't overhear their conversation. Tate was speaking and gesturing, a look of worry on his face. He pointed to the truck and said something. That was when the others reacted to something. Steff put his hands on his head, looking up at the night sky in shock. Miles and Blayne looked like someone had kicked them in the gut. It took everything I had not to open the door to hear what was being said. All three of them glanced at me through the windshield before nodding at something Tate said, then they disappeared, walking away from the truck.

Tate got into the driver's seat and started driving us home. The silence was palpable. Normally, I'd have been uncomfortable, but it was sort of welcome. I needed time to think and process everything that had happened today. Tate gripped the steering wheel like his fingers were a vise. He was still angry about everything that had happened, but there was something else on his face. A battle or an argument was going on inside his head. It was evident in the way his lips twitched, and his eyes squinted. Like he was mentally evaluating some decision.

After going about ten miles, he sighed. Without looking at me, asked, "What did Emily say to you in the car?"

My heart told me to lie, or change the subject, but my brain knew that wouldn't work. Instead, I told him everything. The talk about shifters, the light that came from her hands, the way she'd somehow stopped the car from wrecking, the way Javier had fainted while whispering the word 'dragon.' It was all laid out, and even after I verbalized all of it, it still made zero sense. It was like I was stuck in a different universe or something.

Tate's grip on the steering wheel grew tighter the longer I talked, his knuckles going white. When I finished, he asked, "Are you afraid of me?"

His voice was like that of a little boy asking if his mom was mad at him for breaking some rule. He sounded small and broken-hearted. It would have been sad and heart wrenching, if the answer wasn't so difficult for me to summon.

Skirting the actual answer, I said, "Well, you're being super intense. And I have to admit, shit's a little weird. What did Emily do to the car? How did the four of you take out like a dozen armed guards without getting hurt? And why in the fuck were your eyes glowing? That's the big one."

"I love you, and I would never hurt you," Tate whispered.

He loved me? It was the first time he'd said those words to me. It was the first time a man had professed love for me since Sam died. My breath caught in my throat, unable to form words. So many emotions surged within me then. Fear, excitement, terror... maybe my own love for him. It was too much. Too much for one day.

He went on. "Remember, I promised to keep you safe. I will not fail. I stand by my word." He glanced at me, and his eyes were glowing again. I sucked in a gasp. "Don't be afraid. Not of me. And not of anyone else. They'll protect you with their life."

"They? Who's *they*?" I asked.

Tate was silent for several seconds before he shrugged and said, "You'll know soon enough."

The rest of the ride was quiet. We were both wrapped up in our thoughts. There was no way to know what Tate was thinking. My own mind spun through so many possibilities that it was almost an endless parade of nightmares. By the time we finally pulled into the driveway, I was mentally, emotionally, *and* physically exhausted.

"The girls have no idea you were taken. I'll leave that up to you if you want them to know," Tate said. "Once you get in and have the girls settled and into bed, come over to my place. I've got a lot I need to tell you. No more secrets."

I glanced at the dark outlines of his house, then at mine with the bright windows. One looked depressing, the other looked warm and inviting.

"Aren't you coming to my house? Why would you stay over there?"

A miserable, heartbroken look slid across Tate's features. He looked awful when he whispered, "You may not want me around the girls once I tell you everything."

Not knowing how to respond to that, I nodded. His answer scared me, but there was nothing to do now. I'd have to wait to find out what the hell was going on in an hour or two when the girls were asleep. Without another word, I unbuckled my seatbelt and got out of the truck. As I walked up the path to the door, I heard Tate back his truck across the street and into his driveway. Before I opened the front door, I made the decision not to tell the girls what had happened. There was too much to deal with, without me needing to explain the whole story and calm them down. It was for the best, and it would only exhaust me further. I wasn't sure if it was the right call, but it was what I was going to do. Before I stepped inside, I glanced back at Tate's house. It was still dark, but now somehow ominous. A chill went up my spine, and I closed and locked the door as soon as I was inside.

Chapter 29 - Tate

The early fall night was pleasant. There was a cool breeze coming down from the mountains, and it helped cool me off. Sitting on my back patio, I thought about all the time I'd spent with Harley and the girls. In some ways, it had been the best months of my life. Having people to come home to. People who wanted me around, and were, maybe, beginning to love me. There had never been anything like it. Now, all that might be over.

The guys and I had discussed things earlier. There might be a loophole to the spell Emily had cast. If I rejected my bond with Harley, I was as good as dead. Not just dead, but a painful, agonizing death. I didn't want to do that. Not only because, obviously, I didn't want to die screaming. That was a given. The main reason was that I loved her. Because I loved her, I didn't want her to turn into a shifter. Our loophole was that if Harley rejected me, maybe the spell would be broken. If she rejected me, and the spell was broken, then perhaps later on, we could get back together.

I would never walk away from her and my boy. That was non-negotiable. I would be there to help raise him. I would teach Harley about raising whelps—what we called child dragon shifters. She would need me. I, and my dragon, were sure the baby was going to be born a shifter. For the most part, raising a shifter child was the same as a human child. The issue came about when dragon shifters hit puberty. Our version of puberty, anyway. Sexual maturity still came at the usual time. Twelve or thirteen. Dragons hit shifter puberty at five years old. There was no way a human mother could handle that type of challenge. The eyes began to glow when their emotions got too high. They produced excessive amounts of heat from their bodies if they couldn't control it. I would have to teach him how to control all the things that would happen to him. Only I could show him how to ignore the base instincts that would be like a raging storm inside his mind.

That alone, even if I wasn't in love with her, would require that I stay in her life. She could reject me, and stay safe, but I would always be there for them. It really might be the best option. Life as a shifter was hard enough being born one. There was no way I could imagine living your whole life as a human, and then suddenly, without warning, becoming one. Would Harley go crazy? Accept it? Kill herself? Any scenario, and a hundred others, were possible. It was too hard to even think about.

I heard the front door of Harley's house open and close. My hearing wasn't as good as a wolf shifter like Miles, but it was still incredibly well attuned. My keys were already in my hand, so I stood and walked around my house to the front yard. My heart was hammering away in my chest, and it only got heavier when I saw Harley. She was walking toward me, her hands twisting the hem of her shirt.

"I'd like you to go somewhere with me," I said.

She glanced back at the house, then said, "I'm a little worried about leaving the girls. Especially with what happened today."

"I totally understand that. I took precautions. All the guys are nearby watching the house. Miles is upstairs in my room, Blayne is down at the end of the cul-de-sac in a sedan, and Steff is hiking the woods behind your house. They'll be even safer than if you were there. They will die for them if need be."

She sighed and shook her head. "Tate, how can you know that? Men don't usually die for people they barely know."

I looked her in the eyes. "They're more than just men." Without letting her respond to that, I said, "Will you come with me?"

Her face was a window to the war going on in her mind. I watched her weigh the benefits and consider the arguments. Thankfully, after a few seconds, she said, "Okay."

The drive was nearly silent, which was good. I wasn't sure I could have had a long conversation with the struggle going on inside me. My dragon was not happy with my plan. For the first time in my life, I could feel that it was angry with me. It was afraid that if I went through with what I planned, Harley would for sure reject us. Even the thought of that made my dragon almost jibber with panic. I had to remind it that all this was for Harley's safety—that doing this may be the only way to keep her safe. Sadness washed over me, all of it emanating from the dragon. I apologized to him mentally. *I'm sorry. It's the only way.*

We arrived at my usual shifting location. High up in the mountains. There was great deer hunting up here. It was a special place for me, and I couldn't think of a better place to bring Harley. We got out of the truck and walked side-by-side, not speaking. Once we got a little way into the woods, we found the clearing I knew well. Harley looked at me in a way I couldn't even describe. It was like she was trying to see *through* me, as if she was trying to see something deep inside me.

"Emily kept calling you a shifter. Is that... true?"

I nodded, too afraid to speak.

"What does that mean? Like, a shapeshifter? Like in some movie or something? Are you supposed to be a werewolf?"

"Not a werewolf, no. Not me, anyway. But yes, it's what you're thinking."

Harley stared at me for several seconds, then her face broke into a huge manic smile, and she started laughing. Blinking, I took a step back, not sure what she was laughing at. She continued laughing, big belly laughs, until she began crying. The laughter became almost hysterical. She put her hands in her hair, and took a huge deep breath to calm herself.

She walked in a tight circle, mumbling to herself. "What the fuck is even happening? Am I going crazy? Wait, that guy that captured me said he saw a dragon. Is that what you are? What's happening, what's happening, what's happening?"

Harley was on the verge of a breakdown. I couldn't let that happen. I stepped forward and put my hands on her shoulders. "Calm down."

Harley slapped my hands away, startling me, and pointed a finger in my face. Her voice was venomous. "Don't you tell me to calm down. Don't fucking do that. Do you have any idea what I saw with Emily? She held a car in the air like some goddamned wizard. I thought I was going crazy. You don't get to tell me any damned thing until I know exactly what's happening."

Harley was still crying, but this time it wasn't hysterical tears, it was tears of fear and anger. I was worried about the baby and what all the stress might be doing to him.

Holding my hands up, I said, "Okay… it's okay. I don't want to make you more upset. I'll just take you home. We can forget the whole thing."

Harley was only five-foot-six, petite, and unassuming. Still, when she took two steps toward me, snarling and enraged, I felt a twinge of fear. I resisted the urge to jerk back.

She slapped my chest. "You aren't taking me any-fucking-where until you tell me why the hell your eyes glow, and how Emily can shoot forcefields out of her hands."

Most of Harley's rage seemed to melt out of her, and she sagged in exhaustion. Now that she was calmed down, I took her hand and led her to a small outcropping of rocks and sat with her.

I took a breath and jumped into the story. "So, there are secrets about the world you and your kind aren't aware of. The unnatural is not easy to accept. I *am* a shifter. My kind have roamed the earth for centuries, thousands of years, really. We are magical creatures, and due to that magic and how dangerous we are perceived to be, we usually stay in our human form. We integrate into human societies. After some time, we really seem to be more human than beast."

"We actually changed to keep our secret hidden. We are born as human babies now instead of eggs. We don't even get to know our beast until several years after we're born. Our son will be born a shifter. I can already feel it."

Harley was trembling and put a hand to her mouth. "What are you talking about? How is this real?"

"There's more. There is a group, they've been around for centuries. We simply call them Hunters. Their creed, their very reason for being, is to eradicate every shifter on earth. They hunt us, and kill us like the animals they think we are. Emily is... Jesus, this is complicated... she's a witch."

Harley's eyes went wide. "A witch? Like, magic wand? Poof, abracadabra? Harry Po—"

"Yes, and no. Emily is a witch but, as you saw, there's no need for a wand. Her power is from within. She's in league with a band of hunters. They've already captured and killed several of us in the surrounding area. We think she got close to you to kill me, Steff, Blayne, and

Miles. We're all shifters. Miles is a wolf shifter, Blayne is a panther, Steff is a bear."

Harley said, "The guy who had me prisoner in the mansion, before he fainted, he mumbled something about a dragon. Was that you outside?"

I nodded. "We got to the mansion and were attacked. When I'm in my dragon form, my scales are impenetrable to man-made bullets. I shifted to protect myself as well as… get my rage out. Shifting hadn't been part of the plan. We'd intended to go in quietly and try to get you out without anyone knowing we were there. Things got out of hand."

Harley stared at me. The look on her face told me she didn't believe it. There was a part of her that wanted to, I could almost see it in her eyes. The problem was there was too much *stuff* in her head to keep her from fully accepting—thousands of hours of school, untold documentaries, hundreds of books, magazines, and articles, that claimed reality and the world were only what science said was possible. Everything she'd ever been told pushed her against believing. Witches weren't real, werewolves were the stuff of movies, dragons were myths. I had to show her. There was no other way.

I stood and took a few steps away. Looking into her eyes, I said, "Remember, I love you. I love you so much. My dragon loves you, too. We would never hurt you. Ever. Please don't be afraid."

Before she could say anything, I shifted. My arms elongated and stretched out into wings. My skin slipped away, replaced with bright scales. My jaw expanded, my teeth sharpened and became rows of fangs. In seconds I stood before her, a fully formed dragon straight out of a story book.

I could feel my dragon's excitement and also trepidation. It'd never been so worried. I could sense how terrified it was that Harley would run screaming. Rejection would be almost unbearable to my dragon—to me as well.

Harley looked up at me as I towered above her, and started laughing hysterically again. "I'm hallucinating. That has to be it."

My dragon leaned down and pressed his snout gently to her belly. She gasped, feeling his warm scales against her body. I waited there, with our head bowed, touching the baby inside her. I waited for her to call me a freak, a monster. Waited for the rejection I was certain was coming.

Instead, she placed a hand on my head, sliding her fingers across the ridges of scales, and with wonder in her eyes, she simply said, "Oh."

Chapter 30 - Harley

The analytical part of my mind told me this couldn't be real. There was no scientific reason that what I was seeing could be real. My eyes told me it was all reality, but my brain was arguing, almost frantically, that it was somehow pretend. What my brain couldn't argue against was the heat of the creature in front of me. The feel of its scales. The eyes that looked at me the same way Tate did. I was touching a dragon, and that dragon had been my boyfriend a few minutes ago. There was no way to explain that away.

Finding my voice, I said, "This is surreal. Does it hurt when you change?"

The Tate-dragon gave its head a shake. Negative. A giggle escaped my lips. I pressed my lips together, silencing another round of hysterical laughter. One more outburst like that, and I might not recover. I did not want to give birth in a mental ward, screaming about human dragons.

Reality set in. My baby? It was going to be born like Tate. This was all real, and my baby was going to be a shifter. I leaned forward, holding the dragon's head to keep from falling over. I was lightheaded. Already, I'd realized the dragon meant me no harm. Leaning on it for support seemed the most natural thing in the world. Something I would have thought absurd just fifteen minutes ago.

Not only was it not a threat, but it seemed to want to be as close to me as possible. Its winged arm was already arching around, trying to cradle me. The creature appeared to take pleasure in touching me, or me touching it.

Wait, no, not a creature. Not really. It was Tate. As hard as that was to believe, it was true. This really was Tate. I caressed the snout again, gently sliding my hands across the smooth scales.

A soft, keening sound emanated from the dragon's throat. Whatever the sound was, it was beautiful, and I could feel it all the way down in my bones. As if the sound somehow matched the frequency of my body, I was connected to it. With that connection, I was awash in the dragon's emotions. A waterfall of emotion crashed across me, almost too much to comprehend. The things that stuck out in that tumult was the dragon's fear and worry. But the thing that stuck out the most, was the love it felt for me.

Too tired to stay standing, I sat down. The dragon curled on the ground around me. Working through everything I'd learned today, I tried to make sense of a world where things like this existed. A long time went by as I tried to gather my thoughts.

"Tate, can you come back? So, we can talk?"

The dragon whined in sadness, but after a few seconds, there was a soft breeze, and Tate was again sitting next to me. He looked just as he had before the change. It was almost too hard to believe that he and the massive beast that had been here seconds before were the same being.

I looked at him for a long moment. "How long did you intend to keep this secret from me?"

Tate cast his eyes down, unable to meet my gaze. "I never intended to tell you. Not until I found out you were pregnant and that the baby was mine. I realized that I needed to tell you. I could already feel that the baby was going to be a shifter. You'd need to know, and you'd need my help."

"What's the difference between a human and a shifter baby? I've raised two daughters, why would I need help with a third child?"

"The children are the same, but once they hit a certain age… well, things can get difficult if there isn't an elder of some sort to guide them and teach them how to handle the emotions, the powers, all of it." He took my hand. "Look, if you decide you don't want to be with me, I totally understand. If you decide that, I'll be out the door and gone the moment you say it. I will not abandon my child, though. I'll still be in your life, helping you raise him and guiding him on all it means to be a shifter."

The direction of the conversation had gone to a place I didn't like. "Tate, are you breaking up with me?"

Tate frowned at me, a confused look crossing his face. Awkwardly, he said, "I… uh… thought you were the one who was gonna break up with me."

I almost laughed. "Why the hell would I do that?"

Tate looked genuinely surprised.

"This is all very shocking. So, don't get me wrong. It's, like, a lot. It'll take a while for my brain to grasp what's happening. But can you really tell me that by you being a dragon, that will change how you love me, or the girls, or the baby? Will it change what type of a person you are or the father you'll be?"

He shook his head. "It changes nothing. Not a single thing."

"Well, there's the answer. There's no reason for me to leave you, or for you to leave me. We're in this together."

Instead of the joyous look I'd expected to spread across his face, Tate looked like I'd told him I was dying.

Before I could ask what was wrong, Tate said, "Emily cursed me. All four of us. The other guys and me. She cast a spell that forced me to find you, and connect with you as a mate. If I claim you as my mate, the curse will turn you into a shifter, too. If you reject me, it'll kill me. I'll die. She was trying to get us to mate with other shifters. To bring us together so she could kill more of us at once. Something went wrong with the spell. I'm sorry, Harley."

Emily? She did this. His story made me shake with rage. That bitch! She'd tried to ruin my life, tried to kill Tate and his friends. What kind of a person did that? My hands were clasped so tight that my nails nearly drew blood.

Tate seemed to think my anger was directed at him. He looked on the verge of tears. "I understand. It's best if you reject me. Just get it over with. It'll keep you from becoming a shifter. It'll keep you safe."

"That's not up for you to decide, Tate. I get to live my own life. I get to make my own decisions. Emily is not in control. Not of you or of me. I love you, and she can't change that."

Tate's eyes softened. "Can you repeat that?"

I took his face in my hands, gently cupping his cheeks. "Tate, that spell may have brought us together, but nothing could *force* me to love you. Which I do."

Tate sighed. "I hope that's true. I was starting to wonder how strong that spell was."

I laughed. "Well, it's true that I hated your guts when we first moved in. You were kind of a dick. All my feelings are genuine. I *really* didn't like you. Now, I *really* do love you."

Tate pressed his lips to mine for a quick kiss. "I just want to keep you safe. Shifter hunters can be dangerous."

Before we could say anything else, leaves rustled behind us. Tate and I both spun to see Emily walking out of the forest. Tate growled and put an arm across my chest, pushing me behind him for cover. That growl made my heart skip a beat.

Emily put her hands behind her back. "Hello, Harley. I'm so sorry I had to deceive you. I never meant to get a human involved in all this. I was only in town to hunt shifters." She nodded toward my belly. "But there is the problem with the demon spawn you're carrying in your womb. It would be best for you and the world in general if you took care of that before it's born. It's more humane to do it now, rather than wait until it comes out."

Tate roared, and in a flash, shifted back to his dragon form, blocking me from Emily with a wing. Emily stumbled backward, a look of surprise bright on her face.

"You are a stain on the earth. A virus that needs to be cleansed. Hunters are coming for both of you." She looked around Tate and shouted to me, "I do care for you, Harley. I don't want you to become a beast. I don't want you to die if you don't need to. Please. Please reject this *thing*. Reject him and take your girls and run."

Tate roared at her again and swiped his tail in her direction. She was too far away, but the point was made. Emily walked backward slowly. She kept her eyes on Tate, shaking her head. "I'm going to make sure you die slow. Slow and painful."

Without another word, she spun and ran into the forest. As soon as she was out of sight, Tate shifted back and guided me to the truck. He looked around, making sure no one had followed us, and opened the passenger door.

He grabbed my hand. "Are you absolutely sure this is what you want? If you accept me as your mate, the connection between us will only grow stronger, more intense. There's no turning back after that."

I heard what he was saying. I understood it and what it meant. I pulled him close and kissed him hard. It solidified my answer once and for all. I chose him. He was right, there was no turning back.

Chapter 31 - Tate

After hearing the plans Emily and the hunters had, we needed to make our own plans. The first thing we needed to do was find out who Emily was working for. It was obvious that she wasn't the leader of the hunters. For one, she was a witch. Yes, hunters hated shifters and were hellbent on killing all of us, but they were suspicious of any supernatural entity. They might work with a witch to further their goals, but there was no way a group would follow a witch. Second, she seemed to be following someone else's plan. Nothing about what she'd done so far was what I would have expected from a witch leading a team. It was like the hunters had used her to go on the front lines, do as much damage as she could, and they were set to come in and sweep up whatever was left.

The morning after I told and showed Harley what I was, I invited the guys over to explain everything. They sat in the living room while I relayed the interaction with Emily. The spell, the hunters, the fate that awaited us. All of it.

Miles put his face in his hands, then looked up and said, "So at any moment, one of us is going to meet our fated mate? Just like that? Then we have to choose between dying or turning the person we love into a shifter?"

Steff looked at him and nodded. "That's exactly what he's saying."

"What if we kill her?" Blayne said.

A few weeks ago, we would have all been horrified by the idea of murder. After finding that mutilated body in the woods and dealing with Luis's men, we were harder men. It was scary how quickly you could go from a peaceful person to someone who would kill. It took surprisingly little for that change to happen.

"If we kill her, maybe it'll break the curse. Right?" Blayne asked.

That was a possibility, but we couldn't be sure. What if we killed her, and the only way to break the curse was to have her undo it? Then we'd be stuck. We'd also be murderers. Looking around at them, it didn't look like any of us was ready for that. Not even Blayne, who'd brought it up.

There were too many unknowns when it came to witches. Even those who'd had dealings with them in the past didn't know a lot. We had the witch Miles knew, Siobhan, but she was like a roving gypsy. Way too hard to find or contact for help. It would take days for Miles to find her again. We didn't have that kind of time.

"Look, before we decide anything, we need to find her or the hunters," I said.

"How?" Steff asked.

"Emily has to be nearby. She keeps popping up, and nothing Miles has found shows her living in town. My thought is that she's holed up somewhere in the forests around town. We look for her there. Based on where Harley's house is and how fast she found me and Harley at my shifting location, I've got a fairly good idea where she might be living. It's still a huge area, but we can look faster than humans can."

"So, we become the hunters?" Miles said with a shit-eating grin.

I pointed at him. "Exactly. Someone needs to stay to watch the girls, though."

Blayne raised his hand. "I'll do it. You guys are the better trackers."

After it was decided, Miles, Steff, and I left the house and drove to a pull-off on the highway. The area I wanted to search was probably fifty square miles, and would take humans weeks to search. With our heightened speed and senses, I hoped to search all of it in a day. Maybe two.

Miles and Steff shifted and sprinted into the forest. My dragon was too damned big to shift in daylight, but I was still much faster than a human. I ran beside Miles's wolf and Steff's bear.

Eventually, we split up to cover more ground. I followed my senses, searching for the scents of magic. We were out there for hours, meeting up every thirty minutes to discuss what we had or hadn't found. It started to feel like it would never end, or that we'd find nothing. We didn't even have a cell signal this far out to even check in with Blayne.

As the sun slipped lower in the sky, and right before I'd planned on calling the search off for the day, Miles howled in the distance. It was an excited and urgent sound. He'd found something. I sprinted toward him as his howls echoed across the forest. Emily might have heard it, but wolves and wild dogs were common in these woods. I came upon him in a small clearing an instant before Steff came rumbling out of the trees in his bear form. He and Miles shifted to human, and Miles grinned at us.

"You guys smell that?" he asked excitedly.

Steff and I both raised our noses to the air, pulling in the scents of the surrounding forest. My enhanced sense of smell worked incredibly well. I could smell the leaves, the rich earth, and about a mile away, a deer was taking a shit. Like I said, I had very good senses. Beneath it though, there was an undercurrent of something strong and sharp, like burnt flowers. Magic. We looked at each other, victorious smiles spreading on our faces, cutting through the dirt and sweat caked on our cheeks and foreheads.

Stalking through the woods toward the smell, it got thicker and more pungent. We were close. My vision was the strongest of all of us, and I saw it first. A shadowy structure in the distance through the trees.

"I see something." I waved at them to follow me.

Three hundred yards later, we knelt behind a growth of underbrush and gazed out at what I'd seen. It was a small wooden cabin. The exterior was black, and the building looked to be hundreds of years old. I laughed when I saw it. There couldn't have been anything more cliché.

"Looks like an evil witch's cabin from a storybook," I whispered.

"Literally what I was thinking," Steff said. "What do you guys think? Is it made of gingerbread?"

"Do you think she's inside?" Miles asked.

I shook my head. "I wouldn't think so. She's too smart for that. She may even know we're here. We might be walking into a trap. I'll check."

Stepping out from behind the overgrowth, I shifted. My dragon form would be strongly protected against any spell Emily cast toward me. It was the safe way to go. Still, I kept my long sinuous body close to the ground, moving toward the house as stealthily as my massive body would allow.

The closer I got, the more abandoned the house looked. It didn't appear as though Emily had used the cabin for very long. It did look fairly ancient, though. I crawled up onto the porch, my talons clicking on the wood. My first glance into the dusty and cloudy windows showed me that the cabin had been ransacked, like Emily had left in a hurry. Tables and chairs were turned over, books lay strewn across the floor, and broken glass piled against one wall.

Ready to turn back and tell the guys what I'd seen, my body tensed. There, on the floor, something was protruding from around a corner—a pale arm ending in a decidedly feminine hand and fingers.

I shifted back and sprinted to the guys. Gasping, I said, "Looks like there was a struggle. I can see someone lying on the floor. We need to go in."

Without another word, I led them across the forest and into the cabin. Kicking the door down and bursting inside, Steff and Miles shifted, ready for battle if one was waiting inside. Instead, we found a deathly quiet room. The turned-over furniture was everywhere. It looked worse than it had from outside. The hand was right where I'd seen it. I pointed it out to the others.

Steff and Miles shifted back, then stepped toward it. We rounded the corner and looked down. Emily's lifeless eyes stared out at us from the floor.

"What the hell?" Steff asked. "How did this happen?"

Carefully kneeling down, I touched her neck, feeling for a pulse I knew wasn't there. Sure enough, she was dead, and her skin was cold. A bit of her skin flaked off under my fingers. Her body was deteriorating fast, almost like it was turning to dust.

Miles saw it. "There's no way to know how old she was. Witches can become close to immortal. I think her body is decaying years and decades in a few minutes."

The house fell deathly cold then, right when Miles finished speaking. I stood, getting away from the body, not knowing what was going to happen. Steff's breath came out in icy puffs as the temperature dropped further. Then, a massive *whoosh* sound erupted from Emily's body, and it burst into blue flames.

We jumped back a step, but the flames weren't hot. They were cold. Being near them was almost like holding your hand over a big block of ice. Somehow, the flames were consuming her body but were cold at the same time. Before I could even process how weird that was, something even stranger erupted from within the flames. Emily.

It wasn't actually Emily, but some projection of her. She hovered above the rapidly burning corpse of herself, and stared at us. Her mouth was moving, talking, but I couldn't hear what she was saying. Either her spirit was too weak, or the sound of the roaring flames was too loud.

Seeing that we didn't understand, she seemed to gather herself and spoke again. This time, the sound of her voice carried across the room to us. "You don't have long. The hunters are coming."

"Did they kill you? I thought you were working with them," Miles said.

She sneered at him. "They killed me because I wanted to spare Harley. No matter what, I did come to care for her. Even if she is carrying a shifter baby. They decided she was unclean and had to be taken care of. I was trying to find a counter spell to break the one I'd created. I tried and tried, but there is no cure. No way to break the spell. It'll keep going until its purpose has been fulfilled. There is no stopping it until you've all found your mates or been killed before then. When they discovered I was trying to reverse the spell, they came for me."

She was starting to fade, the flames growing weaker as her body rapidly turned to ashes. I could see the panic in her eyes. The great unknown was rushing upon her, and she was afraid. No matter how ancient or powerful you were, there was one thing that made every living creature equal. Death.

Emily looked at me. "The necklace, Tate. The opal. Make sure Harley wears it. I filled it with protection spells. If she's wearing it, and the hunters try to hurt her, it will automatically cast a shield of protection around her. No one will be able to get to her. Do it, Tate. Do it, and prepare for a fight, because there's one coming. A storm is on the horizon, and you'll have to survive it to save Harley. To protect your baby."

Without another word, her body collapsed into ashes, and the flames extinguished. She vanished. Standing there, looking at what was left of her, we were speechless. Steff even knelt to try to touch the ashes, but they too vanished, almost as though they were snowflakes melting into the floor. There was nothing left to prove that Emily Heath had ever been on this planet.

There was nothing else for us here, other than the knowledge that at least one threat was now out of the way. The hunters still remained, though. Hunters who were powerful enough to kill a witch as strong as Emily. It was terrifying, and we brooded in silence as we headed back to the car. The drive home was equally silent. I was fearful and worried. There was no way to know what my friends were thinking or feeling, but I had to assume they felt the same.

We got back to Harley's and informed her and Blayne about what we'd found at Emily's cabin. Everything we'd seen and heard, including everything Emily's spirit had told us before she vanished. After our story, Harley looked at me, and tears began to well in her eyes. She came to me and wrapped her arms around me, resting her head on my chest.

"Are you okay?" I asked, stroking her hair.

She nodded. "I'm crying for Emily. She died trying to protect me. She wasn't a good person, but in the end, she was trying to do something right. Maybe if she'd had enough time, she could have changed. Maybe."

Not long after the guys all left, Harley and I went to bed. While I brushed my teeth, Harley sat in bed, trying to read. When I sat down, she set the book aside and put a hand to her head as though she'd just remembered something important.

She touched my arm. "Things have been so crazy the last couple days, I forgot to tell you. The DNA test results came back. Good news."

I looked at her and smiled. We'd already known the baby was mine. Having definitive proof was good, though. One less thing to think about as I worked to protect my new family from these hunters. It also gave me one more thing to shove into Ortiz's face. First, I left him with a lawn and mansion full of men who were nearly dead. Those men, once recovered, would be so terrified that they'd all run back to New York. There was nothing Luis could do to bring them back.

We turned the lights off, and Harley fell asleep quickly in my arms. I stayed awake for a long time, staring at the ceiling, thinking. I'd made it very clear to Ortiz that I was not a man to be fucked with. I still needed him to know what would happen if he came near Harley and the kids— my kids—again. Between keeping them safe and Luis' life? Death was the easy option.

Chapter 32 - Harley

After Emily's death, Tate seemed much more on edge as the days passed. It seemed the stress was starting to wear on him. Even small things irritated him, and he was snippy with the team at work. Even me asking what he wanted for lunch made him snap. He, of course, apologized immediately. Still, it was draining seeing him wound so tight. As scared as I was about what Luis or the hunters would do next, I was starting to hope that the other shoe would just go ahead and drop. I wanted to get it all over with and see where the cards fell.

That morning, Tate was in a marginally better mood. We were making breakfast, and the girls had just come down from their rooms. Jordyn was watching cartoons, which always drove Mariah crazy. She thought they were both too old for them, but I liked that Jordyn was holding onto her childhood as long as possible, even though she was already boy crazy.

Mariah sat on a kitchen stool. "Mom, do you think it would be okay if Jordyn and I had a sleepover at our friend's house?"

Without turning from the eggs I was cooking, I said, "Which friends?"

"The Davidson girls. Remember? They're the sisters who are the same age as Jordyn and me. Our birthdays are almost the same, too."

I was still wary of letting the girls out of my sight, especially after the kidnapping. I stared hard at the scrambled eggs, trying to think of some way to talk the girls out of wanting to go. It would be safer if they stayed home, but I didn't want them to know something was wrong.

Tate, putting bread into the toaster, said, "It should be fine. Let them go."

My head turned toward him so fast my neck cracked. Let them go? A sleepover? Was he out of his mind? I nearly had a panic attack if one of the girls went out to check the mailbox.

He must have seen the look on my face. He started the toaster, then stepped close so the girls wouldn't hear.

He pressed his lips to my ear and said, "It'll be fine. I still have guys watching them. And they know their ass is grass if anything happens to my girls."

His girls. I didn't correct him, because honestly, he was right. They were his. He cared for them and loved them. Not for the first time, I thought about how serious he was about us. He'd jumped in with both feet, and now it was hard to even remember life without him. The girls deserved someone like this. Someone who loved them as much as he did, who would protect them with everything he had. He wouldn't do anything, or allow them to do anything, that would put them in harm's way.

"Okay, that's fine. Find out what time this little get-together is supposed to happen so I know."

The girls were both ecstatic. It had been nearly a week since they'd really been able to do anything other than go to school and come straight home. The two of them barely ate any breakfast, they were too busy talking about what they were going to do that night. It was all I could do to get them out the door before the bus came.

Tate spent the better part of the day walking around inside and outside the house with his phone to his ear. He kept barking orders to everyone on his staff. His voice was always gruff and angry. The only time he was cordial was with his three friends and us. I stayed out of his way, but it sounded like whoever he was dealing with wasn't doing things the way he wanted.

It was awful seeing him so stressed out. I'm sure his team didn't enjoy that their usually relaxed and calm friend was being such a dick to them. I wanted to do something nice for him. Something that might pull him out of the foul mood he was in.

He'd just hung up one of his calls, and I said, "I'm going to run to the store real quick."

He smiled. "Okay." He nodded at the door, "He'll go with you."

Confused, I walked over and opened the front door. Steff was sitting on our porch, reading a magazine. Blinking in surprise, I looked back at Tate.

"Really? How long has he been out here?" I asked.

"Since right after the girls went to school. Why?" He didn't look mad or irritated. It was the *new normal* until all the dangers were dealt with.

"Even though I'm wearing this?" I pulled my shirt down to reveal the opal necklace Emily had left me.

"I'm sure that will protect you in some way, but a shifter will protect you better. Besides, it's Steff, you know him. I could have gotten one of the guys you haven't even met yet."

I rolled my eyes. "Fine. Come on, Steff."

Steff drove. I decided to use Steff's friendship with Tate to gain some much-needed info. I wanted to make him a nice dinner to get him out of his funk.

"So, Steff. Here's the deal. I really want to make Tate his favorite meal."

He nodded as he drove. "Okay, sounds nice."

"Anyway, during one of our late-night chats, I remember him saying that the only thing he really misses about home was his mom's cooking. He almost never talks about his past or his family, so when he said that, I knew it was something important. In all the years you guys have been friends, can you remember him ever mentioning something his mom might have cooked that he loved?"

Steff tilted his head, obviously digging through his memories. After several seconds, he finally said, "I do remember something once, way back when we first started out. We were sort of hard up. It was before we got the security firm up and running. We shared this shitty little apartment. The heat didn't work, so we had to just walk around in layers and plug in space heaters to not freeze to death at night. Never could get the damned landlord to fix the freaking thing. Anyway, for about three days, he grumbled about missing his mom's vegetable stew, he joked that it was more meat than vegetables. He said it was the one thing that could... what did he say?" He squinted, trying to remember, then his eyes widened. "That's it. He said it was the one thing that could warm a cold heart."

That was perfect. It was at least a place to start. It was moving further into fall, and the evenings were getting cooler. It still wasn't really stew weather, but it was close enough. It might be the thing that would bring a smile to his face and help ease some of his stress.

I tried to talk Steff into waiting in the car while I shopped, but he wouldn't hear of it. So, I did the shopping with a massive muscled bodyguard shadowing me. I had no idea what kind of ingredients Tate's mom might have used, but I knew he didn't like mushrooms, so I grabbed everything else I could imagine going into a vegetable-and-beef stew.

Steff stood off to the side while I paid and got the three bags. I was checking the receipt as we walked out the door when Steff pushed an arm into my chest and steered me behind him, like he was protecting me. I looked up from the receipt and saw Luis leering at me around Steff's shoulder.

"Back up, motherfucker," Steff growled.

"Well now, if it isn't my long-lost lady love," Luis said, ignoring Steff.

I'd been through enough shit, and the last thing I needed was this. I leaned around Steff. "Luis, you're a piece of shit. You need to get a life and get the hell out of here. I don't know why it won't sink into that thick skull of yours, but we are over. Have been for the better part of a year. So please, do us all a favor and fuck right off."

Luis's eyes slid down my body as I spoke, and locked onto my growing belly. The look of hunger on his face jarred me. It was like he didn't hear a damned thing I'd said.

He pointed his chin at my stomach. "You need to stop playing these games and come home. You're carrying the Ortiz family heir in your belly there. This Podunk shithole town is not the place for an Ortiz boy to grow up."

I knew what I was going to say before I opened my mouth, and it was going to feel good. "The baby isn't yours, Luis. I got pregnant after I finally found out you were one big, walking, talking STD waiting to happen. Cheating on me every chance you got."

He sneered at me. "Nice try. You're trying to piss me off. You'd never jump into bed with another man so soon. No way you could move on from me so fast."

"You've got a major ego problem, Luis. You aren't God's gift to women, even though that's how you live your life. Besides, I had a DNA test done. You are one-hundred percent not the father. There is nothing between us, no connection. You can go home and get out of my life once and for all."

Luis's face went red, and he looked angrier than I'd ever seen him. He jabbed his finger in my direction. "What a fucking whore. Spreading your legs to the first damned meathead who whips his cock out. Fucking slut. I was right to fuck your car up. When I found out you were running around with some jackass cocksucker." He laughed. "You really downgraded baby, you'll never get a man like me again."

From a car behind Luis, three more men got out and slowly walked toward us. I didn't let it show, but I was getting scared. I didn't really know what a shifter could handle, but four guys versus Steff didn't seem like very good odds.

With his men now at his back, Luis said, "You aren't even worth my time. Besides, you'll come crawling back eventually."

"Don't hold your breath, asshole," I said. "Or, on second thought, you should hold your breath. A half hour sounds just about perfect. Then you'll be out of my life for good."

Luis held up a finger. "Watch your mouth, bitch. I'll fuck you up. Make that pretty face not so pretty anymore, then you'll regret playing me."

Steff stepped toward Luis, getting right up against him, almost chest to chest. That shocked Luis. As though he couldn't remember the last time someone had invaded his personal space.

Steff leaned in, his forehead nearly touching Luis's. "*You* need to watch *your* mouth. Understand?"

Luis found his footing again and shoved his chin forward. "Who the fuck are you? And what are you going to do about anything?"

Steff growled, deep in his chest, an inhuman terrifying sound. Luis and his three goons took a fearful step back, and a flash of fear crossed their faces. "Ask your boys who were at the mansion about what my friends and I can do."

I had no idea what the guys had done at the mansion that night, but it had looked like a war zone. None of Tate's guys had even looked winded or injured. I would have enjoyed hearing what the men who had recovered said about what went down. Luis and his men took another couple of steps back.

Luis leaned forward and spat on the ground in front of us. "Fuck the both of you. Trash."

He turned and got into his car with his men and revved the car before pulling out of the parking lot. Steff kept his eyes on them until they were out of sight. Then he helped me into his car and started the trip back home. I could only imagine how Tate would react when we told him. So much for my special dinner putting him in a better mood.

Once we got there and Steff gave him a run-down on the altercation, Tate went ballistic. I'd never seen him so angry. I was glad the girls weren't home because his eyes started glowing.

"That motherfucker doesn't know what he's in for," Tate bellowed at one point.

Steff looked at me and rolled his eyes. "Tate, bro, go outside. Get some air. Shit, man, I know it's daylight but head off into the woods for a shift if you need to. You've been kind of a dick the last few days. No offense, but it's true. You need to get whatever is boiling up inside you out."

"I've been fine. Who the fuck are you to say that?"

Steff didn't look offended. He merely crossed his arms. "You know, maybe the girls were desperate to spend the night somewhere else because of your shit mood. I wouldn't want to hang around you like this."

The anger on Tate's face fell away almost at once. He looked like Steff had kicked him in the stomach. He stopped pacing, a heart-wrenching look on his face. "Have the girls said anything? Is that true?"

I sighed. It was best to be honest. "They did mention yesterday that you've been a lot grumpier than usual."

Tate flinched. Literally flinched, like I'd slapped him. His eyes went cloudy, and he wiped at them roughly. He coughed. "I think you're right, Steff. I need to blow off some steam."

He walked over to me and kissed me. It was a long kiss, hard and intense, but not passionate. This wasn't a sexy kiss. It was a kiss that said *I'm sorry*. He pulled away and put his hands on my shoulders, staring into my eyes. "I'm sorry I've been such an asshole lately. I'll be back in a while." He looked at Steff. "Don't leave her alone. Not for a second."

Steff saluted him sarcastically and locked the door behind Tate. We exchanged an awkward look, then I went to the fridge. I could still make Tate his special dinner. Hopefully, it could still lift his spirits a little.

Chapter 33 - Tate

It had damn near broken my heart to hear that the girls hadn't wanted to be around me. That I'd become so much of an ass that the people I was bonding with couldn't stand to be in the same house as me. Making it worse was that I knew exactly why I was so damned edgy. That fucking spell. Every day that went by without claiming her sent my body into agony. The pain wasn't even something I could explain. It was some painful, irritating malaise that screwed with my emotions. The longer I held off, the angrier I got.

My dragon didn't help things. I wasn't quite feral yet, but things were slowly going that way. Over and over, like a chant, it repeated: *mate, mate, mate, mate.* Anytime I wasn't paying close attention, the dragon tried to take things into its own hands. Just the night before, while cuddling up against Harley, I awoke to find myself nuzzling her neck, my fangs already protruding, ready to bite and claim. The dragon didn't really understand why we couldn't do what we were being drawn to do. I had to be on my toes all the time—something else that had me mentally exhausted and put me in a shit mood. It was getting harder and harder not to sink my teeth and cock into Harley and claim her.

The hope that the curse might vanish once Emily was dead was wholly incorrect. The pull I felt and the pain in my body as I resisted, showed it was still in full effect. My feelings for Harley, and hers for me, were real. We weren't being forced to love each other. Our choice in the matter had been taken away from us, though.

At this point, I really thought that she might accept it. Even the possibility of her becoming like me didn't seem to terrify her the way I thought it would have. The problem was that she was pregnant. None of us knew what might happen to her or the baby if I claimed her while she was expecting. She was still three months away from giving birth. Ninety days of waiting, in slowly increased agony. My patience was being pushed to the edge, but I would have to shoulder the burden and struggle.

I pulled over about ten miles from Harley's house, hoping I was far enough away from any prying eyes that I could safely shift. It had been years since I shifted in the daylight, but I knew it was worth it as my body morphed.

The freedom of body and mind that came when I shifted was almost enough to make me forget all my problems.

The breeze poured across my body and my wings as I rose into the air. Swooping low across the tops of the trees, then lifting high into the air on a warm updraft released some of my tension. A dragon's face couldn't smile, but in my mind, I was grinning from ear to ear, finally relaxed.

My dragon had been cooped up and was stressed out. Mostly from me holding us back from claiming Harley. It needed the release as much as I did. So when a flock of geese heading south for winter appeared on the horizon, I let him have his fun. The godawful honking sounds and the blood and feathers that erupted made the dragon happy and excited. His belly full, and our emotions content for the moment, we made our way back to the car.

Once I was back in the car, I was calmer and a lot more relaxed. The stress was still there under the surface, but it wasn't as bad as it had been. Regardless, I wasn't going to stop pushing until all my girls were out of harm's way. We'd hoped Emily could help with at least getting the hunters off our backs, but so far, there'd been no success.

The day after we found her body, all four of us had returned to her cabin. We'd searched everywhere, looking for clues or information, any hint of Emily's life. Blayne had found a stack of old identities under a loose floorboard. Yellowed birth certificates, passports, and tax forms. Even an ancient paper driver's license from the nineteen-thirties. She really had been much older than she looked.

Everything we found showed that, for the most part, she'd simply tried to live a normal life. Nothing there revealed to us why she hated shifters so much. Or why she would align herself with hunters. On my way back from my shift and goose buffet, the answers began to appear. Blayne called.

"Tate? You free?" he asked.

"Yeah, I guess. What's up?"

"Get to the office."

"Can I ask why?"

Blayne sighed. "Miles's friend just showed up. She's got info on Emily."

A cloud of smoke poured from under my tires as I pulled the truck into a violent U-turn and sped toward the office.

"I'll take that sound of squealing tires to mean you're on the way?" Blayne asked.

"Five or six minutes. As long as I don't get pulled over."

"See you in a few."

Less than five minutes later, I pulled into the office parking lot, barking my tires as I slammed it into park. Attempting to stay professional, I didn't jump from the car and run inside. Instead, I did a weird speed walk and had to bite my tongue not to scream when I punched in the wrong code at the front door. Inside, Kennedy said hi and leaned across her desk, showing me a clear view of her ample cleavage, but I didn't even glance toward her. I made my way down to Miles's office and found the guys in there, with Siobhan sitting in Miles' chair.

Steff closed the door behind me as I entered. Siobhan looked much as she had when we first met her. Aloof, and powerful. They waited for me to take a seat before they started.

"Okay, now that everyone is here, can you tell us what you found out?" Miles asked.

Siobhan nodded. "It took some digging, and a lot of questions. I'll be honest, I don't usually get involved in the issues of other supernatural beings. This spell, though? It intrigued me. I wanted to know who had created and cast something so singularly interesting."

"Interesting?" Steff blurted out. "We might all die. Is that interesting?"

Siobhan looked him steadily in the eye. "Honestly, yes."

Steff looked nonplussed and closed his mouth, deciding he didn't want to ask any more dumb questions.

Siobhan continued. "There is an old warlock in the north woods of Michigan I have sporadic contact with, but he has an almost encyclopedic memory when it comes to witch culture and history. I gave him your physical description and a detailed recounting of the spell she cast. Almost immediately, he gave me a name. Emiladia Wardlow."

From within her robe, she extracted a piece of paper. She unfolded it and set it on the table for us to see. It was a photocopied image of a painting. It looked old, maybe from the sixteen or seventeen hundreds. The woman in the painting was young and lovely, dressed in clothing that had been fashionable then. Staring out at us was the face of Emily Heath.

"Holy shit," Blayne whispered, holding the paper up to examine it closer.

"She was the youngest daughter of the Wardlow clan. The clan had been working with a splinter group of dragon shifters. Something had happened, and they were slowly going feral. The Wardlow clan was trying to develop a new spell that could hold off the process, maybe even cure them from going feral."

"It seems, the process took too long. One day, while Emily was away in a neighboring valley collecting medicinal and magical herbs and roots, the dragons succumbed to the feralization. They attacked the clan's small village." Siobhan swiveled her eyes to me, and said, "It was a complete and total destruction. Men, women, children, babies, all of them. Emily returned some hours later and found that everyone she knew, everyone she had ever cared, ever loved, had been murdered, mutilated, partially devoured—"

"Okay. We get it," I said as shame and guilt tried to bear down on me and crush me.

Siobhan raised an eyebrow. "Obviously, Emiladia was... distraught, to say the least. She became known in most Wiccan circles for her robust and unflagging hatred for shifters, especially dragon shifters. It was part of the reason my friend knew exactly who I was looking for. Her hatred for your kind was without equal."

I buried my face in my hands. I hadn't thought I could feel bad for Emily. This story changed that. A group of dragon shifters had taken everything she loved. If a witch had come to Lilly Valley and killed all my friends, Harley, and the girls, took everything I cared about? Could I have done the same thing she did? Would I become some shifter vigilante scouring the world, hell-bent on killing every witch I found? I wasn't sure, but I now understood her hatred, especially for dragon shifters. Most hunters had something similar happen in their background. It made it more understandable. I'd still destroy them if they came near my family, but it didn't make me any less empathetic.

"That's pretty much all I know." Siobhan turned to Miles. "I'll assume our dealings are done for now?"

Miles, who looked like he might be sick after hearing the story, nodded. "Yeah. If I need you again—"

"I'll *allow* you to find me," Siobhan said and swept from the room, leaving the thick scent of magic in her wake.

"Harsh stuff," Steff said, rubbing his face.

"Yeah. No fucking wonder she wanted us all dead," Blayne said. "How does this help us, though? Does it?"

"It helps us get inside the heads of the hunters. We know how determined they all are," I said. "If all of them have something like that in their past, some stupid ass feral shifter did something like that, they'll die like a dog on a bone. These won't be guys who'll shit their pants as soon as they see us shift. It does help," I said.

I stood to go. As I grabbed the door handle, Miles asked, "You going home?"

I nodded. "I have a lot to think about."

Without another word, I stepped out and walked to my car. The drive home was a total blur. I almost missed the turn into the neighborhood. I nodded at Terry as I pulled into the driveway. He was sitting in his sedan, keeping watch on the house. There was so much going on in my head that I almost didn't notice the smell of food when I stepped into the house. I closed the door and sniffed the air. A wave of nostalgia swept across me at the scent.

I hadn't smelled that in close to twenty years. It was almost exactly like my mom's stew. How the hell? My stomach roared out, rumbling so loud that Harley heard it from the kitchen. She peeked around the corner, saw me, and smiled.

"Hey. I was working on dinner."

"I can tell." My voice was thick with emotion. "How did you get my mom's recipe? It smells just like hers. Wait, how the hell did you even know about her stew?"

Harley grinned. "I prodded Steff for information. He knew very little, so I took what he said and did my best. I wanted to make you happy."

In that instant, looking at her, food was the last thing on my mind. I walked toward her and said, "Put it on low, so it doesn't burn."

Harley saw the look in my eyes and did exactly what I said. Before she could get out of the kitchen, I picked her up and carried her to the bedroom. I gently eased her onto the bed and pulled my shirt off.

Harley looked at me and smiled as she unbuttoned her pants. "What do you think you're doing, mister?"

After I stripped my pants down, I looked at her and growled, "I'm going to show you how hungry I really am."

I was on her in a second. The desperation of my dragon surged within me, making things move faster. There was no foreplay here. Just lust and desire. I kissed her hard, sliding my tongue along hers. I slipped my hand down to her breast and took her nipple between my fingers, drawing a gasp from Harley. Our kiss deepened as I lifted her off the bed, wrapping my arms around her.

Harley's hand worked down between us, and she took my cock in her hand, stroking it gently. I sighed into her mouth and fought back the desire to claim her then and there. I could even feel the ache in my jaw, and my fangs wanted to erupt from my gums. Instead, I rolled her over onto her hands and knees.

I knelt behind her and slid my tongue into her, sweeping it back and forth. Harley moaned in pleasure and rested her forehead on the bed. I wanted every part of her, and I wanted it right then, but I also wanted this to last. I slid my tongue up and circled her asshole, making her gasp. She seemed to like it, so I slid my tongue in slow, luxurious circles until her pussy was dripping wet. Harley was pushing her hips against my face, and I slid a finger inside her while I kept moving my tongue on her ass, making her sigh with pleasure.

"Take me," Harley groaned.

My dragon responded by screaming a roar of joy inside my head, and I went to my knees and pulled her hips back to meet my cock. I slid into her pussy and clutched her ass. The sight of her bent over, begging me to fuck her, released an animal urge within me. I began thrusting, unable to hold back any longer. I leaned down and bit her between the shoulder blades, not enough to break the skin or claim her, but enough to satisfy the dragon for a few minutes. Instead of wincing from the bite, Harley moved her hips back against me, slamming her pussy onto my cock. My mind reeled into a passionate infinity.

Leaning forward, still thrusting, I stroked her hair and murmured, "Are you close?"

Harley whimpered slightly, then said, "Uh, huh. Fuck me, Tate, make me come."

As though I needed an invitation, I thrust faster, harder. Pulling her onto me, an explosive feeling built rapidly in my balls. I groaned as Harley started to convulse beneath me.

"God," she screamed.

I wasn't there yet, I kept moving, hearing Harley's breath grow ragged and gasping, as she began to come a second time. Her hands clutched at the sheets as she called out my name over and over. Finally, after I'd given her all I thought she could handle, I came. My body nearly burst as the ecstasy washed over me like warm honey. My thrusts slowed until I had to drop to the bed beside her. Harley's body was still twitching, and her breath came in short irregular spurts, but the smile on her face let me know that she'd enjoyed it as much as I had.

Moments later, after she'd recovered, she rested her head on my chest. My heart was still hammering away inside. She grinned at me and stroked my stomach.

"You know, if I'd known that would be the reaction, I'd have made that stew a lot sooner."

Chapter 34 - Harley

The night before had been pretty mind blowing. I had a pleasant ache all over, almost like I'd had a work out. I could even feel the bite marks on my back where Tate had bitten me in the throes of passion. It had been the most animalistic and intense sex we'd ever had, but something had been a little off. Tate had been fighting, struggling with something the entire time. He never said what was going through his mind, and I didn't know what to do about it. If he couldn't tell me before or after the amazing night we'd had, there was no way he'd tell me now.

Before I could go deeper into those thoughts, a bang sounded at the door. Freezing with the coffee pot in my hand, I stared at the door, scared of who might be out there. Another three loud bangs rang out. It wasn't the gentle *tap-tap-tap* of a friendly neighbor dropping off a Bundt cake. This was loud, aggressive pounding. Tate was still upstairs finishing his shower, but he had super-duper shifter hearing or whatever. He surely had heard the knocking. He'd be down in a few seconds. It would be safe to at least check the camera, see who was out there.

Putting the coffee pot aside, I stepped over the control panel and punched the icon for the doorbell camera. My jaw dropped, and fear flooded my body. Miles was outside. It was Miles, but not quite the down-to-earth and immaculately dressed man I'd come to think of as a friend. Instead, Miles was barely holding himself up against the wall beside the door. His hair was hanging limp against his face, smeared with blood. Not only his face, but both of his hands were bright red with blood, as though they'd both been dipped in a tub of red paint. His right hand held him up, while the other was pressed to his side, where more blood was oozing out, dripping onto my welcome mat.

I was screaming Tate's name even as I was disarming the security system. I could hear his feet slamming against the floor. I got the door unlocked and swung it open. Miles looked even worse in person than on the camera. He looked at me through a haze of pain and exhaustion. I grabbed his arm and helped him into the house. He collapsed to one knee inside the foyer as Tate leaped the twelve steps from the upper floor. Like a gymnast, he landed almost silently on his feet, wearing nothing but a pair of basketball shorts. His hair was still wet, and his body gleamed with water. Tate's eyes went wide with panic when he saw Miles.

"No." Tate gasped as he fell down on his knees next to his friend.

Miles was already sinking lower to the floor, grunting in pain and rolling onto his back on the tile. Tate took one of Miles's bloody hands and clenched it in his. I'd taken several steps back, not sure what to do. All I was able to manage was to look on in horror, unable to take my eyes away from the blood spreading out beneath him.

"Harley?" Tate bellowed. "My phone."

The strength of his voice snapped me out of my daze, and I ran to the kitchen counter where he'd left it before going to take his shower. I walked toward him with it, but he shook his head.

"You do it. My contacts, there's one labeled *Doc*. Dial it, give him the address. Now."

Quickly scrolling through his contacts, I found the one he said and dialed. It rang twice before a voice answered.

"Yes, Tate?"

A stream of words vomited out of my mouth. I hadn't realized how freaked out I was until I started talking.

The man on the other end of the line said, "Whoa, whoa, who the hell is this? Where's Tate? What's going on?"

Taking a breath, I composed myself and said, "Tate is here, but Miles is hurt. He's hurt badly. There's blood everywhere."

Tate was trying to keep pressure on the wound at Miles's side, but he turned and yelled, "Tell him it's silver. Silver."

"He says to tell you that it's silver," I said, not sure what that meant. Silver bullets? Was that really a thing? Like in the really-real world?

The voice on the line murmured, "Shit, I got it. Where are you? Lilly Valley?"

I rattled off the address. He hung up. I called Steff and Blayne without being told, knowing they'd want to know as soon as possible. Then I put the phone down and grabbed kitchen towels to help put pressure on the wound.

I applied pressure, and blood immediately soaked through the wound. This was not good. It was a lot of blood. Who knew what a shifter could survive, but he needed help as soon as possible. The fact that Tate had a secret doctor on speed dial told me that they must not use regular hospitals. Maybe there was something about their physiology that would tip off humans? But wasn't that better than death?

Miles was gasping for air, like he'd run a marathon. He put a hand on Tate's shoulder and murmured, "Tate, man, I don't wanna die."

Tate looked at him, his eyes full of rage. "You aren't gonna die. You're too fucking stubborn to die, dammit. Now shut up."

Miles laughed weakly, then went serious. Tears spilled over his cheeks, mixing with the smears of blood. "I'm… I'm really scared, brother."

I felt like I was intruding on something intimate, so I kept my head down. My own eyes were burning, tears threatening. Everything was moving incredibly fast, and I was helpless.

Tate's voice grew calm. "I know, Miles. I know. Doc will be here soon."

Five minutes later, I heard the thump as a car door slammed, and a man burst through my front door. He moved so fast that I barely saw his face. He and Tate lifted Miles and ran him upstairs to my bedroom, slamming the door behind them. I stood in my kitchen, staring at the blood on my hands for several long seconds before I ran to the sink and vomited. After I cleaned my face, I rinsed the sink out and spent a full three minutes washing my hands, trying to get the blood out from under my nails.

I'd just turned off the water when Blayne and Steff ran inside. Both of them slid to a stop and gaped at the puddle of blood on the floor. Their faces went ghostly white. Steff looked at me, and for a second, he didn't look like the big badass who had intimidated Luis in the grocery store parking lot. He looked like a little boy, desperate to hear that the worst hadn't happened.

I gestured weakly toward the stairs. "They're in my room. He's... he's still alive... I think."

Before they could move, the most bloodcurdling scream erupted from the top of the stairs. It was like nothing I'd ever heard in my life. If someone died and went to hell to be eternally tormented, that was the sound I could imagine them making. Gooseflesh erupted across my arms and back. Without another word, the two men pounded up the stairs and disappeared. Again, I was left alone. I thanked God the girls were at school.

I grabbed a roll of paper towels and attempted to clean the blood off the floor. I was half way through an entire roll when another scream echoed from upstairs. I tensed. The scream was inhuman, excruciating, and soul-rending. Then, almost seamlessly, it changed from the scream of a man to the howl of a wolf. The baby was kicking like crazy, no doubt he could hear the sound as well.

Just as quickly as it came, the sound cut off. It didn't slowly fade out, it stopped completely, leaving me in silence. Dread filled me. I sat there, my hands once again bloody, the mess on the floor only half cleaned, and stared at the dark hallway at the top of the stairs.

When no one came out, I busied myself with cleaning. It seemed so silly and unimportant. A man I knew and was becoming friends with was upstairs in my bedroom. He was bleeding out and possibly dying. Cleaning was trivial, but I had to keep my mind off whatever was happening up there.

Once the main puddle of blood was cleaned up, everything else was easy. Five minutes later, the tile floor in front of the door looked like nothing had happened. There was some staining in the grout, but I would worry about that later. I was washing my hands again when the bedroom door opened. I dried my hands and walked to the foot of the stairs, dreading the worst.

Tate was walking down the stairs, slow and almost shambling. He looked like he was in a daze, and his eyes gazed out, unfocused and almost dead. His hands were covered in blood. The way he looked gave me the impression that things had gone badly. I put a hand to my mouth and breathed in a gasp.

Tate's eyes moved to me, and he saw the look on my face and shook his head slightly. "He's asleep. He's not dead."

'Oh, Jesus," I said, breathing out in relief.

"Uh, Doc got the silver bullets out. Blayne and Steff held his arms, I held his legs. It was… it was bad."

"I heard," I murmured.

"He gave him a drug that will stop the silver from spreading through his body, but he'll be in pretty excruciating pain until what's already in him works its way out."

Tate stepped down and looked at the stains in the grout. He really was like a zombie. I wasn't sure how to interact with him. Would he fly off the handle and start screaming? Break down in tears? I didn't know. Cautiously, I stepped forward and took his hand. He wrapped his fingers around mine absently, then followed as I led him toward the guest bathroom.

He let me undress him and help him into the shower. I cleaned his hands and arms, washed the blood from his face, and then helped him get out and dried off. The whole time he didn't say anything. He was in shock. Once he was dry, I wrapped my arms around him and held him, not sure what else to do. After a few seconds, he hugged me back, squeezing me tight.

"I'm sorry," he whispered.

"For what?" I asked.

"Men bleeding out on your floor, magic curses, shifter babies? I know this isn't what you signed up for. I've turned your entire life upside down. I should have just paid for your drink that night in New York and let you be. You'd be better off without me. I'll have to buy a new mattress, by the way."

I kissed his chest and looked into his eyes. "Tate, none of that matters. Even now, after everything, I'd choose you."

He looked at me for a long moment. The look on his face slowly faded from surprise to something softer. "I love you so much, Harley. I promise you, I'm going to put an end to this."

Not long after Tate got redressed, Miles called out for him from upstairs. Doc came down while Tate was in and spoke with Blayne and Steff before leaving. The man was as much of a mystery as he'd been when he arrived. I wondered who he was and whether he was also a shifter.

Tate came down twenty minutes later and sat with me, across from Blayne and Steff to finally relay what had happened.

"Miles was on watch duty today. He said he was doing a patrol around Harley's place. Totally normal as far as he could tell. He was in his wolf form to cover more ground faster. He was about a hundred yards from the back porch, out in the woods, when he got shot. The hunters saw him and jumped him. He never knew they were there."

Blayne sat forward, frowning. "But he would have smelled them. If they were within a half mile, he would have smelled them."

Tate nodded. "Yeah, that's what he thought. Miles said that even when they were right there on top of him, he couldn't catch their scent. They've figured out some way to mask it. The way deer hunters stand over campfire smoke to cover their scent. I have no idea how they did it. He'd be dead if he hadn't already been shifted. There were three of them, and they pumped two more bullets into him before he ripped off one of their arms with his teeth."

Ripped his arm off? I felt my gorge rise and swallowed hard. The thought of it was horrible. The other horrible thing was that the hunters had been so close to my house—right out there in the backyard.

"We need a plan of attack. We have to go after these fucks right now. As soon as possible," Tate said.

He sounded off kilter. Probably from the shock of seeing Miles almost die. I didn't want him to go off halfcocked and end up with a silver bullet between his eyes. Blayne and Steff looked like they were thinking the same thing I was.

I put a hand on Tate's arm. "Tate, you haven't been yourself lately. I don't want you guys running off and getting killed because you weren't being careful."

He glared at me. "I know what I'm doing. Don't tell me my business," he snapped.

I jabbed my finger into his chest. "Right there. You just made my point for me. You've been on edge for days."

Steff stood. "Bro, she's right. What the hell's going on with you? I don't even live with you, and I can see you're wound so tight you're about to pop."

Blayne nodded. "Yeah, man. You've always been the most chill out of all of us. This?" He gestured toward Tate. "This isn't you."

Tate huffed a breath out his nose, like a bull. At first, he looked like he was going to argue, but his face fell after a few seconds. His shoulders slumped, and he tilted his head back to look at the ceiling.

After a moment, he looked back at us. "It's you, Harley. I'm starting to go feral. I need to claim you, and I'm holding back. It's starting to break me."

Steff and Blayne both looked uncomfortable with the admission. I was surprised. I hadn't realized he'd been struggling so much with it. Then my mind went back to the hickeys he'd left on my body over the last few weeks. The bite on my shoulder the last time we'd had sex. It started to make sense. He'd been forcing himself not to claim me all this time, and it was damn near driving him mad.

"I don't want to hurt you. I'm not sure what might happen if I do it. Something could happen to the baby or you. I don't know anyone who's ever claimed someone while they were pregnant." He sighed. "We haven't even talked about the fact that Emily's curse is going to change you into a shifter when I claim you, and what the hell might happen with that. It's too much to even consider doing it. Not until the baby is born at the very least."

With everything that had happened over the last week or so, I hadn't even had much time to think about that part of it. Being turned into a magical creature? It was kind of appealing in an idealistic-teenage-fantasy sort of way. But it was also terrifying. Like standing on a cliff and staring out into the void.

"Tate," I said, "I don't think you have until December. Look at yourself."

He sliced his hand through the air like a knife. "No. This is non-negotiable."

Heat rose in my cheeks. He was making decisions that included me, but wasn't taking my thoughts into account. Nothing pissed me off more than that.

"Listen, this isn't just about what you want. I get to have a say in my life, too," I said. "Plus, I don't want to see you in pain. I don't want you putting yourself or anyone else in danger because you're going feral and can't think straight. It's for the best, and I'm ready. You need to claim me."

Steff still looked uncomfortable. "I think she's right."

"Me, too," Blayne added.

Tate looked beyond angry at all three of us. "What are you talking about? Harley, what if I claim you and something bad happens to the baby? How can you... shit, how can I live with myself if that happened?"

"I have the necklace Emily gave me. I won't take it off. I know she meant it to protect me. I'm sure it will protect the baby."

Tate, unmoved, shook his head. "No, not happening. I'm not giving you my bite. Too much could go wrong."

I couldn't be there anymore. He wasn't listening to reason, and I needed to get out of the room to cool off. I stood, but before I walked away, I pinned him with my gaze. "You're being selfish. You need to think about your pack and your family. If you aren't at your best, if you're too stressed or preoccupied with the desire to claim me, then you're putting all of us at risk. Miles almost died. What if Steff dies next time because you were too slow? What if…" My breath caught in my throat, but I pushed forward. "What if the hunters kill Mariah or Jordyn because you've gone feral and can't do anything to help them? You need to think long and hard about whether *that* is something *you* can live with?" Without waiting for his answer, I stomped out of the room.

Chapter 35 - Tate

My anger rose as I watched Harley leave the room. It wasn't directed at her. It was at myself, it was at Emily, it was at the hunters and Luis. Everything was fucked up, and I couldn't get my head to stop spinning to make a good plan. I stood and paced the room, trying to expend some extra energy.

Blayne shook his head in exasperation. "Tate, dude, you have to admit Harley has a point. We're going into battle with these hunters, and you are definitely not at peak performance. You see that, don't you?"

I heard him and bit down on my tongue to keep my mouth shut. I didn't want to spout some retort at him without thinking. I needed time to think, but shit kept happening that prevented that.

"You realize that if you get killed because you're too busy worrying about this curse, you'll leave Harley and your unborn son totally unprotected," Steff said.

I spun on him and snarled, releasing a deep throaty growl. Instead of flinching back, Steff merely raised his eyebrows, looking more irritated than afraid.

Blayne scoffed. "Again, you're making our point for us."

The snarl on my face slipped away. They were right. I wasn't at my best. It wasn't even that I was angry. I was terrified. I was trapped in my own skin, ready to tear free. I wasn't scared of the hunters. I was scared at the thought of losing Harley or losing the baby. I couldn't imagine the pain I'd feel if I took the girls' mother from them. This fear was all that was stopping me. There'd never been a human that turned into a shifter. There was nothing to go off of. No case study, no legend, no text books. Nothing. We were going in blind. I had no way of knowing if I should jump off the cliff or walk away.

Upstairs, I heard murmuring. Miles was talking. Without a word to Steff or Blayne, I walked up the stairs and rounded the corner. I'd assumed that Miles was talking in his sleep. Instead, I found him awake, speaking with Harley. She was sitting on the edge of the bed, away from the bloody portion.

Freezing where I was, without them seeing me, I listened to what they were saying.

"I like the paint job too, by the way," she said, gesturing to the blood stains all over the bed.

Miles smiled, even though he was still obviously in pain. "Yeah, sorry about that. I told them to put me in the bathtub, but they wouldn't listen."

"It's fine. Tate already said he'd buy me a new mattress. Between you and me, I'm going to work him over and get one of those really expensive, top-of-the line, heated and cooled ultra-lux beds."

Miles chuckled, then winced. "Take him for all he's worth. I do his taxes for him, I know how much he's got." The smile fell from his face. "Harley, I'm very thankful for you."

"For what?" she asked, her brow furrowing.

"You've made Tate happy. You can't understand how grateful I am for that. He's my best friend, but I really can't remember him ever being truly happy. You and your girls have broken through that armor he's built around himself. He's actually living a life. He's not just slugging his way through it anymore. He's a great guy, the most loyal friend I could ever imagine. He deserves happiness. He deserves peace, and you gave him that. Thank you."

My eyes burned, and I put a hand to my mouth, holding back a sob. I'd never heard Miles talk about me like that. I never knew he was so worried about me. Sometimes I forgot that other people were watching. My friends were invested in me as much as I was in them.

Miles added, "I know he's not been himself lately. I'm still worried about him."

Harley took his hand. "I'm doing all I can to help ease his mind. The problem is, Tate is a stubborn bastard."

Miles laughed then, actually laughed. It was cut off by a wince and hiss of pain. He dragged in a breath. "You aren't wrong. But I think if anyone can ease his mind, you can." Miles's eyes fluttered closed. As he slipped off to sleep, he murmured, "I can't lose him. I can't lose my brother."

My chest was aching as I watched Harley lay Miles's hand gently back on the bed. This was the hardest decision I'd ever had to make. It was like my whole life was culminating in what I was about to choose. Harley turned and saw me standing in the shadow of the doorway.

She stood and walked toward me with a determined look on her face.

She pressed up against me in the hallway. "I'm not going to let you put us in danger, Tate. I *know* everything will be fine. This is the way things were meant to be. I want your bite. Claim me."

My dragon nearly forced a shift after hearing that. It was going crazy with need and lust. My cock was already getting hard hearing her say those words. I knew what would happen if my instincts overcame me. And that terrified me.

"You need to stop talking," I whispered.

She looked me in the eyes. "I accept you as my mate."

Those words almost snapped me out of reality. I went into a fugue state and didn't even remember taking her hand and leading her back to my house. There was a vague memory of Steff and Blayne saying something as we left. The walk across the street happened in a blink. One minute, we were stepping out the front door of Harley's house, and the next, I was slamming the door of my bedroom. The dragon, the animal inside me, was taking control.

The house felt almost alien to me. I'd spent so little time there it had begun to no longer feel like my home. My home was with Harley and the girls, but for this, we needed privacy. My decision had been made the moment she said she accepted me as her mate. It was time.

Harley sat on the bed as I stood above her. She ran her hands across my stomach and chest. Blood pounded in my ears, and I could actually see the veins in her neck. They pulsed, calling to me. Screaming for my venom. For the part of me that would claim her—change her forever. The fear was still there, and I tensed, trying to hold off for a few more minutes. My vision narrowed, and all I could see or hear was my mate. There was only Harley. Nothing else.

She seemed to see me struggling for control. She looked up at me and whispered, "Don't fight it, Tate. I want this. Claim me. Make me yours."

My eyes shifted, the gold glow reflecting off Harley's face. A knowing smile spread across her face, and I started tearing her clothes off. It was manic, almost out of control. She tugged and tore at my clothes. The neck of my shirt ripped as she yanked it off my head, and buttons popped off her shirt as I yanked it open, revealing her breasts.

Scooping her up and moving her farther up the bed, I settled atop her and kissed her hard. Our tongues twisted and fought playfully as my hand moved gently across her belly. After drifting across the tuft of hair between her legs, I slipped a finger inside her, making her moan. Her nails dug into my back as I latched my lips onto her neck. I sucked at the soft flesh there, moving my finger in and out of her.

My cock was throbbing, almost aching, it was so hard. Harley's hand brushed between us and took me in her hand. I breathed out a heavy sigh as her fingers stroked me, making my dick pulse harder. I didn't know it was possible to be that hard, to want someone that much. I looked into her eyes and saw the need there, saw that deep down, beyond everything else, she wanted me. Me. All these years after my family turned their back on me, someone actually wanted me.

Needing her more than ever, I pulled my hand away and nestled myself between her legs. I took my cock and grazed the head against her clit, moving back and forth. Harley arched her back, lifting her hips.

She gazed into my eyes with so much love and murmured, "Now. Make love to me, Tate."

Groaning, I slid into her, her warmth enveloping her. Her breasts pressed against my chest and my hips began to move. Harley slipped her hands up into my hair, and her eyes rolled back in her head as I began thrusting faster and harder. My lips grazed across her jaw and neck, the dragon screaming at me to do what we both wanted.

"Do it, Tate," she gasped, barely in control. "Take me. Claim me!"

The dragon roared, and my own voice echoed its cry. I clamped my teeth onto her neck, my fangs already out. I sucked in a mouthful of her blood and injected her with my venom. I could almost feel that part of me coursing through her body. The connection was already forming, and I'd never felt anything like it. I came, grunting and burying myself deep inside her as my body shuddered. Harley screamed my name and slammed her hips into me over and over, fucking me even as I was locked in motionless pleasure. Moments later, her own body vibrated and shook beneath me, a wordless moan erupting from her throat. We collapsed against each other, heaving and panting, overcome by what had just happened.

Not sure if I'd done it right, we lay there, holding each other, waiting for… something. I'd never done this before. Even if there hadn't been a curse, I wouldn't have really known what would happen. My body knew how to claim someone—it was instinct. Just like a man or woman knew how to have sex even if they'd never seen it or been taught. Other than that, I didn't know what might happen.

I laughed. "I feel so much better. The feral feeling, it's gone."

Harley caressed my face and nodded, a faint smile growing on her face. I pulled her close to me, the bond between us growing with every second, unbelievably powerful. I put my hand to her chest, feeling her pulse.

I pressed my face to hers. "Our hearts are beating in sync."

"I feel different," she whispered.

Nodding, I said, "It's the mating bond. I kind of thought you'd have shifted by now. The wound on your neck is already closed up and vanished. It definitely worked." It was true, but there was a faint scar where my teeth had torn her skin. A scar that would permanently mark her. Just enough for me to see, to know that she was mine forever. My dragon purred with satisfaction.

Before we could drift off to sleep, a heavy fist pounded at my bedroom door. The explosive sound snatched our bliss and peace away. There would be only one reason for someone to come over here and interrupt this. Something had happened.

Before I could ask who it was, Steff screamed through the door, "Tate! The hunters are here. They're in Harley's backyard."

Chapter 36 - Harley

Tate threw my clothes to me, and we got dressed as fast as we could. Once we stepped out of the bedroom, Steff was there waiting for us. The look in his eyes could only be described as anxious rage.

"They started calling to us from the woods out back. Humans wouldn't have heard it. I'll be damned if Miles was the first of us to hear them. He started yelling at me and Blayne. As soon as I saw them out there, I busted my ass over here to get you." He glanced at me and Tate awkwardly before adding, "Hope things went… well?"

"Yeah, we're good. What do they want?" Tate said.

"Haven't said. They kept saying they wanted all of us there before they'd talk."

The walk across the street was much different than the one we'd taken a few minutes before. The woods behind my house, which had always looked quaint and lush compared to the concrete and steel of New York, now seemed dark and intimidating. In those trees, Miles had been attacked. Danger stood among those shadowy branches and leaves.

We walked into the house and locked the door behind us, not wanting to be flanked if that was their idea. Blayne joined us, and we walked toward the back door. Before we opened it, Tate took me by the shoulders and looked me in the eyes.

"If things go badly, you need to get the hell out of here. My truck is out front with the keys in it. You run, you get the girls, and you get the hell out of here. Don't look back."

I looked into Tate's eyes. In my heart, I knew I could never leave him, especially after what we'd just done. After the deep, unending connection we'd made. I knew what he needed to hear. I looked back at him and nodded my head firmly in assent. He still didn't look comfortable letting me come outside, but I think he wanted me where he could see me. He unlocked the door and swung it open.

We stepped out, and I could see a single man in the distance, about twenty yards from my back porch. He had a rifle slung across his shoulder, but it was hanging to the side, not in his hands. His arms were crossed, and he had what I would call a prickish smile on his face. I hated him on sight, like I probably would have even if I didn't know he wanted to hurt us. This was the type of person you would cross the street to avoid.

Tate stepped in front of all three of us and called out, "Do you have a death wish? Is that why you're here? Because if so, by God, I'll grant it."

The man rocked back on his heels and laughed. "Looks like you're the one with the death wish. But no, we didn't come here to fight you. We all know the kind of magic you dragon shifters possess. Shit, you by yourself could roast all of us in a second."

I noticed rustling branches and limbs, then another six hunters appeared near the leader. Fear spiked deeper into my chest. So many? They all had guns. Could the guys take this many? I had to keep reminding myself of the mansion. There had been twice this many men there. Of course, those men had thought they were going to fight humans. These hunters knew exactly what they were up against. That had to make them more dangerous.

"You need to know there's a war coming. We plan on ridding the world of every one of you abominations. That's what we came to let you know. Say your goodbyes.

Get your houses in order, because we're coming. You'll die…" he jerked a chin toward my stomach, "…and your filthy fucking devil spawn will die, too. I'll happily grind a baby shifter into the dirt with my own—"

So fast. My God! I never knew anything on earth could be so fast. One moment Tate was standing in front of me, the next, he was roaring in rage, and was twenty yards away, holding the man in the air by his throat. It had caught the hunters off guard. They all took a half second to realize what had happened before they raised their rifles and pistols at Tate.

The leader waved them off and croaked out, "Weapons down. The boss wants the dragon for himself."

Tate started to squeeze the man's throat. "I should fucking end you right here. Right now. Pop your goddamned head off. You threaten my unborn child? Maybe I should go ahead and shift, then fucking devour you alive."

Hearing something like that would have made me piss my pants. But this man must have had balls of steel, or maybe he was totally off his rocker. Instead of begging for his life, he started laughing. His face grew redder by the second as Tate squeezed. The guy seemed to have no fear.

"If you kill me, shifter, you won't know the flaw in Emily's curse."

Tate threw the man to the ground. The guy rolled on the ground there for a few seconds, retching and coughing, rubbing at his throat.

"You are a scary son of a bitch," he said, after getting his breath back.

"What damned flaw?" Tate asked.

The man stood and took a few steps away from Tate. He pointed at me. "The flaw is her. Emily got sloppy and was going native. That's why we had to put that magical bitch down. She got close to Harley. She tried to reverse the spell but couldn't. Instead she cast a new spell of protection. Each one of you nasty motherfuckers is going to be fated to mate to a human. None of you get to be with other shifters. But her new spell will protect those women. At least as long as they accept you *things* for what you are."

He looked like he wanted to be sick, as if the very idea of a human wanting to be with a shifter was too much to stand. He was a bigot of the highest caliber. He made *me* want to be sick.

He then held up a finger and smiled a dark, mischievous smile. It made my skin crawl seeing it. "Just 'cause we can't hurt you ladies, doesn't mean we can't make your lives miserable. And we very much plan on making your existence a living hell. At least until the boss decides it's time to end your unnatural lives. You see, this is your warning. To get all the humans in your life out of here before it gets really bad. I've seen the young girls who live here. They haven't been sullied yet. They deserve to go on and live good human lives. This is your one chance to get them out of here. Do what you need to before we come back."

He took a step closer to his team, and they all began to try and fade back into the woods. He pushed his rifle back behind him and rested his hand on the pistol at his hip. He and Tate stared at each other, each radiating hatred back at the other.

The man flashed a feral smile at me. "One thing Miss Shifter-fucker. That protection for mates only covers humans. Once you let one of these filthy beasts change you? Protection is gone."

Without hesitation, he swiftly pulled the pistol from his holster. Time seemed to slow as he raised the barrel toward me. Tate roared out in rage and shock. The pistol bucked in the man's hand. There was time for me to think of all the things I'd done, all the people I'd loved. My girls' faces, their first cries when they were born, the first time my son kicked in my womb, the moment Tate said he loved me.

In less than a half second, the bullet slammed into my chest. There was a massive flash of light and a pop like an electrical conduit blowing. I was thrown back, stumbling, but I remained on my feet. The bullet, smashed and warped, fell to the stone patio. The slight *plink* sound was the only thing I could hear. I looked at my chest, looking for a bullet hole. Instead, I saw the opal necklace Emily had given me.

"Fucking damned witches," the man screamed and turned to run, his team following.

Steff and Blayne leaped into action, sprinting into the woods after the hunters. I eased myself down to the ground. My hands and body shook. I should have been dead. A bullet should have ripped through my chest, bursting my heart and blowing a hole out my back. I *would* be dead. If not for Emily.

Tate knelt next to me, his eyes as bright as flashlights. I'd never seen them like that. His face was a mask of rage and worry.

"Are you okay?" His voice shook as he spoke.

Gunshots echoed from the forest. I tried to ignore them. I looked up at Tate and touched the necklace. "I am. I'm fine."

There was a deep bass growl from behind Tate. We both turned to look, and the biggest grizzly bear I'd ever seen erupted from the trees. It had to be a thousand pounds, if not more. Behind it came a thickly muscled panther. The creatures skidded to a stop. The bear turned into Steff, and the panther morphed into Blayne.

Even after watching Tate become a dragon, after seeing what they'd done to Luis's men, hearing the stories, and knowing it was all true, my jaw still dropped. I was still shocked that all this was real. Magic was *real*, but so was the danger that came with it.

Blayne put his hands on his knees, sucking breath. "They got away. They had a truck waiting in the woods. I ran as fast as I could, but I couldn't catch them. They took some shots at us while they went."

"Assholes nicked me," Steff said, fingering a bloody scratch on his shoulder. "I'll live."

Once we were sure they were gone, we went inside. Tate secured all the windows and doors and checked and double-checked that the alarm system was on while Steff and Blayne helped bring Miles downstairs. They set him up on the couch, and I was surprised at how much better he looked. It made me wonder if shifters healed faster than humans.

Tate, finally sure the house was secure, sat with us. "Okay, good news. I don't think the hunters are going to make any more moves very soon."

"Why do you say that?" Miles asked, frowning in confusion.

"Well, the guy made sure to let us know that there's someone bigger in charge, who wants me for himself. They know I'm a dragon, and that will require they take their time planning. I think this whole thing today was their attempt to kill Harley or one of you three." He nodded toward Blayne, Steff, and Miles. "They wanted to do something that would send me over the edge and make me easier to take down. That whole plan went to hell. They'll have to drop back and be more careful with the next plan."

"We can't let our guards down, but I think we've bought some time. For now, the danger is moving away from us. It's coming back, but not immediately."

Steff pointed at my necklace. "So, I guess the witch wasn't all bad after all. Did you guys see that thing?

Tate raised his hand and gently thumbed the opal around my neck. I could see the look in his eyes. He was as thankful for Emily as I was. Even in death, she'd saved my life. It made me more heartsick. Maybe she could have truly changed if she'd had a little more time. I wished she was here, even for only a few seconds, so I could tell her how grateful I was to her.

Chapter 37 - Tate

I had one more job to do. It needed to be done before I could ever relax. It had been a couple of days since the hunter attack. Miles was almost back to normal, his shifter healing had brought him back better than I'd thought. None of us had ever seen someone get shot full of that much silver and survive. Saying I was grateful was an understatement.

Harley was still on edge, but I'd actually grown calmer and less tense. In my opinion, not only had Emily saved Harley's life, she'd also scared the hunters off for even longer than most of the others thought. I'd told them I thought they'd be gone for a couple of months, but deep down, I thought it would be even longer. The spell that had stopped the bullet had probably scared the shit out of them. They hadn't known about that, which gave them something else to consider. The hunters would have no idea what other spells or curses Emily might have cast before she died. There were no others, as far as I knew, but *they* didn't know that. They would be like dust in the wind for a while. Maybe even years.

When I voiced that thought to Harley, she said, "They'll still be back. Aren't you worried?"

I shook my head. "I can't be worried forever. I truly think that, for now at least, the danger is gone."

That night in bed, I told her about the job I had to take care of, hiding the truth as much as I could. "I've got to fly out tomorrow. I've got a thing I've been putting off. Should only be gone a day or two."

She looked at me, and I could feel that strange connection we had now. There was the weirdest thought that she knew I was hiding something, but she could also tell it was important and not to push. She nodded. "Okay. Be careful. That's all I ask."

Before we fell asleep, I whispered, "Don't worry. Nothing is going to keep me away from you for long."

The next afternoon I landed at La Guardia Airport. I'd only brought a single backpack for the trip. I hadn't been lying when I said I'd only be gone a couple of days. I took a taxi to The Plaza Hotel. On the ride, I pulled out my phone and dialed the number Blayne had been able to dig up for me.

It only rang one time before there was an answer. "This is Luis, who the hell is this?"

"Ortiz?" I asked.

A long moment of silence filtered over the line before Luis said, "Oh, if it isn't the homewrecker. How are you doing, cocksucker? Has Harley dumped you yet? Did you call to let me know she was on the way back to me?"

"I want to meet. You name the place. We need to get things settled," I said, not rising to his insults.

"Brass balls on this one. Okay, we can do this," he said and then gave me an address near the docks in Hell's Kitchen.

"When? I can be there in two hours."

"Be there in an hour. Otherwise it's off." He hung up without waiting for an answer.

I'd let him choose the location because it would give him a false sense of security. He'd think he had the upper hand. He and his men would be sloppy and unprepared. Harley's last few months of pregnancy should be as stress-free as possible. This trip would ensure that. I leaned forward and tapped the glass, getting the cabbie's attention. I gave him the new address and sat back to enjoy the ride.

I got to the location twenty minutes early. I had the taxi drop me off a few blocks away and walked the rest of the way, scoping out each alley and around every corner. I didn't think they'd have anyone out this far to intercept me, but I wanted to cover all my bases. The spot was what had once been a warehouse—right on the waterfront that looked like it had been bought and renovated into some high price condos and penthouses. There was a doorman at the entrance. My trained eye could see the bulge of a pistol beneath his suit jacket.

He saw me walking up and said, "Are you Mr. Mills?"

I nodded. "I have an appointment with your employer. Ortiz."

The man glared. "That's *Mr.* Ortiz to you."

I gazed nonchalantly into the guy's eyes. "Are you gonna take me to him or not?"

"You're an arrogant bitch, ain't you? He told me about you. Arms up, I gotta pat you down."

I did as he asked. He rifled through my backpack, only finding a single change of clothes and some folders and papers. He opened the door and led me to the elevators, where he pushed the button for the top floor.

As the door closed, he grinned at me. "See you soon."

On the ride up, I pulled the folder out of my backpack and tucked it under my arm. When the door opened, I set my bag on the ground just outside the door. The penthouse was beyond gaudy. It was like Ortiz had eaten all his money and then shat it out all over the place. Zebra-skin rug, gold-trimmed lights, original oil paintings that didn't match or make sense in the space. It was what a child would do to try and *prove* he was rich. Ortiz would have been better served if he'd thrown a bit of his money at a good interior designer.

I rounded the corner and found myself in what I had to assume was the living room. Ortiz sat on an armchair in front of a massive gas fireplace. Two large muscle-heads flanked him. Another three guys stood or lounged around the room. They all had the affectation of being wholly unconcerned that I was there, but I could smell the anxiety and excitement coming off them. They were ready for a fight and looking forward to it.

Ortiz adjusted himself and grabbed a glass of what looked like whiskey off the table beside his chair. It was hard not to think he'd chosen that chair because it looked a little like a throne. I stifled an eye roll as I stopped ten feet away and stared him down.

Luis looked around at his men. "This, my friends, is the guy who decided he could shove his cock into my woman." He took a sip of his drink and then gestured around the room. "How can you give Harley a life half as good as this?"

I snorted. "What? This gold-plated trailer park? You don't know shit about Harley. Material things like this don't mean shit to her. And neither do you."

Luis smiled even more broadly, but I could tell I'd pissed him off. "Very funny. Very funny." He looked at the men to his left and right. "Didn't I tell you? Bowling balls between his legs. Well, courage can sometimes be confused with stupidity. I'll still give you props for having the guts to do this like a man. Much more commendable than waiting for me to sneak up behind you and put a bullet in your head."

I gritted my teeth. "Is that what you did to Harley's husband?"

A flutter of surprise passed over his face, but he kept his composure. "Who? Sammy? Don't know nothing about Sammy boy. Of course…" he glared at me, "…when a man has something I want, the gloves come off."

Ready for this to be over, I said, "I'm here to tell you to fuck off once and for all. Harley is mine. The baby is mine. Her girls are mine. You step one foot in the whole *state* of Colorado, I'll know, and I will not hesitate to end you."

Luis's face went red with anger. He downed the rest of his drink and then waved a hand. "Joey, handle this fucker, will you?"

The big guy to Ortiz's right stepped forward. I watched the big man step toward me. He was around six-four. Maybe two-hundred-thirty pounds. I could see scars on his knuckles, but none on his face. He was a fighter. A fighter who'd probably never lost. I tossed my file folder to the side as he got closer, freeing my hands.

He swung at me without preamble, hoping to catch me off guard. I pivoted and spun, grabbing his outstretched hand and twisting the arm up and back. There was a thick, meaty *pop!* as his shoulder popped out of its socket. The big man hit the floor, squealing like a pig, slapping at his chest and clutching at his shoulder, now sunken at an unusual angle. I kicked him in the face, knocking him out and silencing the godawful shrieks.

Ortiz leaned further back in his seat, obviously surprised. The men around the room had all tensed. They evidently hadn't anticipated their friend Joey going down so fast. Ortiz waved a hand at me, and the other four men rushed me.

The first guy kicked out at my stomach. I grabbed his foot before it hit me and drove my own foot into the knee of his other leg. The knee cracked and buckled backward. The man fell, screaming and clutching his ruined leg. A second goon grabbed me from behind, getting me in a headlock. Using my superior strength, I levered my hips, bending and spinning. He flew over my back and slammed down on the ground. I brought my foot down on his face, putting him to sleep.

The last two guys attacked me at once. I ducked out of the way of their punches and swept my leg under the guy on the right, dragging his feet out from under him. He fell over into his friend, and they both collapsed into a heap. I grabbed one by the hair and slammed a fist into his face three times before he went limp. The other had scrambled back to his feet and was grabbing for my shirt. I caught his outstretched hand and twisted my wrist, grabbing and snapping his two middle fingers back, breaking them. He hit his knees, cradling his hand and screaming. I spun and slammed a kick into the side of his head. A deafening silence fell over the room.

I straightened my shirt and glanced up at Ortiz. The look of arrogant unconcern had vanished. Now he looked afraid. Terrified beyond measure. He kept stealing glances at the desk fifteen feet away. I had to assume that he had a firearm over there, but he'd fucked up. It was too far away. He had no further recourse.

I stepped toward him slowly, stopping to grab my folder again. I walked to Luis and towered above him, glaring down at him like the insect he was. It was all I could do not to shift and show him exactly what he'd been screwing with all along, but I held my composure.

From the look on his face, I could see that Luis really believed I was here to kill him. He was shaking, actually shaking, like a cowering dog. There was still a hint of anger in his eyes, but fear overwhelmed it. His breath was coming in quick ragged hisses. I slapped the folder down on his lap with a bang.

I sneered at him in disgust. "Not such a big man once you realize who you're dealing with, are you?" I pointed at the folder, "My friends and I are good at digging. Better than the cops. Better even than the FBI. With the stuff we have in this file, we can end your life. The tax forms alone? If I send them to the IRS, you'll be gone for twenty-five years, easy. Remember, that's how they got Capone. The other stuff? Well, I guess you should be happy New York doesn't still have the death penalty."

"Here's the deal. You stay the fuck away from Harley and the girls. You stay on this goddamned side of the Mississippi, and forget all about us. You do that, and this information never goes anywhere. Can we agree on that?"

Luis had regained some of his previous courage, but underneath, I could still tell he was afraid of what I might do. He adjusted in the seat and opened the folder. He read the first few pages, turning them slowly. His face went pale. He paged faster, the paper snapping and popping in his hands as he flipped through all the information we had on him. Finally, he looked up at me, and I knew we had him.

Gritting his teeth, he said, "Fine! Get the hell out of here. Go back to your precious little lady. Tell her not to come crawling back when she's tired of you. Keep this shit quiet, and we got a deal."

All I did was nod. I turned to leave, stepping over the unconscious bodies I'd left in my wake. I pushed the button for the elevator and grabbed my backpack again. The ride back down the elevator was much more fun. A weight had been lifted off me. The door opened on the ground floor with a ding. When the doorman saw me, his jaw dropped. I walked past him without even glancing in his direction.

The air outside was cool and crisp. It felt good after what had just happened. My flight out wasn't until the next morning, but I thought I might try and change to an earlier flight. Things had gone faster than I thought they would.

There was one other thing I wanted to do before I went back home, though. So, I hailed a cab and gave the driver the name of the place I wanted to go. As we drove, a light drizzle began to come down outside. The lights of the city ticked by, and I allowed myself a sigh of relief.

A few minutes later, I stepped through the doors of the lounge and took a seat at the bar. It was the exact same stool I'd sat on months ago. Across the bar was the spot where I'd first set eyes on Harley.

The bartender put a beverage napkin down in front of me, and said, "What can I get you tonight, friend?"

"Whiskey sour, no ice."

"On it, boss."

He returned with the drink moments later, and I sipped at it for several minutes. Continuing to stare at the spot where Harley had been sitting, I felt the nostalgia. The way my heart had warmed, and the stirring of my dragon, how beautiful she looked, it all came back. It hit me that even then, on that night, I felt the pull toward her. She was meant for me.

I downed the rest of the drink and looked around one last time at the place where it all began. Then, I stood and placed twenty dollars on the bar. I gave the place one last glance and smiled to myself. I left and went back home to my family.

Chapter 38 - Harley

It was December, and it had been almost two months since Tate had claimed me. I still hadn't shifted. On one hand, I was happy. I had enough to worry about without transforming into a giant dragon. On the other hand, I couldn't figure out why it hadn't happened, and was ready for the shift.

I knew it had done something to me. Over the past few months, my senses had heightened astronomically. I could hear and smell things I never could before. Small things, like telling the difference between the scents of different types of wood—like the dining room table smelled different than the kitchen cabinets. I didn't even know different woods could smell different, but there it was.

My body was also more connected to my baby. His magic was like a warm glow coming from inside me; it was actually something I could feel. The same was true of Tate and the guys. Something connected us that hadn't been there before. There was no way to adequately explain it, but even though I hadn't turned into a dragon, I knew I was no longer human.

Mariah and I were sitting on our porch watching Steff and Tate carry boxes across the street to his house. Our house now. We had decided to move into his place. It had an extra bedroom that would work as the baby's nursery. His home was bigger in general, and we would all have more room. I'd already messaged Maddox to tell him thanks for the home the last few months, but we'd be moving by the end of the month.

Jordyn was carrying a box and talking a mile a minute to Blayne about where to put all the things in her new room. To his credit, Blayne never lost the smile and did exactly as she asked. I was truly at peace and happy, even though I knew danger was still looming. Right now, however, there was nothing that could stop me from soaking in as much happiness as I could.

A smile slipped onto my lips as Kayden helped Mariah haul her desk across the street. The boy had become a pretty normal staple at our house. He was obviously smitten with Mariah and fell over himself doing anything and everything to make a good impression with me and Tate. The fact that he was over so much had forced me to have the dreaded *talk* with Mariah about protection for sex. Her face had been flaming the whole time, but she'd promised to come to me if she ever thought she was ready for the next step with Kayden. After the talk, I believed she would.

A sharp cramp tugged at my belly, and I winced. I rubbed at the spot and ignored it. I'd been having Braxton-Hicks contractions for weeks now, and it was becoming routine at this point. The baby was due soon, but I still had a few weeks. At least, I'd thought that was the case.

A few minutes later, another contraction hit me. Painful enough to make me sit up in surprise. Not wanting to freak anyone out yet, I sat and waited. Three more contractions came. When the fourth one hit, I knew things were about to start happening.

"Tate!" I called across the street.

He stopped and put the box down. "Yeah?"

"Car. Now."

"Car? You need to go to the store?" Tate asked dumbly.

Steff smacked him on the back. "No, numb nuts."

Tate glanced at him as another, more painful contraction had me bending over in pain. Realization washed over Tate's face, and he sprinted toward me. Less than three minutes later, I was in the car, trying to breathe through the pain. This wasn't my first rodeo, I knew what to expect and how to handle it. Tate, on the other hand, was close to losing his damn mind. The stoic and calm man I'd grown to love was now freaking out. It got to the point that laughter bubbled out of me.

I placed a reassuring hand on his arm. "Stay calm, big guy. We're gonna be fine. You'll be an amazing daddy."

Three hours later, Tory James Mills was born. As I lay in bed, exhausted, sweaty, and sore, I smiled as I watched Tate pace the room slowly, holding his son. He was in love the first instant he saw him. I could see the love radiating from his eyes. Adoration, pride, and happiness seemed to radiate out of Tate's face as he watched Tory sleep.

After he laid him in the heated bassinet, he stepped over to me and took my hand. He kissed my knuckles, then pulled something out of his pocket. Before I could see what it was, he slid the ring onto my finger. Even in my fatigued state, I gasped and put my other hand to my mouth. Tate had claimed me, as a shifter. But I was born in the world of humans. In that world, a ring on a finger signified something equally as powerful as claiming.

Tate said, "I've taken you as mine in the ways of shifters. Now I want to take you as mine in the way of humans. I want you to be mine in every way possible. I want you to have my last name. I want you to be with me forever. Harley, will you marry me?"

As the tears flowed, I was barely able to get the words out. I managed, "Yes, yes, yes," while sobbing and laughing at the same time.

I slept better that night than I'd ever slept in my life. Content with my baby in his bed beside me and my new fiancé napping on the couch across the room. My body was already feeling better. With the girls, I'd been in pretty significant pain for days. As I slipped off to sleep, I decided there were several benefits to being a shifter.

Less than a week after we got back from the hospital, I called for Tate. I'd finished feeding Tory, and I was feeling feverish and dizzy. Sweat poured off my body, and my skin felt like it was on fire.

Tate came in seconds after I called. When I told him what I was feeling, his eyes went wide. "It's time."

"Time for what?" I asked.

Without answering, Tate leaned out and called across the hall, "Mariah! I… uh… your mom wants to take a walk in the woods. Can you watch the baby?"

"Yeah, sure. I guess. Weird, but whatever," Mariah called from her room.

The woods? Oh shit. My skin was burning and itching too much for me to ask questions, but I had a pretty good idea what he meant. He helped me up, and I leaned on him as we went outside. My body was fully healed from giving birth, but my legs were like jelly. My hair was soaked with sweat by the time we got to the backyard and into the forest. We got to a semi-open area in the trees, and Tate eased me down onto my knees in the moss.

"Okay, Harley, look at me. You need to relax and find that other part of you. The magical part deep inside. Do you feel it?"

I was shaking with fear and excitement. I could sense something. A warmth deep inside my mind and chest. There was something else there as well. I'd never experienced it before, but it was like something else was inside my mind. Something somehow both foreign and familiar. It was scary, but not in the way I'd imagined. It was a similar fear I had just before giving birth.

"I'm not sure how it'll work for you, since you're human, but it should be similar," Tate said as he rubbed my back.

Closing my eyes, I focused on the sensation, pushing deeper into myself. Like the layers of an onion, everything that made me who I was peeled away slowly. Inside, deep down and brand new, something else rose up to greet me.

"Trust the dragon, Harley. She's part of you, she won't hurt you," Tate murmured in a soothing voice.

Doing as he said, I relaxed my last defenses. Opening my body fully to the new entity that had been born out of my soul, I freed the dragon within me. When I did that, my whole essence was immediately filled with fire. Not a destroying or painful sensation. It was a warm blanket. A loving hug from a lost relative. With my eyes closed, I still sensed the way my body was morphing and shifting. When I finally lifted my eyelids, I looked out at the world through wholly different eyes.

My wings stretched out, and I tilted my head around on a thick, muscled neck to inspect my new body. The other presence was right below the surface, like a twin sibling. I loved the dragon the way I loved myself. It was amazing to have this gift, for that was exactly what it was—a gift. Tate gazed up at me with pride, awe, and love. Within seconds, he himself had shifted. Leaning close to me, he pressed his snout against mine.

Deep in my mind, telepathically, he whispered, "You are so beautiful. I'm so grateful for you."

Not only could I hear his thoughts in my own head, but they sounded more sincere. Not that he didn't mean it when he spoke, but through the mind, things were purer. I nuzzled against his neck and sighed.

Chapter 39 - Tate

The girls decided he needed a half-year party the summer after Tory was born. The idea of giving a kid a six-month birthday party seemed pretty strange. If I was totally honest, I thought it was stupid, but everyone else in my home thought it was an important milestone, so I was outvoted.

We did the whole bit, cake and all. After the lunch of burgers and dessert, Mariah scooped up her brother and walked around with him. The older girl made baby noises and talked to him. Even from here, I could see the way he stared at her, like she had hung the moon herself. I'd never seen a baby look at someone with so much love like Tory looked at his sisters. He loved them, and they loved him. It filled my heart with joy. For the hundredth or so time, I wondered how I'd gotten so lucky. So blessed.

Jordyn followed Mariah out to the front yard where a blanket was set up. They lay Tory down and played with him while Harley and I sat on the porch, watching them. They were far enough away that they wouldn't hear us speaking.

I leaned over. "We'll need to tell them soon. About me, and Tory. About you."

Harley looked at me, and the anxious look she always got when we talked about this reappeared. She sighed and fidgeted with her hands.

After several seconds, she said, "I'm worried they'll be afraid of me."

Glancing out at Jordyn and Mariah, I knew the answer to that. "They are smart and strong young ladies. They'll take it in stride. They know that you would die for them. They won't fear you. At the end of the day, no matter what, you are their mom. Mother is the first and most precious of words children learn. Simply because they get older doesn't mean that changes."

"You're right. We'll figure out a time," Harley said, a serene smile on her face.

Taking her hand, I played with her wedding rings with my thumb. After all these months, it was still surprising how some simple jewelry could make me so happy. The rings on Harley's hand were a symbol of what I had. Of happiness.

Once dusk came, I called Steff over to watch over the girls and Tory, then took Harley back to my clearing. Our clearing now. The evening was clear and warm, the sky that beautiful purple that comes right as the sun goes down. My heart was at peace, but down the line, danger would return. The hunters wouldn't be deterred forever. It was part of why I tried to get Harley out here as much as possible. To learn how to use her dragon to its full power.

I had no intention of letting her be in the final battle, whenever that came, but by God, I'd make sure she was ready to defend herself and our children if it came down to it. That was what we usually did when we came out here, but tonight was different. As we shifted and took flight, we simply flew together. This night was for us. To swoop and dive, to enjoy the breeze under our wings. Here with my mate, my wife, we could just fly. So we did.

Chapter 40 - Steff

Baseball, man, freaking baseball. Summer was my favorite time of the year. It was when I could get back to the thing I loved most. The world's greatest game. I coached the Lilly Valley city pee-wee team every year. I loved it. If I'd wanted it, I could probably get a job coaching older kids pretty easily, but there was something about the little ones. Teaching them the love of the game so young felt sacred, so I stayed where I was.

Today was when all the new kids arrived for the first practice. With all the issues of the last few months—babies, gangsters, hunters—it had slipped my mind to go over my roster. Today was the first chance I had. Thankfully, the volunteer assistant coach had taken care of things while I handled all the personal stuff.

I'd been at the field watching warm-ups. The assistant coach was already there. I waved and made my way over to him.

"How's our new team looking?" I asked. I'd coached the team to pee-wee league champions over the last five years, so I had a lot to live up to.

Coach nodded toward the field. "The two over there doing grounding drills were in the lower level last year, so they've already got a jump start. Should have several who can handle the game pretty well."

As he spoke, my eye caught a kid running laps around the bases. His hair caught the light of the sun and reflected the same bright coppery red of my own. The same copper red every man in my family had had for as many generations as I could remember. Watching him run, my thoughts went somewhere else for a second before I returned to the conversation. The kid turned a corner, and I saw the last name printed on the back of his jersey. *Knight.*

My stomach seemed to drop out from under me.

There was something about that kid that was familiar. I held a hand out. "Can I see that roster?"

He handed it to me, and I glanced down at the list of names until I found him. Short stop, Aiden Knight. A quivery feeling hit me in the guts, but I handed the clipboard back and told the coach to go ahead and get a couple of innings of practice game started.

I watched the kids play, keeping a keen eye on the Knight kid. He was only nine years old, like most of the kids, but he was talented as all hell. Looked like me at that age, diving for grounders, good swing, great arm. We'd have another damned good season if the practice was any indication.

After practice was over, I stood near the dugout as the parents came up to collect their kids. Greeting the parents at the end of practice was my little ritual. It made it easier to coach a kid if you knew who was in the stands watching them. The next ten minutes were spent shaking hands, laughing, and discussing the season with parents. Then, out of the corner of my eye, Aiden bolted toward the parking lot. Glancing over, I saw who he was running to, and my heart nearly stopped.

The boy jumped up into the arms of a beautiful woman. She was the woman who had been my entire world. Once upon a time, anyway. I glanced from her smiling face to Aiden, and back to her again. The math did itself in my mind and came up with an answer that made me dizzy. I might have been sick right then, but I had to keep up appearances.

Her name was April. She'd been the love of my life. I'd lost her a long time ago. Roughly nine years ago to be exact. The timing was right. If I allowed myself to dwell on the fact, it became much more possible. Could it be? Dear God, could it actually be?